THE CELESTIAL BLADE

G.L. BREEDON

KOSMOSAIC BOOKS

Copyright © 2013 by G.L. Breedon
All rights reserved.
ISBN-10: 0983777764
ISBN-13: 978-0-9837777-6-2

For more information:
www.kosmosaicbooks.com

TIMELINE OF THE CELESTIAL PILGRIM

(Dates in Origin World notation)

2075 CE — First contact of humans with another intelligent species, the Shilloo.

2101 CE — Humanity joins the Constellation of Species becoming the tenth (of what would eventually be twelve) intelligent species known to exist in the Milky Way Galaxy.

3145 CE — An interstellar signal is received from the Andromeda Galaxy indicating another group of intelligent species exists in the Milky Way's closest galactic neighbor.

3295 CE — The starship *Celestial Pilgrim* is launched to make contact with the senders of the signal from the Andromeda Galaxy.

5289 CE — The *Celestial Pilgrim,* after a nearly two-thousand year long journey, nears its destination.

Excerpted from *The Kellish Book of Known History*

CHAPTER 1
CRUMBLING CASTLE

Wyconna (Wi-KON-Ah): The name given to the human section of the starship Celestial Pilgrim *by its inhabitants. The name comes from the oldest living tree on the Origin World. Wyconna is 10,000 km long, giving it a square area of 31,416,000 km, making it slightly larger than the Origin World continent of Africa.*

The Traveler's Guide to Wyconna, 23rd Edition

The clouds above the thin forest obscured the moon and stars beyond them, leaving just enough light to make out the castle on the hill. The moon was not real, nor were the stars. They were merely projections provided to comfort those creatures used to living under a moon and stars.

But the clouds were real. And far beneath the clouds, in the crook of the valley, stood Jeddu and Kylla, a light drizzle falling on their moonlit faces. Thin and tall for their thirteen years, Jed stood half a hand shorter than Kylla, his dark brown skin a mild contrast with her deep olive complexion in the bluish-white moonlight.

"It's really here," Kylla said, pushing her sandy hair from her chestnut eyes and wiping raindrops from her forehead.

Jed looked up at the crumbling castle on the hill above, wondering if the walls might fall down and crush them in an avalanche of stone. He never really believed the stories about the old castle. He had assumed they were tall tales told to lull small children to sleep. When he and Kylla had learned that this year's school trip would be to the shores of Lake Kenno'Cha, near the rumored resting place of the ancient abandoned castle, they had spent weeks planning a midnight mission to explore the ruins.

"Let's get up there before we lose the moonlight," Jed said.

Kylla took one look up the hill and glanced sideways at Jed. "Race you."

Jed and Kylla ran pell-mell up the hill, zigzagging between the wide slabs of granite and thin, wispy trees. As usual, Kylla took the lead before they were halfway up the hill. Kylla held the hem of her cotton dress high above her knees, her thin legs flashing in the moonlight. Jed tried to suck in more air to power his already tiring legs, but he knew it was hopeless.

Kylla loved to race. And she nearly always won. Jed was not the only boy she bested in contests of physical strength on a regular basis. He was merely the only one who didn't resent her for it.

Unsurprisingly, Kylla reached the top of the hill first. Hands on her hips, she waited for Jed to catch up. Breathing heavily, Jed stopped beside her and bent down, placing his hands on the knees of his woolen trousers as he sucked in air.

"Couldn't we…just…walk…someplace…for once?" Jed panted.

Already beginning to breathe normally, Kylla smiled at him. "Where would the fun be in that?"

"The fun," Jed said, "would be in not feeling like I needed to puke."

As he calmed his breathing, Jed took a moment to survey his surroundings. The castle wall curved gently, completely encircling the towers within. A singsong rhyme all the Kellish children sang telling the story of the castle came to Jed's mind.

Once there was a castle made of stone,
Walls round and white as bone
But stones crumble and walls fall,
And bury treasures beneath them all.

Though white as bone, the wall of the castle was in no way complete. Sections of the wall had collapsed over the many years since its construction and now there were large gaps easily big enough for Jed and Kylla to climb through.

Jed motioned toward the nearest fissure in the wall and started walking.

"Let's go."

Kylla followed silently. The immensity of the adventure they were on finally began to sink into Jed's thoughts. If the story about the ruined castle was true, the other stories might be true as well. Stories of magic swords and precious jewels. And a monster. He hadn't forgotten the stories about the monster.

Jed stopped in front of the gaping hole in the wall and looked to Kylla to see if her competitive streak was still strong.

"Want to go first?" Jed asked.

"Only if you're afraid to," Kylla replied with a sweet smile across her face.

Jed frowned. He hated it when she outwitted him.

He climbed over the large stones of the fallen wall, careful to maintain his footing. Not wanting to seem anxious, he didn't look back to see if Kylla followed him.

The pile of rubble sat a few meters high and it took only moments to climb down to the other side. At the bottom of the pile of stones, Jed found himself in a large courtyard, the three towers of the castle rising above him.

Each tower stood nearly fifty meters tall and sat equidistantly from the circular wall and from each other. A row of two-story buildings connected the towers to the wall, splitting the courtyard into three sections and leaving the space between the towers empty.

Or almost empty. A dark mass was barely visible at the very center of the courtyard. The castle towers seemed to drench the courtyard in shadows, lending an eerie atmosphere to the grounds the full moon above could do nothing to dispel. As Jed stared into the blackness between the towers, something brushed his shoulder.

Leaping back and sucking in a quick breath, he saw Kylla standing beside him.

"Jumpy?" she asked, grinning.

"Not funny," Jed answered. "You go first next time."

Kylla brushed off the suggestion with a shrug. "Which one?"

"The stories all say the treasures of Lord Narrish are hidden beneath the tower closest to the gods," Jed said, mentally bringing to mind the stories he had studied about the castle.

"Whose gods?"

"The stories never say. Maybe it will be clearer from the center of the courtyard," Jed suggested.

"You mean where it's darkest," Kylla said, staring into the blackness between the towers.

Jed slid his knapsack off and opened it to reveal a small lantern. "I swiped this from Mrs. Lemmick's tent. Let's hope she doesn't need to use the latrine in the middle of the night." Pulling a small box of matches from his pocket, Jed struck one and lit the lantern, holding it up as he slid the straps of his knapsack over his shoulder again.

Jed looked at Kylla in the lantern light and smiled. Kylla smiled back and they both laughed. They were frightened, but excited. This was what bound them together more than anything. The love of adventure, of seeing something new, something they weren't supposed to see. Facing fears, and daring each other to leap beyond them.

They walked slowly through the courtyard, their footsteps echoing loudly on the stones beneath their feet. As they passed the base of the towers and stepped into the shadowed inner square, a chill passed through Jed. He shivered and stopped.

Swallowing, he turned to Kylla. "Did you feel that?"

"Yep," Kylla said, looking over her shoulder. "No wonder they say it's haunted by the spirits of dead warriors."

"You always know the right thing to say to calm my nerves." Jed frowned and began walking again, quickly fading into the darkness, even though he carried the lantern ahead of him.

Startled to be momentarily alone, Kylla leapt to catch up with Jed. Walking slowly but steadily, they soon arrived at the exact center of the inner courtyard, the mystery of the shadowy shape revealed by the dim light of the lantern.

They looked up at a massive statue of a man with a sword locked in vicious combat with a large creature three times his size. The creature had four spiral-shaped horns erupting from its head and a large set of bat-like wings sprouting from its back. It had the face of a ram, but the body of a very large and powerful man. The two figures seemed frozen in the final, fatal moments of a deadly battle.

Jed let out a long, quiet whistle. "It's true."

"Is that Lord Narrish?" Kylla asked as she walked around the statue, examining it from all angles.

"Yes," replied Jed as he followed her around the stone warriors. "The monster is the Morikon, a blended beast created by the dark gods. Lord Narrish is said to have fought the beast in battle for three days, finally defeating him on the morning of the fourth day. The stories say he was so impressed by the courage of the Morikon that he refused to kill it, and instead forced it to guard his treasure."

Kylla stared up into the eyes of the Morikon, two black crystals inserted into the stone skull of a ram, as Jed lowered the lantern. "This is what we're supposed to find if we uncover the treasure?"

Jed joined Kylla's gaze. "That was all nearly two thousand years ago, but if the stories are true, the Morikon is said to guard the treasure until Wyconna's end…until the *Celestial Pilgrim* no longer sails between the stars."

Kylla stepped away from the statue and looked around. It was even darker now, the moon hidden by one of the castle towers.

"How do we find the treasure?" Kylla asked.

"The poem describing the treasure says it lies within the tower that is nearest the eternal gods above."

"Do you remember what it says, exactly?"

Jed closed his eyes and thought back to the many times he had read the stories of the Old Ones in a well-worn book called *Tales From the Before Time* he kept hidden beneath the floorboards under his bed. Originally written by a teacher name Pannu Hyth nearly four hundred years ago, it had been a banned book in the Kellish communities for most of that time.

But, it seemed, Jed's grandfather possessed a heretical streak deep enough for him to bury a copy in the attic of his barn, which was where Jed found him hiding it one rainy afternoon. Sworn to secrecy, Jed had gobbled up every story in the book many times over the last two years. He knew nearly every word by heart.

Opening his eyes and looking up at the statue of the Morikon and Lord Narrish locked in battle, he recited:

"Sunlight rose on the fourth day
And Lord Narrish beat the beast down.
Beneath his sword the Morikon lay,
Their blood mixed and crusted brown.

Such a fierce warrior the Lord would not slay,
For upon this the gods would frown.
So he cast it beneath the tower clay,
To guard his treasured crown.

And there beneath the tower gray
The eternal gods forever looked down,
And the Morikon slew all who came its way,
Keeping safe the triple mantled crown."

Kylla turned her gaze from Jed to the stars above. "That's it," she said.

"What's it?" Jed asked.

"The stars," Kylla answered. "The eternal gods are the stars."

"A constellation, you mean?" Jed said, remembering the different ancient Origin World names for the patterns of the stars.

"Exactly," Kylla said, thinking aloud. "When the builders created the ship, they chose the stars from each traveler's home world to project in the night sky. For us humans they decided to use the Origin World so the stars above us would always remind us of where we came from and how far we had travelled."

"But each culture on the Origin World had its own stories," Jed said, following her gaze up to the stars.

"So, who were the gods of Lord Narrish?" Kylla asked. "If we knew his gods, maybe we could find them, or one of them, in the stars above."

Jed thought about this. In his mind he flipped through the stories of the *Tales from the Before Time* page by page, seeing each one and looking for a clue as to Lord Narrish's gods. In his mind's eye he saw an illustration in the margin of the story of the Morikon — a simple woodcut of Lord Narrish kneeling before an altar with four bowls upon it. The first bowl heaped high with dirt, the second with a flame leaping up from it, the third filled with water, and the fourth apparently empty.

"The elements. Lord Narrish's gods were the embodiment of the elements," Jed declared, rather proud of himself for seeing the connection.

"So, where above these towers are there stars that resemble earth, wind, fire, and water?" Kylla asked, more to herself than Jed.

Jed craned his neck back. "The stories showed an engraving with four bowls, each containing an element. They went in order starting with earth, then fire, then water, then air, so maybe what we're looking for…"

"Are four stars in a row," Kylla said, pointing to a row of four stars directly above one of the towers. "Those four stars are part of the constellation Aries, or the ram. And the Morikon is part ram and part man."

She looked down from the stars and smiled at Jed, obviously excited that her love of astronomy, so disparaged by her parents and her teachers as being unsuitable for a girl, had finally proven to be useful.

"Good work, Ky," Jed said, grinning back at her. "Together, this should be easy."

Jed started off across the shadow-filled courtyard toward the designated tower, Kylla right beside him. The call of a strange bird, or what Jed hoped was a bird, rang out along the stone walls around them.

Glancing at Kylla, he quickened his pace, and in moments they stood before the doorway of the tower beneath the eternal gods above.

CHAPTER 2
TOWER TRICKS

Celestial Pilgrim: The exploratory starship launched by the *Constellation of Species of the Milky Way Galaxy in response to a trans-stellar message from an apparently intelligent species in the Andromeda Galaxy. The starship is tubular in shape and is 100,000 km long by 1000 km wide, giving it an internal area of 314,160,000 km², or slightly more than half the surface area of the human Origin World. Traveling by means of Sentient-created space-time wormholes every hundred years, the* Celestial Pilgrim's *journey is estimated to take approximately 2000 years to complete.*
The Encyclopedia Wyconnica, 112th Edition

"Astronomy compels the soul to look upwards and leads us from this world to another."
Plato (427– 347 BCE), *The Republic*

The doorway at the bottom of the tower was simply that, a doorway. What must have once been a massive door standing nearly four meters high was absent. Scraps of wood and iron lay about the courtyard, giving some indication the door had been nearly half a meter thick. Jed held the lantern up high as he and Kylla stepped through the doorway and into the darkness within the tower.

The base of the tower spanned some fifty meters in diameter. The interior of the first level was divided into eight wide chambers, each separated by a large, open archway that allowed the light from Jed's lantern to flow easily from one room to another. The archways acted as supports for the weight of the tower above, but seemed so slender the open chambers appeared in danger of collapse. The absence of windows created an atmosphere of claustrophobia in no way dissolved by the expansiveness of the space. In the center of the tower a large, circular stone staircase ascended to the upper reaches of the keep.

Jed and Kylla walked silently along the dusty stone floor, stepping into the first chamber to the right, examining the remnants of what had once been a series of opulent rooms for greeting guests and dignitaries. Age-blackened tapestries depicting once famous lords and ladies, the forgotten regents of a long dead kingdom, covered the walls of each chamber. Along the walls sat various curved cabinets that no doubt once held ornaments of state, but which were now empty and rotted to the point of disintegration.

Kylla and Jed touched nothing, sticking to the center of each chamber, paying close attention to every shadow and the echoes of their footsteps within the stone walls of the tower. Finally, they had circumambulated the entire series of chambers and returned to the entry hall. As they walked to the spiral staircase in the center of the chamber, Kylla spoke the first words either had uttered since entering the tower.

"What are we looking for now?"

"A passage that leads beneath the tower to the treasure chamber," Jed said as he tried to peer up into the darkness of the spiral staircase.

"You mean we have to go underground?" Kylla asked, her voice breaking just a little. "Why didn't you mention that?"

"After what happened in the cave last summer, I didn't think you would come," Jed replied truthfully, hoping that Kylla would stay and see the adventure though.

Jed saw Kylla's face flush in the dim lantern light with the memory of how she had panicked when the entrance to the cave they were playing in the previous summer had collapsed. Kylla could climb any tree without fear, but she hated confined spaces and had never wanted to explore the cave.

But Jed had insisted. He had led them out through another entrance at the end of the cave and never mentioned Kylla's frantic tears, neither then nor later. Partly because he knew how much it embarrassed her, and partly because Kylla was the bravest person he knew, and if he had stopped to think for one minute her fears of suffocation and death were well-founded, he might easily have panicked himself. Having now mentioned the unmentionable, Jed held his breath as he waited to see what Kylla would do.

"Well," Kylla said, inhaling deeply, "as the *Book of Kell* says, '*The bitter salt of your fears are best dissolved with the pure water of action.*' How do we get below the tower?"

Jed sighed in relief and waved the lantern around the chamber. "I don't know. I thought there might be a door, or a secret passage, but the walls between the rooms and even the outer walls seem too thin."

Kylla squinted and slowly looked around the chamber. Jed could see her silently judging the thickness of the walls, the distance between the supporting archways, and the curvature of the spiral staircase.

Kylla's father was the town stonemason and master carpenter, and he had taught her all he knew about load-bearing walls and the intricacies of creating structural stability with stone and wood. Jed knew Kylla's naturally mathematical mind took to problems of engineering and construction with an ease that caused her father both immense pride (that his only true progeny understood the subtleties of his profession even better than he did) and also grave concern since math and science were frowned upon in the Kellish community, especially for young girls. The Kellish people had long ago abandoned nearly all technology and lived a simple life with little regard for anything more progressive than a horse-drawn carriage.

Fortunately, Kylla was only ever concerned with her father's appreciation of her talents, and always ignored his admonishments that "decent young girls don't concern themselves with how much weight a center beam will hold before falling on her mother's head." To Kylla, such mathematical flights of fancy were her favorite daydreams.

Jed watched Kylla, knowing better than to disturb her when her mind was working on a problem. For a brief moment he wondered what he would ever do if she wasn't at his side in moments like this. The thought evaporated when Kylla spoke.

"You're right about the walls being too thin for a secret passage. They are. But that staircase is thicker than it needs to be. Look."

Kylla grabbed Jed's arm and cast the lantern light up into the staircase. "The staircase above doesn't have a back wall. It doesn't need it. See how the stone is reinforced with iron beams?"

Jed followed her line of sight, but not her line of thought. "I see it, but what does it mean?"

Kylla pulled Jed around into the next chamber, and then the next and then the next until they stood before the back wall of the spiral staircase.

"See," Kylla said, "on the ground floor the spiral staircase has a back wall. But it doesn't need a back wall, so my guess is on this side, the staircase continues down into the lower level. It's brilliant, really. It's hidden in plain sight. Right where no one would think to look."

"You thought of it," Jed said, placing a hand on her shoulder.

"Yes, well, I don't think like most folks," Kylla replied, clearly pleased with the realization her statement was true. "There must be a latch or a lever of some kind that allows part of the wall to move. We have to find it before we can find the stairs."

Jed carefully placed the lantern on the floor where it would provide them with ample light to search for the latch as he and Kylla began to run their hands over every centimeter of the wall.

"Here," Jed said finally, bending down to place his hand on a stone near the floor. "There's no mortar around this stone."

Jed pushed the stone with all his strength and it slowly slid inward. As the palm-sized stone grated against the surrounding rock, he heard a muffled clicking noise, and a large door-shaped section of the staircase wall swung out ever-so-slightly.

The gap between the door and the wall was just barely enough to slide a hand between. Jed and Kylla wedged their fingers into the gap and pulled with all their combined strength until the doorway was wide enough for them to squeeze through.

Jed grabbed the lantern and slipped into the narrow secret passage. He found himself standing at the top of a wide spiral staircase, the twin of the one above. Kylla stepped through the passage to stand beside him and stare down the seemingly endless steps into the pitch-black darkness below.

"Well, at least it's not a cave," Kylla whispered, taking the first step down the stairs. Jed hurried behind her, holding the lantern out, its light revealing only a scant few meters of what lay below them.

His heart pounding in his chest, his breath catching in his throat, Jed felt Kylla do something she had never done in all the years of their adventures together — she reached out and took his hand. He did not look at her, but squeezed her hand in the darkness, thankful again that she had been the one brave enough to admit, even with such a small gesture, the depths of their mutual fear.

The spiral staircase went down and down, their footsteps clacking against the stone, turn after turn, leading them deeper and deeper beneath the tower.

Eventually, the monotonous rhythm of their descent began to calm them a little. Their breathing became shallower and their eyesight adjusted to the darkness. The repetition of step after step even lulled Jed into relaxing his grip on Kylla's hand, but neither felt so calm, or so brave, as to break the connection.

Finally, after what seemed to Jed like ten or twenty minutes, but was in reality more like three, they came to the bottom of the stairwell and found a door. Or, more accurately, what was left of a door. Someone long ago had tried to blast their way through the two-meter-high wood and iron door. That attempt to break through the door had been partially successful, leaving it tilted and twisted at a precarious angle, wedged into the rubbled remains of the stone doorframe.

"Doesn't look like we're the first to make it here," Kylla noted, staring at the ruined door.

"Doesn't look like they made it out, either," Jed said, immediately wishing he hadn't. "Maybe we can push the door and squeeze through that hole," he offered, hoping to distract from his previous statement.

Kylla nodded her agreement and Jed knelt down near the hole between the door and the wall. Stretching his arm out, he slid the lantern through the hole so it would be on the other side, waiting for them.

Jed watched Kylla calculating the weight of door and the likelihood of the wall collapsing further while she crawled beneath it. "If I push from down there and you pull here, it should move just enough for us to slip through," she said.

"Right," Jed said as he grabbed the edge of the door and pulled. Kylla knelt down and wedged herself partway into the hole. Grunting as his muscles strained against the weight of the door, Jed watched Kylla push from below.

Suddenly, the door began to move.

"Quick, Jed!" Kylla shouted, trying to squeeze through the opening as Jed hurried to slide in behind her. But he was too slow, or she was too quick, or the wall was simply too unstable, because before they could do anything about it, the stone wall crumbled above them and the door pivoted, crashing down with a thunderous clang.

Jed opened his eyes and found himself face to face with Kylla, lying side by side, trapped beneath the massive bulk of the door and hemmed in on all sides by the jagged ruins of the collapsed wall. Craning his neck back, he could make out the light of the lantern seeping through a crack just big enough for a head to peak through.

Jed stayed silent a moment, taking in the sudden change in events and trying to remain calm, if for no other reason than to impress Kylla and encourage the same response.

"Are you hurt?" Jed asked.

"No," Kylla replied. "Are you?"

"There's a big rock on my leg, but nothing feels broken."

Jed struggled against the rocks beside his head. "I think we're trapped, though. I can't bend my arms much in this position. Can you move enough to budge these rocks?"

"I can't move anything." Kylla said as she tried to shift the rock nearest her head with no effect. "Jed."

"Yes."

"We might really be in trouble this time," Kylla said, a true hint of fear suffusing her voice as her breath started to quicken. In the dim light from the lantern, Jed could see Kylla was beginning to panic.

This was much worse than being trapped in a cave. The darkness, the pressure of the heavy door above, the stones from the wall all around...he saw tears welling up in her eyes and sensed a scream building in her chest. Jed tried to calm himself and keep a cool head, but the sight of Kylla's distress added to his own mounting fear of confinement and only served to weaken his belief in their eventual escape.

"Don't worry, Ky," Jed said, trying to sound confident, as his voice cracked. "We'll think of something. We always do."

Suddenly, the sound of something moving in the darkness and scampering over the top of the door threw them into silence.

Jed listened, trying to figure out what the creature might be while trying not to imagine something dangerous. Then, the light from the lantern vanished and a head appeared in the crevice that was their only source of light and escape.

Losing all sense of composure and forgetting any mutual rivalry, Jed screamed at the top of his lungs, joined immediately by Kylla. They both continued screaming, vainly hoping the shadowed head would go away, but it remained, and eventually their screams faded and fell away into a dumb silence.

"If this is the best idea you can come up with, then you are really lucky I decided to follow you."

"Fallon!" shouted Kylla, relief flooding her voice at the sound of her little brother's words.

Fallon pulled his head back from the crevice just enough to let the light of the lantern reveal his face. "Why didn't you just push the door over and walk over the top of it, instead of trying to go under?" he asked innocently.

Unlike Kylla, Fallon was dark skinned with curly, close shaved hair. He was smaller than most eleven-year-olds and his hand-me-down wool clothes hung loosely on him, but his large brown eyes radiated a sensitive intelligence.

"Because," Jed replied, "we didn't know the wall was going to collapse."

Jed was thankful Kylla's adopted little brother had followed them yet again, but he was also a little miffed Fallon was once more saving them from their own carelessness. Just once, Jed wished an adventure would go exactly the way he planned it.

Fallon disappeared from the opening in the stones. Jed heard him rooting around in the rubble.

"There's a strip of iron plating that has come unbolted from the door," Fallon said over his shoulder. "I'm going to use one of the stones from the wall as a fulcrum and see if I can raise the door enough for you to crawl out."

"How did you find us?" Kylla asked.

From her tone, Jed knew she was impressed with her brother's attention to the physics of the problem facing them.

"I followed your tracks."

Fallon grunted as he set his small frame to heaving the long iron plate from the crumbled rocks. "It was pretty easy. Like when Jed's grandfather taught us to track deer that time."

"But how did you know we were leaving camp?" Kylla persisted. Jed, too, wondered how her brother always knew what she was up to.

"I had a dream," Fallon replied. "You were standing the middle of a wheat field and holding a large stone above your head, and then something whispered 'help her,' and I woke up. I always trust my dreams. So I slipped out of bed and went looking for you and when I saw you were gone, I went back and got dressed and followed your footprints in the dew until I reached the woods. It's funny, but I wasn't scared running through the woods alone. The trees felt like friends."

Fallon dragged the iron plate to the edge of the door and went to fetch the largest stone he could manage to slide across the floor. He worked in silence for a few minutes.

Jed could hold his curiosity no more. "How did you know which tower we were in?"

"That was easy," Fallon said behind grunts. "The poem of Lord Narrish and the Morikon." Fallon recited it as he shoved the stone into place.

"Beneath the eternal gods above,
Guarded by the Morikon's power,
Rests the Triple Crown treasure whereof,
Lord Narrish built his mortal tower."

Jed's mouth fell open as he heard Fallon recite the words. "How did you know the poem?" he asked, astounded that anyone other than himself would have heard of it.

"Well," Fallon said a bit sheepishly, "I saw the *Tales from the Time Before* in your bag one day while you and Ky were swimming in the pond and I read it while you weren't looking. I didn't figure you would mind. Especially if I didn't tell you."

Jed couldn't figure out which was more annoying — that Fallon had been sneaking looks at his secret book behind his back, or that he had apparently managed to memorize the entire thing in one furtive reading.

Actually, Jed did know. He would gladly have shown the book to Fallon, whose interest in the history of the starship and their ancestors was as deep as his own. However, it had taken Jed weeks of reading and re-reading to memorize the best sections of the book. Fallon's mind was simply too deep and too quick to compete with.

Even his sister, whose subtle mastery of mathematics was always getting her unwanted attention in the classroom, could not match Fallon's innate grasp of numbers. If he weren't so young, his brilliance would simply have been annoying, but combined with his age and size, his intelligence was infuriating. Less so for Jed than everyone else, but it still stung his pride a bit to be so easily outpaced when it came to his favorite subject.

Fortunately, Fallon was used to this, and in most circumstances simply pretended to be a little less bright than he actually was. But when he was distracted, he sometimes forgot to hide his brilliance.

Fallon continued to explain while heaving the iron plate on top of the stone and placing it near the door to give better leverage to his fulcrum.

"The poem seemed to be referring to a constellation, or set of constellations, and the only one that seemed to make sense was from the illustration in the book. Four bowls, four elements, equals four stars, and Aries the Ram was the constellation above. Then, once I was in the tower, I just followed your footprints through the dust.

"Okay. I think I'm ready."

Fallon had lifted the long end of the plate above his head, balancing the other end on the stone and sliding the edge of it under the lip of the fallen door. He would only need to pull down on the elevated longer end of the iron plate, and hopefully the door would move. He raised his hands above his head and took a deep breath.

From beneath the door, Jed could hear the sounds of his exertion, and he could feel the door shudder and move slightly above them. He turned his head to see Kylla's face full of expectation and fear. His hopes were just beginning to rise when the door suddenly dropped back into place.

"I can't move it," Fallon said, frustration obvious in his voice. "I don't weigh enough."

The bitterness of his words hung in the air. Jed knew Fallon was constantly being teased by the other children for being small even more so than for being smart. He could pretend to be less intelligent to fit in, but he could never pretend to be bigger or stronger. Jed could see tears begin to well up in Fallon's eyes.

"Don't worry, Fal," Kylla said. "I've got an idea."

"Yeah?" Fallon asked, sniffing.

"Yeah," Kylla said, confidence filling her voice.

Jed was just as relieved to hear this as Fallon, because he had no ideas for getting them out of their predicament.

"Fallon," Kylla asked. "Is the beam above the doorway still intact?"

"Yes," Fallon said, looking up through the dim lantern light to a heavy, twenty-centimeter-wide wooden beam that had braced the walls where the door once swung.

"Good," Kylla said. "I have some rope in my bag. Find a place on the edge of the door to tie off the rope."

"Brilliant idea, Ky," Fallon exclaimed as Kylla shrugged off her knapsack and passed it out through the crevice to Fallon.

"What idea?" Jed asked, completely confused by their apparent formation of a plan without his slightest comprehension.

"We're going to use the support beam as a pulley," Kylla replied, her eyes beaming with excitement in the shadows. "Fallon will throw the rope over the beam and attach one end to the edge of the door. Then he'll pass us the other end and we'll pull on the rope while he pulls down on the iron plate. With the iron plate acting as a lever for the stone fulcrum and the extra pull from the rope, we should be able to move the door."

"Well," Jed said, "I don't care whether it works or not, I'm still not going to listen to you lecture about how much fun physics is."

Fallon quickly set about the task of tossing the rope over the beam and securing it to the edge of the door. There was a crack in the wood near the point where the iron plate was wedged beneath the door. Fallon tied a large knot in the end of the rope and then jammed the length of rope just above the knot into the crack so the bulk of the knot would hold the rope in place.

Jed watched through gaps in the stones as Fallon completed his task. He turned to look at Kylla, crammed beneath the door, their dusty and sweaty bodies pressed close together. For a moment, Jed found himself thinking how pretty Kylla looked.

Which was a preposterous thought. He realized, suddenly, if he were trapped like this with Syrra Kallinn, he would probably try to kiss her. But then, he'd be happy to kiss Syrra any day, as he had nurtured a terrible crush on her for the last two years.

But the idea of kissing Kylla, however pretty she might be, seemed just plain silly. It would be like kissing his sister — if he had a sister.

Kylla, he was sure, was wishing she was trapped beneath the door with his brother, Tallu. It was no secret to Jed that she had been in love with Tal since she was a little girl. Of course, she had never said anything about it to anyone, especially Jed, but he saw the way she always doted on every word Tal said when they were together.

"Ready in there?" Fallon asked as a rope was tossed through the crevice, snapping Jed back from his thoughts. He smiled at Kylla as they each grabbed the rope.

"Let us know when," Kylla said, drawing the rope taunt, jockeying with Jed to get a better grip.

"Now," Fallon said as he pulled himself up at the end of the iron lever, using all his body weight to bounce up and down to try and budge the door.

Kylla and Jed pulled on the rope with all their strength. It wasn't easy because of their position and the angle of the rope, but after only a few seconds of effort, they could feel the door begin to move above them. They pulled harder, drawing the rope down and the door up.

Fallon's feet touched the floor and he drew his legs up, trying to keep his full weight on the lever. The door had risen by nearly twenty centimeters, giving almost enough room for Jed and Kylla to squeeze through the crevice.

Suddenly, the shifting of the door caused the stones holding it in place on one side to crumble. The door slid to the side, and Jed and Kylla scrambled through the opening as Fallon fell to the floor under the iron plate. Fallon rolled the iron plate off himself and rubbed his chest as Jed and Kylla ran to him. Kylla swept him up from the floor and wrapped him in her arms.

"Thank you, little brother," Kylla said, kissing him.

"You carry our water again," Jed said, using the old Kellish phrase denoting when one person was beholden to another.

"Yes," Fallon said, smiling as he disengaged himself from his sister's grasp. "Maybe next time you'll include me in your adventures from the start."

"Then how would you be able to save us?" Kylla asked as she kissed him again.

Jed picked up the lantern from the floor and swung it around, getting a good look at what lay on the other side of the door they had been trapped under.

Kylla and Fallon followed his gaze and the light of the lantern. Before them stretched a short corridor, and even in the darkness they could see that several other corridors branched out from it.

Jed took a tentative step into the corridor, peering into the darkness. He could just make out where the passageway ended and turned to the right.

CHAPTER 3
LABYRINTH LAIR

"While the labyrinth is a common symbol in several Origin World cultures, representing spiritual progress, the most famous example is that of the Greek myth of the Minotaur, a half-man, half-bull creature trapped in a labyrinth by his father, King Minos. Pledged to kill the Minotaur, the Athenian Theseus fell in love with the King's daughter, Araidne, who gave Theseus a ball of thread to find his way out of the labyrinth."

Famous Myths of the Origin World,
Halbread Wallace, Helios Press, 3rd edition

"Like Adam, I was apparently united by no link to any other being in existence: but his state was far different from mine in every other respect. He had come forth from the hands of God a perfect creature, happy and prosperous, guarded by the especial care of his Creator; he was allowed to converse with, and acquire knowledge from, beings of a superior nature: but I was wretched, helpless, and alone."

The words of the 'Monster' in Mary Shelley's novel,
Frankenstein (1818 CE)

"It looks like a maze," Kylla said, sounding depressed at the prospect of wandering through endless, dank corridors beneath the ground.

"A labyrinth," Fallon said knowledgeably. "A maze has right angles. A labyrinth has curved walls and leads to the center. The stories said the treasure was in a labyrinth guarded by the Morikon."

"Right," Jed said, putting the lantern down as he slid his backpack off and rummaged through it. "In ancient times, on the Origin World, labyrinths were used to guard treasures. They were also used by spiritual seekers. The journey through the corridors of the labyrinth became a journey for contemplating the world within."

"You seem to know an awful lot about labyrinths," Kylla said. "Any idea how to get to the center?"

"Without a map, we'll have to find our way like anyone else…one turn at a time," Jed said.

"We could be lost forever in there," Kylla said. It was clear from the look on her face she was thinking about cutting their losses and retreating from this particular challenge.

"That's why I brought this," Jed said, holding up a large ball of twine. "We'll tie it to something out here, and then we'll always be able to find our way back."

"That's a smart idea," Fallon said.

"I got it from an old legend from the Origin World," Jed said as he tied the twine securely to a large rock. "There was an ancient king who imprisoned a creature that was half-man, half-bull in a labyrinth, just like Lord Narrish did with the Morikon. And there was a young warrior who went into the labyrinth to kill the monster, but knowing he would get lost, a princess gave him a ball of thread to find his way out again."

"I've never heard of that story," Fallon said with interest.

"My grandfather told it to me," Jed said, pleased to finally know something that Fallon seemed unaware of. "I'm guessing that Lord Narrish had heard the story as well."

"Well," Kylla said, picking up the lantern, "let's get started. We have to be back before dawn or Mrs. Lemmick is going to serve us for breakfast."

They walked side by side down the ancient corridor, the lantern casting a bubble of light around them. The air in the labyrinth was cool and they stayed close together as much for warmth as for safety.

They turned left, then right, found a dead end and then backtracked to start again. Jed took a small pad of paper and pencil from his pack and began drawing a map of their progress. They made their way slowly, by trial and error, inching closer and closer to the center of the labyrinth.

It took much longer than they had expected, and after a time Jed forgot to be concerned about wandering through an underground maze on their way to a treasure potentially guarded by a mythical beast. Instead, he found himself impatient from continually retracing their steps.

Fallon seemed impatient for another reason.

"How much oil is left in that lamp?" Fallon asked.

Kylla examined the lamp and grunted in annoyance. "Not enough," she said. "Maybe another hour's worth. Maybe less."

Jed held his hand-drawn map up to catch the lantern light. "I think we're close. We're getting closer and closer to the center. It can't be much longer," he said, leading them around the next corner.

Jed was, in fact, correct. They were extremely close. So close that the very next turn led them into a wide-open space in the center of the labyrinth.

With Kylla holding the lantern high, they walked into the chamber, seeing a tall, circular altar of stone raised upon a dais and encircled by stairs at the center of the room. Shoulder to shoulder, they edged closer to the altar, Jed's foot just touching the top of the stairs.

They froze as they heard a deep rumbling sound. However much it reminded Jed of a massive thunderstorm, he nonetheless recognized the voice of something very large and powerful.

"You are much smaller than I expected," the voice said, shaking the walls of the chamber and causing Jed's heart to vibrate in his chest. "You may turn around."

Shaking with fear and terrified of what they would find, Jed, Kylla, and Fallon slowly turned to face the Morikon. The statue in the courtyard some fifty meters above their heads did not do the Morikon justice. It was larger than the beast depicted in stone.

Even though it was still seated on a massive throne, the four twisted horns of its head nearly touched the curve of the domed ceiling. To stand erect, it would have to stand in the center of the room where the ceiling was highest.

This seemed to be the Morikon's intention, as it raised itself up from the throne onto its massive, tree-trunk-like legs while flexing the biceps of its enormous arms. As the Morikon stepped closer to the light of the lantern, the ground shaking with each footfall, the reddish black of its scale-like skin could be seen stretched tight across its muscled flesh.

Finally, the head of the Morikon emerged from the shadows near the ceiling, blood-red eyes peering out from the face of a ram. Not really the face of a ram. It was a face blended between that of a man and a ram. Animal, yet humanly familiar. There was something about the reddish eyes that, despite their color, also seemed vaguely human.

Jed, Kylla, and Fallon trembled as the Morikon rose up and towered above them, smiling a crooked, beastlike smile. It slowly spread its enormous, leathery wings. The sight of the Morikon looming five meters above them induced as much vertigo as fear, and Jed and the other two fell back onto the stairs.

"You have come for the treasure," the Morikon said matter-of-factly, its deep basso profundo voice echoing throughout the corridors of the labyrinth. The sound of their breathing, rapid and panicked, was the only initial response the three adventurers could manage. Then, surprising Kylla, Fallon, and especially himself, Jed spoke.

"You can't possibly still be alive," Jed croaked.

The Morikon settled its gaze entirely upon Jed, its lips curling in what might have been a smile but seemed more like a snarl.

"You are observant," the Morikon said. "And you are correct. I am not alive."

Sighing so deeply that the sound shook the children's clothes, the Morikon gently folded its wings tight to its back and slowly stepped backward, collapsing into the mammoth stone throne. The room shuddered with the impact of the Morikon's weight into the giant chair.

Kylla and Fallon looked at Jed, amazed the Morikon had retreated at such a simple statement. Jed wondered where this new conversation would lead them, because he found himself speaking again.

"You're techne," Jed said, suddenly grasping something he had always subconsciously known about the stories and legends of Wyconna.

"Again," said the Morikon, "you are correct."

The Morikon rested its massive head in its palm, its elbow propped up by the arm of the throne. "My predecessor was alive. All of my predecessors were alive."

Glancing at them, Jed could see that Kylla and Fallon also understood now. This Morikon that sat before them on its throne was not the first Morikon, or the real Morikon. It was some kind of machine. Some replication of a living thing. Techne — a thing made through technology.

Kylla found her voice enough to squeak out a question. "Did Lord Narrish fashion you?"

"Lord Narrish fashioned all of my kind," the Morikon replied.

"But why would Lord Narrish create you or the living Morikon?" Fallon asked. "The Morikon, you, or whatever came first, nearly destroyed his kingdom."

At this the Morikon laughed, the deep sound of the creature's painful mirth shaking the walls of the chamber, freeing dust from the ceiling to cascade down over the room.

"Lord Narrish made the first Morikon to keep the people under his rule. To strike fear in their hearts that something might destroy them. He fashioned it from bits of myths and legends, living animals, and humans. He was a scientist before he became a lord of a kingdom. He understood more than most do about how to blend the biology of different creatures.

"So he created a monster to keep him in power. For Lord Narrish was not of this land. He came from further toward the ship's bow, banished by his own people for his abuse of technology. He needed to convince the local people, people who had long since forgotten they lived on a ship sailing between the stars, that he was the chosen one, the one destined to be their Lord and Master.

"And so, after creating the Morikon, he fought a mock battle with the creature, deliberately hobbling it in its combat against him, seeming to defeat it and save the kingdom. Then, with the people under his command, the towers of the castle were raised, the labyrinth was built beneath the ground, and the first Morikon became imprisoned by its creator to guard a paltry treasure." The Morikon sighed, the sadness of its story obviously affecting it deeply.

"But what about you?" Fallon asked. "What happened to the original creature, and how did you come to be trapped here?"

"Because he was from the techne culture, Lord Narrish lived much longer than any of his subjects. Nearly three hundred years, in fact. However, his creation was not as healthy as he. The first Morikon barely lived past its second year. But Lord Narrish needed his monster, so he tried again. And again, and again. Twenty-seven Morikons in all. The weakest lived barely a month, and the final one managed to survive nearly sixty years. Eventually Lord Narrish tired of his toiling and set about to create me. A creature that would not die, because it was not alive."

"And when Lord Narrish died, you were trapped here," Jed said.

"Not trapped in the way you mean, small human. But imprisoned, nonetheless. Although the corridors of this labyrinth are too small for me, I could force my way from this place.

"But where would I go? Here in these lands I am a monster. A creature from stories told to frighten children. And in the techne lands, I am an abomination. A relic from a dark age forged by a twisted mind. I am a singular creature, separate from all else." The Morikon paused and then spoke again, clearly reciting the words of something memorized.

"Hateful day when I received life!.....Accursed creator! Why did you form a monster so hideous that even you turned from me in disgust? God, in pity, made man beautiful and alluring, after his own image; but my form is a filthy type of yours, more horrid even from the very resemblance. Satan had his companions, fellow-devils, to admire and encourage him; but I am solitary and abhorred."

The Morikon lowered his head a moment.

"That's from Mary Shelley's *Frankenstein*," Jed said, looking up at the Morikon with sadness. It was one of the few novels from the Origin World Kellish children were allowed to read.

"I suppose I should not be surprised the Kellish teach that particular work," the Morikon said with a gentle laugh, but which still rumbled like thunder directly overhead.

"Is there nothing the Sentient can do for you?" Kylla asked, clearly sympathetic to the plight of this massive monster seated before her. "Surely it can help you?"

"I spoke with the ship's sentient about this many years ago," the Morikon replied. "It assured me I could transfer my mind to another form. An artificial form, of course, but something less intimidating. A human form, even. However, I have grown accustomed to this body, this shell. And Lord Narrish, whatever his many faults, built me well. I have lasted for more than a thousand years, and I will likely last many, many more. And maybe, when the *Celestial Pilgrim* has reached its destination, I will find a world where I can roam free, where the only treasure I guard will be my own company."

The sudden mention of the treasure reminded Jed why they were there, huddled together in the dank air of the labyrinth's center chamber.

"Is the treasure still here?" Jed asked.

"Yes," the Morikon said, "the treasure is still here. Many have come to claim it, and I have turned them all away. But none have come for several hundred years. To be honest, I could have given it to any of them. The control Lord Narrish exerted over me ended with his death. But I knew if I relinquished the treasure, there would be no more hunters coming to find it. So, I used my powers, which are many, and planted in their minds a grand story of how they came to the castle and found no Morikon and no treasure, just dust and ruins. Eventually, my story worked so well no one came. And then I was alone. Until you arrived, crashing through my outer doors.

"You are the youngest who have ever come."

Jed suddenly understood how they might walk out of the castle carrying the treasure of Lord Narrish. They would have to do the one thing no one had ever thought to do.

"Morikon, we have come a great distance, and we have nearly died in our attempt to find the treasure of Lord Narrish, but we know we cannot take it from you by force or trickery. So we ask you humbly, will you give it to us?"

The Morikon was silent for a long time, the only sound in the room his heavy breath, or what might have been breath, as surely a techne monster did not need to breathe.

"No one has ever asked for the treasure before," the Morikon said. "I was placed here to guard it, but the man and people it belonged to have long since passed from this existence. Once I no longer guarded it for others, I guarded it for myself, in the hopes it would provide some contact with the outside world, even if it was a violent and hateful contact.

"However, I have been alone these many years, and the ship we live upon will soon reach its destination, and you are but children, and the first to show any interest or concern for my own being, and there are three of you, which seems to me to be some sort of providence, so yes, I say, you may have the treasure, such as it is."

The Morikon gestured to the altar on the raised dais behind them, indicating the location of the treasure.

"Thank you," Jed and Kylla said simultaneously.

Fallon gave a small bow and nod of thanks to the Morikon, and then all three slowly turned and walked up the stairs of the dais to the altar. At the top of the stairs, the altar spread out before them some two meters long and a meter wide. It was covered with a long, faded green altar cloth, embroidered with Lord Narrish's coat of arms: a man doing battle with a half-man, half-ram beast.

In the center of the altar, spaced equally apart, were three items. Three items so simple that Jed, Kylla, and Fallon turned to each other in confusion. Surely this was not the treasure, for on the altar lay a long but simple dagger, a stone the size of a walnut pierced by a leather thong through a hole in its center, and a small, leather-clad book with the symbol of a labyrinth burned onto its cover.

From behind them, the Morikon spoke, its voice reverberating around the chamber. "Each item you see before you once belonged to a single man. A man who had been chosen by the Sentient itself to begin a new order of Servants of the *Tannett*. He was the first Tellandor priest. Apa'Tu Kana-Shaan. By all accounts, he was a prime example of the holiness of the Tellandor Order."

Jed knew this story from *The Tales from Before Times*. "Apa'Tu went on a pilgrimage to the Merrick towns of the Notesch Valley to stop the feuds and wars between them and bring the *Tannett*." Jed looked at the dagger before him. "But he was never heard from again. The legends always say he sat down one day in prayers and meditations and never arose. That he is still there, praying somewhere in a cave in the Mannigor Mountains."

"He may still be in prayer," the Morikon said, bitterness in his voice. "But not in this plane of existence. Lord Narrish invited the humble priest to be his guest at a private dinner. Hoping to convince Lord Narrish his experiments and projects did not reflect the best of humanity and of the nature of life, the priest agreed. But, Lord Narrish was not interested in sermons from a priest. He believed in no power higher than that of his own mind. Which turned out to be an irony that drove him mad.

"You see, he poisoned the priest Apa'Tu so he could steal the items you see before you and possess their powers. But what he did not realize is that in killing the priest, he had killed the only person who could teach him how to use them. He came here to this room every day until he died, struggling to unlock their secrets, but his mind was not strong enough to provide the key to their powers."

The Morikon was silent and the chamber felt eerily quiet. Not knowing what else to do, Jed reached out and took the dagger before him. Following his lead, Kylla reached out to take the stone necklace, and Fallon picked up the small leather book.

Slowly, somewhat dismayed their adventure had brought such a seemingly paltry reward, Jed turned again to face the Morikon, who greeted them with a snarling smile. "Not the treasure you had expected?" the Morikon asked, its deep laugh echoing around the room.

"No," Jed said, looking at his dagger as he and the other two descended the stairs to stand before the Morikon's throne. "We were expecting something a little more...valuable."

"There is more value in what you hold than you might expect," the Morikon said, his voice dropping to an even lower register. "If you study them, and learn how to use them, they will reward you beyond any simple treasure of gold and jewels. That tome in particular has been my constant and only companion, and I will miss it greatly.

"And now you must go. Dayrise is nearly upon the land, and you must return to your people."

"Dayrise!" exclaimed Jed, picking up the lantern from the floor and seeing how low the oil had burned. He turned to the giant ram-man-beast on its throne and quickly kneeled, Kylla and Fallon following his lead. He knew the creature was not alive in the same way he was alive, but he felt sorry for it all the same. Whether of flesh or techne so advanced he could not even conceive of it, Jed could sense the Morikon's *humanity*.

"Thank you, Morikon," Jed said. "We are forever indebted to you for this gift, and we will one day find a way to repay it."

"Yes," added Kylla, her heart clearly going out to the creature she had been terrified of such a short time ago. "And we will visit you when we can."

"I would like that very much," the Morikon said, meeting their gaze with his crimson eyes.

Jed, Kylla, and Fallon quickly stood and strode toward the entrance of the labyrinth, Jed leading the way with the lantern. At the edge of the chamber entrance, Fallon stopped and turned to the Morikon. "May I ask one last question?"

"You may."

"Is it true that you can breathe fire?" Fallon asked.

The Morikon laughed its deep rumbling laugh as it tilted its head back. Jed and Kylla stopped and looked back just in time to see a giant burst of crimson flame erupt from the Morikon's mouth and fill the inner chamber of the labyrinth. Fallon ran toward them, excitement, fascination, and fear mixed in equal proportion on his face.

"You couldn't have asked it a sensible question?" Kylla said, noticing her little brother's hair was slightly singed.

"I wish I'd thought to ask him that," Jed said, smiling at Fallon as he stuffed the dagger into his knapsack, holding it open as Kylla and Fallon did the same with their treasures.

The three ran back along through the labyrinth corridors, following the trail of twine around curves and corners until finally they arrived breathless at the collapsed door. Scrambling over the rubble of the door, they quickly mounted the stairs of the grand spiral staircase. The staircase seemed twice as long going up as it did going down, but they could see a faint light coming from the top of the spiraled steps and they knew full dayrise was not far away.

Finally, they climbed the last step and found themselves once more in the tower. Racing through the enormous tower door, they ran across the inner courtyard, seeing again the statue of Lord Narrish and the Morikon. Even in the dim, pre-morning light they could make out the ram-like face of the creature, and again, Jed felt sorry for it.

"Lord Narrish was an evil pile of kedrop," Kylla said, making a face at the stone lord.

"He was probably insane," Jed conjectured as he blew out the lantern and shoved it into his knapsack while he ran.

"He forgot what it meant to be human," Fallon said simply.

They raced from the inner to the outer courtyard, through the massive fissure in the castle wall, and down the steep hill upon which the castle stood. Stopping to catch their breaths briefly at the bottom of the hill, they gazed upward where, high above them, the sun-tube running the length of the ship gradually brightened, revealing the upward-sloping inner curve of the ship's tubular shape. Port and starboard, the ground curved up, fading out of sight behind the haze of the atmosphere, circling back like a planet turned inward upon itself. Toward the stern sat a range of impossibly high mountains, while toward the bow the interior of the ship seemed to go on forever.

"We'll never make it back to the camp before full dayrise," Fallon panted.

"We'll have to run the whole way," Jed said, already trying to think of a good excuse for the three of them to be emerging from the forest as the other students were emerging from their tents.

"I love a morning run," Kylla said, taking the lead and sprinting toward the forest. Exchanging looks of exasperation, Jed and Fallon started after her, knowing they would never be able to keep up.

By the time they made it back through the forest, around the beaches of Lake Kenno'Cha, and to the edge of the school camp, it was already full dayrise and the students were having breakfast at a series of tables fashioned from thick wooden planks with log stumps for stools. Their teacher, Mrs. Lemmick, stood at the head of the table issuing instructions on the day's itinerary.

Jed pointed to the table at the side of the main cabin where the last of the students lined up to get their breakfasts from the cook, Mr. Ninnos. Jed slipped his knapsack off and began to sneak through the bushes toward the food table. Kylla and Fallon followed suit. They quickly reached the corner of the cabin and, pausing to make sure no one was watching their entrance, casually stepped from the bushes to take their place in line at the buffet.

Jed smiled at Kylla and Fallon as he grabbed a plate and heaped it high with scrambled eggs and finnick sausage. Having filled their plates, they walked nonchalantly toward the table farthest from Mrs. Lemmick, who seemed completely preoccupied with informing the students about the intricacies of seddal fishing, which was apparently the big assignment of the day.

"It's like we were never gone," Jed said with a smirk as he placed his plate on the wooden table.

"Jed. Kylla. Fallon. How nice of you join us." The three swallowed bits of half-chewed sausage as they looked up to meet Mrs. Lemmick's steely gaze. "Seeing as you missed roll call this morning, and seeing as Mr. Ninnos found your beds empty when he woke the other students for breakfast, maybe you would like to tell us were you have been all night?"

All though it had been phrased as a question, it wasn't.

In the end they were punished with more chores, both during the camping trip and once back in the village, but everyone, Mrs. Lemmick included, believed the lie that Jed told. Because he simply told the truth. Or most of it, anyway. He had been on the verge of fabricating some enormous concoction of a lie when he realized as long as no one knew about the dagger, the stone, the book, and the

Morikon, the punishment, whatever it turned out to be, would make everyone happy. And so, Jed, with Kylla and Fallon chiming at the appropriate places, told some of the truth, but not all of it.

He told about the journey to the castle and the towers, but he made Kylla's finding of the correct tower have nothing to do with astronomy or constellations, but all to do with angles and the position of the stars. And he explained how she did the same thing to find the secret staircase. Then he described the long walk down the staircase, being trapped under the door, and how Fallon had saved them.

And when he told them about using twine to find their way through the labyrinth, he made it sound like something he had thought of on the spur of the moment and he was lucky to have a ball of twine in his pack. Of course, he said nothing about the Morikon and the treasure. Instead, when they finally got to the center chamber of the labyrinth, Jed explained, it was empty, long since robbed of any valuables. Their whole miserable journey, he said, left them running home empty-handed.

From the look she gave him, Jed couldn't tell if Mrs. Lemmick thought he was lying about coming home with nothing or simply lying about the entire story. She punished them, however, as though every word were true. Their fellow students, on the other hand, the ones who were Jed's real audience, did believe. And they thought it was an absolutely brilliant adventure. Jed, Kylla, and Fallon's standing among the other students rose in direct proportion to how far it fell with the teachers. Even Fallon, usually picked on daily, found that for the next few weeks, the other kids treated him especially well.

Mrs. Lemmick, for her part, openly vowed never again to let Jed tell any story of his misdeeds in a public setting. She would be lucky, she said, if the whole school didn't turn up missing the next morning. As far as she was concerned, this was the last educational trip she was going to chaperone.

So, Jed, Kylla, and Fallon spent the next three days of the camping trip helping prepare and serve meals, washing dishes, digging latrines, chopping wood, and hauling water in buckets from the creek. The fact they didn't complain, and seemed even to be enjoying themselves at times, only served to annoy Mrs. Lemmick more, and encouraged her to add to their chores. They were so exhausted by the end of each day they never managed to sneak a single look at the treasures the Morikon had granted them.

On the fourth day, they began their journey back to the village and, by nightfall three days later, they wearily dragged themselves through the doors of their homes and into the arms of their parents. Of course, Mrs. Lemmick immediately informed their parents of what had transpired, and the three were soon engaged in another round of grueling chores, this time dragging on for weeks. But that night, their first night back, they nonetheless risked further punishment and snuck out of their homes to meet at the old hollock tree, the place where they always met at night when planning an adventure.

CHAPTER 4: ARTIFACT EXAMINATION

"The town of Bannek lies at the sternward edge of the Notesch valley. It is not only the first of the Kellish towns to be established but is also the closest to the Pinnak Mountains, and thus to the rest of Wyconna proper. The town is rather large for a Kellish community, numbering some 300 men, women, and children. There are currently 52 Kellish communities spread mostly along the sternward side of the Notesch Valley. Unlike the Merrick towns, some 50 kilometers aft of the Pinak Mountain range, the Kellish are a largely gentle people, practicing both the avoidance of technology, which is the cornerstone of the Kellish philosophy, and the interfaith practices of the Tannett, *the holy book of the Tellandor Order."*
From *The Encyclopedia Wyconnica,* 112th Edition

Sitting beneath the hollock tree, its wide, drooping branches and long, sinewy leaves shielding them from the sight of any possible passersby, Jed, Kylla, and Fallon examined their respective treasures. Jed held the blade of his dagger up to what little moonlight seeped through the leaves while Kylla placed the leather thong with the stone over her head. Fallon flipped slowly through the small leather book, each page completely blank.

"Can I see the dagger?" Kylla asked.

"Sure." Jed handed her the blade. "I'm not sure it was worth all the trouble. It's just a dagger."

"That's not what the Morikon told us," Fallon mumbled, barely looking up from the pages of the book. "He said they were powerful artifacts if you knew how to use them."

"That just it." Jed sighed. "Lord Narrish had them for years and never figured out how to use them. How are we supposed to figure it out?"

"I don't know." Fallon closed the book and examined the cover, running his fingers over the symbol of a labyrinth burnt into the leather.

"Maybe they work together somehow," Kylla said, removing the leather necklace with the stone from around her neck. Holding the stone in her left hand, the leather thong dangling between her fingers, she held the blade with her right hand and closed her eyes in concentration. Jed watched silently as Kylla's hands slowly moved together. Fallon was concentrating as well. But his concentration was directed at the book in his hands. Kylla's hands, holding stone and blade, gently came together with a faint clink. She opened her eyes. Jed looked at her hands.

Nothing.

"It was worth a try," Kylla said.

"Maybe if we each hold one," Jed said, holding out his hand.

"Maybe I should have the dagger," Kylla said, staring at the artifacts she held.

"It's my blade. The Morikon gave it to me," Jed said.

"You just happened to end up standing in front of it. It was completely by chance you ended up with the dagger," Kylla replied.

"But the stone looks better on you," Jed said, immediately wishing he hadn't. To say that the stone looked better on Kylla was to imply the stone was a feminine item, and it made her look more feminine for wearing it.

Kylla hated looking feminine. She was always teased by the other girls for being a tomboy, and it was all her mother could do to force her into wearing a dress. A bow in her hair was the sort of thing to send her into a frenzy.

"It does not look better on me," Kylla said, clutching the dagger tighter as she tossed the stone to Jed. Jed caught the stone in his right hand and grabbed Ky's wrist with his left.

"This isn't fair," Jed said.

"I'm not wearing that stone," Kylla said, gritting her teeth. "Besides, I'm better with knives."

"Then I could use the practice," Jed said, sensing he might have to wrestle the blade from Kylla and even if he managed to succeed, he might wish he hadn't. "You can wear it inside your blouse. That way no one will ever know you have it with you. You can't go around town wearing a dagger."

"I can always keep it in my knapsack," Kylla fumed.

"We can share them," Jed said, finally hitting on an idea he knew Kylla couldn't refuse. While he wanted the blade for himself, in a way, Kylla was right. The only reason he had the knife was because he happened to be standing in front of it when he walked up to the altar in the center of the Morikon's labyrinth. It could just have easily ended up going to Kylla or Fallon. Jed looked in Kylla's eyes and knew he had won the argument. Kylla was headstrong, like himself, but she also had a potent sense of justice.

"Will you two stop fighting? I've found something."

Jed and Kylla turned to see Fallon holding up the book in the pale moonlight beneath the tree. They glanced back at each other.

"Deal," she said. "You keep it this week, and I'll keep it next week."

"Deal," Jed said, grinning as he claimed the dagger. Kylla palmed the stone, wrapping the leather thong around her left wrist.

"What is it?" Jed asked, stepping closer to Fallon.

"Look," Fallon said, pointing to the cover of the small book.

"Where did those words come from?" Kylla asked in surprise as she leaned in to examine the book.

"They just appeared," Fallon said, referring to the two lines of text now etched into the leather cover beneath the symbol of the labyrinth.

"Did you do something to it?" Jed asked as he gently touched a finger to the cover.

"No," Fallon replied. "I was just staring at it. Thinking."

"What were you thinking about?" Kylla asked as she placed a hand on her brother's shoulder.

"I was thinking about what the labyrinth meant. And what the book might be. I was just staring at it, concentrating, letting my mind relax when all of the sudden these words slowly appeared on the cover like something emerging out of a fog."

"You realize what this is, don't you?" Jed said, barely able to contain his excitement.

"Yes," Fallon replied, his breathing quick and heavy as Kylla read the words on the cover aloud.

"The *Tannett: A Book of All Faiths*," Kylla said softly, shivering a little as a gentle breeze stirred the branches of the tree.

"It belonged to the first Tellandor priest, Apa'Tu Kana-Shaan," Jed said. "It must be the first copy of the *Tannett* ever to exist on Wyconna."

"But why are the pages blank?" Kylla wondered aloud.

"To keep it safe," Jed said. "My grandfather said when the Sentient first established the Tellandor Order and decided to use the *Tannett*, it upset a lot of people, so to guard the book, and the priests, the pages must only reveal themselves to the right people."

"Not the right *people*," Fallon said. "It reveals itself to the right *mind*. You have to train your mind to be able to see the words."

"So, if the book changes based on the mind of the person holding it," Jed said, fully realizing the implications of the artifact, "that means it must be techne."

"Which also means," Kylla added, clearly seeing where Jed's logic was leading him, "that the dagger and the stone might be techne, as well."

"And to master all three of them," Fallon concluded, "you have to master your mind."

"Which makes sense considering the teachings of the *Tannett* and the Tellandor Order," Jed said.

He lifted the dagger up into the moonlight beside the book Fallon held, and Kylla raised the stone in her hand. Standing there beneath the hollock tree, holding the mysterious artifacts from the labyrinth between them, Jed, Kylla, and Fallon separately pondered their futures.

How powerful were the dagger, stone, and book? What powers did they possess? And how long might it take to train their minds to be able to unlock and master the secrets of these ancient items? Most importantly, how could they manage all of this without their parents or the town finding out?

Jed, as usual, had a plan.

The next morning, he woke to the sound of his mother rapping a large, wooden mixing spoon on the door of his room. It was her morning ritual for rousing her two boys from slumber.

"Time to get up, Jed," she said as she walked back down the hall and headed downstairs to finish making breakfast.

Jed blinked sleep from his eyes and sat up in bed, scratching his pillow-mussed hair. Looking out of the single small window, he could see the sun-tube beginning to brighten to its early morning intensity. Yawning, he swung his feet around and placed them on the cool wooden slats of the floor.

Standing up, he scratched his back beneath his long, white sleeping gown and walked to the small table in the corner of his room. The room was only his alone until his elder brother returned, at which time Jed would be back to sharing the room with the loudest snorer in the Notesch Valley. On the table sat a large pitcher of water and a wide ceramic basin. Pouring the water into the basin, Jed proceeded to splash the cool, refreshing liquid over his face and head.

Dressing quickly, Jed thought about his brother, Tallu, and wondered when he would be coming home. After a year of absence, Jed missed his brother more than his adolescent pride would let him admit. Tal had turned seventeen a little more than a year ago and promptly left home for his Landdesh.

Landdesh was a long-standing tradition among the Kellish peoples. When a boy or girl turned seventeen, he or she was allowed to leave the Kellish towns and the Notesch valley to explore the other societies aboard Wyconna, the human section of the great starship they all inhabited. The purpose of Landdesh was for young adults to learn about other cultures and societies so they could then return home to make a final decision about whether or not to continue living the Kellish life.

If, after seeing what other ways of living were possible, Kellish youth decided to leave their homes and the valley, they were free to do so, but under the condition that they only return to visit their families once every five years. If, on the other hand, they decided to stay and live the Kellish life, they would become full members of the community. Every Kellish teenager was required to make this choice upon reaching adulthood.

Jed wondered what Tal's choice would be. He was already three weeks late in returning home, and the thought had passed silently between Jed and his parents that Tal had possibly already made his decision.

Jed didn't believe it, though. Tal was always too much the good Kellish son, the one who did his chores without being asked and who truly seemed to enjoy working in the fields all day long. He hadn't even been excited about his Landdesh journey. He considered it more of a duty than a holiday from the daily drudgery his younger brother so abhorred.

Jed felt fairly certain what his own decision would be when the time came. As much as he loved his parents and his brother, he couldn't imagine staying in Bannek. He knew that Kylla and Fallon would make the same choice.

Finished dressing, Jed ran downstairs and out to the barn, making a quick but necessary stop at the outhouse. His stomach rumbling with hunger, Jed attacked his morning chores with an uncharacteristic vigor. He gathered up some eggs, took them to his mother, grabbed a pail of slop for the hogs, filled the trough with hay for the cows, and made sure Looee, the family horse, had a fresh bag of grain. Then he dashed across the lawn, up the front steps, through the door, along the entryway, across the kitchen, and slid into the seat next to his father just as his mother placed a large plate teetering with pancakes in the center of the table.

"How many times have I told you not to run in the house, Jed?" his father said in a stern voice.

"About a million," Jed replied with as much impishness as accuracy.

"Well then," his father said, locking eyes with him, "let's not make it a million and one." His father's face broke into a quick grin as he tussled Jed's hair, which was another of the morning rituals in the household.

Jed's father, Kannu, was a large man, standing nearly two meters tall, with wide shoulders, well-muscled from his many years farming the land. His hair and complexion were both a deep chestnut brown, like Jed's, and his face, while wrinkled from countless hours in the sun, nearly always held a smile. But it was his eyes of bright bluish hazel Jed thought distinguished his father. He communicated far more with those eyes than he ever did with words.

His mother, though she, too, had what Jed thought to be beautiful eyes of deep golden brown, was the more talkative one of his parents. She was tall as well, and while not nearly as tall as her husband, she stood a good half-head taller than most women in the town. She had a dark olive complexion, and her hair was a deep rich auburn that appeared nearly black when not in direct sunlight. Gray strands might appear from time to time, but Jed noticed they rarely lasted more than a day on his mother's head.

However, it was the sound of his mother's voice that always came to mind first when Jed thought of her. She had a sweet, gentle tone, just half an octave lower than one would expect, giving her speech a melodious quality that lingered long after she had finished speaking. In fact, her name, Ranna, meant 'lovely voice' in the dialect of her ancestors.

"Let us bless this meal," she said, looking from her husband to Jed as they all bowed their heads. Nearly all Kellish prayers were said silently, and the blessing before meals was no exception. Jed closed his eyes and repeated the standard blessing from the *Tannett* to himself.

"May those who grew this food have love and peace.
May the spirits of those animals whose lives were taken for this food have love and peace.
May those who prepared this food have love and peace.
May all those who partake of this food have love and peace.
May all beings have love and peace."

Jed opened his eyes to find his mother placing two pancakes on his plate while his father passed him a small dish with scrambled eggs. "Thank you," he said as he reached for the syrup, poured some, and began shoveling the contents of the plate into his mouth.

"Hungry this morning?" his father asked.

"Starving," Jed said around a mouthful of egg.

"Don't speak with your mouth full," his mother admonished.

"Sorry, Mom," Jed said, trying to time his reply so as to have an empty mouth without sacrificing the speed of his engorgement.

"Do you think he'll come today?" his mother asked aloud to herself as much as anyone else. There was a hint of sadness, or maybe fear, in her voice, which she covered by taking a sip of breakfast tea.

"I'm sure he'll be home by the end of the week," his father said, glancing up from his plate and just briefly catching his mother's eye. "Boys come back late from Landdesh all the time. It's not that unusual."

"It's unusual for Tallu," his mother said.

Tallu hated to be late for anything. He had always been punctual to a fault. Which Jed considered to be a fault, if for no other reason than because it always made Jed look bad when he was late, which was almost always.

"Maybe he got lost," Jed offered, wishing for his brother's safe return, but secretly hoping for a little more time as the center of family attention…and as the sole resident of the bedroom.

"The Sentient keeps an eye on every boy and girl out on Landdesh," his father replied. "If he were lost, the Sentient would find him."

"Which is all the more worrisome," he mother pointed out. "If he's not lost, maybe something happened to him."

"Well, I could ask the council to petition the Sentient to find him," his father said, his dislike of petitioning the Kellish council for anything evident in his voice.

"A good idea, Kannu," his mother said. "The council's weekly meeting is tonight. You could go to them after you finish in the fields."

Jed saw by the look on his face that his father had completely forgotten the weekly council meeting was that evening. His father could not now change a plan that he himself had suggested, so he merely grunted.

Jed knew it was not from lack of concern over Tallu's well-being that his father wished to procrastinate petitioning the council. It had far more to do with the fact his father had been passed up three times in a row for inclusion in the council.

The council was made up of six men and six women over the age of forty, elected once each spring. Jed's father had felt certain he would be selected to participate in the council at least once since he had turned forty, but the council's membership had changed only slightly in the past twenty years, the people of Bannek preferring familiarity over new ideas.

"Good then," his mother said, obviously happy her concerns had been addressed, even if indirectly. Jed knew she had been worried even before Tallu had failed to return at the end of the required time.

Any mother is likely to worry when her eldest child goes out into the wider world alone for the first time, but for the last month or so, a mood had settled over her that no one could ignore. A look of dread came over her face whenever Tallu was mentioned. Jed knew his mother sometimes had premonitions that were farsightedly accurate. She called it "having a feeling" about things. It usually meant she knew something would break before it did, or that people would be stopping by later that same day. As he stuffed the last bite of egg into his mouth, it occurred to him that his mother "had a feeling" about his brother's delayed return.

Swallowing harder than he had intended, he noticed how quiet his parents had grown. Jed shattered the inner thoughts of his silent parents by pushing his chair back from the table with a loud squeak.

"May I be excused?" he asked. "If Ky, Fallon and I are late for class just once we have our restitution chores doubled."

"Yes, you may be excused," his mother said, visibly whisking the darker thoughts from her mind as she smiled at her youngest son. "That, I hope, will teach you the value of listening to your elders, and the importance of following the rules the next time some wild adventure pops into your head."

"If we're lucky, Mom," Jed said as he got up from the table and kissed her goodbye.

His father tussled his hair again as Jed grabbed his books from the countertop and headed out the back door. His father lowered his voice, but Jed still heard the words as he stepped outside. "If we're lucky, he'll be too tired to get in any more trouble."

"I can't imagine we'll ever be that lucky," Jed heard his mother say as the door closed behind him.

CHAPTER 5
CONVERSATION OF
ENERGY

Sentient: *A sentient is an artificial intelligence created from both living tissue and electro-mechanical components. All sentients are conscious in a way that is indistinguishable from the consciousness of other intelligent species, such as humans. Sentients of sufficient size and complexity are capable of warping the space-time continuum in a manner that creates an Einstein-Rosen bridge, or worm hole, between two points in space, allowing instantaneous travel between said points. The phrase "The Sentient" is used to describe the sentient formally called Axeon, who guides and controls the starship* Celestial Pilgrim.

The Encyclopedia Wyconnica, 112th Edition

Jed ran down the dirt road between the trees, past his father's fields of wheat and corn and his neighbor, Mr. Gander's, fields of barley. He met Kylla and Fallon near a thicket of winnick bushes.

"Morning," Kylla said, leaping onto the road to run beside Jed.

"Mornin'," Jed replied, grabbing the tied bundle of Fallon's books from his hands so the younger boy would have an easier time keeping up.

"Thanks," Fallon said, his attention focused on making his legs go as fast as possible. They heard the school bell from down the road and picked up their pace slightly. They always ran to school in the morning, both because Kylla loved to run, and because Jed was usually late.

As they ran, Jed thought about his plan for the three of them to study the artifacts without their parents finding out. His plan was simple, but it required a great sophistication of timing.

In the Kellish towns, when someone violated the rules and laws of society, the response was not what was traditionally considered punishment in the rest of the ship. In the Kellish philosophy, "wrongdoing" was to be corrected with "right doing." The Kellish believed in the "Three Rs": Reflection, Regret, and Restitution. When someone did wrong, whether it be breaking laws of the valley or a simple household rule, they were compelled to follow the path of the Three Rs.

They would first be given time to reflect upon their transgression, to see how it had caused suffering for others, and how it had affected the community. Then they would be given time to cultivate regret for their actions. As the ancient Kellish saying went, "*Without regret, there can be no reward.*" By reward, the Kellish elders had been speaking about the transformation of one's heart and the birth of the desire to make restitution for one's improper actions. Restitution generally meant making things right with the one who had been wronged.

For instance, if a young boy stole a freshly-baked gyllen berry pie from his neighbor's windowsill and got caught not long after with crumbs of pie on his face and stains of berry filling on his shirt, he would first be sent to his room to reflect upon how his selfish theft deprived his neighbors of their pie and shamed his family. Then, hopefully, his reflection would produce a feeling of regret. It might take a while, and he might need to be guided to it by his mother, but eventually the regret would arise.

Not guilt. Kellish had little use for guilt. It was largely unproductive and, in their way of thinking, more than a little self-centered. One could feel guilty and never do anything about it, but regret motivated action, which was where restitution came in.

In this case, restitution would mean baking pies for the neighbors. Seven pies to be exact. The Kellish held the number seven to be sacred. Restitution was traditionally made seven-fold.

For repeat offenders, there was often added a fourth 'R' of 'Rehabilitation,' which could mean many things, depending upon the infraction. It usually took the form of contributing to the community, and in the case of the stolen pie, the second theft for that particular child, resulted in a week of painting fences.

Extra chores seemed a fine penance to Jed, particularly because the chores fit perfectly into his plan. He, Kylla, and Fallon would perform their work each day after school at twice their normal pace and then sneak off to the Hollock tree to study and train with the artifacts.

After years of making regular restitution and engaging in frequent chores, the three companions had established a leisurely pace for their work. No one would now expect them to perform their tasks any faster than usual, but by doing so, they could gain themselves nearly an hour a day to unlock the secrets of the blade, the stone, and the ancient *Tannett*.

The three runners reached the edges of the small town and slowed their pace as they loped toward the town square and the old schoolhouse. They waved hello to everyone they passed, the same people they saw every morning on the way to school. Men in woolen britches with suspenders and white cotton shirts. Women in long, dark blue, gray, or brown dresses with their hair tied back. The baker, Mr. Golssom. The mason, Mr. Lallway. The reverend's husband, Mr. Vannesh. The potter, Ms. Needsen. The blacksmith, Mr. Bannit. And the grocers, Mr. and Mrs. Opplis.

The town square was not very large, but then again, Bannek was not a big town. In the center of the square sat a small pool of water with a statue of a woman in the center, looking skyward, her hands clasped in prayer at her chest. This was Jindow Kell, the founder of the Kellish way of life. She had been a scholar from the elite cities who decided to try and create a life without the technology she felt her fellow humans had become overly dependent upon. At the base of the statue an inscription read:

Follow the faith of your heart,
Guiding knowledge with wisdom,
And reach for the stars within.

We come to seek what reason cannot find
We come to worship the whole of human faith
We come to build a life apart
So that we can build a life together.

It was considered impolite to run in the town square out of respect for the statue of Jindow Kell, so Jed and his friends ceased their light jog as they crossed the square toward the school. Nearly two dozen other children did the same as the school bell continued ringing.

Their steady pace brought them to the steps of the schoolhouse and beneath the ever-mindful gaze of Mrs. Lemmick, her pale blue dress wrinkled like the light pink ribbon holding back her long, gray hair.

"Good morning, children," she said, adjusting her glasses. "You look sleepy. Are the extra chores keeping you up late?"

"No," replied Jed with a smile of innocence.

"We were up late studying," Kylla said, her mouth making a gentle smile.

"Very late," Fallon added, clearly trying his best to make sure his smile did not break into a laugh. They waited until they passed Mrs. Lemmick and their backs were to her before they allowed their smiles to turn to smirks and silent giggles. Mrs. Lemmick's "Hrrumpgh" of suspicious disgust came out sounding more like a fly had lodged in her throat, resulting in a mild coughing fit.

Jed took his assigned seat next to Kylla and Fallon and waited for Mrs. Lemmick to stop coughing and begin class. Usually a teacher would have separated three students such as Jed, Kylla, and Fallon for fear of them disrupting the classroom, but Mrs. Lemmick had discovered, against all common reason, that the three seemed to behave better and actually learn more when placed in close proximity to one another. Yet another mystery about Jed and his friends she had openly resigned herself to never understanding.

Classes proceeded as normal. Because the schoolhouse only had one room, all of the students, regardless of age, were taught together.

This required Mrs. Lemmick to be an attentive and inventive teacher, a feat she usually managed with surprising ease.

She was helped by the children, of course. The older children assisted the younger children with their studies and explained the lessons to them, with the exception of Fallon, where this system was reversed, much to the annoyance of the older students.

The school day began with a science lesson, which was Kylla's favorite class after mathematics. Of course, because it was a Kellish school, the science lessons tended to be of a practical nature and applicable to their lifestyle. Thus, in learning about the physics of force, the children would be taught about pulleys, and how the water wheel of the granary converted the force of the local stream into energy for grinding grain. Or how the strength of the wind was harnessed by the local windmill for a similar purpose.

While Jed certainly was thankful for the lesson on the pulleys and levers that Kylla and Fallon had so wisely made use of, he had yet to see how harnessing the wind was going to be useful to him.

The lesson that day was about energy, and as it turned out, was far more helpful to Jed, Kylla, and Fallon than learning about pulleys and levers. The morning's class explored how plants use the energy of sunlight and carbon dioxide from the air to grow. Mrs. Lemmick sat at her desk as ten-year-old Missii Deffoo stood at the head of the class and read from *The Big Book of Kellish Science.*

"The process by which plants harness the power of light to transform carbon dioxide into food and further growth is known as photosynthesis. Plants absorb light through their leaves, which have a special chemical called chlorophyll in their cells. The chlorophyll absorbs red and blue light and reflects green light, which is why the leaves of plants look green. The cells of the plants use the energy of the light plus the carbon dioxide they breathe in from the air to combine with water and create starch or glucose, which is used by the plants to grow more leaves or fruit. The main by-product of this chemical process is oxygen, which plants give off into the atmosphere. In this way, plants and animals, including humans, help form a symbiotic ecological

cycle, with plants using the carbon dioxide animals breathe out and releasing oxygen animals need to breathe in."

Missii continued to read, explaining how animals' bodies use oxygen and glucose to create energy in their cells. Jed looked over and saw Kylla writing furiously in her journal, which he thought was odd since Kylla never took notes in science class. Jed leaned sideways to read over her shoulder as she wrote.

"If sunlight powers plants, what does that imply? Sunlight, real sunlight, comes from stars. If we lived on a real planet in a solar system, like the Origin World Earth, it would orbit a massive star called the sun. This star would send its energy in the form of photons toward the planet, where it would warm the water and the atmosphere and, if they had evolved, be used by the plants covering the surface. A star obtains its energy from fusion, where hydrogen, the most common element in the universe and the one stars are almost entirely composed of, is crushed at the center of the star, creating so much pressure and heat that the atoms of hydrogen are 'fused,' together in a process that releases massive amounts of energy and light.

"But we don't live on a real planet. We live on the Celestial Pilgrim, a tube-shaped starship sailing between galaxies. The light that's falling on my desk through the window of the schoolhouse did not come from a sun but from the sun-tube far above my head that runs the length of the ship. But where does the sun-tube get its energy from to create the light within the Celestial Pilgrim? And, for that matter, where does the Celestial Pilgrim get its energy?"

Jed could tell from what she had written that much of it was learned by surreptitiously reading banned books in the town library when no one was looking, because it certainly wasn't in The Big Book of Kellish Science.

Her face flushed with excitement, Kylla turned to Jed and Fallon. Fallon looked at Kylla with a twinkle in his eyes. "It's an interesting question, isn't it?" he whispered. Fallon had apparently reached the same conclusion as Kylla.

"What's an interesting question?" Jed whispered. As usual, he was a step behind when matters of science were floating about.

Kylla leaned over to whisper back. "If the artifacts can change form, like the book, and if they have powers like the Morikon said, where do they get their energy?"

Jed blinked in silent response. Glancing at the old pulley and weight-powered clock in the corner of the room, Jed realized the school day had many hours to go before they would be released. He had no idea what the answer to Kylla's question might be, but he couldn't wait for the day's lessons and chores of restitution to be finished so they could find out.

After finishing school and their chores they gathered beneath the hollock tree to examine the artifacts again. Slender blades of grass shifted in the mild breeze, brushing against the polished blade of the Tellandor dagger, lying on the ground. The artificial sunlight from the giant glowing tube 500 kilometers above reflected off the blade and into Jed's face.

"How long do we need to wait?" Jed asked.

"Who knows," Kylla replied. "Maybe this won't even work."

"It's been twenty minutes," Jed said.

"They were underground for centuries," Kylla said. "Who knows how long it could take for them to regain power?"

Jed, Kylla, and Fallon sat in a small semicircle in the low grass of the fields behind the Hollock tree. The dagger, the stone, and the book rested on the ground before them, each placed before its guardian.

"I don't think it has anything to do with sunlight," Fallon said as he pulled the book closer. He touched the edges of the book and the hidden inscription appeared beneath the symbol of the labyrinth on the cover. Opening the book, he stared at the blank pages. They remained empty. "It was a good idea, but I think their energy comes from someplace else."

"We don't even know what they do," Jed said. "How are we supposed to know what energy they need?"

"Maybe if we figure out what they do, that will tell us where they get their power," Kylla said.

"And maybe it's the other way around," Jed said, picking up the dagger and peering at it intently. "Maybe we need to know what powers them to know what they do."

"Maybe we power them," Fallon said as he looked up from the book.

"How do you mean?" Kylla asked. "With body heat?"

"With our minds," Fallon suggested.

They were all silent for a while as they considered this possibility. Obviously the book, the ancient *Tannett*, responded to Fallon's mind. And while it seemed a fantastic notion, Jed knew in the wider world outside the Notesch Valley, fantastic things happened all the time. Science and technology had progressed several thousand years beyond the limited scope of its teaching and use in Kellish society.

Jed considered the idea thoroughly. In a way, it was not especially surprising. Jed and Kylla knew better than anyone Fallon's mind was special. While Fallon hid his intelligence from most people, Jed suspected Fallon also concealed the true depth of his mental abilities, even from his sister. It was difficult for Jed to admit, but he knew that even at a young age Fallon could access levels of knowing that Jed would never in his life experience.

It was with this thought in mind that Jed handed Fallon the dagger. "Try the dagger, Fallon," he said. Fallon accepted the blade into his hands, clearly surprised at how light it was. "If you can make the book work, maybe the dagger or the stone will respond to your mind as well."

"But I can only make the title appear," Fallon said. "The inside of the book is still blank."

"And maybe the dagger is easier to control, or power, or whatever," Jed replied.

"Maybe we should all switch," Kylla said. "Maybe we have the wrong artifacts." She handed Jed the stone and took the book from Fallon.

They sat there in the late day tube-light behind the Hollock tree and stared intently at the artifacts before them. Jed held the stone in his hands, focusing his attention on it completely. Kylla likewise held the book, trying to make the letters that had disappeared as soon as it left Fallon's hands reappear for her. Fallon clutched the dagger in both hands and gazed at himself in the reflection of the blade.

A constant light breeze wafted around them, shifting the branches of the Hollock tree and causing the long, drooping leaves to slap together slightly like some mild, vegetative applause. A rabbit hopped quickly across the clearing, pausing in the middle for a long moment to stare quizzically at the three young humans before it spotted a hawk high above and hurried upon its way. The light from the sun-tube began to fade, signaling the onset of nightfall an hour away.

"I don't know what to think about," Jed said, breaking the long silence with a sigh of frustration.

"Neither do I," Kylla said, setting the book down impatiently. "I know what it's supposed to say, but I can't get it to do anything."

"Just relax your mind," Fallon said. "Don't try to think. Listen to what the book is saying. What it might be saying. Listen with your mind."

"Hmfff," Jed grunted. *How do you listen to something that doesn't make any sound*, he thought, beginning to toss the stone from one hand to the other. He closed his eyes, challenging himself to catch the stone as he chucked it between his hands without the aid of sight. It was the sort of challenge he gave himself all the time, to see if he could do something as well with his eyes closed as he could with them open. Sometimes he would walk through his house with his eyes closed, testing his memory of where everything was until he would knock something over, and his mother would admonish him to literally watch where he was going. Sometimes he even closed his eyes when he was running with Kylla to see how long he could manage before tripping over some unseen object or unevenness in the road.

Eventually, Jed stopped counting how many times he had tossed the stone between his hands. He let himself relax into the rhythm of the soft slapping sound the stone made as it hit his palms. He had no idea how much time had passed, but suddenly he noticed his left palm did not make contact with the stone after he threw it from the right. Opening his eyes, he expected to see the stone lying in the low grass near his legs. But the stone was not on the ground.

"Look," Jed whispered, amazed.

"Yes, look," Kylla said, holding up the book for the others to see. "I got the title to...wow!"

Kylla had indeed managed to make the title appear on the cover the book, but Jed's feat seemed impossible by comparison. The stone she had been wearing secretly beneath her blouse for the last several days floated gently in the air between Jed's two open palms, the leather necklace hanging down limply beneath it.

"How are you doing that?" Kylla asked in amazement.

"I have no idea," Jed replied honestly.

He looked over to see Fallon staring at the stone and smiling. "I told you," Fallon said. "You just have to listen."

Turning his gaze back to the blade of the dagger, Fallon's smile widened, and for a moment in the dimming light, Jed thought the blade seemed to shine. Then suddenly it glowed. The blade of the ancient dagger in Fallon's hands radiated a bright, deep blue light, casting a pale hue upon Jed and Kylla and creating shadows on the grass behind them in the dim evening light. Jed was so startled that the stone stopped hovering between his hands and fell to the ground. Fallon slumped a bit with a slight sigh and the glow of the blade faded away.

"That was amazing," Kylla said. "Both of you."

"I was afraid to hold it any longer," Fallon said. "It seemed to want to grow brighter and hotter and I was scared what might happen."

"I know," Jed said. "I had a similar feeling. Like there was much more power there in the stone. That it could do so much more than hover."

"It's like that with the book, too, isn't it, Fallon?" Kylla said. "Like there's a great ocean of knowledge waiting to burst into your mind."

Fallon looked up at the dimming sun-tube above them. "It's getting dark, but I think we still have time."

"Right," Jed said, knowing immediately what Fallon meant. He took the book from Kylla and handed the stone to Fallon. They wouldn't be home until dark, and they would all be in trouble for missing dinner, but they had to know if they could each unlock the separate powers of the artifacts.

As the sun-tube dimmed to its nighttime setting and the artificial projection of the Milky Way appeared in the darkened sky above, the silhouette of the Hollock tree in the empty field could be seen from the road. Fortunately, there were no travelers that evening to see the two large bursts of bluish light that erupted from behind the tree, one about five minutes after the other.

CHAPTER 6
LATE FOR SUPPER

Excerpt from Jed's Journal:

"I'm worried about mom. She can't stop talking about Tal. Can't stop worrying about him is more like it. And Dad isn't much better. Only he worries by never mentioning Tal unless Mom mentions him first. It's enough to drive me crazy. Because I can't do anything about it. Tal is late.

It worries me, too, the more I think about it. Where is he? What is he doing? Could something be wrong? He's never late for anything. And he would never be late if he knew Mom would worry. And he knows Mom will worry. Which just worries me all the more.

And I'm worried about the artifacts the Morikon gave us. What do they do? What can they do? And what can we do with them? I wonder what Tal will say when he sees them. He better not think about telling Mom and Dad like he did that time when Ky and I took the horse and wagon for a ride. How was I supposed to know the wagon wouldn't make it across the creek bed? Maybe we just won't tell him. No, Ky would never be able to keep a secret like that from Tal. She's so weird around him sometimes. Like she's always trying to impress him with all the things she can do. Like math, of all things! Who cares about math!"

Jed did indeed return home late for supper.

In Jed's household, the evening meal was considered greatly important. It was a time for the family to talk and discuss the day each had experienced, as well as settle issues that arose on a regular basis in any family. Attendance was mandatory. Jed's excuse of having harsh and demanding chores around school and town were not met with sympathy by either his mother or father, particularly since this evening his grandfather had attended supper.

Although he did receive a small wink of sympathy from his grandfather, it didn't stave off the application of the three Rs. It was determined Jed could reflect upon the rudeness of being tardy by eating alone, and he could cultivate regret and make restitution by doing the dishes. Rehabilitation could wait until recidivism was displayed. Which meant, Jed knew, he'd better not be late for dinner again this month, or he'd be cooking meals for weeks thereafter.

That evening, however, Jed was too ecstatic about the results of his training with the artifacts, especially the blade, to be at all bothered about extra chores. He wolfed down his dinner and set to washing dishes straight away.

As he scrubbed the pots and pans and plates, he remembered the sight of the ancient blade in his hands, glowing deep blue in the darkness behind the tree. Fallon had been right, there was the sense of an enormous power in the blade, but it had taken every ounce of Jed's concentration to keep the blade glowing faintly for a few seconds. Whatever else the blade might be capable of, it would take many weeks, if not longer, for Jed to unlock its secrets. Fallon might have an easier time of it, but he seemed far more interested in the secrets held by the ancient book.

He desperately wanted to rush upstairs to his room and practice again with the dagger, but he, Kylla, and Fallon had agreed it was too risky to practice with the artifacts anywhere except at the Hollock tree, together. Anything could go wrong alone. Their parents might discover them, the artifacts might behave in a dangerous manner — anything.

As he placed the final plate in the wooden dish rack, Jed noticed he could hear the voices of his parents and his grandfather from the living room. Quietly, he took the dish basin to the back door and poured the dirty water onto the grass. Returning to the kitchen, his brother's name caught his attention.

"Tal's a bright boy," Jed heard his grandfather say. "I'm sure he'll be just fine."

"The council of elders assured me they would send a message to the Sentient immediately," his father said.

"But what if the Sentient can't find him?" his mother replied, worry and fear evident in her usually dulcet voice. "Maybe it doesn't care. It's not like it's a human being. It's not like it has feelings or compassion. It's just a cold, calculating machine."

"Maybe," his grandfather replied, "but it has managed the safety of our people, and all those aboard the *Celestial Pilgrim*, for nearly two thousand years. I'm sure this sort of thing happens all the time."

"But why does it have to happen to our son?" his mother asked.

"Well, at least with Tal we know it probably wasn't his idea to be so late in coming home," his father said.

"But with Jed, you know he's going to be late, so you don't worry as much," his mother countered.

At the mention of his name, Jed could feel his ears burn hot with self-consciousness. He wondered how his parents would react if he were several weeks late coming home from Landdesh. Would they be as worried? As worried as they were for Tal? Some deep-seated sense of sibling rivalry reared up within him, but it didn't get very far as he suddenly realized how worried he was for his older brother.

"At least for the first hour or so," his mother finished. He was sure, in that moment, his mother would be just as worried for his safety as his brother's.

"Speaking of the younger one, why don't you stop lurking in the kitchen and come walk me home?" his grandfather said.

Jed was always impressed with his grandfather's perceptiveness. It came, he supposed, from years of tracking and hunting animals in the valley. Jed stepped into the room, the dripping dish basin still in his hands, his cheeks flushed with embarrassment.

"You might want to remember, the next time you're eavesdropping," his grandfather said with a smile, "that silence can be just as revealing as noise."

Jed nodded silently as he realized his grandfather had been listening to the sound of him washing the dishes and had known when the noise ceased that Jed was likely to be listening from the kitchen.

"I don't think you need to give him any advice on how to misbehave, Father," his mother said.

"I'm just trying to make sure the boy doesn't get in any more trouble than he already does," Jed's grandfather replied.

"You might try teaching him not to listen in on conversations of adults in the first place," his mother said.

"He has a right to know what the situation is with his brother," his father said, looking at Jed, a hint of sadness in his eyes.

"What is the situation with Tal?" Jed asked.

His parents were silent. They looked at each other, and then at Jed.

"Why don't I explain it to you on the walk home?" Jed's grandfather said softly, his words eliciting an audible sigh of relief from his mother.

It was clear to Jed that neither of his parents really wanted to share the depth of their worry with him. Jed's grandfather hugged his mother and father good night and headed out the back door. Jed placed the dish basin in the kitchen and took an oil lamp from the counter.

"Don't dawdle on your way back," his father said. "We'll have an early day with the summer festival tomorrow."

"Stick to the path," his mother added.

"I will," Jed said, striking a match and lighting the lantern before closing the door.

Jed held the lantern near his waist as he and his grandfather stepped off the back porch of the house onto the thin dirt path leading off between the fields of corn. The lantern light cast malevolent shadows along the cornstalks, but holding the lantern low, as his grandfather had taught him, kept the light from his eyes and left his vision more attuned to darkness.

Often when they made this short, nighttime trip, they did so without the aid of the lantern so Jed could learn, as his grandfather said, how to see without seeing. His grandfather's house was nearby, only a half a kilometer through the fields and past a copse of birch trees. Jed's mother and father had repeatedly offered to share their home with the elder family member, but Jed's grandfather had always refused. His excuse was that a household only needed one man and one woman, but Jed suspected that it was more likely that his grandfather simply valued his independence too much.

Since Jed's grandmother died two years ago, his grandfather had taken to wandering the countryside whenever he wasn't in the fields. He always told his daughter and son-in-law he was off hunting, but even though he would be gone days at a time, he rarely ever came home with any game. This was odd, in that he was known as the best tracker and hunter in all the Kellish towns.

Jed and his brother had, in fact, spent much of their childhoods leaning the art of tracking and hunting from their grandfather. While their father was an excellent farmer and could make nearly any crop produce twice what his neighbors' fields did, he was rather hopeless at hunting. However, because the family raised several cows, a handful of pigs, and a flock of chickens, his father always managed to place meat on the table.

During their hunting trips, Jed's grandfather would teach Tal and him how to read the small clues every creature left behind as it passed through a place. They learned how to find tracks in hard earth, how to see the passage of an animal in the way leaves and branches were bent, how to smell the difference between where an animal had been and where it had not, and how to sense the presence of another living being, even when no outward sign was visible. His grandfather was a master of this particular skill.

Jed thought of these lessons as he walked beside his grandfather, feeling a powerful heat well up in his chest. Swallowing hard, Jed turned to the old man.

"He is coming back, isn't he?"

"I'm sure you'll see him again."

"Do you think something's happened to him? Mother thinks so. Maybe something bad."

"It is very possible."

Jed hadn't been prepared for that amount of honesty. He was hoping his grandfather would reassure him and settle his fears. But he should have known better. His grandfather didn't believe in avoiding things, but rather in facing them head-on.

"I wish I could do something. Something useful."

"You can," his grandfather said, smiling for the first time on their walk.

"What?"

"You can help ease your mother's concern by giving her no more reason to be concerned about you. No more adventures to castles, no more turning up late for supper, no more fights with classmates, no more…"

"It's Kylla who starts the fights!" Jed interjected.

"Then keep her from starting them." His grandfather frowned. "I never should have given you that book to read. I indulge you too much."

"I don't feel indulged when I'm painting the Hall of Light and doing extra chores." Jed frowned as well.

"Fortunately, your parents and the town are wise enough not to make my mistakes."

His grandfather smiled suddenly and reached a hand out to ruffle Jed's hair. The action reminded Jed of Tal doing the same thing a little over a year ago, just before he walked down the path away from the house, the first steps on his journey out of the valley.

"Do you think he's in danger?" Jed asked, his voice breaking slightly.

"Your brother, unlike other family members, is not one to be late or inconsiderate," his grandfather replied. "If Tal knew he could not make it home by the end of his Landdesh, or if he had chosen to stay away a bit longer than usual, he would have sent word. The fact he didn't leads your mother and father to suspect he is in danger. That is why your father requested the council to contact the Sentient and ask for help in finding Tal."

"What will the Sentient do?"

"I am not sure," his grandfather said, slowing his pace slightly. "From what I understand, the Sentient is able to determine the location of every boy and girl on Landdesh at all times. It may know where Tal is even now."

"But what if something happened to him? What if he's hurt and can't tell anyone?"

His grandfather stopped and placed a hand on Jed's shoulder. "We have no way of knowing what has happened, Jed. All we can do is pray. And trust in the Sentient to find him. And trust in Tal. Your brother is far more capable than most. Maybe, like me, he has met his future wife and is simply taking a little extra time to convince her to follow him home."

Jed looked up into his grandfather's gentle face, the soft light from the lantern revealing the sadness in the old man's eyes. Sadness and longing. Jed's memories of his grandmother flooded his mind, coated in an amber glow of the love and affection she had always generously bestowed upon her only two grandchildren. Jed missed his grandmother terribly and could not imagine how much her absence pained his grandfather. How much would it hurt them both to never see Tal again? The thought was one Jed dared not hold in his mind too long. He hugged his grandfather tightly, warmth welling up unexpectedly in his face for the second time that night.

"I'll see you tomorrow," Jed said, turning away quickly, embarrassed, as most boys are, to have his grandfather see such an emotive sign of his love.

"Good night, boy," his grandfather called after him as Jed ran back down the path toward his own house.

Stopping near the porch of his home, Jed turned back to look across the fields and saw his grandfather staring up at the night sky and its projection of stars. Sighing for a moment, Jed also looked up, knowing his grandfather was thinking again of his grandmother.

Looking at the stars made him think of Tal. Where ever he was, Tal would be seeing the same stars that night. Unless something had happened to him. Unless he was in danger and needed help. His grandfather and his parents seemed convinced the Sentient could help Tal if he were in trouble, but Jed was not so sure.

He had heard stories of the Sentient's abilities, but trusted more in his own. Wyconna, the human section of the starship *Celestial Pilgrim*, was massive, but Jed was very good at tracking and finding things. After all, he had found Lord Narrish's castle, and the labyrinth, and the Morikon, and the treasure of the ancient book, necklace, and dagger. If he needed to, he would find his brother as well.

Rubbing his eyes, from dust, he told himself, Jed glanced again at his grandfather, still staring up at the heavens, and turned to go inside.

CHAPTER 7
SUMMER FESTIVAL

"Harmony in all things should be our aim. By living closer to nature, by living off the land as our ancestors did, so many millennia before us, we achieve this harmony in a peaceful fashion.

"Many years ago, long before humanity left the Origin World, there was another group of people who intentionally abandoned the technological wonders of the day to remain closer to nature and live simpler lives. These people were called the Amish, and they were guided as much by their faith as by their conviction that technology would not and could not help them become better human beings.

"All throughout Wyconna, societies are dividing themselves along the lines of how they use technology and how they worship. While we will abandon the majority of technology, we should not abandon faith. We will instead embrace all faiths to the extent this is possible. For this reason, while every individual faith will be welcome in our community, we will primarily follow the core teachings of all human faiths as assembled by the Tellandor scholars in the Tannett — The Book of All Faiths.*"*

From *The Book of Kell*, Jindow Kell, founder of the first
Kellish community

The next morning was the day of the summer festival, and Jed was up early helping his father with the farm chores. As his father slopped the pigs, Jed cast a mix of corn and wheat onto the ground of the pen behind the chicken coop. The chickens pecked at the grains as Jed's father set the slop bucket down and walked over to join him.

"Give me a hand with the eggs while they're feeding," Jed's father said.

"Okay," Jed said, following his father into the coop. Jed paused inside for a moment, letting his eyes adjust to the dim light filtering through the gaps between the wooden slats of the walls. The potent smell of dried chicken droppings filled his nostrils and he wrinkled his nose. He grabbed an egg basket from a hook on the wall and joined his father in collecting eggs from the hens' nests.

"I know you're worried about your brother," his father said, looking at him over the rows of nests. "We're all worried. But I don't want you getting it in your head that there's something you should be doing about it. The Sentient will find Tallu. I'm certain of it."

His father paused, holding the basket of eggs in both hands. Jed had not taken his eyes off the nests and eggs.

"Look at me, Jed."

Jed placed the last egg in his basket and looked up at his father.

"It's okay to be worried. It's okay to be afraid. But fear is not a wise mind. We can't act out of fear. And we can't surrender to it." His father looked down at the basket of eggs in his hands. "If I acted out of fear, I'd be running over the Pinnak Mountains looking for your brother. And that wouldn't help him, or me."

Jed wasn't exactly sure what his father was trying to tell him. Had his father somehow guessed at Jed's thoughts from the night before? He decided to answer the way he always did when faced with ambiguous statements from his parents.

"I understand."

His father looked up from the eggs to stare into Jed's eyes. "Good." He sighed slightly, then smiled. "I'll finish up here. You run along to clean up and help your mother."

"Yes Sir," Jed said, handing over the basket of eggs and sprinting out the door of the chicken coop, happy to be free of the foul odor, but with the confusing words of his father still rumbling in his head.

Behind the house, across from the barns and animal pens, sat a small table with a large washbasin and a misshapen bar of lavender scented lard soap. Next to the table stood a rain barrel from which Jed scooped water and poured it into the basin. Grabbing the soap, he washed his hands thoroughly. The Kellish way of life did not have much use for technology, but it was very insistent upon hygiene.

Rinsing his hands, he emptied the basin by tossing the water into the yard and turned to walk into the house through the back door. Even before he entered the kitchen, the smell of fried eggs and warm biscuits made his mouth water.

"Smells great, Mom."

Jed's mother turned from the wood stove and wiped the sweat from her brow with the back of her wrist. On the windowsill behind her sat three large, green-apple pies cooling in the morning air.

"Did you wash your hands?"

"Yes," Jed said, taking a set of cloth napkins from a drawer and placing them on the table. He returned to the drawer and started taking out silverware.

Suddenly his mother was standing beside him. Beginning to smile, he turned to her, his smile freezing midway as he saw the tears brimming in her eyes. Without warning, she grabbed him and crushed him to her in an embrace far stronger than he would have expected her capable of.

"I know you are worried about your brother," she said, clearly fighting back tears.

His mother's words, echoing his father's just moments before, made Jed realize how worried his parents were about Tal, and how worried they were Jed might be worried. All of that worrying was beginning to make him worry. But it wouldn't be helpful to let his mother know.

"Tal can take care of himself," Jed said, his voice muffled by his face being crushed into his mother's bosom.

"He's just a boy," his mother said, stifling a sniffle. "And he's so trusting. So honest. So upright. Why couldn't he be more like you?" She crushed Jed tighter than ever.

Jed's head began to feel like a walnut on the verge of being cracked open, but he marveled at what his mother had just said. All his life everyone always said how much they wished he could be more like his older brother, and how upstanding Tal was, what a wonderful son he was, and how Jed could learn a thing or two from his behavior…on and on and on until Jed had begun to resent his brother just for being who he was, because Jed was not appreciated for who *he* was.

But here was his very own mother wishing that Tal was more like Jed. He didn't know what to say.

"Mom, you're crushing my head."

"Sorry, dear," his mother said, releasing him as she placed a kiss on his forehead.

Jed wiped his face. "It's okay, Mom."

A look of concern suddenly crossed her face. "Oh, dear, I hope you didn't take what I said the wrong way. It's not that I don't love you as much as your brother, or that I don't worry about you, or that…"

"Don't worry, Mom," Jed interrupted as he grinned. "It's the best thing anyone has ever said to me."

"Oh. Well then…that's good," his mother said, smiling back. "Of course, simply because I think your brother could benefit by being a bit more like you, and I do mean a bit, that shouldn't be taken as any sort of encouragement for you to be any more like yourself than you already are. Understood?" Her gentle voice had dropped an octave in emphasis.

"Understood," Jed said, still grinning as he finished setting the table.

"Who understands what?" Jed's grandfather asked as he and Jed's father stepped through the door, following the scent of breakfast and looking hungry.

"Yes," Jed's father added somewhat suspiciously. "What is Jed understanding now?"

"We were just coming to an understanding," his mother said quickly, "that Jed would be helping serve breakfast, so why don't you both sit down and we'll eat? We don't want to be late for the opening ceremony of the festival."

Jed looked at his mother, who winked at him as she turned from the table to pull the biscuits from the oven.

Naturally, Jed was late for the opening ceremony of the festival. He and his family had met Kylla, Fallon and their parents on the road into town. Kylla had suggested she, Jed and Fallon run ahead to save seats. The adults accepted this idea enthusiastically. Unfortunately, because Kylla loved to run, she did not always take the most direct route between two points.

As a result, Jed found himself running beside Kylla and Fallon as they dashed along an old dirt path behind the Hall of Light. Up ahead they could see the last of the townspeople walking through the large open doors.

"How could we run ahead and still be late?" Jed panted.

"We're not late if the doors are still open," Kylla said, laughing as she ran faster.

"Look," Fallon said, pointing as he gasped for breath.

Jed looked to where Fallon pointed and saw Pastor Vannesh stepping out of the front door of the old building that served as the town office. She lifted the hem of her robes and walked briskly toward the back door of the Hall of Light across the street.

"Perfect," Kylla said. "If Pastor Vannesh is late, we can't be late."

"Pastor Vannesh is never late," Fallon said. "Maybe something is wrong."

It didn't take Jed long to figure out what that might be.

"The Sentient's voice box is in the town office."

Kylla and Fallon didn't need to be told what that meant. Jed had never seen it, but everyone in town knew there was a wooden box in the town office allowing the Sentient to talk to the town council. If Pastor Vannesh was late, if could be because she had been speaking with the Sentient.

Speaking about Tal.

"We can ask her about it after the ceremony," Jed suggested as they skidded up to the entrance of the Hall of Light.

Townspeople and folks from neighboring Kellish towns packed the Hall of Light. The summer festival was a celebration that brought much of the valley together. Of course, it was not really summer the way it would have been if they had been living on a real planet, but the Sentient had long ago established a cycle of 365 days and manipulated the weather to simulate the yearly seasons Jed's distant ancestors had known.

In the Notesch Valley, the Kellish celebrated the arrival of each season with an elaborate community feast, for which every townsperson brought one or more home cooked items. A commencement ceremony, held in the Hall of Light, preceded each festival feast.

Jed, Kylla, and Fallon, still breathing heavily, scooted into seats near the front, saved for them by Jed and Kylla's mothers.

"Run ahead to save seats," Jed's mother whispered. "I can't believe I fell for that."

Jed was about to say something when Pastor Vannesh, looking a bit winded, stepped up to the lectern at the front of the room. Jed gave his mother an apologetic smile and turned toward Pastor Vannesh.

While women's roles in the Kellish society were unequal in many ways, one area of undisputed equality was in worship, where it was held that men and women had fully the same access to the Divine, and thus fully the same right to be a pastor.

The pastor was a tall woman in her fifties with long salt and pepper hair, respectfully pulled back. Her wide smile softened the angular features of her face.

"Let us take a moment and pray, each in our own way," she said, her deep yet feminine voice carrying easily throughout the hall. Placing her hands together, she bowed her head, and the congregation silently did the same. Every *Tannett* service began this way, in silent prayer, allowing each person of faith to meet the moment in his or her own fashion without imposing anything upon them.

Raising her head, Pastor Vannesh spread her arms wide and smiled at the congregation.

"Welcome, everyone. It is a joy to my heart to see you all here on this beautiful morning. As you know, we are gathered today as a community to celebrate another change of season, another turn of the endless wheel of life. This is a moment for us to reflect upon the past and to plan for the future. It is a time for us to recognize how, just as each season blends one into the next, and each year melds into the following, our lives also change, both by growing older, and growing older together.

"Over a thousand years ago, our ancestors came to this valley to establish a new way of life, a new way of being human.

The first of the Kellish people, led by Jindow Kell, settled here with two guiding principles — abandon technology in order to create a simpler way of life, and embrace all faiths by following the teachings and principles of the *Tannett*.

"This is the life our ancestors bequeathed to us and it is to their hard work and self-sacrifice that we owe the harmony, prosperity, and grace that define our present lives. Their springs became the summers of our lives, just our summers will become the autumns of our children's futures. In turn, their autumns will fall to winters of their children, who will grant springs to their offspring.

"And so, I ask you to hold in your hearts and minds a blessing of thanks to our wise and long toiling ancestors as we recite together the first lines of the *Tannett Shannha*."

After Pastor Vannesh spoke, the congregation began to recite in unison.

"Faith hides like the oak within the acorn
Waiting to blossom into maturity,
When it will see the sacred in all things,
The Divine as the Ground of all being and becoming."

The *Tannett* had been created and assembled by a great scholarly woman priest named Vallha Natuur nearly a thousand years before the *Celestial Pilgrim* set forth on its voyage. She created it in the hopes of providing a bridge to help the different faiths learn from one another and embrace the universal truths each taught.

The *Tannett Shannha* was the central text of the *Tannett*. It was a set of poetic, multi-faith prayers and meditations outlining the seven principles of the *Tannett* and providing an easy daily practice that could be engaged in alone or in communion with fellow worshippers of all faiths.

Normally, a festival ceremony began with a full recitation of the *Tannett Shannha* and took nearly an hour, but today Pastor Vannesh led them in the recitation of only the first few verses. Jed thought it odd, as did many of the townspeople, who looked among themselves, clearly concerned with the sudden change in the traditional pace of the ceremony.

If Pastor Vannesh noticed the concern of her congregation, it did not show in her voice as she continued to speak.

"The Hindu *Rig Veda* teaches:

'Let your aims be common,
and your hearts be of one accord,
and all of you be of one mind
so you may live well together.'

"And the Buddhist *Dhammapada* proclaims:

'Happy is the unity of the Sangha.
Happy is the discipline of the united ones.'

"And the Christian *Bible* says:

'My house shall be called a house of prayer for all peoples.'"

Pastor Vannesh smiled and looked up from her notes.

Only three quotes, Jed thought. That was also odd. Pastor Vannesh loved to quote from the *Tannett.* Usually she was good for at least twelve quotes on an occasion such as a seasonal festival. While Jed would normally have been thrilled to witness an abbreviated festival ceremony, he felt certain Pastor Vannesh hurried though it for a reason, and he could not help relating that reason to the Sentient's speaker box in the town office and therefore to, Tal.

"Our ancient ancestors wrote these words," Pastor Vannesh said, "and they are just as true today as they were thousands of years ago. We can only treasure and respect our community by fully embracing it and immersing ourselves in it, for a community can only be as strong as its members intend it to be. Without our intention, without our contribution, without our dedication, it will rot and disintegrate like a fallen tree. But if we nurture it, if we nurture each other, its roots will become deeper, its flowers will bloom, and its branches will reach far into the future. So let us continue this nurturing by celebrating together the arrival of another season."

Pastor Vannesh then did something that surprised Jed even more than the abbreviated ceremony. She smiled once more, bowed to the congregation, then turned and walked from the hall through the door behind the altar.

The townspeople looked around in confusion as they stood up and began shuffling out of the hall.

"That's peculiar," Jed's mother said, raising an eyebrow.

"And so short," his father added. "The pig won't be done roasting for another hour."

"Hmm," his grandfather said, frowning as he stared where Pastor Vannesh had disappeared out the back.

Jed said nothing. He had no desire to explain his suspicions to his parents. It would only make them worry more. And Jed was now concerned enough for his whole family.

That anxiety only intensified when he realized, a few minutes later, that Pastor Vannesh had vanished. Normally she would have greeted the townspeople as they left the Hall of Light, but she was nowhere to be found. No one had even seen where she had gone. Speculation swirled among the townspeople when Pastor Vannesh had not returned in time to say the blessing at the start of the festival feast.

"Where do you think she went?" Kylla asked later as they stood in line at a long banquet table draped in dark green cloth.

"The better question is why she left," Fallon said, eyeing a large plate of sila-root salad.

"If it had something to do with Tal, then what I really want to know is, when she'll be back?" Jed said.

Kylla and Fallon stared at him in silence. There was nothing they could do but wait, and they all knew it. Knowing he could not assuage the apprehension he felt, Jed decided it was best to act normal, and nothing was more normal than overeating at a festival feast.

The feast was well attended and well supplied. Each townsperson brought at least one passing dish, and Garrif Kinsom had donated a pig for roasting. Laid along a wide wooden table sat sweet meat pies, fillendall casserole, roasted hannock seeds, mashed meffron tubers, fresh vegetable salads, steamed beans, baked beans, three-bean surprise (made with four kinds of beans), a large chocolate cake, and assorted pies.

Everyone sat at long tables or on blankets in the grass. Jed and Kylla's families ate together, sitting on a large blue tablecloth Jed's mother kept especially for such occasions.

The adults engaged in their usual conversations. The men listened to Jed's grandfather tell his hunting stories and debated the trading value of this year's surplus harvest while the women traded recipes and talked about how lovely their neighbor, Ninnet Kinnsom, looked in her peach colored dress, wondering how she had managed to dye the cotton that particular shade.

The celebration went on well past sundown and into the night. As the tube-light dimmed and the shadows of the buildings grew thick along the village streets, several men lit a large bonfire at the edge of the town square.

The wood burned brightly, flames leaping high into the darkness. Jed watched his father and mother dancing in the firelight with their friends and neighbors, grinning to himself. His mother was smiling, truly smiling, for the first time in weeks. He wished Tallu was there to see it.

Kylla and Fallon emerged from the crowd behind Jed, taking his arms and dragging him into the swaying crowd. The three joined hands, dancing in a circle as they encircled the fire, laughing and humming along to the song his mother sang as she spun in his father's arms. Her clear and strong voice rose above the sound of the instruments and carried over the fire and into the town square where people who were not dancing quieted to listen. It was an old song from the first feasting day when the Kellish families celebrated the first harvest of their first year of living in the valley.

Sweat and toil in the midday sun
A farmer's work is never done
Never time for fun and games
The fields call our names

Harvest time will soon draw near
The close of another planting year
Soon will be the time for Winter's flames
The fields call our names

As the dancers grew tired, more and more townsfolk hugged their neighbors, said their goodnights, and drifted home. Jed and Kylla's families did the same, walking together along the quiet dirt road leading to their homes.

Kylla held hands with her father, giggling as she teased him about the structural stability of the new barn he was building for the Litton family on the other side of the river. Her father threw his head back and laughed as he hugged her close. Fallon walked beside his adopted mother, holding her hand and smiling silently at a joke they seemed to share without exchanging words.

Jed watched Kylla and Fallon with their parents as he walked beside his mother and father, who were speaking softly and holding hands as they often did on nights like this. Jed was torn for a moment, feeling that he was too old, as a boy, to be holding hands with his parents and feeling a bit jealous of Fallon for his younger age.

Fortunately, his mother dispelled such thoughts by tossing her arm around his shoulders and pulling him tight to her side as she kissed him on his head, pausing a moment, as mothers often do, to breathe in deeply, smelling his hair, reassuring herself on some primal level that his scent was correct, and this was indeed her child. Jed's grandfather walked a pace and a half behind, slowly, not so much from his age as from the two flagons of summer ale he had consumed that night.

They soon reached the fork in the road that led to their respective households, and the two families said goodnight. The women hugged each other as the men exchanged firm handshakes, and the children called goodbye while they turned and walked to their homes.

Jed was a little ahead of his parents and grandfather along the wagon-furrowed path, enjoying the feel of the cool night breeze on his cheeks, which were still a little flush from dancing. He noticed two visitors sitting in the shadows of his front porch, silently watching the family approach the house.

Jed stopped in his tracks, not sure what to do — not sure who the shadowed strangers were or what their presence on the front porch meant at this time of night. He did not need to wonder long. As his parents came up behind him, the two strangers stood up, stepped off the porch and into the front yard. One of them was Pastor Vannesh.

The other stranger was also a woman, a little older than Pastor Vannesh, probably in her late sixties, her hair a dark silver gray, shorn close to her scalp. Her skin was deep ebony, like the robes of the cloak she wore and her long, thin face looked beautiful in the dim light of the half-moon above. In one hand she held a tall wooden staff, its crown tipped by a sphere covered in interlaced gold circles.

Jed's heart beat faster as he saw the mysterious woman, his mind racing a dozen directions at once. The elderly woman standing beside Pastor Vannesh was clearly a Tellandor priest, and her presence could only mean one thing.

CHAPTER 8
MYSTERIOUS MESSENGER

"The Tellandor Order is nothing less than a threat to the very existence of our civil society. If this band of proselytizing priests is allowed to roam the whole of Wyconna unfettered and unchecked, I guarantee we will see the decline of all religious belief, not just that of our particular faith."

From a sermon by Pastor Lin'Aptack, of the Greater
Wyconna Church of the Stars, 345 AL (After Launch)

"Evenin', Pastor," Jed heard his father say.

"Evenin', Kannu," Pastor Vannesh replied. "I've brought someone to see you. This is Shann'Ka Qa'Lea Unna'ta, a priest of the Tellandor Order. Sister, this is Kannu Hinnsah and his wife Leenna, their son Jeddu, and Leenna's father…"

"Raneel," Sister Qa'Lea interrupted. "The elder Kellish and I have met," she continued, sending a hundred new questions buzzing through Jed's mind as he looked from the priest to his grandfather.

"Do you have news about Tallu?" his mother asked, clasping her hands together and bowing slightly, the anxiety in her voice clearing away all other questions hovering in the night air.

"Why don't we go inside?" Qa'Lea said.

"Is something wrong?" his mother asked, her beautiful voice cracking as tears welled in her eyes.

"I do not know what may or may not be wrong," Qa'Lea said, her voice adopting a gentle and soothing tone that seemed to place Jed's mother at ease. "I believe your son to be alive, but it is complicated, and it would be best if we could discuss the matter in a more peaceful setting."

"Yes, of course." Jed's mother swallowed back her tears. "I'll make some tea."

"And we have plenty of food if you are hungry from your travels," Jed's father added.

"That would be most appreciated," Qa'Lea said, following Jed's mother up the stairs of the porch. Jed's grandfather, still silent, quickly stepped ahead of the group and held the open the door for Qa'Lea and the others to pass through.

Jed's mother served tea with leftover meat cake. Meanwhile, Jed's father lit all the lanterns in the house and placed them around the kitchen, resulting in a bright gauzy glow that cast away any and all shadows, which, as Jed thought about it, was probably the intent — to cast out shadows and possible bad omens, leaving only light and truth, and hopefully news of their eldest son his mother would be able to bear.

"Now," Qa'Lea said, as she raised her head from silently blessing the food and drink placed before her, "the news I have of your son is not good, but neither is it all bad." Jed could see his father take his mother's hand beneath the table and wished he could do the same. "Firstly, I do believe that Tallu may be in danger," Qa'Lea said. "It is not certain, but it is more likely than not."

"What kind of danger?" Jed's mother asked, her voice a near whisper.

"He has disappeared from the Sentient's view," Qa'Lea answered. Jed's parents were silent at this news, briefly exchanging confused glances.

"Maybe you should explain what that means," Pastor Vannesh said.

"Yes, I'm sorry," Qa'Lea said. "When any Kellish child leaves the Notesch Valley for their year of Landdesh, a very small device, so small you could not see it with the naked eye, is surreptitiously implanted beneath the young person's skin."

"You put techne in my son," Jed father said, his eyes narrowing. "You know that this is against our beliefs."

"It was not I, but the Sentient who did this," Qa'Lea responded, her voice stern and calm. "But you are correct. A small amount of techne was placed in your son, as it is placed in all of those of the Notesch Valley who leave the confines of its mountains. No permission is asked because most would refuse, and therefore, never be allowed to leave the valley."

"There are some who know," interjected Pastor Vannesh. "I knew. And most of the council members know. It is a compromise. Our safety, not our customs, is the Sentient's primary concern."

"The device is removed when the children return to the valley," Qa'Lea said. "They are never aware of its presence. It allows the Sentient to know exactly where the child is at all times and to monitor the child's health. In the event of an accident or an emergency, the Sentient can make sure the child receives prompt assistance.

"It is not intended to be an insult to your customs and beliefs. It is intended to protect you beyond the walls of this valley."

"But it has failed to protect Tallu." Jed's mother stared at Qa'lea.

"Yes," Qa'Lea said, the sternness of her voice falling away to reveal a depth of compassion that had been hidden behind her professionalism. "In this instance, the techne seems to have failed. It is not unheard of for the tracking device to become inactive or for a mild injury to damage it. However, something more peculiar has happened.

"Because it is not uncommon for Kellish children to return late from their Landdesh, or to decide not to return at all, the Sentient was not concerned when your son's year beyond the valley walls lapsed. It was only when you made a request to your local council for the Sentient to investigate your son's whereabouts that it became important. The Sentient immediately located the position of the tracking device, which should have indicated the location of your son precisely. However, when the Sentient sought to establish a visual confirmation using other means, it was determined the tracking device had been removed from Tallu and placed on another young man of a similar age and physical description."

"You mean our son truly is missing?" Jed's father asked.

"Yes," Qa'Lea said, her eyes never leaving Jed's parents.

"And someone has taken him," Jed's mother said, crying openly now for the first time. Jed's father, tears at the edges of his own eyes, placed his arm around his wife. Once again, Jed wished he sat closer to his parents so he could seek their comfort for the sharp pain beginning to grip his chest.

"You believe he is still alive, though," Pastor Vannesh said, trying to provide some measure of hopefulness.

"Yes," Qa'Lea said, adjusting the tone of her voice yet again to project a sense of optimism. "We have no reason to believe that Tallu is not alive, although the Sentient does feel he may be in danger."

"But the Sentient will be able to find him?" Jed's father asked.

"Not directly," Qa'Lea answered. "That task has been extended to me, and I assure you, all of you, I will find Tallu."

Jed looked into Qa'Lea's eyes and saw a determination and sense of power that seemed to him inexhaustible. He realized Qa'Lea was no mere gray-haired old woman. She was a Tellandor priest of considerable knowledge and experience and a formidable force to be reckoned with.

"But we are so far away," Jed's mother said. "I know you have means of travel much faster than our own, but wouldn't it make more sense for a priest who is closer to look for our son?"

"Under the circumstances, speed is not an asset," Qa'Lea said. "There are several priests near where your son disappeared, and more where the Sentient believes him to be now, but unfortunately, not all of them can be trusted."

"Tellandor priests not trusted," Jed's grandfather said, speaking for the first time, his face hardening against the fear now palpable around the table.

"The Sentient believes Tallu has been kidnapped by a faction of Third and Fourth Generation Crew Members who are attempting a mutiny," Qa'Lea said.

A sudden silence fell over the table as they all digested the implications of Qa'Lea's words. Jed racked his mind for everything he knew about the crew members and the conflicts between the different generations. He knew when the *Celestial Pilgrim* embarked upon its journey there had been a Primary Crew assigned along with the Sentient to ensure the success of the voyage.

These crew members were intended to see the journey through to its completion. With a combination of lifespan-enhancing technologies and a form of timeless sleep, the Primary Crew members would take shifts of several decades each, rotating in groups, to ensure all of them arrived at their destination.

Naturally, as time passed, these Primary Crew members had children, many of whom became part of the command hierarchy of the starship. But their status was never equal with that of the Primary Crew members, their parents.

In important decisions, the opinions of the Primary Crew members were always given greater weight. This, unsurprisingly, created a great deal of tension between the Primary Crew and their descendants. If Jed understood Qa'Lea correctly, the Third and Fourth Generation Crew Members were plotting to take control of the *Celestial Pilgrim* and the human section, *Wyconna*. It reminded him of his father's frustration with the older members of the town council, but on a much grander scale.

"The world beyond this valley," Qa'Lea said, bringing Jed's attention back to the discussion at the table, "has become dangerous, in subtle ways. Those who have kidnapped Tallu will expect the Sentient to search for him. This the Sentient will do. And the investigation will show that Tallu apparently drowned in a boating accident."

"That's preposterous," Jed's mother said, confused and a bit offended. "Tallu is an excellent swimmer."

"I'm sure he is," Qa'Lea said. "But that is not the point. The purpose of this official investigation is to convince those who abducted Tallu that the Sentient is no longer looking for him. This will make it easier for me to unobtrusively search for your son and find him. Unfortunately, in order to avoid attracting attention to myself and my real mission, I will be forced to travel very slowly, pretending to be on my usual teaching pilgrimage. This will decrease the speed with which I can find and rescue Tallu, but it will greatly increase my chances of success. If those who have taken your son believe the Sentient and I are close to finding him, it is possible they will harm Tallu, and we do not want to risk that."

"Why did they kidnap him?" Jed asked, the words escaping his lips long before he remembered his manners and the presumption that Kellish children his age should remain silent when adults were discussing important matters.

"That is a very good question," Qa'Lea said, looking Jed directly in the eyes for the first time. Jed felt himself falling into those brown eyes for a moment, lost in the depth and radiant magnetism of what lay behind them. "We do not know for certain, but I suspect he was simply in the wrong place at the wrong time and saw something he was not supposed to."

"But why keep him?" Jed's grandfather asked. "And to what end?"

"That is the real question," Qa'Lea said, looking around the table at each member of the family in turn. "It is possible, even likely, his kidnappers plan to make use of him in some way to further their cause. That is why swiftness, however slow-footed it must be, is of the essence.

"And that is why I must leave you. I begin my journey immediately. Thank you for your hospitality and your patience. I assure you, I will do everything in my power to bring your son home to you. I will be in touch again when it is possible."

With this, Qa'Lea stood up suddenly, bowing with clasped hands to the family and the pastor. She briefly touched Jed's grandfather on the shoulder as she strode to the door, opened it, grabbed her staff from where it leaned against the wall, and left the house. The door closed quietly, leaving everyone around the table looking at it, wondering, each in their own way, what the future would bring.

CHAPTER 9
DESTINY DEPARTURE

"Henceforth, all genetic modifications of humans will be guided by the principles established in High Council Edict 1142. Genetic modifications to all nonhuman creatures not set forth in High Council Edict 1143 are hereby banned and prohibited under penalty of law. Furthermore, all creations of new species from existing or artificial genetic material are governed by High Council Edict 1145 and prohibited without express permission of the High Council."

Summary of the New Gene Laws, High Council, First Generation Crew, 545 AL.

"Security is an illusion. Life is either a daring adventure or it is nothing at all."

Helen Keller 1880–1968 CE (Origin World dates)

Jed's mother was distraught and inconsolable after Qa'Lea's abrupt departure. Jed's father tried to calm her, but he was too worried to be of much use. Pastor Vannesh attempted to reassure them Tallu's safety was in the best of hands. Qa'Lea and the Sentient were sure to return him unharmed. Patience and prayer were the best courses of action.

Jed's grandfather was oddly silent, saying nothing for the longest time before suddenly professing his exhaustion and excusing himself to head home. Jed accompanied his grandfather, the two walking in silence for most of the way.

When they reached the edge of his grandfather's yard, Jed finally mustered up the courage to speak.

"Do you think she'll find him?" Jed had asked.

"I have no doubt she'll find him," Jed's grandfather said as he looked up at the false moon in the night sky. "The question is," Jed's grandfather continued, wincing at his words even as he spoke them, "whether or not she'll find him alive."

"You think he's in that much danger?" Jed asked, looking up at his grandfather's face, still tilted skyward.

"Qa'Lea is one of the oldest, most experienced and most powerful Tellandor priests in all of *Wyconna,* if not the whole of the ship. If the Sentient has assigned her this task then the danger must be very real and very great."

"You've met her before." Jed said, remembering what Qa'Lea had mentioned.

"Yes, I have." His grandfather looked down from the stars and into Jed's eyes. Jed saw the memory of both sadness and pleasure mixed on the old man's face. "I met her first when I was a young man of about sixteen. She was on a teaching pilgrimage and stopped in town for a month. She doesn't look a day older than she did then. Don't know how old she really is. I asked once, but she only smiled at me and said that time was an illusion. I was terribly smitten with her, even though she was much older. Of course I knew it was hopeless. A Tellandor priest's vows and all that.

"Then she left town one day, and I grew up enough to see that your grandmother's charms, while entirely different, were just as enticing. I saw Qa'Lea a few times throughout the years, always looking the same, and me looking grayer and older each time.

"When your grandmother passed, Qa'Lea was kind enough to take some time to tutor me on my retreat practice. It meant a great deal to me. She is an amazing teacher. An amazing woman." Jed's grandfather wrapped his arm around Jed and drew him close. "I'm sure she will find your brother. He may be in danger, but his life could not be in better hands."

Jed walked back to the house slowly, already knowing what he would do and how he would do it. When he returned home, he found his mother and father holding each other at the kitchen table. Pastor Vannesh had left. Jed approached his parents to hug them goodnight and his mother clasped him to her chest, crushing the air out of his lungs. She was no longer crying, but the tears of the night were still wet on her face, and when Jed felt them against his own cheeks, he could no longer keep in check the emotions that had been mounting within him ever since Qa'Lea appeared on their porch.

Tears flowed down Jed's face as he sobbed at his mother's breast. His father wrapped his arms around both of them, and they stayed like that until sheer exhaustion forced them to bed.

But Jed didn't stay in bed long after his parents said goodnight. He waited until he heard their bedroom door close before silently slipping from his blankets. He began packing his knapsack with everything he thought he might need on the journey ahead.

The first thing to go in his bag was the ancient dagger. He did not know what he would need it for, and hardly wanted to imagine, but he knew he would need the primeval blade if he was going to follow Qa'Lea and help rescue his brother.

Jed slowly opened the window of his bedroom, a faint creak gently escaping into the moonlit night. Slipping the strap of his knapsack over his head and securing it around his shoulder, Jed slid one leg over the windowsill, as he had so many times before when sneaking out of the house after dark, and placed his right foot firmly on a thick branch of the maple tree in the backyard. Swinging the rest of his body out onto a branch, he looked back briefly to make sure the note he had written his parents was clearly visible on his pillow, held in place by the large polished rock he normally used as a paperweight. Taking a deep breath, knowing what was ahead but not knowing what it might entail, Jed shimmied down the tree and sprinted across the yard.

A short time later he stood beneath the windows to Kylla and Fallon's rooms tossing pebbles at their windows. Moments later the three gathered in the shadows of the nearby barn as Jed recounted the story of Qa'Lea's arrival and the message she brought about Tallu's disappearance. As he explained his plan, he realized he would need to convince them not to follow him. It wasn't an easy task.

"It's too dangerous," Jed said for the third time.

"Which is exactly why you need me with you," Kylla retorted.

"Why you need both of us," Fallon added.

"I told you, you're not coming," Kylla said to Fallon. "It's too dangerous."

"Which is why neither of you are coming," Jed said.

"If you go, she goes," Fallon said. "And if she goes, I go."

"This is ridiculous," Jed said, turning to leave.

"You need my help," Kylla, said, grabbing Jed's arm.

"He's my brother," Jed said, confused by his conflicting desires to both protect Kylla and Fallon and to have them accompany him on the most dangerous adventure of his life.

"We all love him," Kylla said, squeezing Jed's arm harder. He could see the tears she was holding back and knew what she meant.

"We all need each other," Fallon said, placing a hand on each of their arms. "All three of us are meant to go."

"What do you mean?" Jed asked, curious at the tone in Fallon's voice.

"I think the three of us are supposed to go together," Fallon said.

"I don't understand," Kylla said.

"It's always the three of us," Fallon said. "Three is a very powerful number. Haven't you wondered why there were three artifacts in the labyrinth? Why not two, or four? There were three, and each suits us in some way, I'm sure of it. And the three artifacts are intended to be used together."

"Are you saying it was destiny?" Jed asked, his heart beating quickly.

"You think it was all planned?" Kylla asked, looking into Fallon's eyes as they blazed intently in the shadowed light.

"Destiny isn't planned." Fallon said. "But when it happens, when events align in a way that shows a clear path, you have to follow that path. No matter where it leads."

They were all silent for a moment. Jed and Kylla knew in their hearts, Fallon was right. It made sense on a level that transcended logic and reason. For once they could glimpse themselves as parts of something larger. Even if they could not yet discern what that something was, they knew clearly their parts had to be played together.

Kylla and Fallon quickly ran back to their house and quietly stuffed their knapsacks for the journey. They took food from the kitchen and left a note for their parents. Jed felt grateful. He had been too concerned he might alert his parents of his departure if he had snuck downstairs and raided the family larder for supplies. Ten minutes later, all three headed out on the greatest adventure they could ever have imagined.

Jed's plan was to track Qa'Lea at a distance for the first few days. He reasoned if they stayed four to six hours behind her, they could easily follow her trail while not alerting her to their presence. If Qa'Lea became aware of them too soon, she would surely force them to return home and they would never find a second opportunity to sneak out of town. But if Qa'Lea was well along her journey, Jed figured she would not dare take the time to accompany them back to their homes. Time, as Qa'Lea had said, was of the essence, and Jed was counting on the Tellandor priest judging it more important to swiftly reach Tallu than return Jed, Kylla, and Fallon to their parents.

Beneath the artificial light of the half-moon above, they followed Qa'Lea's tracks down the main road and out of town. Jed knew in general what the elderly priest's path would be, so he hoped this would make it easier to track her. The main road from town met up with the Kiffen'Ur Trail, which led toward the Pinak Mountain Range that separated the Notesch valley from the Winsomm Valley and the rest of Wyconna proper. But the Kiffen'Ur Trail did not lead all the way to the mountains. It stopped dead at the edge of the Atrum Forest. There was no trail through the forest and up to the Sanshu Pass, which was the easiest way through the mountains.

This absence of a navigable path was intentional. The idea was to keep the valley safe and out of view of individuals from the more technologically advanced societies who might be tempted to breach the mountain walls in search of some sort of sightseeing adventure.

For the most part, this natural defense succeeded. A group of curious folk would wander into a Kellish town every few years, but once the townspeople alerted the Sentient, if it was not already aware of their intruder's presence by other means, the sightseers were escorted back to the lands from which they came.

The only difficulty in all this arose when the Kellish children leaving the valley for their Landdesh year were taken to the mountain pass because there was no clear path through the forest to follow. The Kellish children's guides, of whom Jed's grandfather was often the leader, would choose a different way through the forest each year. On their return, the Sentient would usually send a guide with the children to get them through the mountain pass, back through the forest, and on their way home.

Because of all this, Jed knew tracking Qa'Lea to the forest would be relatively easy. Following her through the forest would not be nearly as simple. He also knew if his father and grandfather set out to find them, there would be little chance of escaping. Everything Jed knew about tracking and wood sense he had learned from his grandfather. Even if he, Kylla, and Fallon entered the forest at different points and backtracked in an attempt to confuse their trail, his grandfather would see through the ruse as easily as looking through glass. His grandfather had, after all, shown him that trick just last summer.

With Kylla and Fallon silently at his side, following Qa'Lea's faint footprints in the deep dust of the road, Jed tried to calculate what the chances were that his father and grandfather would follow them. While it seemed almost certain they would try to catch him, Jed doubted the men would venture past the mountain walls of the valley. It seemed more likely they would turn back and request the Sentient to find the children and return them. Central to Jed's plan was not allowing Qa'Lea to become aware of them until they had reached the Sanshu Pass.

It was a dangerous gamble. If Jed failed to track Qa'Lea properly through the forest, they might easily come out in the wrong spot and have no idea where the pass was located. The pass was not easily visible and could only be seen from one spot at the edge of the forest.

His thoughts of possible complications to the adventure he had embarked upon with his friends were temporarily suspended as the main road met up with the Kiffen'Ur Trail. Jed realized they must have been walking for several hours.

"Can we stop and rest for a bit?" Kylla asked, recognizing, as Jed had, just how far from town they had come.

"We can drink a little," Jed said, reaching in his knapsack for his goat's bladder water skin. "Now that we've reached the Kiffen'Ur Trail, we are less likely to run into anyone, but I want to make sure we reach the forest by dayrise."

Jed took a swig of water. Wiping his lips, he passed the skin to Kylla, who took a deep draught before passing it to Fallon.

"How long until we reach the forest?" Fallon asked, handing the water skin back to Jed after taking a few large gulps of the cool liquid.

"Two hours," Jed replied. "Maybe three."

"Then we should hurry," Fallon said. "When the moon fades there is only an hour until dayrise." Jed and Kylla looked to the placement of the artificially projected moon in the sky and realized Fallon was right.

"How quietly can you run?" Jed asked the other two.

"I've never tried to be quiet, just fast," Kylla responded.

"Well, be as quiet as possible," Jed said as he began to lope as silently as he could down the trail. "We want to reach the forest before the sun sees our hides, but we don't want Qa'Lea to hear us. Luckily the wind is against us, so it won't carry our footsteps to her ears."

Trying to stay as light of foot as possible and breathe as softly as they could, Jed, Kylla, and Fallon ran down the packed dirt of the Kiffen'Ur Trail toward the Atrum Forest, toward daybreak, and toward destiny.

CHAPTER 10
TO HUNT AND BE HUNTED

"The ecological composition of bacterial, viral, plant, insect and animal life within the confines of the human section of the Celestial Pilgrim, *commonly called* Wyconna *by its inhabitants, was assembled from a wide selection of possible components, most from the human Origin World, and some from planets colonized by the human species. This mix is under the constant supervision of the Sentient and a panel of Primary Crew ecologists to ensure that the ecosystems of the human section remain in something close to a balance, although periods of chaotic ecological unbalance are necessary for the long-term survival of the artificial environment as a whole. By and large, genetically modified organisms are strictly controlled for introduction to any particular ecological sector."*

From *The Encyclopedia Wyconnica, 112th Edition*

The Kiffen'Ur Trail was, in truth, little more than a slender path winding around the hills and through the fields of waist-high wild grass covering the lower plains beneath the Pinak Mountains. An occasional stand of trees and frequent clumps of bilder bushes dotted the landscape, but, in general, the horizon was open and unobstructed.

This was largely the reason Jed, Kylla, and Fallon were making such haste to reach the forest. The wild grass of the plains was tall, but not tall enough to offer any protection from those who might see them. If dayrise came upon them before they reached the forest, it would only take Qa'Lea glancing back over her path to discover she was being followed. Assuming she had not yet reached the forest. If they had been following her through denser vegetation, Jed might have been able to judge her distance ahead of them by the character of broken weeds and such, but the trail, while not often traveled, was ancient enough that there was little plant growth inhibiting the progress of any traveler.

Jed kept his gaze constantly roaming between the dirt tracks, the path of the trail up through the low hills, and his two friends behind him. He looked at Kylla. He could see even she was beginning to tire from the constant running. Fallon, several paces behind, looked positively exhausted, his diminutive stature working against him. Jed knew making it to the forest in time would be close. Turning back to the trail and looking down, he frowned, suddenly coming to a complete stop. Kylla crashed into him.

"What's wrong?" Kylla asked, seeing the look on Jed's face as he continued to stare at the ground. Fallon finally caught up and stopped, bending over and breathing heavily as Jed looked up from the trail.

"The tracks are gone," Jed said.

"What do you mean, gone?" Kylla asked. "Where could they go?"

"Qa'Lea left the trail early," Jed said.

"Probably to throw off anyone who might be following her," Fallon added between labored breaths.

"Maybe," Jed said. "Or maybe she knows another way to the Sanshu Pass."

"Or maybe another way through the mountains," Kylla said, thinking aloud.

"If we lose her now, we'll never be able to catch up," Fallon said as Jed began to backtrack along the trail, his face bent down close to the path.

"We're not going to lose her," Jed said, barely concealing his irritation at the suggestion.

The artificially projected moon was already fading, its dimming light lending little help to Jed's quest to find where Qa'Lea's tracks left the trail. Kylla and Fallon followed silently behind him, knowing they were of little use to Jed in discerning Qa'Lea's direction. Jed's skills in tracking would have made it a relatively simple task in the daylight to distinguish Qa'Lea's footprints from those of himself,

Kylla, Fallon, and older tracks that lay beneath theirs, but in the darkness, he found the task frustratingly difficult.

"I can't see the trail well enough," Jed said, bending closer to the ground.

"We could light a candle," Kylla offered.

"Someone might see it," Fallon countered.

"I need more light somehow," Jed said as he stopped and stood up.

"Maybe more moonlight will do," Kylla said.

"How do you suggest we create more moonlight?" Jed asked, turning to see that Kylla was already digging into her knapsack.

"With this," Kylla said, pulling a white sheet from her bag. "I thought we might be able to use it for a distress signal if we got in trouble."

"Brilliant," Jed said, watching as Kylla handed one corner of the sheet to Fallon. "Still, you better keep it low so no one can see it above the kull grass."

Kylla and Fallon unfurled the sheet carefully between them, dividing it into half its length and keeping it just at the top of the grass, angled to reflect the dimming moonlight onto the trail at their feet. Jed bent back down, eyes to the ground, and walked slowly back the way they had come. After about ten meters, he stopped, stood up, and looked around. Stepping quietly from the path, he examined the ground and grass to one side of the trail, and then he looked at the other side.

"What a devious old woman," Jed said, standing up once more.

"What's the matter?" Kylla asked. "You can't find the trail?"

"Oh, I'll find it," Jed said. "Eventually. Her trail ends here, but she didn't enter the grass. She must have back backtracked, walking backward in her own footprints. I'll need to check the grass along the trail on both sides to see where she might have gone in."

"But you can definitely find it," Fallon said as more of a statement than a question.

"It's not about *finding* it," Jed said, beginning to walk along the edge of the trail, examining the tall grass for signs of entry. "It's about how *long* it takes me to find it. That's her whole point. Not necessarily to throw someone off the trail entirely, but to make them waste much more time finding it again than was expended in creating the diversion. What took her less than a minute could take us an hour."

"We don't have an hour," Kylla said.

"I know," Jed said. "Hold that sheet to the side of me so I can see better."

Kylla and Fallon followed Jed slowly along the trail as he moved from examining the tracks in the trail itself to the possible signs of tracks in the kull grass. Even with the added moonlight reflected off of the sheet, it was too dark to tell where footprints had been impressed twice, which would have indicted exactly where Qa'Lea had jumped off the trail.

Then it occurred to him Qa'Lea may have done just that. Jumped off the trail. In his mind's eye he saw the elderly priest's tall walking stick leaning against the wall.

"Devious, devious, devious," Jed said aloud.

"What now?" Kylla asked, obviously annoyed at being relegated to holding a sheet for her part in solving their current problem.

"She must have used her walking stick to vault over the edge of the grass," Jed said.

"I thought you said she was old," Fallon said.

"She's old, but she's spry," Jed said, moving quickly along the edge of the trail, knowing now what he was looking for, and knowing he had already seen it.

"Here," Jed said, pointing to a small divot in the mossy ground at the edge of the trail. "I saw it earlier, but I assumed it was a hole for a mole or something."

Stepping through the tall kull grass, Jed examined the ground and the vegetation beyond the trail. "You can pack up that sheet," he said, grinning. "She went this way."

Kylla wadded up the sheet and stuffed it in her knapsack as she and Fallon followed Jed into the tall grass of the plains. While their progress was not as swift as before, following tracks through tall grass versus the trail posed little problem for Jed and slowed them only slightly.

Tracking, as Jed's grandfather had taught him, was like reading. One had to know how to read the ground below and the landscape around oneself. Nature arose in certain patterns, and animals or humans that passed through a space would leave a mark in those patterns one could interpret, like writing. Jed's grandfather likened it to walking into one's house after someone else had been there. If you were attentive, you could tell what they had done by what they had moved or left behind.

The key to tracking was twofold: First, knowing what the landscape looked and smelled like when undisturbed, and second, knowing what signs a creature might leave in passing through it. Jed's grandfather had taught him how to discern the difference between a blade of grass broken from the wind and one bent from the passing of a deer, how to see a pawprint or footprint in the hardest ground or the softest moss, how to tell how long ago the mark had been made, and how to know which dropping came from which animal. Jed had practiced his grandfather's lessons until tracking had, indeed, become like reading for him.

When he was reading, he found himself in another world. His mind focused on the words in front of his eyes and the world around him ceased to exist to his senses, the world in his mind becoming as real as anything he had ever known.

Tracking was the reverse experience; his mind so focused on the world around him that his thoughts and motions all seemed to be part of the landscape he moved through. It was one of the few times when he felt his mind and heart were truly at peace.

But, on that night, too near morning, even though he was immersed in reading the language of the landscape before him, he didn't feel at peace. They had lost a precious amount of time and dayrise was now even closer than ever.

Jed tried to press the pace as much as possible, fearing Qa'Lea might have pulled the same trick again and knowing they would never make it out of the kull grass of the plains before dayrise if they had to waste more time on false trails.

But they were lucky. The trail ran true, and dayrise cast its crimson-tinged light upon them just as they found themselves at the edge of the Atrum Forest.

Stepping into the Atrum Forest was like walking back into night. The fir trees were so tall, and the canopy of their branches so tightly woven together, little daylight ever reached the forest floor. A mere forty meters into the forest, the light from the plains behind them faded to near darkness. Jed remembered his grandfather once telling him the word *Atrum* meant *dark* in some ancient language. It certainly lived up to the name *dark forest*. Fortunately for Jed, the thickness of the trees above meant the vegetation along the forest floor was much drier than the grass of the plains, making it easier to see the path Qa'Lea had taken through the black woods. Although the light was dim, the trail was clear enough to follow. Not that Qa'Lea apparently had any interest in making her trail easy to track.

Kylla and Fallon close behind him, Jed continually checked and rechecked the signs of the trail, attempting to see where Qa'Lea tried to lead potential trackers astray. Several times the trail split where Qa'Lea had backtracked along her own footprints, and several more times she used the pole to vault away from her tracks, even using stones in the forest floor to balance the walking stick and make the trick more difficult to decipher.

However, each time the trail split or seemingly disappeared, Jed soon found it again. He pursued his quarry with relentless devotion. At times, he would suddenly hear himself muttering, "Devious, devious, devious," under his breath.

They stopped occasionally to briefly rest, drink a bit and eat dried meats, but Jed feared if they paused too long he might lose the trail. Not that the trail might go cold, but that he might lose his vision for seeing it. He had never spent this long tracking anything, and staying in the mental space required for the task was beginning to drain him. It didn't help that they had not slept all night and were all well beyond the limit of what they had previously known as exhaustion.

He also knew if he lost the trail, it would be the end of their attempt to help find Tallu. While he could follow Qa'Lea's trail, he had no way of knowing where the Sanshu Pass was. If he lost the trail, they would have no choice but to turn around and follow their own tracks back out of the forest. It was a great deal of pressure, and Kylla and Fallon seemed to understand this, barely saying a word as the three of them progressed through the forest.

Late in the afternoon, so near dayfall that visibility within the forest had been reduced to only several meters, Jed came to a stop. Kylla and Fallon were used to this and silently paused behind him.

Jed began checking the ground closely, moving outward in a spiral pattern, as he had so often that day. Kylla and Fallon had seen the routine so many times it seemed normal. Jed had found the spiral pattern quicker than paying attention solely to Qa'Lea's footprints. He assumed she had used the walking stick again to leap clear of her current trail, but after several minutes he stopped and looked at Kylla and Fallon while scratching his head.

"I can't find it," Jed said.

"Maybe you're just tired," Kylla said.

"Maybe we should rest for a minute," Fallon offered.

"No," Jed responded. "It's gone. I can't find anything within ten meters."

"Maybe she doubled back," Kylla suggested.

"No, I checked," Jed replied.

"What do we do?" Fallon asked. "We can't turn back."

"I know," Jed said as he sat down, his legs collapsing beneath him as much from frustration with himself as exhaustion. "If we don't find her trail..." he began to speak, but the emotion behind the thought of having to leave the search for his brother to the hands of others overwhelmed him, and he fell quiet.

Kylla sat next to Jed and placed her hand on his shoulder. "We'll think of something, Jed. We always do."

Jed didn't reply. He looked past Kylla and into the forest, suddenly feeling a wave of hopelessness flood over him. He felt like he had let them down, that he had let his older brother down. But he didn't want to give in to that emotion, not yet. There had to be something they could do.

He turned to see that Fallon, his energy completely spent, had fallen onto the soft forest moss and was already snoring gently. Somewhere above them a bird squawked and took flight. The sound of wings beating the air slowly faded as it flew away from them and through the dense maze of trees, a curving gold pattern spread out across its wings.

Jed noticed Kylla staring at the branch where the bird had been. The branch, like many of the branches, was only two or so meters above the forest floor and jutted up against the branches of its neighbors. Kylla looked down at the ground and then back up at the branch. A smile crept across her face, and looking back down, she smacked Jed's arm so hard he fell over sideways.

"What was that for?" Jed asked, rubbing his arm.

"Just how spry is this old priest, anyway?" Kylla asked, the grin on her face growing larger.

"Well," Jed said, "she's been hiking all night and all day, playing leap frog through the forest every thirty minutes, so I'd say she's in better shape than we are."

"If she climbed a tree," Kylla said, "how far do you think she could manage to get by swinging from one branch to another?"

Jed shot up to his feet so quickly Kylla yelped in surprise. Fallon, waking up in response to the sound of his sister, raised his head and looked around. "What'd she do this time?" he asked.

"Something devious," Jed replied.

"You really like that word," Fallon said, standing up.

"He's just annoyed because he's following someone as devious as he is," Kylla said.

"And fortunately, I'm traveling with someone who is even more devious than I am," Jed said, smiling at Kylla.

"I'll assume that's a compliment," Kylla replied.

"Naturally," Jed said. "Now help me find where she climbed back down to the ground."

"Climbed back down to the..." Fallon started to say and then looked up into the trees. "Oh. I see. She *is* devious."

It took them nearly twenty minutes of searching in separate spiral loops along the forest floor to find where Qa'Lea's footprints suddenly reappeared, but once they had, the trail was clear and straight. It was apparent to Jed that Qa'Lea either didn't believe anyone could follow her after such an elaborate diversion, or she no longer felt she could afford the time to take such precautionary measures.

They made good progress again, and Jed estimated Qa'Lea was only five hours ahead of them. Soon, however, nightfall came, and it was too dark to follow the trail. They decided to make camp for the night and rest, hoping not only that Qa'Lea would do the same, but that if Jed's grandfather and father were following, they would do likewise.

CHAPTER 11
NIGHT VISION

Excerpt from Kylla's Journal:

"It's late and very, very dark here in the Atrum forest. Jed and Fallon have fallen asleep next to the fire, so I thought I'd take a moment to update my journal. I'm so tired, I don't know if I can manage to write much more. Only to say how scared I am. My eyes are so tired I can barely make out the words I'm writing by firelight. I can't decide if I'm more tired or scared.

Not scared of the forest so much as scared for Tal. I don't know what I'll do if something bad has happened to him. We have to find him. And soon. Everything Jed said makes it seem like we might only have days left. We should have started out weeks ago when Tal was only a few days late. We should have known. I should have known. If something happens to Tal, I'll never be able to tell him…well, you know what I'd tell him if I had the courage to tell him.

If I thought for a moment he might understand. That he wouldn't think of me as a child. I'm not a child. That look he gives me sometimes, like I'm the little sister he never wanted. Oh, I want to strangle him when he gives me that look! If only he wasn't so cute when he was giving it. I'm so worried. And so tired. I must sleep. I hope Jed was right about there not being any creatures in the forest. He always chooses the worst times to be wrong."

Using the underbrush of the forest, a few fallen branches, some dry moss, and a piece of flint from his knapsack, Jed started a small fire. With the forest as thick as it was, there was little chance of the light from their fire being spotted, either by Qa'Lea or by anyone attempting to follow them.

Sitting by the fireside, they eagerly devoured a simple meal of dried meat, cornbread, hard cheese, and apples. They passed the water skin between them, eating in silence. They were so exhausted from their journey, they needed all their energy to concentrate on eating, and had little left for conversation until their hunger had been sated.

"We should get some sleep," Jed finally said as he wrapped the remainder of their food in a piece of cheesecloth.

"Should we take turns watching?" Kylla asked before taking one last sip of water.

"Watching for what?" Fallon asked, looking around at the pitch black forest beyond the fire.

"I don't know," Kylla said, glancing around at the darkness beyond the flames. "Things."

"What sort of things might be running around in a pitch-black forest at night?" Fallon asked, the tone of his voice indicating his vivid imagination was presenting numerous, unpleasant possibilities.

"Wild things," Kylla replied as she busied herself with repacking the food into her knapsack, obviously trying to forget what she had just suggested.

"There are no dangerous animals in the forest," Jed said, trying to muster as much authority into his voice as he could manage. "Besides deer and a fox or two, there are only small animals in the forest."

"What about wolves?" Kylla asked, gazing into the darkness between the trees.

"Or bears," Fallon said, scooting himself closer to the fire.

"The wolves stay in the plains where it's easier to hunt," Jed said. "And the bears stay in the mountains near the streams. There's nothing to worry about as long as we keep the fire going and stay close to it." Jed tossed two more thick branches on the fire and lay down close to the flames, using his knapsack as a pillow.

Kylla and Fallon looked at each other for a moment and then, shrugging, did the same. They arranged themselves to one side of the fire facing out into the woods, their backs to the small blaze. Although it was still technically summer, the night air mild in the plains, deep within the woods it had a definite chill. They wrapped their arms around themselves to preserve their warmth.

Even though Jed was as tired as he could ever remember being, he did not immediately fall asleep. In fact, he found it impossible at first to even close his eyes. Regardless of the conviction with which he had stated their safety, the impenetrable shadows beyond the light of the fire played with his imagination. It was all too easy to envision something lurking behind a tree or a small scrub from a dim firelight flickering to and fro.

Shadows shifted and shapes seemed to change before his tired eyes. And the sounds of the forest, while its animals were supposedly asleep, seemed to be more alive than during the day. Insects chirped, trees creaked as they swayed in the gentle wind moving among the treetops, their branches clicking and clattering against one another in an incessant cascade of sound. It was not long before Fallon had shifted position to be closer to his sister. "For warmth," he said.

Jed quickly shifted to join them, the three of them lined up, facing away from the fire, Kylla's sheet spread over them for additional warmth. Soon after, Jed fell sound asleep.

He woke with a start. While Jed's body didn't move, his eyes bolted open. He tried not to breathe as he gathered his senses, attempting to figure out why he was awake, and where he was. He quickly remembered the journey from home to forest and just as quickly realized the cold air against his back meant the fire had burned out.

But that wasn't why he was awake. There was something else.

Something at the edge of his mind made him uncomfortable. A warning of sorts. He wasn't sure *how* he knew, but he knew.

They were not alone in the forest.

He tried looking around the trees to see what might be lurking in the shadows, but it was too dark, and Kylla's head obstructed his field of vision. Lying on his side, he could see nothing. And with his heart now pounding in his chest, he couldn't hear anything moving, although the hairs standing up on the back of his neck told him otherwise.

Slowly as he could, he slipped the hand of his free arm into his knapsack, searching for the one thing he knew might give him an advantage. As his fingers probed his pack, he gently nudged Kylla with his knee and whispered to her as quietly as he could.

"Ky, don't say anything."

Her sudden change in breathing told him she was awake. "Something is in the trees."

"Where?" Kylla asked, the fear in her voice almost masked by a whisper.

"I can't tell," Jed whispered back. "If we move at the same time, we might scare it away. Wake Fallon."

"I've been awake for two minutes," Fallon whispered. "It's behind us."

The chill along Jed's back grew more intense as he began to imagine something large and unpleasant just behind him. Then his fingers found what they had been searching for.

"Wait for my signal," Jed whispered.

Slowly pulling the dagger from its sheath in the knapsack, Jed rolled beneath the sheet, pretending to still be asleep. As he turned, he kept his eyes open just a fraction, trying to see what might be in the forest. What he was looking for wasn't hard to spot. In fact, it was all too easy to see. Frighteningly easy.

There in the darkness of the forest trees, some five meters past the cooling red embers of the fire, stared a blue pair of impossible eyes. Impossible because they were glowing.

Jed had seen the eyes of many animals in the darkness of night and knew that the glowing of their eyes was just reflection of the light around them. But Jed had never seen an animal with blue eyes, nor eyes as large as these, and there was no light this deep into the forest that could be reflected now that the fire had burned down to near ash.

Incredible as it was, there was something in the forest with large, unnaturally glowing, blue eyes staring right at them. And whatever it was, it seemed to be huge, because the eyes were nearly a meter from the ground, and Jed could discern the faint outline of a wide, bulky shape within the trees.

"Now," Jed said aloud, nearly screaming, not taking time to muster his courage for fear his courage would fail, as he and his companions launched into action.

Flinging the sheet aside, Jed leapt to his feet, followed swiftly by Kylla and Fallon, each of them yelling at the top of their lungs, Jed brandishing the ancient dagger, Kylla wielding a branch intended for the fire, and Fallon holding a large rock.

The possessor of the glowing blue eyes was not impressed, nor frightened away. The blue eyes, shining in the night, continued to stare impassively at the three Kellish children.

Now that his own eyes were fully open, Jed could see more clearly the beast that beheld them with its gaze. Its eyes really did glow from some sort of internal luminescence, and this glow partially illuminated the features of its face and even some of its body.

Its face seemed like some strangely compacted cross between a very ugly dog and a vicious bear. Its body, barely visible under the shadowy glow of its eyes, was also compacted and seemed like a gnarled mass of muscles on four stout tree stumps. It was a hideous creature, and even more repulsive as it opened its fang-filled mouth and uttered a low, guttural growl.

Jed, Kylla, and Fallon subconsciously retreated two steps from the source of the growl and raised their weapons in defensive postures. As the creature's growl ended, Jed noticed how quiet the forest had suddenly become. There were no insects chirping, and even the familiar clacking of tree branches seemed muted.

"Leave!" Kylla suddenly yelled, shaking her large stick.

The glowing blue eyes slowly, silently blinked once in response.

Yelling at the top of his lungs, Fallon stepped forward and threw his rock with all his might.

As many a schoolyard bully had been chagrinned to discover, Fallon, while small and scholarly, also possessed a surprisingly strong arm and a deft accuracy with a hurled object. So it was a shock to all three that, instead of the rock bouncing off the head of the blue-eyed creature staring them down, it simply disappeared with a quick, snapping noise.

Fallon stepped back a pace, trying to figure out what had just happened when a sharp crunching noise met their ears, solving the mystery.

The creature was eating the rock.

Kylla gasped slightly and stepped in front of her younger brother to defend him against any possible retaliation by the creature. The monster growled again, louder this time as it moved forward from the shadows.

Not knowing why, or even what he was doing, Jed suddenly stepped up to meet the creature, his right arm raised and the dagger pointed directly at it.

"Go!" Jed shouted in a voice that seemed to command much more authority and convey far more threat than he had known he possessed. The creature, however, did not pause, and as it came toward them, they could all see that it was, indeed, nearly a meter tall standing on four feet, and that its muscled mass must weigh nearly three hundred kilos. Its spiked hide stretched tight around its massive limbs. It was clearly a creature capable of killing nearly anything in its path, and it did not seem at all concerned by the threats from the three young Kellishers before it.

The creature took another lumbering step forward, and as Kylla pulled Fallon close, Jed shouted again, this time placing both hands on the hilt of the dagger.

"I said, GO!"

The creature stopped, its eyes suddenly fixated on the blade of the dagger, which had also begun to glow blue. As the creature paused to consider whether to attack or retreat, the blade of the ancient dagger began to blaze with a brilliant blue light so powerful that Jed could feel the heat of it against his face and was nearly blinded by its brilliance. The blade blasted forth a sword like light that engulfed Jed, Kylla, and Fallon in its glow and seared the spiky skin of the creature.

Then the glow of the blade faded, and was gone.

Gone as well was the creature.

Jed slumped and lowered both his arms, letting the dagger dangle in his right hand. Kylla and Fallon reached out to steady him.

"That was brilliant!" Fallon said.

"Yes," added Kylla. "That was amazing! How did you do that? The blade has never been that bright before."

"I don't know," Jed replied honestly. "I guess I was just scared. I don't even remember thinking about the dagger, only feeling frightened of whatever that thing was. Then suddenly the blade was glowing and I found that if I concentrated on it, on the blade instead of the fear, it got brighter and brighter. And then it stopped."

"Well, it's a lucky thing you did whatever you did or that thing would have been having us for breakfast," Kylla said, looking around the forest to make sure the creature had really departed.

"We can't stay here," Jed said, grabbing the sheath of the dagger from his knapsack.

"I doubt it will come back after that," Kylla said, clearly unenthusiastic about the prospect of resuming their journey before sunrise.

"What's to say that creature is alone?" Jed asked as he strapped the sheath to his side and slid the dagger into place.

Kylla stared at the dagger. The look on her face said she realized Jed was right. They would need to be more careful now that they knew what sort of creatures they might come across in the forest.

"Besides," Jed said, beginning to douse the final embers of the fire with dirt as Kylla folded the sheet, "it's almost sunrise and we have no idea how early Qa'Lea will be up and moving. Priests are used to getting little sleep and rising before daylight."

"There's another reason to leave now," Fallon added as he shouldered his knapsack and looked at the other two. "I don't think that creature was anything natural, and there's never been a technology-created creature this side of the Pinak Mountains."

Fallon, as usual, had said aloud what Jed and Kylla were too afraid to even think about. The creature was definitely a product of technology, which meant its presence in the forest with them was no accident.

"It was looking for us," Fallon said as the three of them stared at each other in growing concern.

They paused for a moment, holding each other's gazes, and then Jed spoke.

"Let's go."

He crossed the remains of the fire and headed into the woods.

"How will you see the trail without light?" Kylla asked. "We don't want to get lost in the forest."

"I'll use this," Jed said as he pulled the dagger from the sheath at his hip and held it out before him. The blade began to glow with a dim blue light as he stepped into the densely packed trees.

CHAPTER 12
HIDDEN PASS

Genetics: The science of genes and heredity in organisms. Genes are the units of heredity that determine different aspects of how an organism will function and develop. The instructions for all life originating on the Planet Earth (The Origin World) are contained in DNA, or Deoxyribonucleic acid. These DNA instructions are found in the nucleus of each cell in an organism's body. In humans, they are grouped together into 23 pairs called chromosomes. Genes are groups of DNA on each chromosome that have instructions for specific biological functions. These genes, or sections of DNA, each code for the creation of specific amino acids, the building blocks of proteins, which are the basis of organic life.

Each strand of DNA is composed of four chemical compounds, or nucleotides, called adenine (A), guanine (G), cytosine (C), and thymine (T). These four DNA bases, as they are known, are arranged in different combinations of pairs along the length of the DNA strand. Each DNA strand is twisted along its axis in what is called a double helix. During reproduction, the strings of DNA separate, each parent contributing a half strand of DNA to the new organism. These new DNA strands, or chromosomes, become the blueprint for the new organism, combining characteristics from both parents.

From *The Encyclopedia Wyconnica, 112ᵗʰ Edition*

Dayrise came not long after they left the camp. The illumination of the tube-light above gradually increased in intensity to mimic the actual rising of a sun on a real planet and Jed resheathed the ancient dagger.

After dayrise, Jed found himself checking the blade at his side repeatedly, as if to reassure himself it was still there. It was important to be aware of their surroundings, to be prepared in the event the creature might return. While Jed concentrated on finding and following Qa'Lea's trail, Kylla and Fallon lent their attention to the woods around them, constantly checking to the rear and sides to see if they could catch any glint of blue eyes, trying to tune their hearing to the low din of the forest, and searching for some aural anomaly that might warn them of a predator's approach.

Jed noticed Kylla frequently reaching up to cup her hand around the ancient stone hanging at her neck. More than once he caught her making it float along with her as she walked.

After several hours, they paused for a late but much needed breakfast of apples and cheese. They did not stop for long, nor did they speak much. They each knew, without saying it aloud, that their course was now determined for them. They had to find Qa'Lea before the creature might find them again, and they could not turn back and head home, even if they wanted to, because the creature was behind them.

They pressed ahead as fast as Jed could find Qa'Lea's trail through the forest. Fortunately, Qa'Lea had abandoned her practice of trying to confuse her trail. Jed had been fearful that with a new day of travel, she might have tried at least one or two tricks, but the trail was easy to follow. He briefly considered attempting to disguise their own tracks at some point, but he suspected the creature following them could smell well enough that even taking to the trees would not offer a sufficient deception.

He plunged ahead, leading them through the forest as quickly as he could, knowing that the sooner they could catch up to Qa'Lea, the sooner they would be safe. Assuming, of course, Qa'Lea could protect them from the blue-eyed creature. Jed's grandfather had held nothing but admiration for Qa'Lea, and the Tellandor priests were long rumored to be recalcitrant but skilled warriors.

Regardless of Qa'Lea's ability to protect them, Jed knew once they were in the Sanshu Pass that the creature could only attack them from the rear, which was not the case while they were still in the forest. The real question was how quickly they could catch up with Qa'Lea. Jed felt certain from the state of the signs he found on the trail — footprints, broken weeds, slightly bent branches and so forth — Qa'Lea was still at least four hours ahead of them. Since her pace of progress had to be nearly equal to their own, if not greater, Jed reasoned the only real chance they might have of catching up with her would be to continue pressing onward once night had fallen and try to reach her while she was making camp for the evening.

It would not be an easy day's hike, and all the more difficult for the lack of sleep they had endured, but with the creature behind them as motivation, it was much easier than it might normally have been to muster the energy to continue walking. The fact that this was not the first adventure for the three was another advantage. While this might have been the most extreme challenge they had faced, they were used to taking risks far from the protective gaze of their parents.

As the morning turned to afternoon, an event marked by the tube-light reaching an apex of brightness and then slowly beginning to dim, the forest finally began to thin, and the incline of the landscape increased. They had reached the far side of the Atrum Forest and began to ascend the lower reaches of the Pinak Mountains.

While their exit from the forest greatly livened their spirits, they now had to climb nearly halfway up the mountain before reaching the Sanshu Pass.

Moreover, tracking Qa'Lea's path became more difficult as the vegetation of the forest gave way to rocky mountainside. However, Jed's grandfather had taught him well how to read the signs of a trail, whether in grass or woods or stone. While there might not be a weed bent or broken, there were usually pebbles or dust one could not help but displace while passing. To the untrained eye, they might seem as though they had been placed there by the wind or rain, but if one knew how to look for a natural pattern from the unnatural, one could see where a person or animal had passed.

Jed was also spurred on by the knowledge that only Qa'Lea knew where the Sanshu Pass was, and if he did not properly follow her trail to it, they would never find the pass on their own.

The progress up the mountainside was considerably slower than through the forest. It was not only the incline slowing them but the difficulty of the terrain. Often, Kylla would push Jed up a slope of rock so he, in turn, could pull her and Fallon up to join him. On more than one occasion, the white sheet served yet another function, acting as a short rope they could use to pull each other up with, overcoming steep outcroppings of stone.

They paused twice more while working their way up the mountainside, breaking to chew dried meat and sip their dwindling supply of water. Remembering yet another old trick his grandfather had taught him, Jed picked up three small pebbles and handed one each to Kylla and Fallon, instructing them to the keep the small stones under their tongues. Although skeptical at first, Kylla and Fallon were pleased to find the presence of the pebble in their mouths kept their saliva flowing and significantly diminished their thirsts.

The ascent up the mountainside was not straight, veering back and forth as it rose. The one clear benefit was they could easily check behind them to see if they were being followed. After a few hours, their nerves began to relax as it seemed obvious nothing could come toward them from out of the forest without taking a significant amount of time to get to them.

By late afternoon, they reached the pass. Of course, because the pass was hidden by the way it blended into the natural formation of mountainside, they did not realize they had reached the pass until Jed followed Qa'Lea's trail almost to the mouth, which was created by the two opposing mountain walls.

Suddenly, realizing what he was seeing before him, Jed came to a stop. Intent on keeping their footing, Fallon and Kylla bumped solidly into Jed's back.

"What?" Kylla said, looking around in the fear Jed had seen something far more dangerous than a mountain pass.

"Look," Jed replied, pointing to the mouth of the mountain pass. Kylla and Fallon followed the line of Jed's outstretched arm but saw nothing.

"Look at what?" Fallon asked.

Jed turned and smiled. "Look from here."

Jed stepped forward and to the side as Kylla and Fallon took his place. They both let out low, audible gasps. The pass was suddenly visible. From Jed's vantage, just a few steps away, the pass was invisible again.

"I wonder if it was built that way," Fallon thought aloud.

"How could you build a mountain?" Jed asked, even as he realized the answer.

"The whole ship was built," Kylla said. "Why not plan the mountains?"

Jed wondered, for the first time, how many things he always took for granted as being natural in their massive world were, in fact, artificial.

"Whether it was planned or not, we'd better get into it as fast as possible," Jed said, resuming his progress toward the pass at an even quicker pace. "If there is something behind us, we don't want to help it find the pass by letting it see us enter."

They scrambled up the last stretch of rocky slope and dashed through the mouth of the pass into a long narrow canyon cleft into the base of two opposing mountain peaks. The canyon floor was only a few meters wide, but largely level, as though it had been worn down by centuries and centuries of travel and weather. Or, possibly as Fallon had hinted, it simply looked that way because it had been designed to look that way.

As they walked along the canyon floor they looked upward, following the rocky walls up to the sky. The walls of the pass in some places were at least twenty meters high and thirty meters wide. The effect of the canyon's high walls and narrow passage below made Jed feel as though they were walking into some massive stone cathedral, like the sort he had seen in books he wasn't supposed to find in the town library.

"It's beautiful," Fallon said, staring skyward and trying not to trip on the small rocks that littered the path of the canyon floor.

"Yes, it is," Kylla said as something moved on the canyon wall, causing her to jump. Jed and Fallon, noticing her reaction, spun around. Jed's hand slid the ancient blade from its sheath in one swift movement.

"What is it?" Jed said.

"A bird," Kylla said. "There." She tilted her head back to look high above them where a bird flew through the canyon walls. "I've seen that bird," Kylla said, pointing to the strange gold markings on its wings.

"There's probably lots of birds like it around here," Jed said, trying to sound rational.

"Not with those wing markings," Kylla said. "I know I've seen it before."

"Maybe it's watching us," Fallon said.

"Let's not get paranoid," Jed said, returning the blade to its sheath and turning to continue into the pass.

"Just because I'm paranoid doesn't mean there isn't a bird following us," Kylla said, walking beside Jed.

"Maybe not," Jed replied, "but there's something much bigger and nastier we know is probably following us, and our best chance of not getting eaten is to catch up with Qa'Lea as soon as we can."

This somber analysis of the situation was enough to silence them all and set them single-mindedly to the task of covering as much ground as possible before nightfall.

To their surprise, it did not take them hours to catch up with Qa'Lea. Only an hour after they had entered the pass, they came around a slight bend in the canyon and found the old priest sitting cross-legged on a rock, her eyes closed and hands cupped in her lap, her walking staff resting across her legs. They were so surprised to find the object of their two-day trek simply seated before them on the canyon floor that the three Kellish children stopped dead in their tracks and stood in silence.

They continued to stand quietly for several more seconds, not knowing what to do now that they had caught up with the Tellandor priest, particularly as she seemed to be in a state of prayer or meditation.

Jed's mind felt suddenly, uncharacteristically, blank. He wasn't sure if they should disturb her and make her aware of their presence. What he would say if they did? He had been so intent on tracking Qa'Lea that he had not had time to give any thought to what he was going to say as to convince her to let them accompany her on the journey to find Tallu. He was spared deciding how to proceed when Qa'Lea, eyes still closed, suddenly spoke.

"Your grandfather has taught you entirely too well the ways of a woodsman," Qa'Lea said, her powerful but melodious voice echoing slightly along the canyon walls.

"You are as skilled as you are determined," she continued, opening her eyes and staring at her three pursuers. The intense gaze of her deep brown eyes mesmerized the three like a snake charming its prey.

"Step closer," she commanded.

Jed, Kylla, and Fallon crossed the short distance of the canyon floor and stood before Qa'Lea. She remained seated on the rock, her knapsack at her feet.

She held their eyes a few moments longer. It felt to Jed like she was weighing them, probing them, searching for something. It reminded him of the examinations Healer Ginnel gave each of the townspeople on a yearly basis. Only in this instance some other part of him was being examined, a part not seen with the eyes, but present nonetheless.

"I believe introductions are in order," Qa'Lea said after some time.

Jed gulped in nervousness, nearly swallowing the pebble he had been carrying beneath his tongue. He coughed and spit the pebble into his hand, an act Qa'Lea noted with interest.

He turned and gestured toward his companions. "This is Kylla. And this is her brother Fallon. They're my friends."

"And good friends they must be to join you on a dangerous journey to find your brother," Qa'Lea said.

Jed struggled mentally for the correct words to convince Qa'Lea to allow them to accompany her. She spared him the necessity.

"Let us dispense with the explanations, the exhortations, and the begging. I had hoped I had shaken you off my trail and that your grandfather would find you and return you home. Regrettably, now that you have reached the pass, it is unlikely your grandfather will follow you into it. As I'm sure you surmised. I am also rather certain that no matter what I say to you it will be impossible to convince you to return home. And, as I made clear to you at your house, we do not have the luxury of time that would allow me to return you to your family myself. The only other option open to me would be to leave you trailing behind me and to try to lose you on the other side of the pass. So, in the interest of your safety, and in finding your brother with all possible haste, I will agree to take you with me."

Jed couldn't help himself. He smiled. He almost laughed, but he instinctively knew it would be a mistake in the presence of those piercing, russet eyes. His did his best to hide the smile, but he was certain Qa'Lea noticed it. He suspected she noticed nearly everything. He stole a quick look at Kylla and Fallon to see that they, too, had looks of relief and excitement on their faces. As he turned back to Qa'Lea, she continued.

"There will, however, be rules," Qa'Lea said. "Rules you will follow without question. The first rule is that you will do whatever I say, whenever I say, without hesitation. Is that clear?"

Jed, Kylla, and Fallon nodded their assent.

"Good. We will no doubt encounter situations where your failure to follow my instructions will result in your endangerment, if not your deaths. And, so that we are perfectly clear, I do not appreciate being placed in a position where I must become responsible for your safety and wellbeing. It will be difficult enough to accomplish the task set before me without being distracted by the requirement of caring for three young children."

"We can take care of ourselves," Jed blurted out before realizing his mistake.

"I'm sure that in most circumstances you are more than capable of fending for yourselves," Qa'Lea said, pointedly staring at the ancient dagger strapped to Jed's hip. "However, this journey is rather more difficult and complicated than the adventures you are used to. Moreover, it will be more difficult for me to pass unnoticed through the land with the three of you in tow.

"Which brings me to our second rule. You will stay by my side at all times, unless I explicitly tell you otherwise. I cannot waste time trying to find you while I am trying to find Tallu. And lastly, if I determine it is too dangerous for you to continue with me, I will place you in the care of someone I trust and you will stay with that person until I return for you.

"Those are the rules. There will be no discussion of them. You do not have a choice in accepting them, and breaking them will have severe consequences. Do you each understand?"

Nodding their heads slightly, Jed, Kylla, and Fallon acknowledged Qa'Lea's rules.

"Good," she said. "Now come here and place your hands upon mine."

The three Kellish children stepped forward and placed their hands on Qa'Lea's outstretched, upturned palm, stacking one hand upon the other, first Jed, then Kylla, and then Fallon.

"Do you swear you will do as I have instructed and follow all the rules I have explained to you?" Qa'Lea asked, staring into each of their eyes in turn.

"Yes," Jed said, speaking first, knowing full well what it meant to swear an oath to a Tellandor priest.

"Yes," Kylla said, staring back into Qa'Lea's eyes, clearly seeing in her the sort of woman she had never before encountered.

"Yes, by all above and all within, I swear," Fallon said, using the ancient Tellandor phrase of commitment and binding, which brought him an even more intense stare from Qa'Lea.

"You really are a 'brightly lit star,'" Qa'Lea said to Fallon, quoting an old Kellish saying.

"Thank you," Fallon said, obviously pleased she honored him with the Kellish words he knew so well.

"I have been told the three of you are something special," Qa'Lea said in a mysterious tone. "However, further introductions will need to wait until we make camp tonight. I want to get as far into the pass as possible before nightfall sets upon us. While we march forward, I will send word back to Pastor Vannesh that you are safe and joining me for the journey to find Tallu."

Qa'Lea stood up, her priest's robes falling to the tops of her leather boots as she took the walking staff in both hands. A small sphere crowned the staff. Dozens of interlacing circles covered the sphere, some raised above the surface and some etched within. Three of the circles were colored gold and linked together around the entire sphere.

Qa'Lea held the sphere in one hand and the rod of the staff in the other. She twisted each one slightly in opposite directions, and the sphere quickly disengaged from the staff, coming to rest in her left hand. She sat the staff on the ground and cupped the sphere in both hands. Holding the sphere to her mouth, she breathed long and deep on it and whispered something Jed could not hear. Then, something very miraculous happened.

The sphere began to change shape…slowly at first, and then more and more quickly until it was no longer a sphere but something else entirely, something that suddenly spread its wings and leapt from Qa'Lea's hands into the air. Kylla gasped, and Jed turned his head to follow the flight of the bird. It was the same bird Kylla had seen in the forest, and the same one that had startled them earlier as they entered the canyon.

"I've seen that bird," Kylla said. "You were spying on us."

"Yes," Qa'Lea replied. "I sent my friend there to see if you were still following me."

"That's how we knew you used the branches," Jed said. "Kylla saw the bird, or whatever it is."

"Ah," Qa'Lea said. "That does explain a few things. I'll need to instruct my friend to be more careful in the future. He loves people to see him fly. He so rarely gets the chance to do so."

"Is it techne?" Fallon asked, fascinated by the level of technology that must be necessary for what they had just witnessed.

"Yes," Qa'Lea said, shouldering her knapsack.

"It seems like magic," Kylla said, still staring after the amazing bird.

"No, it's not magic," Qa'Lea said. "There is no such thing as magic, although there are things that are not techne that people still think are magic."

As she held out her hand, Qa'Lea's staff rose swiftly from the ground to meet her grasp. She smiled at the Kellish children for the first time, a smile that warmed and entranced them. Then she turned and walked deeper in the canyon.

"Come," she said over her shoulder, not bothering to look back. "We have much ground to cover before the tube-light fades."

CHAPTER 13
TRAVELING COMPANIONS

"The Tellandor Order represents the most vile and insidious menace that rational-minded people have faced since the Great Journey began. Their doctrine of spreading faith before reason, of inculcating the innocent with their hodgepodge of religious mumbo-jumbo, places us all in peril because it signals the decline of empirical science and the logical mind."

From a campaign speech by Laphis Andraw Jallin, Mayor and Head Council, New Alexandria, 945 AL

Still stunned and transfixed by the inexplicable act of levitation that followed so close on the heels of the remarkable transformation of the sphere, Jed, Kylla, and Fallon yanked their heads around to Qa'Lea's direction and then pulled their bodies along to follow.

They marched along behind Qa'Lea in silence for several minutes, consumed with their own thoughts and trying to process the fact they had not only succeeded in finding Qa'Lea, but their very determination to do so had convinced her to take them with her. Jed could not help but think about what his grandfather had said about Qa'Lea and his obvious admiration for her.

Jed had been very young when his grandmother passed away, and Qa'Lea was considerably older than his grandmother would have been, but try as he might, he simply could not picture Qa'Lea in a grandmotherly role. She was simply too fearsome. Too dynamic. The women in the town, and in his life, were certainly strong by any traditional definition, but none of them were commanding in the way that Qa'Lea was. He had never met anyone with the presence Qa'Lea possessed, man or woman. It more than impressed him — it impressed upon him a desire. A desire to attain that command himself, because while he always felt out of place and a bit too different, he could not imagine Qa'Lea ever had such feelings. She seemed too focused on what was happening in the moment to be concerned with what people thought of her.

This focus made Jed think of something else. In his mind's eye, he kept seeing the walking staff rise up from the ground and into Qa'Lea's open palm. He repeated the moment in his mind again and again, trying to figure out how she had managed such a feat. She had said it wasn't techne, which meant that it wasn't like the stone necklace's ability to levitate, and she had said it wasn't magic, but she had not said it wasn't deception. Was it some sort of trick? Or had she really made the staff to move at her bidding?

They walked like this, no one saying a word, each ensconced in their own thoughts, until Jed suddenly remembered something important, something Qa'Lea would surely want to know.

"Uh... Ma'am," Jed began and then trailed off in silence, suddenly aware he wasn't sure exactly how he should address someone of Qa'Lea's stature.

"The customary title for a Tellandor priest is Shann'Ka," Qa'Lea said after several moments of Jed's consternated silence. "I am Shann'Ka Qa'Lea, Tellandor priest, Hann'Al School, Ninth Level. However, considering the circumstances, formality would seem a little more than ridiculous. You may simply call me Qa'Lea."

"Thank you, Qa'Lea," Jed said, happy she seemed a hint more friendly than a few moments before.

"But aren't you a priestess?" Kylla asked before Jed could resume telling Qa'Lea what he had intended to say before he found himself tongue-tied.

"No," Qa'Lea said, a slight hint of amusement in her voice. "I am a priest. The fact I am a woman does not change that. You would not call a woman mayor a mayoress, or a woman doctor a doctoress, would you?"

"We've never seen a woman mayor or a woman doctor," Kylla said. Jed noticed the look on Kylla's face. She seemed to be considering the importance of Qa'Lea words in a way that escaped him.

"You live a sheltered life behind these mountains," Qa'Lea said. "Once we pass through this canyon and into the rest of Wyconna, you will see women in every role: mayor, doctor, soldier, farmer, and shopkeeper. Not in all places, but in many."

"What about the men?" Fallon asked, clearly as curious as his sister about the roles people were allowed to fill outside the Notesch Valley.

"You will find men are similarly unconstrained by certain rules. You will see men as teachers, clothes makers, and home tenders."

"How do people ever come back from Landdesh in Kellish towns after they have seen such things?" Kylla asked, obviously fascinated by the wonders that lay ahead of them on their journey.

"Your little valley may lack certain advantages of techne, and it may have strict social customs," Qa'Lea said, "but it has a number of other charms that do, I assure you, compensate those who choose to live there."

Jed could not imagine what those charms could possibly be, and it was a struggle to wretch his mind back from contemplating them and set it on the course he had been on when he first opened his mouth.

"We saw something in the forest last night," Jed blurted out in a rush, fearing the conversation might be steered away from him again. While Qa'Lea gave him a curious glance as she continued to walk, Kylla and Fallon immediately knew what he was referring to.

"What sort of thing did you see?" Qa'Lea asked.

"A beast," Jed said, licking his lips with nervousness at the memory.

"With blue eyes," Kylla added, glancing behind them as she spoke.

"Glowing blue eyes," Fallon corrected, his own eyes wide at the memory.

Qa'Lea stopped and looked back over the children's heads, down along the canyon path. "When did you see this beast?" Qa'Lea asked, the tone of her voice suddenly serious.

"Last night," Jed said.

"It was watching us while we slept," Kylla continued.

"And there was just one?" Qa'Lea asked.

"We only saw one," Jed said.

"And what did you do?" Qa'Lea asked.

"We tried to scare it off by yelling at it," Kylla said.

"Not very effective, I imagine," Qa'Lea said.

"It ate the rock I threw at it," Fallon said.

"A gore-hound," Qa'Lea said matter-of-factly. "They have a taste for rocks. Sharpens their teeth." Again scanning the canyon behind them quickly, Qa'Lea turned and continued hiking into the pass, her pace significantly quicker than before. "We'll need to move faster now," she said. "No time to waste."

Jed, Kylla, and Fallon hurried to catch up with Qa'Lea, as eager to learn more about the creature as they were to ensure they were close to Qa'Lea should it reappear.

"Why is it called a gore-hound?" Jed asked, not entirely certain he wanted to know the answer.

"They are called gore-hounds," Qa'Lea said, "because they do not eat their prey, but tear them limb from limb and leave the pieces behind as a warning to others. Oddly, they are herbivores."

"You mean they eat plants!" Fallon said.

"Yes," Qa'Lea said. "They feed on leaves, grasses, and sometimes roots. While the taste of blood, even the smell of it, is enough to send them into a killing frenzy, they do not eat flesh of any kind."

"What's a creature like that doing in the Atrum Forest?" Kylla asked, the look on her face suggesting she already knew the answer.

"Gore-hounds are used to track and destroy," Qa'Lea said, glancing back at the three. "They were tracking something, very likely either you three or me. The better question, and the one that most interests me at this moment, is why did it not attack you?"

"Jed scared it off," Fallon said, looking at Jed with open admiration.

Jed was both proud of himself and a little frightened at the memory. It occurred to him, as it had not before, how lucky he had been in warding off the creature. It made his palms sweat just thinking about how it might have turned out differently.

"Scared it off how?" Qa'Lea asked.

"With the dagger," Jed said, patting the ancient blade at his hip.

"And how did you convince a beast that size to fear a blade so small?" Qa'Lea queried.

"I made it burn," Jed said, a little shy of admitting to an adult, particularly a Tellandor priest, what the blade could do, and moreover what he had done with it. He hoped that admitting to the use of the ancient artifacts would not get them in trouble.

"You made the blade burn?" Qa'Lea said, turning to look Jed in the eyes.

"Actually, it glowed," Jed admitted. "It glowed blue."

"It was enormous," Kylla added, clearly anxious for Qa'Lea to believe them. "It reached out and touched the beast."

"Yes," added Fallon. "It was the light that scared the creature off."

"I see," Qa'Lea said, seeming to consider a number of possibilities all at once. "You have mastered more of the blade than I would have thought possible for one your age." She turned to Kylla and Fallon.

"You two have tried it as well, I assume."

"Yes," Kylla said.

"But we never managed to make it as bright as Jed did last night," Fallon said.

Jed looked between Kylla, Fallon, and Qa'Lea and decided to keep quiet for the time being. While he was terribly proud of his ability to command the power of the blade, he was still a Kellish boy, and tools of techne, like the blade, were considered dangerous and possibly immoral.

"And how have you made out with the stone necklace and the book?" Qa'Lea said.

There was a slight silence in which Jed, Kylla, and Fallon exchanged glances in an effort to determine who should respond first. Jed decided to take the lead.

"We have been able to make the stone necklace levitate in our hands," Jed said, "and we have been able to make some of the words in the *Tannett* appear."

Now it was Qa'Lea who was silent. She seemed again to be considering many different things all in one moment.

Then she surprised the three by smiling at them and saying, "I suppose the Morikon was right to give you the artifacts. I had assumed it was simply being sentimental in its old age."

Jed, Kylla, and Fallon were stunned by this revelation of how Qa'Lea knew about the artifacts. So much so that it was another several moments before one of them spoke.

"You are friends with the Morikon," Fallon finally said.

"We have been friends a very long time, the Morikon and I," Qa'Lea said.

"How old are you?" Jed asked, remembering the conversation he had with his grandfather but before realizing how rude such a question was to ask of a Tellandor priest.

"My age in time is different than my age in body," Qa'Lea said rather enigmatically. "I was one of the first Tellandor priests, but I have taken several sabbaticals, during which I remained in stasis, for hundreds of years at a stretch."

"That would make you nearly a thousand years old," Kylla said, her mind clearly reeling with the implications.

"Hundreds, actually," Qa'Lea said with a casualness indicating she had long since lost interest in how old she might become.

"But how can you live so long?" Fallon asked, trying to make sense of it. "You aren't techne, are you?"

"No," Qa'Lea said. "I am not techne, although technology has certainly been a benefactor in allowing me to live as long as I have. But many people live this long. Much of the First Generation Crew is as old as myself, and some quite a bit older. I have lived four hundred and forty-nine years consciously, and if you include the time in stasis, which is sort of a suspension of the body in time, then I have been around for nearly fifteen hundred years. Any way you look at it, I am old."

"But then what keeps the Morikon alive?" Fallon asked.

"The Morikon is not alive in the biological sense because it is not a biological creature. It is techne. It is a machine of sorts. And it was designed to last for hundreds of thousands of years, if not longer. But what keeps the Morikon from ending itself? That I'm not certain. I think it may simply want to see how the story ends."

"What story?" Jed asked.

"Ours," Qa'Lea said. "The story of the *Celestial Pilgrim*. What happens when this great ship we live upon finally reaches its destination? And what lies beyond that moment?"

"There's something I don't understand," Fallon said, hurrying to keep up with Qa'Lea's long gait and fierce pace.

"What might that be?" Qa'Lea asked in return.

"Why does the Sentient allow techne, like the Morikon and the gore-hounds, when their creation was so obviously misguided?" Fallon asked. "How could it allow Lord Narrish to create the Morikon and all the creatures before it?"

"Well," Qa'Lea said, "First, those are two separate cases. While the Morikon is techne, the gore-hounds are not. They are living creatures. Creatures designed, this is true, but alive, nonetheless. And the Sentient does not so much allow things to happen as much as things are done without its knowledge.

"Lord Narrish's activities too place in an earlier time when the Sentient's role was merely advisory and the Council of First Generation Crew were responsible for what could and could not be done. They were not very vigilant in watching out for how technology was used. Which is why, and how, so many communities within Wyconna decided to abandon technology, each to a different degree.

"It was in large part the activities of Lord Narrish, and those like him, that led to the creation of the Notsch Valley and the founding of the Kellish and Merrick towns. It was also what led to the Sentient being given responsibility for monitoring how technology is used throughout the ship, and, while vast improvements have been made in eliminating injustices like those of Lord Narrish, the Sentient is prohibited from spying on the population of Wyconna. Therefore, many times it is unaware when things of an unseemly nature are done, such as the bio-engineering of the gore-hounds."

"What is bio-engineering?" Kylla said, dropping her gaze as soon as she asked the question. Jed could tell she was a little embarrassed to reveal their Kellish ignorance of such matters to an obviously worldly woman. He felt the same shame.

"How much science do they teach you in your Kelllish schools?" Qa'Lea asked.

"As little as possible," Kylla said, bitterness in her voice.

"Well, I'll try to make it as simple as possible, and you can look up the details later," Qa'Lea said.

"All living things have a set of instructions that determine how they grow and what they look like. These instructions are like a blueprint for a house. This blueprint is called DNA, and it spells out certain genes, instructions on what cells should be what tissue and what tissue should become which organs. By changing what is said on the blueprint, you change what the living being will become and how it will grow. So, those who created the gore-hounds blended the genetic blueprints for several different animals and then made further changes to accomplish things that do not occur in nature, like the glowing blue eyes."

"But who would do such a thing?" Jed asked, remembering staring into those unnatural blue eyes from behind the blade of the dagger.

"Someone who wants to create fear," Qa'Lea said.

"Well, they succeeded there," Kylla said, looking over her shoulder.

"But there are many reasons people use technology to alter the blueprint of life," Qa'Lea said.

"Why does the Sentient allow it?" Fallon asked. "What good can come of it?"

"Quite a bit of good in the right hands," Qa'Lea replied. "While it is true there are those who will use the technology to create creatures like the gore-hounds, and in some cases creatures much,

much worse, there are also great benefits to the knowledge of how life works on its most essential level."

"So," Fallon said, glancing over his shoulder again, "if the gore-hounds are created, does that mean there might be a flaw in their biological blueprints that might help us if it shows up again?"

"No," Qa'Lea said. "Gore-hounds are not bred and cannot breed. They are all born in a single litter carried in the belly of an unwilling female bear. However, that does not mean they do not have weaknesses, or they cannot be killed."

"How do we kill it?" Jed asked, feeling both anger and fear begin to stir up within his gut as he thought of confronting the gore-hound again.

"If it appears again, it will not likely be alone," Qa'Lea said. "And you will do nothing but run the opposite direction. If the gore-hounds find us, leave them to me." The tone in Qa'Lea's voice held not simply authority, but a sense of power that drove the three Kellish children into a sudden silence. While she might first appear to be a frail old woman of excessive age, it was clear to Jed that if anyone was capable of defeating a gore-hound, it was the Tellandor priest they followed.

This last exchange marked the end of their conversation as Qa'Lea increased her pace, the Kellishers struggling to keep up. The sky above began to dim, the tube-light fading. Qa'Lea was determined to march as far into the pass as possible before nightfall.

As it turned out, the bird that was Qa'Lea's staff-head returned as darkness began to make picking a path through the scattered stones of the canyon floor a dangerous proposition. With the bird returned to its former form and seated atop the long wooden staff, a touch from Qa'Lea's hand caused the staff head to emit a powerful beam of light clearly illuminating the path ahead.

Bearing the staff before her like a lantern held high, Qa'Lea led the three Kellishers through the darkness of the canyon pass well into the night. Though they paused occasionally to rest and snack on their dwindling provisions, their overall pace did not slacken until they could see the artificially projected moon between the canyon walls above them. Shortly after this, Qa'Lea relented and, realizing her young companions could be pressed no further, decided to make camp around a long bend in the pass.

CHAPTER 14
ANCIENT SECRETS

"Our mission, and I use that word with all its implications, is to help the communities of Wyconna, and of the Celestial Pilgrim *as a whole, become whole communities again. We are here to help. To help heal the rifts that created The Great Upheaval. To help spread understanding where there is currently only hatred. To help build again what has been broken."*

Shann'Ka Apa'Tu Kana-Shaan, the first ordained priest of Tellandor Order

The rocky canyon floor was not nearly as comfortable a place to pass the night as the soft moss of the forest, but Jed, Kylla, and Fallon did their best. They found a soft mound of clay at the base of the canyon wall and used their knapsacks to create cushions behind their backs as they rationed out the remainder of their dried meat, bread, and cheese. Qa'Lea took her staff and pressed it into the clay until it stood on its own as though guarding them.

Qa'Lea's food consisted of cheese, bread, nuts, dried fruit, and a bag of roasted corn kernels. Seating herself next to the children on the clay, she offered them some of her rations. Jed hesitated a moment and then took a dried plum, savoring the sweet meat of the fruit, sucking on it for a moment to draw out the flavor before he began to chew. Following Jed's lead, Kylla took a small handful of nuts while Fallon sampled the roasted corn.

"It's too bad we can't build a fire," Kylla said, wrapping her arms around herself against the chill of the night air as she munched on a large kanob nut.

"A fire might warm us," Qa'Lea said, "but it would also draw any gore-hounds right to us."

"We can live without a fire," Jed said. He didn't want to consider what the likelihood of gore-hounds following them into the canyon was. It was probably not a probability, but a certainty.

"Do you think they can come from above?" Fallon asked, looking up between the canyon walls at the artificial stars and moon.

"I doubt it," Qa'Lea answered. "Gore-hounds are fearsome in a fight, but not very nimble. They don't climb well. If the walls of the pass weren't so sheer, I'd suggest we scramble to a ledge for safety. As it is, my staff will warn us if anything approaches."

Kylla took out the stained, dirty sheet from her knapsack and wrapped it around Fallon, Jed, and herself as they continued to eat. Qa'Lea ate in silence, looking at each of the children in turn as if sizing them up yet again. *Mentally weighing us for possible defects*, Jed thought. The three tried their best not to notice the examination. It was not an accusatory stare, but probing nonetheless. The hardness of Qa'Lea's features seemed to soften and her eyes twinkled in the gentle light of the moon. For a moment, Jed could have sworn he saw her smiling.

"You know," Qa'Lea said, "while we can't build a fire to keep us warm, that doesn't mean we have no options for warmth. Why don't you show me what you can do with that dagger of yours, Jed?" Caught off guard by such a request, Jed coughed in surprise, nearly sending a piece of cheese flying out of his nose.

"What do you want me to do with it?" Jed asked, slowly getting to his feet and drawing the dagger from its sheath.

"Show me what you did last night," Qa'Lea said. Jed looked into Qa'Lea's deep, brown eyes and then turned his attention to the blade in his hand. Stilling his mind and clearing it of all thoughts, even of holding a Tellandor dagger and being watched by a Tellandor priest, Jed focused on the blade. Within moments, it began to glow a bright blue.

Kylla and Fallon watched intently, both visibly as nervous as Jed about showing the blade and its powers to Qa'Lea. The blade reached its apex of brightness, casting a dim glow on Qa'Lea's unreadable face. It wasn't a tenth as bright as the night before and Jed feared he had lost whatever skill he might have possessed in the moment of panic which had engulfed him while facing the gore-hound.

But the very thought of the gore-hound brought that moment of fright back to his mind with such clarity, he found the brightness of the blade suddenly increasing like a fire with lamp oil thrown on it. A blazing blue light stretched out nearly three meters from the tip of the blade. Jed was so pleased with his accomplishment that he lost the focus of his mind, and the blue light of the blade winked out of existence.

"Impressive for one your age," Qa'Lea said. "And even more so in that you have managed without any training." Jed couldn't help but smile at the compliment.

"Now you," Qa'Lea said, turning her gaze to Kylla. "Show me what you can do with the stone around your neck."

Kylla swallowed hard as she stood up and Jed sat back down. Slowly, she lifted the leather thong of the necklace over her head and then cupped the ancient stone in her hands. Qa'Lea's expectant stare clearly did little to help Kylla concentrate, but she breathed out slowly and closed her eyes. Within a few seconds the stone levitated several inches above her hands.

And then she did something she had never tried before — she lowered her hands to her sides as the stone necklace remained hanging midair. Staring at the leather strap dangling beneath it, Kylla silently willed the stone to move father away. Gradually, it went through the air until it hovered right over Qa'Lea.

"Wow!" Jed said, unable to contain his excitement at Kylla's performance. Suddenly self-conscious, Kylla lost the connection with the stone and it fell like the rock it was into Qa'Lea's abruptly open and well-placed palm.

"Wow, indeed," Qa'Lea said, seeming to restrain a smile. "There are many novice priests who would have been pleased to accomplish as much after *months* of training."

"It's hard to hold my concentration that long," Kylla said as Qa'Lea tossed the necklace back to her.

"Sorry," Jed whispered as Kylla sat down next to him, barely containing her excitement as she slipped the necklace back over her head.

Fallon was already on his feet and stepping forward, holding the ancient *Tannett*. "I haven't managed to make more than a few passages appear," Fallon said, no hint of disappointment in his voice.

"Show me," Qa'Lea said, gesturing for Fallon to sit in front of her. Fallon sat down, crossed his legs, and opened the book to a random and as yet blank page. "This time," Qa'Lea continued, "don't think of what you might see, or what you want to see, but listen. Listen with your mind."

Fallon turned his attention to the pages of the book. It seemed to take him no time at all to reach a relaxed and focused state. From where Jed and Kylla sat, they could see the blank pages of the open book momentarily become filled with text. The text then became different text and different again, ancient verses fading in and out of existence, glowing faintly in the dim light.

As one page faded into another and another after that, Jed began to get a sense for just how massive the store of text within the techne *Tannett* must surely be. With a sudden shock, he suddenly realized the *Tannett* in Fallon's hands held far more knowledge than a traditional, paper bound volume. While a true *Tannett* might contain the bare essence of humankind's religious and spiritual traditions, Jed suspected the ancient *Tannett* Fallon held in his hands contained the entirety of all human knowledge from before humans left the Origin World until well after the starship Wyconna was upon its journey. This knowledge, the well of all human knowledge, filled him with a strange and exciting kind of joy. He could see Fallon filled with the same delight.

And then he heard a voice. The voice of the ancient *Tannett*.

"How may I help you, young seeker?" the book in Fallon's hands said in a soothing female voice.

Fallon was so startled he literally jumped, nearly dropping the book. Fumbling to catch the book before it hit the ground, Fallon looked up to see Jed and Kylla's astonished faces, as well the unexpected broad smile of Qa'Lea. The priest laughed softly as she stood and gently took the book from Fallon.

"You are all an abbot's dream," Qa'Lea said, her voice tinged with affection. "The Kellish towns have always been a good source of Tellandor stock, but rarely does one find three adepts so talented at such a young age."

"Can you teach us?" Fallon asked, voicing the question that had been at the tip of Jed's tongue and probably in the front of Kylla's mind.

"Are you three offering to join the order?" Qa'Lea asked.

"Well, we're a bit young," Jed said.

"There are those who join the order as young as Fallon here," Qa'Lea informed them.

"Do we need to join to learn?" Kylla asked. It was obvious from her tone she wasn't sure about the idea.

"These are the tools of a Tellandor priest," Qa'Lea said. "They should be wielded by a Tellandor priest."

"But they're ours now," Jed said. "The Morikon gave them to us."

"That he did," Qa'Lea said.

"I'll join the order," Fallon said, his face as serious as his words.

Qa'Lea looked down at Fallon and considered him for a moment. "Yes, I believe you would," she said. "However, that will not be necessary. As Jed has pointed out, while these are the implements of a Tellandor priest, that priest is long since dead and these tools are, by all rights, now yours. That does not, however, mean they do not come with a responsibility. Although that is a dagger at your hip, a Tellandor priest does not see it as a weapon, and it should only be used in the defense of yourself or others in need. And it should never be used in anger. If you can all agree that you will only ever use these ancient implements to help others, then I will school you in their uses. Can you agree to that? Can you swear to it?"

Jed, Kylla, and Fallon spoke simultaneously as they affirmed their agreement. "Good," Qa'Lea said, "Then place your hands upon the *Tannett* and repeat after me." The three placed their hands upon the ancient *Tannett* Qa'Lea held out to them and looked up into her eyes, which were bright and spirit-filled even in the dim moonlight.

"I vow by all that is holy and good," Qa'Lea intoned, waiting for them to repeat her words back to her. "Never to use the tools of the Tellandor priesthood," and another pause for repetition, "to bring harm to any living being," pause for repetition, "except in the defense of my own life or the lives of others."

Qa'Lea held their gazes a moment longer and then lowered the *Tannett*, letting their hands fall back to their sides. "Good," she said. "Now let me tell you a little about what you have rescued from the Morikon's labyrinth. These belonged to the very first Tellandor priest, Apa'Tu Kana-Shann."

"The Morikon told us how Lord Narrish tricked him and poisoned him," Jed said. He had not intended to be rude, but his interruption brought raised eye from Qa'Lea.

"Then I'm sure he also told you these items you now process were the reason for his death," Qa'Lea continued. "And while that does not make them more special in themselves, that sacrifice demands constant care lest you risk tainting the memory of Apa'Tu Kana-Shann's death.

"What's more, the dagger and the stone necklace are precious because they are parts of the Tellandor history. Not simply because of who they belonged to, but because they are no longer used by any priest. A few decades after Kana-Shann's death, the dagger and stone were replaced by the staff, which not only combined the purposes of both items, but seemed less likely to incite misunderstandings.

"Few people think of a priest with a staff as dangerous, while many see nothing but danger in a dagger, regardless of who carries it. And even a stone on a strap of leather can seem like jewelry to those who are wrapped tightly in their piousness. So, you see, to the best of my knowledge, which I assure you is not inconsequential, those are the only Tellandor artifacts of their age remaining intact within the whole of Wyconna. They are singular, invaluable, and irreplaceable, and you must respect them as such."

"If they're so valuable, why did the Tellandor Order leave them with the Morikon all these years?" Jed asked.

"Can you think of a better place to leave something valuable?" Qa'Lea said.

"But then why did the Morikon give them to us if they are so valuable?" Kylla asked.

"I had been wondering that myself," Qa'Lea said, "until I saw each of you use them."

"We're supposed carry them," Fallon said. "It's destiny."

"Destiny is a strong word and a stranger thing," Qa'Lea said. "While you are correct that you are supposed to carry these ancient tools, and I agree with you not only because of what I have seen but what I feel in my heart when I see them in your hands. However much this may be a truth, do not ever confuse destiny with fate. Fate implies the story is already written and we are all just playing out our parts, but destiny is merely the forces of the cosmos tugging us in one direction for a bit of time.

"Now, we need our rest, but I will show you briefly the power of the Tellandor tools."

Qa'Lea turned the cover of the *Tannett* to face the Kellish children and opened the cover. "As you have by now surmised, each of these tools is activated by the power of the mind. By focusing your mind in the right way, you can activate different aspects of the tools' powers."

"The dagger can read my mind?" Jed asked.

"They do not read your mind in the way you suggest," Qa'Lea answered. "They are receptive to the energy of the mind, and respond to it. That is a very different thing. As you know, each of these tools is a very advanced piece of techne. And each of them has the ability to scan the mind of the person holding it and interpret the different states of that mind. Different states of mind, shaded with different thoughts, will create different responses from the tool. The *Tannett* is even more sophisticated. It not only contains a record of everything that has ever been written or created by human beings up until the time of Kana-Shann's death, but it is also a sentient, although artificial, being."

"You mean it doesn't just talk, but it thinks?" Fallon asked, his eyes wide with wonder.

"Exactly," Qa'Lea said. "Every Tellandor priest has a similar *Tannett*, one that will only reveal itself to a mind pure enough to warrant it. The contents of the *Tannett* are hidden because not all the places a Tellandor priest might travel welcome the words of the *Tannett*, particularly not when they contain all the words of human wisdom ever written down."

"But why not?" Kylla asked. "What could be wrong with that?"

"From my perspective, and that of the Tellandor Order, nothing," Qa'Lea answered. "But, there are those who only want to know what they already know, and some people can be hostile to the idea that there might be ideas and words equally as important as the ones they hold dear and sacred."

"But why a sentient book?" Jed asked, still trying to wrap his mind around the idea that a techne book could be a conscious person.

"Because priests usually travel alone," Qa'Lea replied, "and those who travel alone can get very lonely." Reaching within her robes, she removed her own *Tannett*. "This *Tannett*, who prefers to be called Jaan'Ka, has been with me since I was first ordained. It is, in many ways, my closest friend."

"But it's not even alive," Kylla said.

"True," Qa'Lea responded, "but one does not need to be alive to have a mind, and Jann'Ka has always been kind, patient, and caring, if somewhat distracted at times."

"I heard that," Qa'Lea's *Tannett* said in a deep male voice. "I am not distracted, I am busy."

"This is Jed, Kylla, and Fallon," Qa'Lea said, introducing them in turn while pointing the book at them.

"Our solitary journey has become a parade," the book said. "How lovely."

"Yes," Qa'Lea said. "And since you are so busy, I shall let you continue with your tasks." She closed the *Tannett* and returned it to her robes.

"Are they aware of what is around them all the time?" Jed asked, wondering if the ancient *Tannett* might record his every move.

"They are only aware when asked to be," Qa'Lea replied. "Otherwise they busy themselves with the study of texts or projects of their own. However, when aware, they can both see and hear far better than any human possibly could. They can even approximate the senses of smell, taste, and touch, although they have little use for them."

"But why would they need to study texts if they carry the text within them?" Fallon asked.

"Understanding the meaning of a text and knowing the words are two entirely different things," Qa'Lea said as she opened the cover of the ancient *Tannett* from the labyrinth. "This *Tannett* I have spoken to on several occasions while visiting our mammoth friend. Its name is Aaral."

"It is good to see you again, Qa'Lea," the book said, its feminine voice both soothing and musical.

"I hope you are well," Qa'Lea said to the book. "Now that you are no longer bound to the labyrinth, are you sure you won't let Jann'Ka update your records? There is much you have missed these many centuries."

"I suppose," the book said, the tone of its voice suggesting it didn't particularly relish the notion. "I can't say I have much interest myself, but it may be of use for the children."

"This is Jed, Kylla, and Fallon," Qa'Lea said, again making introductions.

"It is a pleasure to finally be introduced properly," the book said. "We have much to learn from each other. We have both lived, shall we say, sheltered lives, for quite some time. It will be interesting to see the world of this ship together."

"We will begin their education tomorrow, as time permits," Qa'Lea said to the book. "But for now, why don't you catch up with Jann'Ka?"

"An excellent idea," Aaral said as Qa'Lea slipped the book beneath her robes to join the other. "My *Tannett* will update the records of yours so there will not be any knowledge you might miss should you need it. And now, let me briefly show you what else you will be learning in the days to come. Stand please, Kylla."

Kylla looked at Jed and Fallon briefly, wondering what might be expected of her, and then stood up to join Qa'Lea.

"Take the stone in your hands," Qa'Lea instructed. Kylla did as asked, and Qa'Lea cupped her own wrinkled hands around those of Kylla. "Now clear your mind and focus on the stone. Imagine yourself as though enclosed in a bubble of light." Kylla closed her eyes. Qa'Lea looked at Jed. "Jed, pick up that large rock and throw it right at my head."

Jed blinked. He wasn't sure if the elderly priest was kidding or serious.

"Right at my head," Qa'Lea repeated, a taunting tone creeping into her voice.

Idly wondering what kind of trouble it could get him into, Jed picked up the large, fist-sized rock at his side and hurled it at Qa'Lea's head. The rock whipped through the moonlight and stopped, hovering mid-air like a fly suddenly caught by a spider's web.

"Look," Qa'Lea said to Kylla, who opened her eyes, at first only a little, and then wide in amazement.

"Am I doing that?" Kylla asked.

"I am guiding you," Qa'Lea said, "but yes." Slowly, the rock lowered to the canyon floor and Qa'Lea released Kylla's hands. "The stone of the Tellandor, or the Celestial Stone as it was called back in the time of Kana-Shann, was given to Tellandor priests to protect them in the event of an attack. It cannot only repel most projectile and energy weapons, but also possesses the power to help the human body heal. Now for the Celestial Blade."

Qa'Lea extended her hand toward Jed and he handed her the hilt of the dagger. She took it in her right hand and it immediately blazed forth with a brilliant blue light.

"This dagger was meant to look harmless, but, wielded by the right person, to be a powerful tool of defense." Qa'Lea flicked her wrist, and the blazing blue blade of the dagger suddenly grew eightfold in length, becoming a brilliant azure sword of light.

"It is tuned more subtly than the other Tellandor tools so it can never be wielded in anger," she said. "But it can be wielded in fear, which is why it responded so well to you last night, Jed. Of course the blade has other uses as well." Qa'Lea took a step toward the

Kellish children, the blade held high, and they instinctively leaned back.

"While we cannot risk building a fire, that does not mean we cannot have some warmth." Qa'Lea aimed the blade at a large boulder to the side of where they had made camp and engulfed the stone in a wave of lightning blue light. Qa'Lea kept the blade aimed at the rock for several more seconds, blue light-flame leaping from the blade to the boulder. Then the light vanished. She flipped the dagger, taking it by the blade to hand it back to Jed, who was surprised to find the metal felt cool to the touch. "Mind the blade of that dagger. In addition to its other properties, it is incredibly sharp and will never become dull."

Jed, Kylla, and Fallon were silent for a moment. Then they noticed the heat being emitted by the boulder to the side of them. As Jed slipped the dagger back into its sheath, they all moved a little closer to this new source of warmth. He felt overwhelmed by the possibilities of what he had just seen and by Qa'Lea's promise to teach them how to master the Tellandor artifacts.

Fallon was the first to speak, bringing back an old question. "Where do they get the energy to do these things?" he asked.

"Energy is everywhere in everything. Within you, me, the air, the rocks, and within the space that exists even at the smallest level between atoms." Qa'Lea smiled. "I'll explain another time. Now you should rest. There is a long march ahead of us tomorrow and you will need all of *your* energy."

Qa'Lea stretched out near the boulder and placed her knapsack beneath her head, seeming to fall asleep within seconds. Jed, Kylla, and Fallon glanced at each other and shifted their positions so they could all gain maximum warmth from the still-radiating stone. Despite the excitement they felt at what lay ahead of them in the days to come, they were all asleep within minutes.

CHAPTER 15
FIGHT OR FLIGHT

Genetic Engineering: *The scientific manipulation of* DNA *to alter an organism's function; or to combine the functions and characteristics of different organisms into a new one; or to create new, previously unknown organisms. Somatic cell engineering refers to the alteration of* DNA *within an organism, the traits of which cannot be passed on to future offspring. Germ-line genetic engineering refers to the alteration of* DNA *of the germ line, or reproductive cells, the results of which will be passed on to offspring.*

For example, somatic gene therapy might be used to correct a deadly defect in a person's genes that causes a blood disease, while germ-line therapy might be used to alter potential height, hair color, skin color, or intelligence of a child, traits that would be passed on to any future children. While somatic engineering is used widely throughout Wyconna, germ-line therapy is highly restricted and used only to correct life-threatening genetic deformities.

From *The Encyclopedia Wyconnica, 112th Edition*

Jed woke with a start, sitting up and blinking quickly to dispel sleep from his mind, his heart pounding in his chest, not knowing where he was or why he was awake. *It must have been a bad dream*, he thought to himself, but he couldn't remember what he had been dreaming, or even if he had been dreaming. Then he heard something that froze his heart — the deep growl of a gore-hound echoing through the canyon walls.

Leaping to his feet, Jed looked around and immediately noticed Qa'Lea was no longer at the camp. Her staff was also missing. The growl woke Kylla and Fallon as well. Jed motioned for them to remain quiet. Down around the bend of the pass, back the way they had come, a powerful flash of blue light cast long, sharp shadows along the canyon walls. Jed looked at Kylla and Fallon in the dim light and could see the same fear he felt reflected back from their faces. He could also see determination.

Silently, the three snuck back down the canyon pass, clinging close to the walls of rock, following the snarls and roars of the gore-hounds. Each clutched the ancient artifact they had been holding earlier that night, the blade of the dagger in Jed's hand glinting in what little moonlight remained. As they came slowly around the bend, another blast of blue light illuminated the night, revealing Qa'Lea facing off against four massive gore-hounds, her staff held before her like a weapon, a stream of blazing blue light flowing forth from the ornate head and blasting a gore-hound through the air and into the canyon wall. The gore-hound fell to the ground and didn't move.

Another gore-hound lay some five meters behind the first. The remaining two gore-hounds leapt in unison at Qa'Lea, who spun the staff vertically and slammed the base against the stone floor of the canyon, a ball of reddish light appearing around her. The gore-hounds struck the field of red light and flew backward as though kicked by a horse.

Although they had not moved since reaching the scene of the battle with the gore-hounds and had not made a noise, Qa'Lea turned to the three Kellish children and shouted in a voice so powerful it literally caused them to stumble backward.

"Grab your things and run!"

Jed, Kylla, and Fallon turned their gaze from Qa'Lea to the gore-hounds, who had recovered and were now sitting back on their haunches, preparing to leap again. Before any of the three could shout a word of warning, Qa'Lea yelled at them again.

"Now!"

Qa'Lea turned to face the gore-hounds, another blast of blue light flashing forth from her staff, missing the gore-hound it was intended for and causing the wall of rock behind it to explode in a cascade of rubble. Not waiting to see what would happen, and suddenly fearing Qa'Lea's wrath even more than the sight of the gore-hounds, the Kellishers turned as one and raced back to the spot where they had made camp.

They gathered up their belongings, Kylla stuffing the sheet into her knapsack while Fallon tossed the strap of his own across his shoulder. Jed grabbed both his and Qa'Lea's knapsacks and within seconds the three were fleeing down the canyon pass as fast as they could. Running in the dim light along the rock-strewn canyon floor was dangerous and after stumbling the third time, Kylla catching him as he fell, Jed drew the ancient blade and focused his mind enough to make it glow sufficiently for illuminating the path ahead of them. The sounds of the gore-hound's snarls continued, but got fainter and fainter as they raced through the pass.

When they had run at least a kilometer, Jed stopped, and they turned in unison to look behind them into the darkness and listen. They could no longer hear anything. No growls, no snarls, no blasts of energy from Qa'Lea's staff.

"Do you think she's all right?" Fallon asked.

"She has to be," Kylla said.

"But what if she's not?" Fallon persisted.

"Then the gore-hounds will be coming for us," Jed said.

And then he heard it. The sound of someone, or something, running along the canyon floor the way they had come.

"It must be her," Fallon said.

"Maybe we should run," Kylla said.

"We can't outrun a gore-hound," Jed said, raising his arm with the dagger before him, the blue glow of the blade growing slightly stronger. Kylla reached into her blouse and removed the ancient necklace, holding the worn, round stone in her hands. Fallon stood between them, not certain what he should do and clearly wishing the ancient techne *Tannett* had some sort of defensive properties.

The sound of the running steps grew louder and louder, and Jed was almost certain they had to be made by two feet and not four, but he clinched the hilt of the blade tighter even so. Then Qa'Lea emerged into the dim blue light of the blade, holding her staff in one hand and lifting her robes with the other, running to meet them. She came to a stop a meter away and stood before them, hardly seeming winded at all.

Without even thinking, all three Kellish children rushed to Qa'Lea and embraced her, speaking so quickly and over the tops of one another that Qa'Lea could barely follow what was said.

"Yes," she said in answer to some question as the three broke away and stood before her. "I am fine. A Tellandor priest who cannot handle a few gore-hounds is a disgrace to the order. And no, they will not be following us again. At least not those four. And thank you, I am glad to find you alive as well." Qa'Lea began walking, her arm falling around Fallon's shoulders as she herded them up the pass. "However, that does not mean we will not be followed by others, or possibly something worse."

"What could be worse than gore-hounds?" Jed asked before he realized he might not want to know.

"Winged Krath," Qa'Lea said, causing the head of her staff to emit a dull blue glow to light the way. Seeing this, Jed let the light of the dagger fade and slipped it back into its sheath. "They are leathery beasts that fly fast and very high. And they have excellent eyesight. They can spot a mouse from ten kilometers up. And, most disturbingly, they were designed to love the taste of human flesh."

"Who would send such things after us?" Kylla asked, unable to keep herself from glancing upward to check the night sky.

"Well, I doubt anyone would send a winged Krath, since there are very few left alive," Qa'Lea said. "But it makes no sense to take chances when they seem to be willing to send gore-hounds into the Notesh Valley."

"But who?" Jed asked. "Who would send the gore-hounds after us?"

"And why?" added Fallon.

"I don't know that they were sent for you," Qa'Lea replied. "I rather doubt it, but it is possible. More likely they were sent for me. And they were sent for me to ensure I do not find your brother, Tallu. Why someone would want that is a much more complicated story."

"Can you explain it?" Jed asked.

"Jed told us what little he could, but it doesn't make much sense," Kylla added.

"I explained some the night before last at your parents' table," Qa'Lea said. "As you probably know from your lessons, when the *Celestial Pilgrim* was launched on its journey, a team of crew members was chosen from among all the different species of passengers to be the Primary Crew, which would be responsible for helping Axeon, the Sentient, ensure safe passage of the starship to its destination.

"The crew would took turns on watch, helping guide the course of internal affairs aboard the ship. With the aid of medical enhancements, much like my own, and the same sort of sleep stasis that has allowed me to pass so many years, the Primary Crew members could see the voyage through from beginning to end. It was important that some of those setting out on the journey be present at its conclusion.

"Of course, the Primary Crew had children, and their children had children, and they all became part of the Primary Crew. But there is a difference between being a First Generation Crew member and a Third or Fourth Generation Crew member, which is how the trouble began.

"The opinions of the First Generation Crew carry more weight and their decisions are final, whereas opinions of the later generations are only taken under advisement. And so it seems the great-grandchildren of the first crew members have begun to tire of being treated like children. There has been a split within the Primary Crew of the ship, with those of the First and Second Generations aligned with the Sentient on one side and those of the Third and Fourth Generations on the other. It appears they are attempting a mutiny for control of the Sentient and the ship."

"Why would they do such a thing?" Fallon asked, a hint of fear in his soft voice.

"Because," replied Qa'Lea, "they believe the First and Second Generation Crew, under the influence of the Sentient, have led the societies within the ship toward a disaster. A New Dark Age, they call it. They feel civilization, all of the civilizations within the ship, have become too unscientific."

"The Kellish are unscientific," Kylla said. "But not the rest of Wyconna."

"What they really mean is that the civilizations among the ship have become too spiritual, or more specifically, too religious. You see, they are of the opinion that only science should be used in guiding human affairs and religion is simply a collection of superstitious tales that retard the natural evolution of the galactic civilization. Which, not surprisingly, was the opinion of many of those who created the *Celestial Pilgrim* in the first place. It was also the opinion of many of the First Generation Crew before their journey began.

"But living for centuries, caring for the lives of millions and millions, and the guidance of the Sentient, changed their minds. The Sentient is, by its very nature, a spiritual being, and moreover one that seeks only to benefit the lives of the other sentient creatures in its care. Even though it is not alive in the way you and I are, *life* is its central concern."

"What do the other crew members want?" Jed asked.

"They want to reestablish the social structures that guided civilizations before the ship began its journey. Today, everyone, regardless of their species or their place in the ship, is allowed to follow their own path, in spite of how they approach science, or technology, or religion, which is why the peoples of Wyconna have such diverse opinions and customs on such matters. But the Fourth Generation Crew Members want to establish a way of life that would be the same for everyone, regardless of their wishes. They wish to create a very orderly, and in my opinion, sterile society. And they wish to do so before the *Celestial Pilgrim* reaches its destination."

"And these are the people who have Tal," Jed said, trying to imagine what his brother's captivity must be like among such people.

"Yes," Qa'Lea replied. "The leaders of the Fourth Generation Crew, and some of the Third, have created an underground movement among the passengers of the ship. A movement called the Iron Hand. Their goal is to create friction between the different societies and religious groups aboard the ship and ultimately to incite violence between them, thus justifying the implementation of their social and cultural plans."

"The Iron Hand has Tallu?" Kylla asked, a hint of fear creeping into her voice.

"I believe so," Qa'Lea replied, her own tone a bit more gentle. "The Sentient suspects Tallu witnessed something he should not have and was therefore kidnapped by the Iron Hand. To make matters worse, the Sentient also believes the Iron Hand has infiltrated the Tellandor Order, which means not all Tellandor priests are trustworthy."

"So how do we get Tal back?" Jed asked. For the first time, he was fully realizing the magnitude of the task ahead of them and the danger his brother was in.

"We will follow his trail," Qa'Lea said. "And when we find where he has been, we will use this knowledge to discover where he is. Then we will free him." Qa'Lea spoke these last words with such authority that the enormity of the task and the sheer improbability of success were washed from Jed's mind, leaving only a grave sense of purpose.

"Once we get Tallu back," Fallon asked, obviously thinking far ahead, "how will you destroy the Iron Hand?"

"This is not a task you need concern yourselves with," Qa'Lea said with seriousness. "And I will not endanger your lives any more than they already are by telling you." Qa'Lea ended the conversation, walking onward through the pass in silence. Jed, Kylla, and Fallon followed quietly as well.

Jed's mind churned with the new revelations Qa'Lea had given them and the firm knowledge of just how much danger he had placed himself and his friends in. While he wondered if he had made a mistake, he could tell from the looks on Kylla and Fallon's faces that the knowledge of Tallu's danger and the threat posed to the entire ship only solidified their resolves to find Jed's brother and free him from the clutches of the Iron Hand.

CHAPTER 16
BEYOND THE VALLEY

Fragments From Fallon's Journal:

"We leave our home not knowing whether we are bound for some unseen glory or possibly some unsung end. We only know why we go. We go because we are who we are. Are what we are. Because we have no choice. We follow Destiny to whatever dark death or bright future awaits us."

"I can't figure out how she made her staff move. I have an idea, but I'm not sure."

"I hate gore-hounds. They make my stomach churn. And they smell bad!"

"I miss my rabbit, Pilco. And Mother and Father. I hope we get to sleep in a bed tonight. Or at least not on the ground."

"Had an idea while walking. I need to ask Qa'Lea what the requirements are for joining the Order. Not now. But maybe later."

After an hour walking in silence, they noticed the first signs of dayrise. Slowly, over the course of another hour, the tube-light increased in intensity. By the time they finally walked out of the mouth of the pass and looked down over the Winsomm Valley on the forward side of the Pinak Mountains, it was nearly full daylight. They paused at the mouth of the pass, as much to drink in the sight of the land before them as to rest.

The Pinak Mountains sloped gradually toward the Winsomm Valley. Rolling hills and tall grass stretched before them for kilometer after kilometer, small stands of trees dotting the fields. A thin waft of smoke rose from the chimney of a farmhouse at the foot of the mountains where the valley turned to grass and hills. Across the valley, at least two days' travel by foot, they could make out a small town. A thin but passable trail led down the side of the mountain from the Sanshu Pass to the valley below. Qa'Lea started down the trail, surefooted as a mountain goat, the three Kellishers falling in behind.

"The owners of that farm are friends of mine," Qa'Lea said, pointing to the farmhouse in the distance. "We'll stay the night there. They have a comfortable hayloft."

"What's that town in the distance?" Jed asked.

"That is Pinukket," Qa'Lea replied. "It's a resort town of sorts."

"What's a resort town?" Kylla asked.

"A town where people go to play and relax," Qa'Lea said. "And in this case, where they go to play and relax without the benefit of technology. The people who go there pretend to live like the Kellish peoples. For a few days, at least."

"Why would people possibly do that?" Jed asked, his voice breaking in incredulity.

"People will do all sorts of strange things if given the chance," Qa'Lea said, the tone of her voice vague and unreadable.

The three Kellishers followed Qa'Lea down the mountainside, Jed trying to imagine a whole town where people did nothing but play and relax, and trying even harder to imagine why they would want to pretend to live like the Kellish. It was hard for him to envision something more bizarre.

The trail split several times as they walked down the mountainside. This was evidently another measure to keep the location of the pass hidden. Multiple trails would slow down and confuse anyone trying to cross the mountains without permission. Qa'Lea, of course, always knew which path to choose. They descended for another hour, occasionally helping each other down particularly steep sections of rock, and then they broke for a brief breakfast. The Kellishers ate all that remained of their food and Qa'Lea again shared some of hers. She assured them her friends in the farmhouse would be more than happy to send them on their way with supplies for the journey.

The descent down the mountainside was uneventful and the effort to reach the farmhouse in the valley below before nightfall necessitated a hasty pace that, because of the hazardous nature of the trail, meant most of the day was passed in silence. Qa'Lea did not want them to become distracted and accidentally tumble down the mountainside, which all three Kellish agreed was very sensible. They did not pause for lunch, but kept moving, passing the water skin between them when they grew thirsty and eating nuts, dried berries, and bread from Qa'Lea's knapsack.

They reached the grasslands of the valley as the tube-light began to fade precipitously, indicating nightfall was imminent. The smells of the grasslands and the valley were a welcome change to the dusty and arid climate of the trail they had walked along all day. The tall kull-grass smelled sweet and wet in the late summer air, and Jed caught the scent of various wildflowers and the occasional stand of bree bushes with their ripening berries. As they walked, Jed and the others casually picked the oblong, reddish berries and tossed them into their mouths, savoring the honey-like juices as they flowed down their throats. The path through the valley soon met up with a road and they followed it away from the mountains and toward the farm.

As nightfall settled in and the waxing moon appeared before a blanket of stars, they finally reached the farmhouse. An old couple, nearly seventy, sat on the porch with their dog when the group walked up the thin dirt path to the farm.

"My word," the old man said. "Look what the night brings us."

"Shann'Ka Qa'Lea, how good to see you," the old woman said. The elderly couple, dressed in rustic clothes similar to those worn in the Kellish communities, stepped down from the porch and embraced Qa'Lea, each in turn. The man introduced himself as Leeno and his wife as Betta.

"And who are your fine young companions?" Leeno asked.

"They are my wards," Qa'Lea replied, still smiling and obviously happy to be in the company of friends. "I am escorting them from their Kellish village to visit their cousin who has left the Kellish way."

"I didn't know the Tellandor order had become travel guides," Leeno said, smiling at the three Kellishers.

"It is a favor for their grandfather, who is an old friend of mine," Qa'Lea said. Qa'Lea made brief introductions of Jed, Kylla, and Fallon, but she had warned them on the journey down the mountainside to say as little as possible to everyone they met, even those who were old friends. Jed, Kylla, and Fallon could all pass for being cousins, but there was no need to strain their cover story by adding embellishments that would come with questioning. Lies, Qa'Lea had noted, while sometimes necessary, usually led to more lies, which usually led to their unraveling. Qa'Lea would do most of the talking and the Kellishers would pretend to be politely silent, which came naturally, considering how tired they were from the previous three days of traveling.

"Why, these children look starved!" Betta said. "I've got a huge pot of stew on the stove inside. You'll join us, I hope."

"We'd be honored and grateful," Qa'Lea replied. "And we'd be even more grateful for the use of the hayloft for the night."

"Don't think twice about it," said Leeno. "I only wish we could offer you a real room, but the house is small and we have only the one bed."

"The barn with be just fine," Qa'Lea said.

They followed the old farm couple into the house, a wave of mouthwatering smells washing over them as they crossed the threshold. Leeno had not exaggerated when he said the house was small. It had only one room — a kitchen on one side, a table in the middle, and a bed against the far wall. The smell of a hot meal made Jed salivate, as he, Kylla, and Fallon sat on the edge of the bed and Betta came around the room with bowls of stew and slices of warm bread.

The adults sat at the table and talked about things they held in common, which apparently was a love of storytelling. With bites of hearty stew and bread jammed hastily into his mouth, Jed marveled at how relaxed and even gregarious Qa'Lea seemed in the company of her friends. For most of their short time together, she seemed stern and single-mindedly set toward whatever task was at hand. For the first time, he could see how his grandfather could have befriended her and could imagine how well they must have gotten along.

After a second helping of stew each, the three Kellishers were having trouble keeping their eyes open and their heads from falling into their bowls. Qa'Lea said goodnight, and, taking one of the oil lanterns hung around the room, led them out to the barn. It was larger than the house and smelled of dry hay and animals. To Jed, it was a familiar and comforting odor. He sprawled next to Kylla and Fallon in the hay, already beginning to doze as he watched Qa'Lea cross her legs, cup her hands, and begin to meditate. Within moments, he was asleep.

When Jed awoke the next morning, he found Kylla and Fallon still asleep, but he could see Qa'Lea outside through the open barn door. Rubbing the sleep from his eyes and brushing hay from his hair, Jed stood up and walked to the barn door, looking out to see it was still early morning. Qa'Lea stood with Leeno next to a cart hitched up to a willug beast.

Willug beasts were large, muscular farm animals, common throughout the region. They had two horns and a thick mat of fur, and often smelled as though they had spent the day rolling in their own manure, which was apparently their way of relaxing after long hours of pulling plows through the fields. In addition, the large hump on their shoulders was a massive water reservoir that allowed them to go two or three days without taking a drink. Although they were ugly, smelly animals, prone to near constant flatulence, they redeemed themselves by being able to pull a plow or wagon all day long with nary a hint of exhaustion. A little slower than a horse at pulling a wagon, and occasionally a bit more stubborn than a farmer would like, a willug beast was a fine farm animal.

Qa'Lea, it turned out, had paid Leeno a small sum to borrow the willug beast, who Betta had long ago named Dung for its smell, and the cart to take them all to the town of Pinukket. Qa'Lea planned to leave the cart and beast of burden with a mutual friend who would return it later in the week. After a hot breakfast of eggs and toast, because Betta insisted they have a real meal at a table before setting off, they were in the wagon and on the road.

The ride not only offered them the opportunity to rest their legs but a chance to learn more about the ancient Tellandor artifacts. As they rode, Qa'Lea at the reins of the willug beast and the Kellishers in the back, she explained in more detail how they could train their minds to activate the Tellandor tools.

"The key to mastering all Tellandor techne is focusing the mind," Qa'Lea began. "Now you've already proven yourselves much more capable than most, and certainly most your age. I will teach you the skills needed to master your minds and focus them on whatever you choose for as long as you choose. Traditionally, novice priests begin by focusing their minds on their breathing, and then moving on to meditations on love and compassion. It is only later that they learn to focus their minds so they can utilize a staff or a sentient *Tannett*. So, we will begin the training of your minds with a simple meditation, and then I will explain how to access Aaral."

"But wouldn't it make more sense to learn about the dagger?" Jed asked. "In case we run into anymore gore-hounds."

"Or the necklace," Kylla suggested. "You said it can heal people, and what if one of us gets hurt?"

"Firstly," Qa'Lea said, "if there are more gore-hounds, which I doubt because they are unlikely to appear while we are near more populated areas, you will do just as you did before and leave them to me. I will do any healing that needs doing as well. Used by an untrained mind, the stone can bring as much harm as healing to a person. Moreover, learning to activate the *Tannett* will help you practice focusing your mind without the risk of accidents. We don't need this wagon going up in flames because someone's mind lost its focus while using the dagger, and I have no desire to be tossed from this wagon because someone has focused a little too intently on the stone." Although they still felt as though their arguments had some validity, Jed and Kylla admitted Qa'Lea's caution made sense.

"Can you teach us how to move things the way you moved your staff the other night?" Fallon asked.

"Maybe someday," Qa'Lea said. "But it takes years of training and only a few are ever capable of it. One's mind needs to be not only focused, but pure, a mind that no longer sees itself as separate from the universe around it."

"How long does it take to gain that mind?" Fallon pressed, clearly fascinated by idea of a mind at one with the universe.

"In my case..." Qa'Lea laughed. "About seventy-three years." Jed watched as Fallon blinked in surprise. As interested as Fallon, Jed realized how difficult a task such training must be and how far from accomplishing it he would be even if he started immediately.

"But, I am a slow student," Qa'Lea continued. "There are those who have managed to accomplish that state of mind in much less time. However, they are rare and special." She gave a glance back over her shoulder at Fallon.

"Now," Qa'Lea said, "let's begin with something simple. Let's see how long you can watch your breath." Jed snorted a half laugh. "It's not as easy as you might think, Jed. I'm not talking about watching your breath for a few seconds, I mean for hours at a time."

"Hours!" Jed said, foreseeing a very dull and boring wagon ride ahead of them.

"Not hours on this occasion, no," Qa'Lea said. "But for an hour at least. To prime your mind for the *Tannett*. Now, make yourselves comfortable back there and close your eyes. Then just breathe. Don't do anything but breathe. Don't try to change your breathing in any way, just let the air flow in and out of your lungs. All you need to do is watch your breath. Just notice it. Notice the air passing in through your nose and passing out. That's it. Just see how long you can keep your mind focused on that one thing — breathing. And when your mind wanders off, as I assure you it will, just bring it back to your breathing."

"You want us to do that for an hour?" Kylla asked, already sounding sleepy from the prospect.

"When I started my training," Qa'Lea answered, "we were required to meditate like this for three hours a day. And that was before breakfast."

"It can't be that hard," Fallon said, leaning back against the side of the wagon and closing his eyes.

"We shall see," Qa'Lea said as Jed and Kylla followed Fallon's example.

For the next hour, Jed and the other two tried their best to keep their minds focused on the task of watching their breathing. Jed constantly found himself daydreaming about using the dagger. His mind would wander off and it was sometimes a minute or more before he realized he was no longer watching his breath. With an effort, he would bring his mind back to focusing on his breathing. In total, he probably managed to maintain less than twenty minutes in contemplation. But it did get easier the longer he persisted. The longest stretch, near the end, lasted nearly five minutes.

Moreover, he discovered that when he was able to focus his thoughts only on the breath passing in and out of his lungs, a sense of peace and calm pervaded his mind. For the first time in days, he felt the tension in his shoulders, built up with every dangerous encounter, relax and dissolve. His mind became pliable. Even when he lost focus and began to daydream, it was easier to bring his mind back to task. His heart felt lighter, but at the same time, more full. When Qa'Lea finally told them the hour was up, Jed opened his eyes to see contented looks on the faces of Kylla and Fallon. He knew his own face presented a similar visage.

"That is the most ancient form of meditation known, not just to humans, but to every species we have ever encountered," Qa'Lea said. "It is the root of nearly all spiritual practices. In fact, in the ancient human language of Greek, 'spirit' means 'air.' So how did you do?"

"You're right," Fallon said. "It isn't as easy as it sounds."

"No," Qa'Lea said. "But it gets easier with practice. And the benefits are numerous. A more relaxed and focused mind, a more open heart, and a deeper sense of the Divine in all things. The first of the seven principles of the *Tannett* and the Way of the Tellandor is that all things are a manifestation of the Divine. All things are sacred. However, to truly be able to see that, we need to still our minds from the normal chatter and daydreams so we can see how the world truly exists. We can only accomplish this by training the mind. Later, we can use similar techniques of prayer and meditation to cultivate the second and third principles — universal love and universal compassion. And by cultivating these positive minds, we can dispel the negative states of mind that we usually cling to, like fear or anger or jealousy."

"But I thought mediation and prayer were the last of the seven principles of the *Tannett*," Jed said.

"Yes," Fallon added. "First is the divine nature of all existence, second is universal love, then universal compassion, fourth is the ethical way to live, fifth is service to others, sixth is mindfulness and peace of mind in all things, and the seventh is the benefit of meditation and prayer."

"An excellent recitation," Qa'Lea said. "However, one should not think of the principles of the *Tannett* in a linear fashion. At the very least, one should think of them as a circle. No one tenet is given greater emphasis. None is the first principle. So, in that sense, meditation and prayer lead directly into the divine nature of all things. And, seen as a circle of seven points, one can imagine each point connected to the others. Therefore, you have a web of connections between the different principles, just as mediation and prayer flows into universal compassion, which flows into ethical conduct, which flows into mindfulness. So, while they are often presented as simple list to be memorized, they are really a pattern to be emulated and lived. That is why they were chosen by Vallha Natuur as the base principles for the *Tannett*, because they are the common ground of all faiths, and just as these principles are interconnected, so too are all faiths bound together by these shared principles."

"That makes so much more sense," Fallon said, leaning back against the side of the wagon.

"Yes, it does," Qa'Lea said. "But at the moment, all you need to worry about is focusing your mind enough to activate the Tellandor tools so you can access their full range of powers. The *Tannett* is the easiest of the three Tellandor tools to access, so take Aaral out and we will practice."

For the next several hours, Qa'Lea guided Dung and the wagon along the simple dirt road and through the rolling hills of grass while patiently instructing the three Kellishers how to activate and access the techne *Tannett*. At first, they took turns passing the ancient book between them, each learning to activate the voice of Aaral. Once they had accomplished that task, they were guided by both Qa'Lea and Aaral in learning to make the words of the pages come to life. As they soon discovered, the techne *Tannett* could make pictures and moving images appear on its pages as well.

As they rode along in the wagon, they learned how to access the vast information at Aaral's disposal and how to search for and find information of any kind. They marveled at the breadth of knowledge contained in the small volume. They had heard of encyclopedias before, as there was a two volume set entitled *The Kellish Encyclopedia* sitting near the front table of their town library. However, whereas the *Kellish Encyclopedia* had been written by determining what knowledge Kellish peoples should not know by omitting it from the text, the pages of Aaral seemed to be the exact opposite, containing all the knowledge and writings of humanity.

Jed's mind boggled at how the techne *Tannett* could possibly contain all the information it did. He imagined fields and fields as far as the eye could see stacked with books upon books. It was so much knowledge, especially after a childhood of being fed only selective information, that they spent most of the lesson swinging between stunned silence and ecstatic excitement.

It became clear that each had their own preferences for knowledge as they probed Aaral's pages. Jed was drawn to the history and literature contained in the book, while Kylla focused almost entirely upon reading about science and technology, and Fallon liked the various philosophies and religious texts of humanity and the intelligent species it had encountered. They remained so engrossed in the *Tannett* they didn't even notice they had reached the town of Pinukket.

CHAPTER 17
FAUX TOWN

Advertisement for vacations in the town of Pinnuket:
"Are you tired of living the good life?

Are you bored with abundance?

Does having every whim met by automated means leave you feeling overly energetic?

Have you ever wondered what it might be like to unplug from the world and step back in time to a slower, more peaceful way of life?

Then come to the stunningly beautiful town of Pinnukett and enjoy life the way the Kellish do! Embrace nature and simple living with all the comforts of a five-star luxury resort. In Pinnukett, you can experience the way the Kellish live without having to give up your real life.

Get back to nature. Get back to the farm. Get back to Pinnukett.

Situated at the far Aft of Wyconna, within sight of the Pinak Mountains, Pinnukett is the ultimate escapist-faux-recreational-lifestyle-immersive experience.

With our discount weekend packages, you won't have to sell the family farm to pay for it!

Access our sentient travel agent today."

"We have arrived," Qa'Lea said over her shoulder. "You should put that away and keep the dagger and necklace handy, but out of sight. There are few who would recognize the dagger for what it is, but there is no need to draw attention to ourselves."

Jed, Kylla, and Fallon did as they were instructed and looked out of the wagon as it rolled into the town. The town itself seemed to be a larger version of their own. There were familiar shops and buildings, a town square, and even a Hall of

Light. Jed noted the architecture and construction of the buildings were almost identical to Kellish design. Only a few small, decorative details seemed to indicate a difference. The Kellish were plain people and rarely used ornamentation in their homes and public buildings. The buildings of Pinukket, however, all had slight floral details along their windows and doors.

The people, too, were different and easily divided into two classes — those who were pretending to be dressed like the Kellish, which could be discerned from the true Kellish by the fact that their clothes were far too new, and those people dressed in a manner the Kellish children had never seen. In fact, what made the second class of people most interesting was that none of their clothes seemed to match. It looked as though each wore the costume of an entirely different land and culture.

"So, people come here to pretend to be Kellish?" Jed asked, staring a little too long at a woman in a swooping and completely impractical white dress, for which he was rewarded with a nasty glare.

"Not only that," Qa'Lea said, "they pay for the privilege to do so."

"They pay money!" Kylla blurted out a little too loud, drawing a glance from a man passing by wearing bright yellow pants.

"To live like Kellish!" Fallon added. All three Kellishers were stunned by the idea that anyone would pay to live the way they did.

"As I explained before," Qa'Lea said, "the societies and cultures of Wyconna are divided largely along two lines; the way people choose to use technology, and the way they choose to worship. Many people in societies that use a great deal of technology find it relaxing, even life changing, to abandon that technology for a short period of time and explore, in a safe way, what it would be like to live the way others have chosen. The Kellish are very well-known for their way of life without technology and much admired for their culture, especially for the fact that they have an extremely open religious society, embracing all faiths. You would be hard-pressed to find anyone willing to pay to live in a Merrick town."

"You'd you have to pay me to live in a Merrick town," Jed said with obvious contempt in his voice. Merrick towns enforced strict social rules on their citizens and dogmatically followed a single religion that saw all non-believers as heretics.

"Yes, but people are still curious about the Merrick and Kellish ways of life," Qa'Lea said. "The Pinak Mountains act as a natural barrier to keep the curious from disturbing the people of the Notesch Valley, but when the Kellish and Merrick settlements were first established, it was very difficult to keep the determined from breeching the mountains. Few of these people were actually interested in following the Kellish way themselves, but that didn't stop their curiosity. When it became apparent how many people wanted to see the Kellish way of life, some very enterprising business folk decided to create this town to duplicate the Kellish culture in a manner that wouldn't actually disturb the Kellish themselves."

"What about the Kellish people of the town?" Kylla asked, looking at a man sweeping the walkway in front of his bakery.

"They are not really Kellish," Qa'Lea said, unable to repress slight smile. "They are paid to pretend to be Kellish."

"Let me get this straight," Jed said, squinting up at Qa'Lea. "People from Wyconna pay to come to a town that looks like it's Kellish and is run by people who are paid to pretend they are Kellish."

"It's called a resort," Qa'Lea answered. "The people who pay to come here sometimes help the people paid to work here, or sometimes they just come to take in the scenery and try the food. Sometimes they just need a break from their hectic lives and think a town without technology will be the best way to rejuvenate themselves. Regardless of the reasons or the strange economics of it all, the town functions to keep people from bothering the real Kellish. Strangely, a few people who have grown up Kellish but decide to leave the Valley after their Landdesh come to work here. You see, the absence of technology is only on the surface. The people who work in the shops and on the farms all have homes here, and most are filled with technology. Even most of the farms use technology where the Visitors, as the paying customers are called, won't notice."

"Is the rest of Wyconna this strange?" Jed asked. As he looked around, he tried to figure out what buildings might be facades for technological marvels that would never be found in a true Kellish town.

"There are stranger things in Wyconna than you can possibly imagine," Qa'Lea said. "And Wyconna is only the beginning of strangeness aboard the *Celestial Pilgrim*." Qa'Lea turned down a side street and away from the main square. "It's time we turned in the wagon and good old Dung here to Leeno's friend. Then we'll get a bite to eat before the daylight is gone."

Qa'Lea guided the wagon along a narrow, winding street, eventually bringing it to a halt in front of a small brick house with a large chimney. "Wait here," she said and climbed down from the wagon. She walked up the short path to the weathered front porch, the door swinging open as she placed her foot on the first step. In the doorway stood a tall, slender man in his mid-forties with long, silver hair. He did not smile as he greeted Qa'Lea, but he did embrace her.

"It is good to see you again, Randal," Qa'Lea said.

"It is good to see you as well," Randal replied. "I hope the Way keeps you well."

"And you," Qa'Lea replied. "Leeno and I have a favor to ask of you."

"And I have something for you," Randal said, looking over Qa'Lea's shoulder at the three Kellishers in the back of the wagon.

"Traveling companions," Qa'Lea said, looking into Randal's eyes.

"Let's step inside," Randal said.

"I'll be back in a moment," Qa'Lea said over her shoulder as she followed Randal into the house.

Jed exchanged looks with Kylla and Fallon, but no one said anything. Randal had not closed the door to the stout little house and Jed had the sense Qa'Lea was watching them from the shadows within.

After a few minutes, she emerged from the house with Randal and headed toward the wagon. "For the remainder of the day, we walk. Thank you for your help," Qa'Lea said, turning to Randal.

"Any help I can offer is always yours," Randal said.

Jed, Kylla, and Fallon climbed down out of the wagon. Randal nodded politely to each of them as he led Dung and the wagon back behind the house to where a large wooden shed stood. The Kellishers shouldered their belongings as Qa'Lea began to walk up the street, back the way they had come.

When they were halfway up the street and well out of earshot of the house and Randal, Qa'Lea slowed her gait. "It would be best if you forgot that man's name, the location of his house, and the very fact that you ever saw him. If you are ever asked, you should say you rode the wagon to town with me and I sold it and you have no idea where."

"Why?" Jed asked. "Is he dangerous?"

"No," Qa'Lea replied. "Just the opposite. I want to make sure that no one who is dangerous ever finds him. He has helped a great deal in our quest at great risk to himself and it would be a shame if any harm came to him."

"How has he helped?" Kylla asked.

"He gave me something," Qa'Lea responded as she led them back to the main street and toward the town square.

"Where are we going?" Jed asked.

"Although Pinukket strives to simulate a Kellish town, there are a few amenities here that no Kellish town would ever dream of," Qa'Lea said.

"Like what?" Fallon asked.

"Like a restaurant," Qa'Lea said.

"What's a restaurant?" Kylla asked.

"A restaurant is a place where people go to pay and be served food," Qa'Lea said. She managed to say it in a tone that was not condensing, but did not manage to keep the slight smile from her face. "There's one near the aft-ward corner of the town square that has very good service and lovely outdoor seating, which is good for private conversations."

"People seem to pay for the strangest things on this side of the mountains," Jed said. He tried to imagine anyone he knew paying someone else to cook for them.

"People who travel far from their homes often do not have the time or the space to cook for themselves," Qa'Lea said. "A restaurant is like an inn, without the rooms."

Jed considered this. While there was no inn in their small town, he had seen one in the Kellish town of Hammur. Traders and tinkers often stayed there. In their own town, traveling folks would stay in a farmer's barn or with friends. But no one would ask for money in exchange for a meal. Even at the inn, a meal was considered part of the price of the room. And he couldn't imagine anyone willingly eating food from an inn without needing to. In the end, he decided not to worry about it and just accept the weirdness of it all. Jed felt certain Qa'Lea was right; he would see things far stranger things than people paying for a cooked meal.

They followed Qa'Lea through the town square and toward a building with several large wooden tables sitting outside under a tall oak tree. They garnered a number of curious glances and a few outright stares as they walked beside Qa'Lea. Jed at first thought it must be because they were with a Tellandor priest but then thought it was because their clothes probably looked more authentic than the *pretend* townspeople. And then he noticed something else.

"There aren't any children," Jed said.

"No," Qa'Lea said. "At least, not in public. Not unless they are children of the paying tourists." Jed made a mental note to look up the new word 'tourist' when he got his hands on the techne *Tannett* again. "There are children here," Qa'Lea continued, "but they are the children of the paid workers and are generally kept at home or in places less public."

"What's wrong with children?" Kylla asked, visibly stiffening at the idea that somehow she should not be seen in public.

"Nothing at all," Qa'Lea said, "but while children are very good at playing pretend, they aren't much interested in getting paid for it, and very few would want to play at being Kellish children all day long. Imagine someone trying to pay you to act like Merrick children all day."

"That'd be perfectly silly," Kylla said, laughing at the thought.

"I agree," Qa'Lea said as they reached the restaurant. The establishment was called The Red Hawk, a fact announced by a large sign painted in black and gold over the door. A young woman in an apron greeted them and ushered them in.

The inside of the building was spacious with large tables and chairs set throughout a wide open space in the middle. Booths with tables and benches built into the walls lined the perimeter. Jed noticed immediately that the woodwork of the tables and chairs was clearly Kellish in design, if not craftsmanship. Kellish furniture was always simple and linear with a repetition of three parallel lines to symbolize the three pillars of Kellish society: family, community, and land.

"We'd like a table in the back garden," Qa'Lea said to the young woman.

"Certainly," the young woman said with a slight smile. She gave the Kellish children a brief, curious glance and then led the way through the restaurant and out to a garden patio.

The garden behind the restaurant was not really a garden the way Jed thought of one. There were no vegetables to be seen anywhere. However, there were a large number of beautiful flowers and even a few small trees. Although the garden had a low wooden fence around it, there was nothing behind the restaurant except a large field of rye that gave way to the rolling hills of the plains. It made for a gorgeous view, and Jed was reminded of summer dinners out behind his parents' house on the long wooden table his father and grandfather had built. For a moment he was homesick, but then he squashed the thought, remembering he wouldn't really feel at home until his brother was there at the table with him.

The woman in the apron seated them in the corner of the garden far away from the only other customers, a young couple holding hands. Qa'Lea sat with her back to the field, facing the inside of the restaurant. The woman in the apron presented each of them with a small booklet of several sheets of paper. Qa'Lea explained these were the menus, and they were expected to choose what they wanted to eat from what was listed inside. She marveled at their enthusiasm for the novelty and patiently explained the less obvious dishes until everyone made their choices. The woman in the apron ran off to the kitchen to convey their preferences to the cook.

Most of the dishes were named after authentic Kellish meals, but a few were obviously intended to make strangers comfortable by replicating meals they were more accustomed to. Jed selected the Bannur meat pie, while Kylla had the summer squash casserole, and Qa'Lea and Fallon both opted for something called a Kellish pasta plate, which Jed was certain was Kellish in name only since he had no idea what pasta might be. However, Qa'Lea assured Fallon it was both tasteful and nourishing, if a bit starchy, and Fallon, always interested in trying new things, was happy to experiment.

"How will we pay for everything?" Fallon asked as he watched the woman in the apron performing the same routine of taking orders from another table inside.

"I have plenty of currency," Qa'Lea said. "You need not worry about paying for anything while you are with me."

"Can you tell us now?" Jed asked, looking around to make sure no one had been seated any closer while he had been engrossed in reading the menu.

"Tell you what?" Qa'Lea asked as she cocked her head toward Jed.

"What Rand....I mean what he gave you," Jed said.

"You are like a dog with a bone sometimes, aren't you?" Qa'Lea said with a hint of a smile.

"You don't know the half of it," Kylla said, grinning.

"As if you have any room to talk," Fallon said, poking his sister with his elbow.

"I imagine it is a fault you each possess to an astonishing degree," Qa'Lea said. Then she reached within the folds of her robe and placed a small leather-bound book on the table before them.

"What is it?" Kylla asked.

"Is it another *Tannett*?" Fallon questioned.

"No," Jed said in almost a whisper. "It's Tal's journal."

CHAPTER 18
DINNER CONVERSATION

"Were it not for the Tellandor Order, and the Sentient's efforts to promote the Order's message of peace and the universal truths common to all faiths, it is unlikely that Wyconna, or indeed the whole of the societies aboard the Celestial Pilgrim, *would have survived the acrimonious near-civil war we now call The Upheaval. Though they have little influence today, some eight hundred years later, we passengers of the* Celestial Pilgrim *owe them all a great debt."*

Why the Tellandor Order is Still Needed,
by Sylvyy Wifless, Common Broadcast essay,
1075 AL (After Launch)

A moment of silence hung over the table like a thick cloud. After a time, Jed reached out and pulled the journal to him. He rested his hands on it but did not open it. The leather-bound sheaves of paper were the closest he had come to his brother in over a year, and the knowledge that it contained Tallu's thoughts and impressions of his journey caused a tightness to grip Jed's heart. He took a deep breath and opened the cover.

"The journal was hidden in a ventilation shaft in a youth hostel in the twin cities of Onnimus-Onnima, several days' travel from here," Qa'Lea said. "The hostel is a place young Kellish often stay while on Landdesh. The person who found it is loyal to the Tellandor Order and made sure it found its way here so I might use it to trace Tal's whereabouts."

"Why couldn't whoever found it track Tal down?" Kylla asked, looking over Jed's shoulder as he flipped through the pages of the journal.

"Because, while that person was willing to risk their life to help the Sentient, the Sentient was not willing to ask for such a sacrifice," Qa'Lea answered.

"Although sending me is a slower method, it is much more reliable. As I said, all of the Schools of the Tellandor Order have been infiltrated. It is difficult to know who to trust, and in some instances, it is best to trust no one."

"Have you read it?" Jed asked, looking up from the journal.

"Only the last entry," Qa'Lea said. "I have scanned the rest of it into my *Tannett* so I can read it as time permits. The task of reading will fall mainly to you, Jed. I do not know if there will be any clues of use beyond those of the final entry, but we may learn something small yet vital from it. You should read the last note."

Qa'Lea reached across the table and flipped the pages of the journal to the final page with writing. Jed stared at the words a moment and then brought them into focus. Kylla and Fallon respectfully leaned back so he could read the words alone.

'I've seen something today. Something horrible. Horrible enough if it was an accident, but I know it wasn't. I saw a man die. Right in front of my eyes. I was walking back to my room tonight after leaving Mirra and her friends. I was alone and the streets were nearly empty. But there were two men talking near Waasl Street where the transport sled comes through and they seemed to be arguing. I ignored them, but then the transport sled was coming, and it always comes too fast, so very fast, and then the one man pushed the other in front of the transport sled. Right onto the sled track. I could see both of them illuminated by the lights of the transport sled, like two big glowing eyes showing me everything.

But the thing is, just before the transport sled hit the man who had been pushed, I saw his face. And I knew his face. I knew who he was. It was the owner of the antique store I had been in last week when I was looking for old paperbound books. It was him, I know it was. And the man who pushed him. I saw him, too. Those eyes. Those eyes weren't normal. They must have been techne of some sort. His eyes were red. I know it sounds crazy, but it's true. It wasn't some trick of the light. His eyes were red. Just for a moment. And then the transport sled hit the store owner. Mr. Gundle was his name. Hit him with an awful sound. And I saw it. I saw him get hit and die. The sled was going so fast it smacked his body and tossed it fifty meters along the track and then, before I could even blink, the transport sled ran over his body.

The train stopped, but it was too late. And I must have screamed, or shouted or I don't know what, because the other man, the murderer, turned and saw me. He saw me with those red eyes. And even with the red eyes I knew I recognized him as well. It was Officer Truun, one of the city law enforcers who works in this sector. The one who had helped me find the art museum my first day in the city. And then his eyes were back to normal and he was after me. I turned and ran. I just ran as fast as I could, up the street and down another, trying to lose him.

He was fast. He closed the distance between us so quickly I thought he would catch me for sure. Then I heard the droning sound of another transport sled. I had run clear across the sector. I saw the sled and ran across the tracks. The sled driver must have seen me and hit the brakes because the sled came to a stop and when I looked back it was blocking the way from Officer Truun, or whatever he is.

I don't know what to do. I'm back in my room now, but I'm afraid that maybe Officer Truun found a way to track me here, or look for me tomorrow. Maybe he's looking for me right now. Or maybe he has other law enforcement officers looking for me. He probably knows I'm Kellish. He must have been able to tell. And the Kellish kids nearly all stay in hostels. Maybe he's coming right now. I'm going to…"

The entry was blank after that. So were all the remaining pages. Jed looked up into Qa'Lea eyes, his own filled with tears he refused to let run down his cheeks. Slowly, he pushed the journal across the table so Kylla and Fallon could read it. No one said anything while they read.

Just as they finished and pushed the journal back to Jed, the woman in the apron arrived with a large tray holding the dishes containing their meals. As she placed the proper plates before each person, Jed took Tal's journal and slid it into his knapsack, placing it next to the dagger.

Qa'Lea thanked the woman and waited until she was out of earshot before turning to Jed. "I'm sorry," she said. "It's clear the murder your brother witnessed is the reason for his disappearance. Undoubtedly, the officer is a member of the Iron Hand. The shopkeeper may have been a member, or he might simply have been someone they were trying to force into cooperation."

"How long will it take us to get to the twin cities?" Jed asked. His determination to find his brother was stronger than ever now that he knew exactly what sort of trouble Tal was in.

"A few days," Qa'Lea said. "We could travel faster, but that would draw even more attention to us. The Sentient's fear, as well as my own, is that if the Iron Hand knows we are looking for Tallu, they may kill him just to protect themselves."

"Then you think he's still alive?" Kylla asked. Her face spoke of determination as much as worry.

"Yes," replied Qa'Lea. "We suspect he is being held so they can use him somehow. More dead bodies would attract attention, and Tallu's disappearance has already attracted more than they desire."

"What about the man with the red eyes?" Fallon asked. "The officer. What was he?"

"Probably just an augmentation," Qa'Lea said. "There are a lot of people in the technology-friendly cities who choose to have their bodies augmented with techne. The red eyes could be decorative, or they might be the result of some enhancement that allows better vision in the dark."

"How soon can we start for Onnimus-Onnima?" Jed asked.

"In the morning," Qa'Lea said. "We will need our rest. And our sustenance." She gestured to the food on the table before them. They had all been so engrossed by the journal and the meaning of it, they had completely forgotten about the meal on the table. Qa'Lea bowed her head in a brief, silent blessing of thanks for the food and the Kellish children did the same before devouring the contents of their plates.

They ate in silence. The entry in Tallu's journal had left them all too worried to make small talk and too stunned to really enjoy the interesting cuisine. It was clear Tallu was in serious danger and they needed to find him as soon as possible.

By the time they finished eating, nightfall had begun and the rolling hills behind the restaurant slowly filled with shadow. The serving woman in the apron placed lit candles on all the tables and around the perimeter of the patio. The candlelight and darkness combined to create an atmosphere of calm that did much, along with a full stomach, to steady Jed's nerves. It seemed to have a similar effect on Kylla and Fallon. They had each known danger in their adventures together, but never something this serious. Plots against the Sentient. Spies within the Tellandor priesthood. The rebellious Iron Hand. It was all much more than they were used to.

Jed's fears only served to steel his resolve to find Tallu and help the Sentient. If what Qa'Lea had said was true, it was not just Tallu or themselves who were in danger, but their friends, and family, and everyone they had ever known. The whole of Wyconna, and even the entire ship, was at risk.

Their server brought the bill and Qa'Lea settled it, taking a small stamp from the folds of her robe and pressing it into the paper of the bill. She then took two small currency chits from what appeared to be the same pocket and handed it all back to the woman in the apron, who smiled and disappeared into the main building of the restaurant. Qa'Lea noticed the curious looks from her three dinner companions. "All expenses of Tellandor priests are paid for by the Sentient. That stamp authorized payment. The currency was a tip for good service. It's customary." As she smiled at them, her smile quickly faded to a frown as she turned in her seat to look out over the dark, rolling hills behind her. Her frown deepened when she looked back around to the table.

"Is something wrong?" Kylla asked.

"There's something out there," Fallon said, answering Kylla's question, but raising one for Jed.

"Gore-hounds?" Jed asked.

"No," Qa'Lea replied. "Something else. I'm not sure what. It may be nothing. But we should get a room at the inn and get some rest. I want to catch the first train in the morning."

"Catch the first what?" Kylla asked.

"A train," Qa'Lea said. "It's how we'll be traveling for a bit. I'd explain, but it will be easier to just wait and see."

Qa'Lea stood up from the table and led them back through the restaurant and to the town square. Oil lanterns on posts set every ten meters or so around the square cast a warm and reassuring glow over the cobblestone street as they exited the restaurant and headed for the inn. The inn was large, well lit, and inviting, taking up nearly as much space as a dozen Kellish houses would have.

As they walked along the street, Qa'Lea kept her eyes on the inn, but Jed noticed that she slowly turned the head of her staff in all directions. He glanced over his shoulder and tried to peer into the shadows of the alleyways between the shops. Just for the briefest of moments, he thought he saw something red in the shadows, something he would have sworn were two crimson eyes, but as he looked more intently, there was nothing but shadow. Turning around, he tried to convince himself it was just his imagination sparked by the entry in his brother's journal, but it wasn't easy.

At the Kell House Inn, Qa'Lea led them inside to a long, wooden bar against one wall where a plump man with thick gray hair and a reddish complexion greeted them.

"Welcome, Shann'Ka," the man said, smiling as he used the formal Tellandor greeting. "We haven't been graced by the presence of a Tellandor priest for quite some time."

"I need a large room," Qa'Lea said. "Big enough for all four of us."

"There is no need for that." The innkeeper smiled. "I can give you a room of your own and a room for the children at the same price as a single room. Consider it a discount for the Order."

"That is very kind of you." Qa'Lea smiled back. "But my request wasn't for budgetary reasons. I am escorting these Kellish children to meet with their cousin, and I do not want to be held responsible if their curiosities lead them to, shall we say, 'wander about'."

"Ah, I understand," said the Innkeeper, grinning even wider. "My grandchildren are just the same. I'll put you in the Regent suite. And the same price as before. You may find a few people in town these days who don't hold a great deal of respect for the Tellandor ways, but my wife and I have always said if it weren't for the likes of you, the whole of Wyconna would have fallen apart long ago."

"You are too kind, Innkepper," Qa'Lea said.

"Landdel's the name," he replied. "How long will you be staying?"

"We must leave in the morning," Qa'Lea said.

"Well then, I'll show you to your room so you can get a good night's rest," Landdel said. "It's up these stairs right here."

Landdel stepped around the wooden counter and led them up to their room. After he had gone back down the hallway, smiling and humming an old Tellandor hymn to himself, Qa'Lea closed the door and locked it. The room was spacious, with two beds, two couches, and two chairs all arranged around a fireplace that was already lit against the mild chill of the night air.

"We wouldn't have gone anywhere, you know," Jed said, a hint of defensiveness in his voice.

"I wasn't worried about you going anywhere of your own volition," Qa'Lea said. "I thought it best that I don't let you out of my sight for other reasons. Now, I suggest you all get ready for bed and then we'll take a few minutes to continue your training before you sleep."

Jed, Kylla, and Fallon washed their faces and readied themselves for bed in record time. As they sat on the edge of one of the beds in the large room, Qa'Lea knelt before them, holding her staff.

"There is something I would like to do that I want to ask your permission for," she said.

The three Kellishers exchanged curious looks before turning their attention fully to Qa'Lea, her eyes flickering in the light of the fire. "As I explained to Jed and his family, when the Kellish leave the valley on their Landdesh, the Sentient secretly uses techne to track them no matter where they go in Wyconna. Tallu's tracking device was disabled, but it has given us an idea of where to begin the search for him. What I would like to do, with your permission, is place a techne tracking device on each of you, so if we ever become separated, I will be able to find you. Do you find that acceptable?"

"Will it do anything else?" Jed asked. "Besides letting you know where we are?"

"No," Qa'Lea said.

"How big is it?" Kylla asked.

"Will it hurt?" Fallon added.

"You will not feel a thing, and it is so small you will never even notice it is there."

"And you'll take it away when we go home." Jed said, more of a statement than a question.

"Of course," Qa'Lea said. The Kellish children looked at each other once more and then nodded their acceptances in unison. Qa'Lea raised her staff in the air and the headpiece glowed a gentle orange, the gold bands brightening in the light. She touched the headpiece to Jed's shoulder, holding it in place for a moment while the light of the headpiece pulsed briefly. Then she moved on and repeated the same procedure on the shoulders of Kylla and Fallon. When she was finished, she stood and smiled. "Thank you. I will sleep much better tonight."

"What happens if we are separated and we need to find you?" Jed said. He didn't really want to think about the possibility of being separated from Qa'Lea, but he knew how even the best of plans could come unraveled.

"You can use Aaral the *Tannett* to find me if necessary," Qa'Lea said. "That will be our first lesson for the evening."

Qa'Lea had them begin by taking five minutes to repeat the breathing meditation they had learned during the day before showing them how to access the *Tannett* and request Aaral to search for her. Afterward, she took the time to show them each how to accomplish making the blade of the dagger blaze with blue-light fire and how to make the stone necklace create a field of protection around the wearer.

Two hours later they had each managed at least a rudimentary mastery of the three Tellandor artifacts. True mastery, of course, would take many, many months, but Qa'Lea had given the essential knowledge that continual practice would enhance and deepen with time.

They stayed up a little longer, Qa'Lea in meditative prayer, Kylla and Fallon exploring the knowledge of the techne *Tannett*, and Jed carefully flipping through the pages of his brother's journal in hopes of finding a new clue to his whereabouts. Although they were all excited by their new knowledge of the Tellandor ways and also fearful of the adventure they were getting deeper in to each day, their exhaustion got the better of them sooner than they expected. Long before Qa'Lea finished her prayers and opened her eyes, Jed, Kylla, and Fallon were all fast asleep.

CHAPTER 19
TRAIN RIDE

Hinduism

"Hinduism is the oldest of the human religions still in practice, originating in the Indus Valley (in what became Pakistan) from 2500 BCE to 1500 BCE. Hinduism has many deities, but all are considered a manifestation of the single Absolute or Ultimate Reality known as Brahman. Popular deities that are worshipped are Brahma, the creative force of the cosmos, Vishnu, the preserving force of the cosmos, Shiva, the destructive or transformative force of the cosmos, and Shakti, the divine mother."

From *The Kellish Book of All Faiths*

Judaism

"Judaism is the second oldest religion still practiced and was founded by the prophet Abraham circa 1800 BCE. Judaism was the first monotheistic religion, believing in a single God who is responsible for creating and maintaining the whole universe. Often translated from the original Hebrew as Yahweh (YHWH), the name of God is never spoken aloud in Judaism. The Jewish faith is guided by 613 mitzvot, or commandments, guiding every aspect of Jewish life from worship and diet to justice and personal conduct."

From *The Kellish Book of All Faiths*

(More information about Hinduism and Judaism can be found in the *Brief Summaries of the Nine Major Human Faiths* at the back of this book.)

Qa'Lea awoke them well before dayrise and suggested they take turns bathing quickly and pack for the journey. Jed was amazed to find plentiful hot water available for bathing by simply turning a faucet knob in the large cast iron bathtub. He wished he had known about the bath the night before and had the time to enjoy a good soak. As it was, they seemed to have little time at all. Qa'Lea hustled them out of the inn and down the street as dayrise began and the tube-light above started growing warm and bright.

They stopped along the way at a bakery to pick up some sweet rolls for breakfast, but eating would have to wait until they were in motion. Qa'Lea led them down another wide street and to a long building built of sturdy wooden logs. Inside they headed for a counter recessed into the wall and Qa'Lea spoke to the woman behind it, taking the stamp from her robes and applying it to a piece of paper the woman placed on the countertop. The woman then handed Qa'Lea four thin strips of paper and Qa'Lea quickly guided them through the building.

"We need to hurry," Qa'Lea said as a loud bell began to ring. "This is the only train for half a day and we can't afford to miss it."

"Where's the train?" Kylla asked. For an answer, Qa'Lea ushered them around a corner and outside where they saw the train. Twenty-some enclosed metal wagons, each one linked to the next, stretched along two thick, metal beams laid into the ground. The wagons were lined with windows and Jed could see passengers already seated inside. At one end of the line of wagons sat a larger wagon with billows of stream coming out of a tall metal chimney. A man with a thin mustache and a short blue cap on his head waved them up the steps of the nearest wagon. The Kellishers followed Qa'Lea aboard.

Within the wagon, Qa'Lea led them down a narrow aisle between rows of well-cushioned seats. "Sit," she said, indicating two rows facing each other. Jed sat next to Kylla and Fallon took a seat between Qa'Lea and the wall of the car.

As they settled themselves, several other passengers entered the car and took seats. A young couple who looked to be recently married sat opposite a middle-aged man and what seemed to be his elderly mother. A man in a rounded hat took a seat facing Jed at the opposite end of the car and immediately buried his face in a book. It was not a paperbound book like those Jed was accustomed to. It was far too slender and didn't seem to contain any pages, but it was the same shape as a book and the man appeared to be reading it.

"Is it a real steam engine?" Kylla asked, surprising Jed. She had been the last to fall asleep and had apparently taken the time to satiate her curiosity about the mode of transportation by looking it up in the ancient *Tannett's* encyclopedia.

"It is and it isn't," Qa'Lea said as she passed out the sweet rolls. "That was real steam you saw when you boarded, but like everything else in this town, it isn't what it seems. The engine doesn't run on coal or wood, but on electricity. The steam is just for show. This train is the main way people get to the town of Pinnuket. People who come here like the atmosphere it creates, even though it's completely out of place, as there has never been a Kellish town that so much as sneezed in the direction of a steam engine. The advantage, of course, is that this train is about ten times as fast as a real steam locomotive."

Just then the train gave a great jerk, and suddenly they were in motion. Qa'Lea gestured out the window as the train slowly pulled out of the station and began to pick up speed along the tracks. Soon the landscape outside the window passed by in a blur and the town of Pinukket was long behind them.

"Can this thing fly off those tracks?" Kylla asked, a bit of anxiety in her voice as the train finally reached a constant speed.

"Not this train and not these tracks," Qa'Lea said. "But was known to happen back when trains were first invented."

"We're going so fast," Jed said. "It couldn't take more than a few hours, could it?"

"Well," Qa'Lea said, "Wyconna is very large and we are not going nearly as fast as you might think. It only seems fast because the fastest thing *you've* ever seen is a wild horse. This train is only traveling at seventy kilometers an hour or so."

"That's more than we walked in two days!" Kylla said, looking out the window again.

"It's comparatively slow for transportation in Wyconna," Qa'Lea said. "But as I said, we need to take a less frequented means of transportation to avoid attracting attention. This train will get us to Concordia by late day."

"What do we do for now?" Fallon asked, indicating his preference by tapping the *Tannett* in his backpack.

"Although this car is nearly empty now," Qa'Lea said, "the train will make stops at several small towns along the way, and I don't think we need to draw attention to ourselves with that sort of activity. However, I believe I have something that can help us pass the time in a constructive manner."

Jed wasn't sure he liked the sound of the phrase "constructive manner". It usually translated as "work" or "chores," and he had no desire for either. Qa'Lea reached into her knapsack and pulled out a leather pouch the size of her hands. Stretching between the two rows of facing seats, she pulled on a round, palm-sized ring set into the wagon's wood paneling. Giving it a tug, a section of the wall slid outward while another leglike section fell forward from that, unfolding a thin but serviceable table between them. Qa'Lea placed the leather pouch on the freshly unfolded table and pulled from it a thick deck of cards.

"Are you familiar with the *Tasheck El Gon?*" Qa'Lea asked.

Jed and the others shook their heads.

"It was created as a teaching aid," Qa'Lea said, "to help spread the ideas of the *Tannett* in a less formal fashion." She spread the cards out on the table. All of the cards had the same illustration on the back, a spiral labyrinth that was the symbol of the Tellandor Order, but each card was illustrated with a picture or image on the reverse side and writing beneath it.

"*The Deck of All Souls,* as it is commonly known," Qa'Lea said, "is a way of teaching about all faiths and beliefs of the human family. Unfortunately, as with most games of leisure, interest in the *Deck of All Soul*s waxes and wanes through the years. A hundred years ago, you couldn't go anywhere without finding people playing a game of the cards. Now, even in the Kellish towns, it's only the older folks who have any interest." Qa'Lea gathered up the cards and shuffled them quickly before dealing out five cards each to Jed, Kylla, Fallon, and herself.

"It's very simple to play," Qa'Lea explained. "There are one hundred eight cards in a deck, and there are twelve suits, or categories, of cards. Which means that within each suit there are nine cards."

Jed picked up his cards and looked at them. He had one that said "Founders" at the top with a picture of a man in yellow robes sitting beneath a tree, his legs crossed and eyes closed. Beneath the illustration, which seemed a cross between a simple painting and something more realistic, were the words, "Siddhartha Gautama: The Buddha." Jed quickly read the rest of the card, glancing up to see Fallon and Kylla inspecting their hands of cards in a similar fashion.

The information on the card was brief and to the point. "490 – 410 BCE (Origin World Dates). Founded Buddhism. Born a prince, he gave up a royal life to become a wandering ascetic. After six years of mediation, he sat beneath the Bodhi tree and achieved Enlightenment. 'Buddha' means 'One who is awake.' Taught the Four Noble Truths: 1) The Nature of Suffering, 2) The Origins of Suffering, 3) How to End Suffering, and 4) The Eight-Fold Path."

Jed looked at his other four cards and saw they were similar. One said, "Prophets and Mystics: Ezekiel." The second, "Symbols: OM:" had a curving symbol as the illustration. The third said, "Sacred Texts: The Koran;" and the final card said, "Other Faiths: The Greeks and Romans."

As Jed continued to examine his cards, Qa'Lea explained the deck and how to use it. "The Twelve suits are: Founders, Sacred Rites & Rituals, Sacred Origins, Sacred Symbols, Deities, Sacred Places, Sacred Objects, Sacred Teachings, Sacred Texts, Sacred Celebrations, and Other Faiths. As I said, each suit has nine cards, each representing one of the nine major faiths. Any guesses what those are?"

"Judaism, Christianity, and Islam, for sure," Jed said, looking up from his cards. "And Buddhism."

"Hinduism, and Taoism, as well," Kylla added.

"And Confucianism and Jainism," Fallon said, laying his cards down on the narrow table.

"And the last?" Qa'Lea asked. Jed and Kylla examined their cards again and Fallon frowned.

"Sikhism?" Fallon asked.

"Good guess," Qa'Lea said, affirming his answer with a smile. "So, each of the nine faiths has a card for each of the eleven of the categories. In the final category of Other Faiths, each card describes an ancient or less popular faith. Now there are several ways to play, but the one I'm going to teach you now is the simplest. To start, you choose how many cards will be in a hand and then deal that many cards to each player. Since this is to be an easy game, we'll start with five cards each, although you can play a game with as many as eleven. Then we take turns drawing a new card from the deck. But as we take one card, we have to give one card back to be placed face up on the discard pile, like so."

Qa'Lea took a card from the deck she had put face-down on the table and placed it in her hand next to the other five cards. Examining them briefly, she chose one card from those in her hand and laid it face-up on the table. It said, "Symbols: The Star of David — Judaism." Turning to Jed, she continued. "Now, since we go around the table from right to left, Fallon's turn is next. He can either take a card from the pile that is facing down or he can take the top card from the discard pile. But he can only take one card. The point of the game is to be the first person at the table to have assembled a hand of five cards, all from the same faith. And, if there are no more cards left in the deck facing down, the person with the most cards of one faith wins. Everyone understand?"

"Seems like a lot of luck is involved," Fallon said as he drew a card from the deck and examined his cards.

"Well, you three are certainly among the luckiest people I have ever encountered," Qa'Lea said as Fallon placed a card on the face-up pile. "There are versions of the game that require more skill than luck, but they are more complicated. I'll teach them to you once you have the basics."

Play continued around the table from Fallon to Jed to Kylla and back to Qa'Lea. As the game went on, Jed divided his attention between reading about the different faiths of humanity, looking out the window at the fields and trees rushing past, and glancing furtively at the other passengers in the train car.

Between learning about an ancient civilization called Greece and their pantheon of gods and goddesses and being curious about the seemingly massive towns in the distance beyond the fields of golden wheat, Jed noticed that one of the passengers struck him as a bit strange. He was a stocky man, slightly overweight but tall nonetheless, and dressed in black pants and a shiny black shirt with a black jacket. A piece of black cloth wrapped around his neck dangled down onto his shirt, and a wide-brimmed black hat sat on his head at an angle.

Even from where Jed sat, he could see the fabric of the clothes was exquisite and probably cost more than all the clothes in his village. The angle of the hat partially hid the man's face, but what Jed could see of it, it didn't look pleasant. He had blocky, angular features with a thick, sausage-like nose and large, bushy eyebrows. The man appeared to have fallen asleep reading a sheet of com-paper.

Jed had seen com-paper for the first time that morning. Qa'Lea had explained that a com-paper was a techne device that, while thin, could present text and images, much like the techne *Tannett*. It could hold large amounts of information and also receive new information and images from signals broadcast throughout Wyconna. People apparently used it to see what was going on in the wider world.

Jed leaned a bit closer to Qa'Lea and lowered his voice to a whisper. "Shann'Ka, there is a man…"

"Yes, I know," she whispered back, before raising her voice and addressing Kylla and Fallon as well. "I think it's time to turn your hands down. It seems I have won the first round."

Qa'Lea gave Jed a meaningful look, one that clearly said he should say no more about his suspicions, as she laid her cards face-up on the table to reveal a hand of five cards all denoting some aspect of the Christian faith. "I was worried for a moment," Qa'Lea continued. "I drew six cards before Kylla finally placed down the sacred symbol card of the cross. Part of the key to this version of the game is paying attention to what cards your opponents are discarding, so you can get an idea of what hand they are trying to assemble. Any guesses as to what you're each holding?"

Jed and Kylla looked at each other quizzically, but Fallon said quickly, almost blurting it out, "Jed is trying to assemble a hand of Islam, while Kylla is trying for a hand of Taoism."

"Very good," Qa'Lea said with large smile. "We'll have to play something more difficult after all. I may actually stand a chance of losing. It may surprise you to discover this, but Tellandor priests hate to lose at cards."

They continued playing hand after hand of the *Deck of All Souls*, Qa'Lea winning each hand, teaching them tips and complications to the game, adding to the number of cards in a hand, certain cards becoming wild and able to be used in any hand, and a new rule about picking up multiple cards from the discard pile.

They played for several hours, occasionally stopping to snack on leftover sweet cakes. Jed soon stopped watching the suspicious man with the hat and began to watch Qa'Lea more closely. He was certain she was keeping an eye on the man, but for the life of him he could never catch her even looking in the man's direction. After a while, he gave up and tried to imitate her, looking at everything but the man in black with the book. After a short time he realized he could pay close attention to the man without ever looking directly at him by using his peripheral vision and carefully selecting where else to look.

The train made several stops over the course of the morning and into the early afternoon. At each stop, Jed glanced in the direction of the mysterious sleeping man in black to see if he might rouse himself and depart the train, but the man seemed to be in a contented and unbreakable slumber. He didn't even shift his position. Jed found it disconcerting. Almost as disturbing was how often Qa'Lea won each game. Jed suspected she had spent a very long time playing with this deck of cards to be so good at every variation of the game.

Fallon was the only one who seemed able to best her, winning two games in a row, which elicited a wry smile from Qa'Lea and resulted in the next round of cards being an even more complicated variation on the game. Tellandor priest or no, Qa'Lea seemed unaccustomed to losing, particularly to a challenger so young as Fallon, who, while pleased with himself, was gracious about winning in a way almost impossible for anyone unfamiliar with Kellish ways to believe.

As the train began to slow down in its approach to the next town, Qa'Lea dealt out the cards for a new game. Keeping her eyes on the cards as she placed them on the table, she lowered her voice to a whisper. "Keep looking at your cards. We're going to start a game, but we are getting off the train at the next stop. When the doors of the car open, Fallon will pretend to have won and begin collecting the cards as though he is going to deal again. Slide the cards discreetly into your bag at the last possible moment. Everyone make sure you have your things. When the door begins to close, we will make our move." She smiled and in a louder voice said, "Now let's see how fast you can learn the Castalle variation."

As he picked up his cards, Jed exchanged quick glances with Kylla and Fallon and struggled against the temptation to sneak a peek at the sleeping man. It was his turn and he quickly pulled a card from the deck and discarded another without even looking to see what his hand was. As the train continued to slow and the card game went faster and faster, only Qa'Lea seemed to take her time to consider her cards before making a discard.

Glancing out the window, Jed saw they were slowly passing through what seemed to his Kellish trained eyes as an enormous town. A few hundred times larger than his own village, it was considerably larger than anything he had ever set foot in and twice the size of any town they had traveled through so far that day.

They passed fields with various crops in summer bloom for several minutes, but these gave way to something he could never have imagined: row after row of long, glass buildings, each at least two stories tall and seemingly filled with green things of various shapes and sizes. Looking closer, which was not easy as the train whizzed by each structure, Jed noticed that they seemed to contain plants. Large and small, some with flowers, some without. What a miraculous thing; a house of glass to hold plants!

Qa'Lea noticed his gaze, which was imitated immediately by Kylla and Fallon. "Greenhouses," she said in a causal but instructive tone. It seemed the tone she most often took when speaking to them.

"They are used to grow plants that require a very special and delicate environment to flourish. This is the town of Concordia. One of the things they specialize in is rare and delectable fruits and vegetables."

Bringing his attention back to the game, Jed noticed it was his turn. Quickly taking a card from the face-down deck, he tossed another from his hand without thinking, and just as quickly returned his focus to the town outside the train window. He noticed Kylla and Fallon were also paying far more attention to the town than the game. At each town they had passed through before, the play of the game had been suspended so the Kellishers could gawk at the buildings and people rushing past the window. The necessity of making it appear like they were not going to leave the train divided their attention.

The town outside the window was unlike the other places they had seen. The buildings of those towns had been constructed from the familiar materials of brick, wood, stone, and plaster, each home or store being a little different, reflecting that they had all been built by hand.

Here, in Concordia, the buildings seemed to have all been built by the same hand at the same time from some material Jed did not recognize. It might have been wood, but Jed could not discern any separate boards or any grain to the material. The buildings were all of different shapes and sizes, and all painted in different colors, some in multiple colors, but there was something about the smoothness of their construction giving them a subtle and beautiful appeal. Moreover, the arrangement of the buildings, which could be discerned even from a moving train, had a graceful flow that seemed natural and elegant to the eye.

Even the streets appeared constructed from some unknown pavement, flat and black, but apparently unmarked by frequent use of fantastically sleek vehicles both large and small. Not that there were many vehicles that Jed could see. Most of the traffic seemed to be people walking, or being carried along on sections of the street flowing and moving of their own accord. All in all, as simple as it was, it was a strange sight for three children more accustomed to dirt roads and simple wooden houses than people being carried along by moving streets past multi-hued homes and stores.

Suddenly the station came onto view and the train slowed to a near crawl. It was Kylla's turn and she and Jed tore their attention from the world outside the window of the train car and back to the card game. Kylla took a card from the deck and discarded another as the train rolled to a complete stop. Qa'Lea then took her turn, taking a card from the pile and laying one down on the discard pile. Fallon quickly snatched up the card Qa'Lea had discarded and laid another in its place. He laid his cards down on the table just as the doors of the train car slid open of their own accord.

"I win," Fallon said, looking up from the cards as Jed grunted aloud, realizing Fallon had indeed won. Apparently, he didn't like the idea of pretending to win.

"Impressive," Qa'Lea said with her head cocked at a slight angle while she stared at Fallon, who immediately began gathering the cards up as though he were going to deal again. Once he had them in a pile he quickly swept them into the deep main pocket of his knapsack, conveniently sitting at the table's edge. Jed and Kylla each slipped their hands beneath the table and made sure they had a solid grip on their own knapsacks. Two people had already exited the train and the last of the four who were boarding slid through the door.

Qa'Lea looked to the three Kellishers. "Now!"

Moving with surprising alacrity and grace, Qa'Lea flowed out of her seat and down the aisle of the car, just reaching the door as it began to slide closed. Holding the door of the train car wedged open with her arms, Jed, Kylla, and Fallon, moving as quickly as only those with much practice of hasty escapes can do, ran beneath her arms and onto the train platform.

Jed turned just in time to see the mysterious man in black, his blocky and deeply creased face revealed in full for the first time, as he rushed down the aisle of the train car. Qa'Lea stepped back and allowed doors to close. She did not even pause to look at the man again; she simply turned from the train and began walking along the station platform, herding the three Kellishers toward the exit with her open arms and her staff.

Jed hazarded another glance back at the man in black as the train began to pull away from the station. The man's face was roiling with barely constrained fury. Jed felt certain the man was going to break through the glass windows of the train car door and chase them down. As the train left the station, quickly gaining speed and taking the mysterious man in black away from them, Jed felt an uncomfortable premonition that it was not the last time he would see that distasteful square face.

CHAPTER 20
NEW CLOTHES

Excerpt from *Good Times and Glad Tidings*, a festival play performed every year on Foundation Day celebrating the establishment of the town of Concordia. Authored by Galadis Five, artificially conscious sentient and playwright, (625 AL to 1566 AL).

Mother Nature: I can't believe you would actually say that! You're so insensitive.

Father Science: Maybe you're too sensitive.

Mother Nature: You've always taken me for granted. Only paying attention to your own needs. Never concerned for how your behavior affects me.

Father Science: I'm just trying to understand you. You can be so mysterious.

Mother Nature: I'm mysterious for a reason.

Father Science: I'm only trying to help.

Mother Nature: Well, you can start by leaving me alone.

Father Science: It's not my fault you were treated badly.

Mother Nature: Who else could be to blame?

Father Science: Well, I, for one, blame Uncle Technology. He's always getting carried away and he rarely thinks about the consequences of his actions.

Mother Nature: But I'm the one who pays the price for his adventures.

Father Science: There must be some way we can all learn to get along.

Mother Nature: Well, Aunt Ecology keeps talking about finding some sort of balance, some sort of harmony between us all, but I think she's a little optimistic.

Father Science: We could try an experiment.

Mother Nature: Oh, you and your experiments!

Father Science: We could start a town, a place where people could try to live in balance between ecology and technology, between nature and science.

Mother Nature: (pause) We could call it Concordia.

A few minutes after their hasty disembarkation from the train, Jed and the others walked along the main street of the small town. It was even more enchanting and beautiful up close than it had seemed from the train. The people were equally fascinating and lovely. The Kellishers recognized something familiar and comforting about the citizens of the town almost immediately. They were each dressed in colorful clothes, as different in hue from one another as the painted buildings they walked passed — men in long shirts with billowy pants and women in swaying dresses that seemed to be wrapped around their bodies from a single piece of cloth, or in some cases, multiple pieces of different colored cloth.

The people themselves were as colorful as the clothes, every shade of skin and ethnic feature visible along the wide central street. The whole of Wyconna was much the same, long since having been segregated in terms of religious persuasion or the use of technology rather than ethnicity, especially the Kellish towns, but even here the contrast was significant. There were always different kinds of people among the Kellish, but rarely so many different people in one place at one time. However, it was the way people moved and spoke to each other that elicited a sense of home for Jed. It was the ease with which people engaged each other and their activities that reminded him of home, far more so than the fake Kellish Pinnuket. Having just narrowly escaped an unknown fate with their hurried exit from the train, the town helped considerably to calm his mind.

"What is this town?" Fallon asked, glancing up at Qa'Lea.

"This is Concordia," Qa'Lea replied, stopping by a small fruit stand and beginning to pick common and exotic fruit from a table as colorful as everything else in the town. "Take some fruit. You'll be hungry soon."

The fruit stand vendor, a thin man in his middle years wearing a bright blue shirt, handed each of the Kellishers a bag made from some clear, lightweight material they had never seen before. As they each picked fruits from an assortment of apples, mangos, cornberries, and plums, Fallon reiterated his question. "You've told us the name, but what do people do here?"

"Yes," Jed said. "There's something about this town that seems familiar."

"It seems more like home than the town that was pretending to be home," Kylla added, popping a reddish dallopberry in her mouth and wincing at its tartness as she chewed.

Qa'Lea paid the fruit vendor and they walked down the center of the street. The central part of town was restricted to pedestrian traffic, no vehicles in evidence. Qa'Lea took a bite of a green-blue apple and tried her best to explain the town.

"Concordia was established some five hundred years ago as an attempt to find a peaceful, sustainable balance between technology and nature. Moreover, it was established to find a way to harness the energy of industry and commerce while allowing everyone an equitable, if not necessarily equal, standard of living."

"That sounds like a Kellish town," Jed said, looking at the different shops they were passing, from something called a barber, to a fish shop, to a cheese shop, to bakers, to stores for things he had never seen.

"Yes," Qa'Lea continued. "In some ways they are like the Kellish people, although few here practice the Way of the *Tannett*. Nearly all people here are either Hindus or Buddhists or Atheists. But many of the guiding principles are similar. The desire to find balance in all things is the same, but here, instead of relying on strict rules to find that balance, the people of Concordia try to find it by creating just enough chaos and activity to be constantly creative. They each strive to take their personal energy and devote it not only to the betterment of themselves, but of the entire community. To that end, they each share in the risks of everyone else, benefiting from their successes and suffering from their failures.

"For instance," Qa'Lea continued, gesturing toward the shops they were passing, "each shop you see along this street is managed by an individual or a family, but all of these businesses are funded and supported by the city itself, and the profits from the businesses are in turn shared with the city. These profits are then used to fund other new businesses, replace those that fail, fund city projects like roads, or support those who are too old to work. So, while everyone pursues their individual talents and desires, they are still something of a collective in economic and social terms.

"You can see it in their housing. Each family builds their own house, or a group of families builds a collection of homes in one structure, but the costs are split with the city so everyone can afford a reasonable and comfortable dwelling. Those who wish for something more lavish can create it by supplying the extra funds themselves."

"So they all work for themselves *and* for the city?" Jed said, looking up at a middle-aged man and woman they were passing, the couple smiling and holding hands. It was a display of public affection that would only ever be seen in a Kellish town by a very young and bold couple. It made him think of his parents, and he quickly turned his attention back to Qa'Lea.

"Yes, exactly," she said.

"But how do they balance the use of technology?" Kylla asked as she watched a family transported by one of the moving sections of the street.

"It is not easy to find balance," Qa'Lea said. "But, they have been more successful than most settlements around Wyconna, although they have experienced periods of both technological extravagance and austerity. Essentially, they try to hold to their motto of '*Technology to ease burdens, not creativity or connection.*' They use technology to make physical labor easier in some cases, but not in others. These moving streets, for instance. They are for getting from one side of town to the other, but people walk whenever they can afford the time to do so. Much of the agriculture is automated, or helped through automation, with the planting and harvesting in the fields and greenhouses around the town accomplished by robotic machines, but nearly every family has a garden that is tended to by hand. They use the most advanced technology for the maintenance of the human body and extension of life, but they refuse to allow it to be used for augmentation or alternation of the human body unless to correct for defects in children.

"Of course, it is not entirely idyllic," Qa'Lea said, smiling down at Jed and the others. "There is always human emotion to contend with on an individual level, and politics to deal with on the collective level. Politics here can test even the patience of a Tellandor priest. The religious persuasion of many the residents has led them to seek out a consensus for most decisions, and their local council, while nominally in charge of the town, must take everyone's feelings on a particular matter into consideration, and all of their decisions must be unanimous. If you have never participated in a council of any sort, I can assure you that reaching a consensus is sometimes more painful than simply having your views completely ignored.

"Ah, here we are." Qa'Lea stopped in front of a small shop with a bright orange cloth awning and smiled down at the three Kellishers.

"What is a tailor?" Fallon asked, reading the words painted on the large glass window of the shop.

"Someone who makes clothes," Qa'Lea said. "The three of you are beginning to stand out too much in those hand-sewn woolens. We're going to find you something a little more fashionable."

"And what is that?" Jed asked, pointing to the side of the shop where a series of images depicting people in different styles of clothing flickered across the wall.

"It's a vis-sheet," Qa'Lea explained. "It's like com-paper, only larger. It's thin and flexible and can be placed on nearly any surface in any shape. It presents any images and sounds that are broadcast to it."

"It looks so real," Jed said, marveling at the images on the wall.

"There are things that simulate reality much more efficiently," Qa'Lea said. "Maybe before this is all over, I'll show you a sensory-sim. Enough gawking. Let's get you some new clothes."

Kylla looked up and stared Qa'Lea in the eyes. "I'm not wearing another dress."

"I wouldn't think of it, dear," Qa'Lea said, holding the door open for her. "I always hated wearing dresses when I was your age. Now, of course, I can't wear them at all, and I miss them terribly. In with you. All of you. I want to catch the next train out of town."

They emerged from the little shop an hour later, each with two new sets of clothes. They each wore a new outfit and stuffed the second outfit and their old clothes in their knapsacks. The Kellishers found it amusing to discover that people would pay someone to make clothes for them. Back home, the women of each family made the clothes, having been taught by their mothers for generation after generation. The shopkeeper, Hallid, or the tailor, as Fallon had insisted on calling him, turned out to be an old acquaintance of Qa'Lea's.

Of course, the tailor did not make the clothes himself, although Qa'Lea assured them he cut an excellent set of robes, or even a dress, when time allowed. But because time was short, Hallid used a machine that created the clothes while the Kellishers watched, manufacturing each a set of loose pants, a long shirt, and a jacket to the specifications of size, shape, and color. The jackets fit nicely over the shirts, having wide-folded cuffs and wooden hooks with loops of cloth to close them up in front. Jed and Fallon had each taken a suit of dark blue, Jed opting for another in deep red, while Fallon chose white, and Kylla took one in emerald green and another in black.

Walking down the street from the shop and back toward the train station, Jed noticed how much more comfortable he felt. Oddly, he also felt a sense of loss. It was as if by shedding the clothes of their hometown he was shedding a part of his identity, a part of who he was. However, the new clothes also made him feel like he was entering a new life. Like crossing a threshold as significant as stepping out of the Notesch Valley and into the wider world of Wyconna. Jed remembered a passage in his brother's journal that had caught his eye while skimming through it the night before.

"I bought a new set of clothes today. They're simple, and not really that much different than what I had been wearing, but they help me fit in. I don't feel like such a freak, such an obvious backwoods bumpkin. People don't stare at me as much, at least not when I'm just walking down the street. I still have so much to learn to fit in, but at least people can't tell from my clothes that I don't belong. Of course it was sad as much as exciting. I realized this was the first time I've ever worn anything that wasn't made for me by my mother. It's like one more connection, one more string attaching me to her, to my whole family, has been cut."

Jed understood exactly how his brother had felt. As he walked beside Qa'Lea, his eyes passing from colorful people to colorful shops and back again, he wondered what his brother was feeling right at that moment. What clothes did he wear, wherever he was? And was he safe? And wasn't that face just a bit too square, and just a bit too wrinkled, and was that suit black?

Jed's eyes went wide, but he kept them moving past the café window where he was sure he had spotted the man in black from the train. It was a struggle of will against body to keep his legs walking at the same pace as before.

"Shann'Ka," Jed said as loudly as he dared, trying to appear casual, "I think I just saw…"

"Yes, I saw him too," Qa'Lea said. "Or one of them. There may be more of them that look the same."

"More of who?" Kylla asked, glancing behind her.

"Don't look back," Qa'Lea said, gently placing an arm around Kylla's shoulders. "We don't want them to notice we've seen them."

"Are there more than one?" Fallon asked, staring straight ahead.

"I'm not sure," Qa'Lea replied. "There may be several. And they may or may not look like the square-headed fellow."

"You mean he has a twin?" Jed asked.

"Not in the strictest sense," Qa'Lea said. "A twin of sorts. A clone. A biological duplicate, genetically identical to the original. The organization, whose name we won't mention in public, often uses them to create confusion in their operations. Although it may also be a techne imitation of a human being, which is even easier to duplicate."

"What do we do?" Kylla asked, visibly reassured by Qa'Lea's arm on her shoulders.

"We must do what they expect us to do, while doing exactly what they do not," Qa'Lea replied.

"How do we do that?" Jed asked.

"Just follow my lead and be ready to run when I tell you," Qa'Lea said.

"Is that always going to be our plan?" Fallon asked, a hint of worry in his voice.

"I very much hope not," Qa'Lea responded, giving Fallon what might have been either a look of irritation or concern. "However, it's the only plan we have for the moment, so just keep walking."

They kept walking, all the way back through the town and to the train station. The old stone station's squat features starkly contrasted the sleek, silvery train that pulled into the platform. The train was far more sophisticated and advanced than the one they rode earlier. Qa'Lea bought passage at the counter and then led the Kellishers across the platform and through the wide open doors of the first train car they came to. The interior design was ornate with smooth lines and minimal linear ornamentation, creating the sensation of swift, powerful speed even while the train stood still.

"Keep walking," Qa'Lea said, herding Jed, Kylla, and Fallon down the aisle and toward the door at the end of the car. "Through the door and into the next car." Jed held the door open and they passed into the next car. And then the next and the next, walking all the way down the length of the train, past luxuriously plush seats full of passengers. Jed and the others tried not to look too closely for fear of finding a face that might be unpleasantly familiar. As they walked, they heard the conductor's voice announcing the train's departure, repeated throughout the train, seeming to come from everywhere in each car at the same time.

"Hurry, now." Qa'Lea said. "Not much time."

They felt the train lurch as they reached the last door of the last car, Qa'Lea stretching out over the heads of the Kellishers to swing it open and shuffle them through. As the door slid closed behind them, they found themselves outside the train on the same sort of small platform they had walked on between train cars, only now the train was beginning to move, and there was not much room for standing.

"What are you waiting for?" Qa'Lea shouted over the roar of the rushing wind. "Jump!" With a slight nudge from Qa'Lea's staff, Jed, Kylla, and Fallon leapt from the back of the train and hit the ground, rolling to absorb the impact of the fall the way they had learned to do when jumping out of trees back home. Qa'Lea landed on her feet right behind them. "This way. Hurry. Run!"

Qa'Lea led them across several sets of tracks and around the cars of parked trains and back to the side of the train station, leaping over a small row of bushes and running across the low grass of a manicured lawn to where the main street into the center of town began. Qa'Lea guided them directly onto the moving street, propelling them toward the center of town at a pace much faster than they could have run.

"What will we do now that we've missed the train?" Kylla asked.

"Riverboat," Qa'Lea said, glancing behind them to see if they were being followed.

"A boat?" Jed said, looking behind them as well. "That's not nearly as fast as a train."

"No, it is not," Qa'Lea said. "Especially not the train we were just on, which is about ten times as fast as the one we took this morning. But this riverboat is no ordinary vessel, and it will be fast enough — if we catch it in time. Walk a little faster."

They did as instructed, nearly running down the moving street, propelled at a speed that clearly thrilled Kylla to near bursting and made Jed wonder what would happen if he were to trip and fall. Fallon struggled to keep up, his shorter legs working hard to maintain the same pace as everyone else. Abruptly Qa'Lea slowed to a stop and corralled them with her staff. "Off here."

They stepped off the moving street, nearly stumbling to their knees with the shift to suddenly steady ground. "Down this street. Quickly. The riverboat is supposed to cast off the same time as the train leaves, but the captain is never on time. At least I hope he's not today."

The Kellishers followed Qa'Lea down the street, smelling the scent of the river they could not yet see. Turning a corner, they came to a street much like the others of the town, only this one had a definite dead end — the river docks sitting fifty meters away. Running down the sidewalk, the slender Concordia vehicles whizzing down the center of the street, they could see the riverboat tethered to the docks, the wide blue Nilus River stretching out behind it.

It was like no boat Jed had ever seen — nearly a hundred meters long and four stories high, with two huge wooden paddle wheels in the middle of the hull, and two large black smoke stacks shooting up five meters above the uppermost deck. Men on the dock began to cast off ropes mooring the riverboat to pier posts, the long wooden gangplank swinging slowly to the side as twin gray clouds billowed up from the smokestacks.

"Hold that ship!" Qa'Lea shouted in a voice that carried down the street and seemed to freeze the crew of the boat in the middle of their tasks. She skidded to a stop at the edge of the gangplank, Kylla right behind her, Jed and Fallon running up close thereafter.

The crewman on the other side of the gangplank stretching over the five-meter expanse of water between the docks and hull of the riverboat gave Qa'Lea an amused smirk.

"Gangplank's up. You'll have to wait for the next boat," the burly, bushy-bearded crewman said.

"We need to be on *this* boat," Qa'Lea said, her voice icy with authority.

"Sorry, priest." The crewman laughed. "Maybe you can take the train."

"Lower that gangplank, Jarrod," a deep male voice called from a balcony four levels above. "And stop snorting like a pig."

Qa'Lea looked up toward the voice, shielding her eyes from the glare of the tube-light, and smiled. On the balcony, near the pilot house, stood a wide shouldered man with gray hair. He wore a white suit with gold buttons down the front of the jacket. He smiled as deeply as Qa'Lea.

"Thank you, Captain Pansho!"

"You are always welcome aboard the *River Queen*, Shann'Ka Qa'Lea," the Captain said as the gangplank swung back into place. As Qa'Lea stepped onto the gangplank and led them across to the deck of the riverboat, Jed gave one last glance backward to see if there might be a man with a blocky face behind them. Seeing none, he turned to look at Qa'Lea, certain she must know everyone useful and mysterious on the entire starship.

CHAPTER 21
THE RIVER QUEEN

Buddhism

"Born a prince, Siddhartha Gautama, (490 – 410 BCE) of the Shakya clan in India became the founder of Buddhism. Buddha means "One who is Awake," and enlightenment, the goal of Buddhist practice, is considered to be awakening to the Ultimate Nature of Reality. Buddha's core teaching was the Four Noble Truths."

From *The Kellish Book of All Faiths*

Taoism

"As much a philosophical way of life as a mystical religion, Taoism (sometimes spelled Daoism) is concerned with bringing human life into harmony with the natural cosmic principle of all existence. The word Tao is usually translated as 'Path' or 'Way,' and refers to the Ultimate Reality and the act of bringing human action in alignment with it."

From *The Kellish Book of All Faiths*

(More information about Buddhism and Taoism can be found in the *Brief Summaries of the Nine Major Human Faiths* at the back of this book.)

The *River Queen* made its way swiftly up the Nilus River as true nightfall began. The tube-light faded from a dusky orange hue to darkness, and the lights of houses along the riverbank reflected out across the smooth surface of the water. Seated at the Captain's table on an outdoor dining deck, Jed stuffed another bite of chocolate cake into his mouth and marveled again at the magnificent riverboat and its amazing captain seated just across the table from him. Small, bright globes of light dangled from wires strung along the deck, giving a pleasant glow to everyone's faces, especially that of Captain Pansho, who laughed again in a deep, echoing voice.

"It's all true, I assure you, every word of it," Captain Pansho said, taking a deep drink of wine from the crystal glass beside his empty plate. They had been invited to dine at the captain's table, and it was a long, rich, and extravagant meal with two soups, one hot of creamed mushrooms, another chilled of tomatoes, then a salad with nuts, dried blackberries, and a cheese made from goat's milk.

This was followed by herb roasted hens stuffed with wild rice and served with small carrots, green hannock beans, and butter soaked potatoes. Next came a small dish of fruit flavored ice, to cleanse the palate as Captain Pansho had said, and finally the creamy chocolate cake with a chilled center of iced sweet cream. It was the most amazing meal Jed, Kylla, and Fallon had ever experienced, exceeding even the festival meals back home. And, of course, the festival meals never had Captain Pansho's stories for entertainment.

Hearty meals were a way of life with Captain Pansho, his wide girth obviously the result of one too many tasty desserts. Although he was somewhat round, he seemed the epitome of health and vitality, his skin darkened from days spent on the open decks of the riverboat, a short trimmed beard of silvery gray rimming his jaw line, and his fiery blue eyes conveying the sense of a powerful life force in him. That force was never so evident as when he was telling stories.

"Of course," Captain Pansho said, grinning from behind his gray beard, "I have another story. One you might find a bit more interesting, as it involves the first time I met your guardian."

"I sincerely doubt they will find that boring incident worth listening to," Qa'Lea said, smiling over a bite of cake.

Her mood upon reaching the riverboat had lightened considerably, and the Kellishers noticed it and took comfort from it. Whereas before, she had always seemed doubly aware of her surroundings and if not exactly tense, certainly firm in her manner, here she seemed relaxed for the first time. Whether it was because they were far from shore and the threat of gore-hounds and square-headed men in black, or because she knew the Captain took exceptional precautions with the security of his riverboat, Jed really did not care. If Qa'Lea was at ease, Jed and his friends could relax as well.

"We'd love to hear the story," Kylla said, taking a sip of raspberry juice to wash down the last of her cake as she glanced at Jed. They had been enjoying the Captain's stories nearly as much as the food, and any story about Qa'Lea would certainly be as good as the cake.

"You should not encourage him," Qa'Lea said.

"Nonsense," Captain Pansho replied. "Everyone loves a good story. And this, I assure you, will show you a side of the good Shann'Ka you have not seen. You see, many years ago, long before I had this gray beard or this big belly, I was barge boat captain, hauling goods up and down the river. One night, well, let's just say that barge boat captains love one another's company, and often when in one another's company, they have a tendency to consume too much of certain beverages they would do better to avoid entirely."

"More truth you have not spoken all night," Qa'Lea said.

"But more truth to come," Captain Pansho continued. "You see, it had gotten very late, I had become very, how shall I put it…"

"Inebriated," Qa'Lea offered.

"Less than usually aware of my surroundings," Captain Pansho countered. "And as I was leaving a less-than-reputable establishment in a rather seamy section of the lower docks in New Laords, I was accosted by four unscrupulous thugs armed with sticks and knives."

"Were you hurt?" Fallon asked.

"Well, my pride was bruised…" Captain Pansho began to reply.

"You mean your head," Qa'Lea said, cutting him off.

"Oh, my head was so soaked in the turpentine they served in that dive my brainpan hardly noticed a thing." Captain Pansho laughed. "Until the next day, naturally. Of course what really saved my head was not the drink, but the appearance, out of the fog like some mythical heroine, of none other than the honorable Shann'Ka Qa'Lea. The four thugs were so surprised, they stopped kicking me where I had fallen and stared at her in amazement, the lights of the dock behind her casting a long shadow over of all of them, her robes seeming to be made of stone and that staff looking three meters tall."

"Every time you tell this story, I become more amazing," Qa'Lea said, a hint of embarrassment finally slipping out from behind her usual equanimity.

"My dear Qa'Lea," the Captain said, raising his glass, "every time I see you, you *are* more amazing." Taking a quick sip, he turned to the children. "And can you guess what she said to the four ruffians? She stepped out of the shadows so they could see her eyes, and she gave them this look, and you should say your prayers you never see this look directed at you, and she said in this sweet voice, 'You gentlemen will give that man back his wallet and leave now.' Just like that. Like she was telling a porter to take her bags.

"Well, as you can imagine, this wasn't received by the thugs with anything but derision. However, it did have the happy effect of inducing them to leave me and turn their attention entirely toward Qa'Lea. Not that I was to be of any help, mind you, but it did give my aching ribs a respite and allowed me to rest my head on the wooden dock and watch what happened next. And what happened next convinced me either I was in the presence of some extraordinary creature from the heavens, or I had truly pushed myself beyond the limits of human consumption for certain liquids."

"The latter, most likely," Qa'Lea said.

"What did happen next?" Jed asked, anxious now that the story seemed near a climax and not wanting Qa'Lea to distract Captain Pansho from the meat of it.

"Why, what happened next is they attacked her," Captain Pansho said. "All at once, with sticks and knives, and not a word of warning. Usually with thugs, you'll find one has a big mouth and likes to test the waters first, but I assume the reputation of the Tellandor priesthood was such they felt idle chatter would only have given Qa'Lea the advantage. Not that she needed it. She already held the advantage. She was so smooth and graceful, it was almost like watching a dance. A very short dance. A few seconds after they rushed her, they were all lying unconscious on the docks, sprawled out like forgotten sacks of grain. And she had not a mark on her. It was a sobering sight. No pun intended, naturally."

"Naturally," Qa'Lea said, stifling a snort of laughter.

"And that was how I first met your lovely guardian," Captain Pansho said. "She kindly returned my wallet, helped me back to my boat, and set me on the straight and narrow." He looked at the glass of wine in his hand and then down at his large belly. "Of course, straight for me is like straight for a river, with a few twists and turns here and there. And I am not nearly as narrow as I used to be, but there is no one you might ask who wouldn't tell you that I am not a better man for having met this gracious priest. May you all be so lucky one day as to see her skills of combat in action."

"Oh, we've seen her fight," Kylla said.

"We know how gracious she can be when provoked," Fallon added.

"Fighting in front of children?" Captain Pansho said, a teasing lilt to his voice.

"It was not like that, I assure you," Qa'Lea said, hardness returning to her tone.

"And who are you fighting these days?" Captain Pansho asked, raising his glass to his lips. "More dockyard ruffians?"

"Gore-hounds," Jed said, realizing as he spoke the words he had broken the spell cast over the dinner by bringing the harsh reality of their situation back to mind.

The Captain nearly spit his wine back into his glass as he coughed and choked. "Gore-hounds. Those two words tell me a story all by themselves." His jovial manner evaporated and he turned his attention fully to Qa'Lea. "I don't have your faith in things unseen, but I do have faith in people. More importantly, I have faith in you. Anything you need, any time, any place, you have only to ask, you know that."

"Yes, I know," Qa'Lea said. "Thank you, Barris. For now, passage to the twin cities will be enough."

Captain Pansho looked at them and brought a smile to his face. "It has been a lovely meal, and it has been good to meet all of you, but I have a riverboat to attend to, so you will kindly excuse me. Stay as long as you like, and order anything else your hearts desire. Your rooms are already prepared and ready for you whenever you decide to retire for the evening."

He stood up, holding the back of his chair for a moment. "You three Kellishers take good care of this priest, she means a great deal to me. I leave her in your care." He bowed slightly, turned and walked back along the open deck, climbing a thin set of stairs up to the wheelhouse from where the riverboat was piloted.

They sat in silence for a moment, each taking in the view of the occasional lights from houses along the river, enjoying the feeling of the breeze from the riverboat's passage on their faces, and glancing up to look at the artificial stars projected in the night sky above them.

"Will you teach me to fight?" Kylla asked suddenly, breaking the mild reverie of the night.

"Me too," Jed added.

Qa'Lea drew her gaze slowly down from the artificial heavens to the Kellishers across the table from her. "What about you, Fallon? Do you want to learn to fight?"

Fallon glanced at Kylla and Jed for a moment and then looked to Qa'Lea. "Not really. But I suppose it would be good to know how. Just in case."

"Just in case," Qa'Lea echoed.

"We're already learning to use the knife and the stone," Jed said. "It would make sense, wouldn't it, to know how to protect ourselves if we don't have them handy?"

"Unfortunately," Qa'Lea said, "it does makes sense." She sighed and placed both of her hands on the table. "I fear I have made a grave error in allowing you three to come with me. However, at this point, I feel we are committed to our course. So, when time allows, in addition to your current studies, I will teach you a little of how to defend yourselves when necessary." Jed and Kylla glanced at each other, trying to hide their grins.

"This is serious business," Qa'Lea said in a tone that stifled the smiles. "Normally there is a long period of training in the arts of the mind and soul before one begins to learn the combat arts. And the same is true for the use of the blade and the stone, or the staff, which is what is taught these days."

"Why is that?" Jed asked.

"Because of the power one can wield over others," Qa'Lea said. "With my staff, or with your blade and stone, you can cause great suffering to other living beings. And with the combat arts, you can cause harm with only your hands. Without properly training your mind to control your emotions, such as anger, and training your heart to cultivate compassion and love, it is all too easy to be swayed by the heat of the moment and bring suffering to others unnecessarily.

"Violence should always be avoided, but it is sometimes necessary to defend oneself and others from those who would do harm to us. There are those, even among my own order, who disagree with this, and believe violence should never be used, even to defend the life of oneself or a loved one. It is a central teaching in many faiths, particularly Buddhism, and the teaching of ahimsa in Hinduism, the admonishment of Jesus to 'Turn the other cheek' in Christianity, and some followers of Jainism go so far as to avoid causing harm even to small insects.

"Unfortunately, these ideals have rarely been lived up to by the followers of many of those faiths." Qa'Lea paused, sighing again. "I have begun to lecture. As much as you need guidance, you don't need a sermon at this point. The reason for this teaching of completely avoiding violence is that without great wisdom, it is impossible to know if the use of violence in defense of others is truly wise and just. And without cultivation of compassion, there can be no wisdom deep enough to make that judgment."

"We need to put the seven principles into action," Fallon said, interrupting.

"Yes," Qa'Lea said, a smile escaping her lips. "Exactly. The principles, fully embraced, protect us from harming others. We arrive early tomorrow morning, so I will give you some combat instruction this evening before bed."

"Can you tell us more about Onnimus-Onnima?" Jed asked, his attention suddenly diverted from learning how to fight, a thing no Kellish child would normally ever be taught, to the next destination in their journey. "Tal's journal mentions traveling there, but he doesn't seem to have written much after he arrived."

Qa'Lea gathered her robes around her against the slight chill of the night air. "In the morning, the *River Queen* will deposit us at the twin cities of Onnimus-Onnima. A thousand years ago, they were one city called Onnimi, stretching across the river and connected by three bridges. The city was unique because of its faith. Not because all of its citizens were required to worship a single faith, as is sometimes the case in cities throughout Wyconna, no, it was special because the religion they worshipped was alien in origin."

"What do you mean by *alien*?" Jed asked, picturing in his mind creatures that were mere legends among the Kellish.

"I mean," Qa'Lea said, "the religion of Onnimi did not originate with humanity, but with a species called the Urris, one of the first alien races to have been encountered by humanity in its exploration of the galaxy. Among the Urris, there was a religion called Onnamare which posited that there were twin forces ruling the universe, one benevolent and one malevolent, but each necessary. The followers of Onnamare felt that by worshipping the benevolent force, a god called Hannish-Onna, they could sway the balance of the universe and create a more just world."

"That doesn't sound dangerous," Jed said, wondering what this new city might be like.

"Of course it's not," Qa'Lea said. "In fact, it is similar to an ancient faith from the Origin World called Manicheism, but the problem began some five hundred years ago when there was a split in the faith of the Onnimi. Within the span of twenty years two sects formed, each having a completely different way of worshipping Hannish-Onna. Within a hundred years, the city was in turmoil and a civil war had begun, each side vying for power and trying to destroy those of the opposite faith."

"That sounds like madness," Fallon said.

"Who would fight over how to worship?" Kylla asked, clearly incredulous at the notion.

"In the past," Qa'Lea said, "before the Long Journey began, many of our ancestors often fought long, bloody wars for far less than a difference in religious belief. However, here on Wyconna, the Sentient is charged with ensuring the safety of all the passengers, and so a truce was forced into place, whereby the city was divided by the faith of its citizens, the Onnimus taking one side of the river, and the Onnima taking the other. This, of course, did not end the conflict, but it did end the majority of the bloodshed."

"Then why are the twin cities so dangerous?" Jed asked, struggling to imagine people fighting because of their faiths.

"Oh, it's not," Qa'Lea said, "as long as you are of the proper faith and on the proper side of the river. Visitors are granted exception but are only barely tolerated. And there are small, violent factions on both sides of the river that often decide to blow up a shop or a transit sled or a boat because they still believe both cities should follow the same beliefs — their beliefs."

"Why would my brother ever want to go to a place like that?" Jed asked, trying to think if he had read anything in the journal that gave a clue.

"I'm not certain," Qa'Lea said. "I have only skimmed the journal, and while he makes no direct statement, I suspect he was following a girl."

Kylla's head snapped back from where she had been looking out over the river. Jed noticed the worried look on her face, but suspected it was for slightly different reasons than his own. Tallu followed a girl. Maybe this girl was the reason Tal got into trouble. Maybe he was in love with her.

Kylla looked over the table at Jed and smiled. He smiled back. She would be asking to read Tal's journal that night for certain.

CHAPTER 22
THE TWIN CITIES

Transcript from *Wyconna Now*, a news and information program broadcast throughout the whole human section of the *Celestial Pilgrim*, anchored by Kellip Furno.

(Tight shot on Kellip Furno standing before aerial image of the Twin Cities.)

Kellip Furno: In our top story today, the city councils of the twin cities Onnima and Onnimus have once again failed to reach an agreement over their longstanding dispute. Legal advisors for both cities have counseled them to break off negotiations and take the case before the High Court of Wyconna in hopes that an adjudicated settlement will be considered mutually binding by both parties. The crux of the quarrel between the two cities is over which one should be allowed to use the prefix "Onni" in its name. Both cities take their names from the original city name of Onnimi, derived from the name of the faith that is the root of the conflict between the two communities, Onnamare. The mayor of Onnimas had this to say about the disagreement.

(Close-up of Mayor of Onnimas standing before the city council.)

Mayor of Onnimus: These heretics of the other side of this light-forsaken river must be brought to their knees and made to see the righteous valor of our city. They must accept that only the true inheritors of the Onnamare way may claim the right to use the Onni in their name.

(Wide shot of Kellip Furno.)

Kellip Furno: The Head High Council of Onnima said this in response.

(Close-up of Head High Council Member of Onnima.)

The Head High Council Member of Onnima: I hope they all rot and burn in an everlasting hell that consumes the whole of their blight-infected city and wipes it clean from the face of the planet!...Umm...I mean clean from the interior of the ship!

(End Transcript.)

Morning came much sooner than Jed and his fellow adventurers were prepared for. Captain Pansho had arranged for the Kellishers to have their own cabin, and while Qa'Lea had at first been reluctant to let them out of her sight, she eventually agreed, showing them how to set Aaral, the ancient techne *Tannett,* to stand guard and give a signal of warning if anyone tried to enter the cabin without permission.

Jed, Kylla, and Fallon had stayed up far too late, practicing the few simple defensive moves Qa'Lea had taught them before retiring to their adjoining cabin. When they finally tired of twisting each other's joints in swinging motions and throwing each other to the ground, they set about to spend more time mastering the ancient Tellandor artifacts.

Jed agreed to relinquish the dagger to Kylla for the evening and gave her pointers on how to will the blade to burst into a blue blaze. He took up learning to master the *Tannett* while Fallon tried his hand at using the stone to create a shield of impenetrability around himself.

It was well past middle night when Kylla and Fallon fell asleep. Jed quietly took his brother's journal from his knapsack and started reading. Kylla had hinted several times throughout the evening that she would like to see the journal, but Jed had simply ignored her intimations. By the time he had begun to read it was already so late that he struggled to keep his eyes open. He fell asleep reading the one passage he could find relating to their destination the following morning.

"Mirra spoke very highly of the Twin Cities, although everyone else I talk to about them just grunts or laughs in my face when I suggest going there. 'A nice place to visit as long as you don't get off the train,' is what most of them say. But Mirra seems to have nothing but good things to say of the cities. Or at least of Onnima. Of Onnimus, she says not a peep. But then, she doesn't talk much to begin with. She's an odd girl. I'm glad I met her, though. She says she's planning on returning home in a few days."

It was with those words Jed fell into slumber, dreaming of the Twin Cities. The cities themselves were nothing like his dreams, as he saw first thing that morning when Qa'Lea pounded on their cabin door to wake them.

He raised his head to look out the glass portal and saw the cities coming into view as the *River Queen* cruised up the waterway. Shortly thereafter, having quickly stuffed their faces with hot rolls of cheese and ham and washed them down with fresh tangerine juice brought to the room by a steward, they all gathered on the lower deck of the massive boat, watching as it came closer and closer to the Twin Cities.

The cities were clearly in competition with one another; each side of the river comprised of one grandiose building after another, matched equally, side for side. Tall buildings of stone and glass flourished along the shoreline and seemed to stretch along wide paved streets deep into either metropolis. If a building towered toward the sky in Onnimus, then there was one to match or exceed it directly across the river in Onnima. If there was a statue in Onnima, then on the shores of Onnimus there was a larger sculpture. The only place this competition ceased was at the docks. The docks occupied a giant floating platform in the center of the river, attached to either shore by a wide bridge. The bridge had once been a single structure spanning the river, but a large section had been cut out of the middle, separating the two halves and the two rivaling cities.

"I thought you said there were three bridges?" Jed asked, looking up at Qa'Lea, who seemed to be paying close attention to the workers gathered on the docks they were rapidly approaching.

"Originally there *were* three bridges," Qa'Lea said absently. "But that was a thousand years ago. The other two were destroyed in the wars that consumed the cities some five hundred years ago. This bridge is all that is left. And as you can see, the cities' leaders still have such distrust for one another that the structure no longer connects them directly. That is why the docks are built in the middle of the river. They don't trust each other enough to have separate docks."

"And a damned silly nuisance it is," said Captain Pansho, stepping up from behind them. "Causes nothing but problems for vessels simply trying to pass through. Too shallow near the shores. Nearly got stranded myself once when the Vice Chancellor of Wyconna River Ways was aboard and insisted on trying to pass a little sailboat blocking the way. Lost my vote in the next election, he did."

"Shouldn't you be in the control room?" Qa'Lea asked as the *River Queen's* paddles stopped and the massive boat gently slid up to the docks and came to a halt.

"Wouldn't want to miss seeing you off," Captain Pansho said with a wide smile. "Besides, the sentient pilot docks this beast better than I ever did. Last time I tried to bring her in manually, I nearly lost the starboard paddles. Insurance company practically insisted I relinquish the landing duties to the sentient pilot."

"Samuel Clemens would have been shocked," Qa'Lea said with a grin.

"He was a better writer than a pilot, I'll wager," Captain Pansho said, laughing.

"Who's Samuel Clemens," Jed asked, thinking the name sounded familiar.

"Look it up with Aaral when you have time," Qa'Lea said.

"What are they teaching children these days?" Captain Pansho said, mock concern in his voice.

"Where we come from, not nearly enough," Kylla said, looking up at Captain Pansho with a face managing to be both sullen and happy at the same time.

"Then you stick close to Shann'Ka Qa'Lea here," Captain Pansho said. "You'll get an education like no other."

"We won't let her out of our sight," Fallon said, obviously remembering what the Captain had told them the night before.

"See that you don't." Captain Pansho grinned and turned to Qa'Lea. "Fair weather and fair passage."

"Fair weather and fair passage to you as well, good friend," Qa'Lea replied.

Farewells said, they walked along the docks toward a set of massive, open boxes at the base of the bridges.

"Which city are we headed for?" Kylla asked, looking between the two as though not sure which might be more unpleasant.

"Onnima," Jed said before Qa'Lea could answer. "That's the one mentioned the most in Tal's journal."

"Exactly," Qa'Lea said. "And I believe I know where we can continue our search." Kylla frowned at each of them. It was clear from the scowl on her face she was trying to figure out some way of sneaking a look at Tal's journal.

They stepped into the large metal box Qa'Lea called a *lift*. A metal and glass door closed and the box began to rise along the outside of the support column for the bridge. The meaning of the name was clear, and Jed marveled at how swiftly they ascended along the side of the support column to the height of the bridge platform. It was dizzying progress for someone who had never been further off the ground than the top branches of a hollock tree. He glanced at Fallon and Kylla and saw the same mixture of excitement and anxiety he felt looking down at the water a hundred meters below. Qa'Lea, he noticed, was frowning.

"After our encounter with the fellow who has the odd-shaped head and his twin," Qa'Lea said, "I've been thinking it might be a good idea if we have a safe word."

"What for?" Jed asked.

"Similar to the way the man who was following us can have multiple copies of himself, it is also possible to copy others," Qa'Lea said. "Or to create the illusion of a copy."

"You mean the Iron Hand could have a copy of one of us?" Kylla said, her eyes blinking at the thought.

"Yes," Qa'Lea said.

"What's the safe word?" Fallon asked, looking away from their progress up the side of the bridge's support column.

"I was thinking of 'theodicy,'" Qa'Lea said.

"What does it mean?" Jed asked.

"It is the philosophical study of the question of how a creator god could be all powerful, all knowing, and all benevolent, and yet still allow evil to exist," Qa'Lea replied. "Not the sort of word to come up in daily conversation around agents of the Iron Hand, but one which is relevant to our cause."

"What's the answer?" Fallon asked. "To the question of theodicy, I mean."

"Who knows?" Qa'Lea said with an ironic smile. "No one seems to have come up with a good answer since Godfried Leibniz posed it some three thousand years ago.

"We have arrived." Qa'Lea gestured toward the door of the lift as it came to a stop and opened, revealing the walkway of the bridge.

The walk along the bridge to the shore of Onnimas was much shorter than Jed had expected. What surprised him most was how little there was to the city. From the landing at the end of the bridge they walked a little way along the grand promenade at the shore's edge, marveling at the massive stone and glass buildings. They cut down a side street, which curved sharply, rapidly closing the shoreline off from sight, and discovered the grand facade of the city's shoreline was exactly that — a facade. Once the shoreline was no longer visible, the city gave way to a sprawling mass of low buildings, none of which seemed to be in particularly good condition. It was as if the whole of the city's wealth and might were focused on presenting a good face to their neighbors across the river with little left for the people actually living there.

Jed, Kylla, and Fallon stayed close to Qa'Lea as she led them from one winding street to another and through one seedy neighborhood to the next. She explained they were headed to the hostel, an inn of sorts, a dilapidated establishment often frequented by people traveling to the Twin Cities with few financial resources.

Kellishers on their Landdesh were common guests there. It was where Tal's journal had been discovered in an air vent by the person who cleaned the rooms. Fortunately this person had given the journal to a local police officer sympathetic to the Tellandor Order. This was how it had managed to come into their possession, being passed from one set of friendly hands to another, guided at a distance by the Sentient's discreet requests.

More striking than the differences between the buildings along the shoreline and those of the city proper was the disparity between the people. While walking along the shore, the people had been very well dressed — men in long, black, single-piece suits and women in long, white dresses. They had seemed polite, though extremely cold and reserved. By contrast, in the city center, while the stark black and white colors dividing men and women were just as strictly enforced, the people themselves seemed less rigid.

One run-down neighborhood began to look much like the next and eventually, while they did not relax, the Kellishers became more accustomed to their surroundings. Coming from the Notesch Valley, they had never seen buildings as tall as those along the shoreline and had been impressed with them. Likewise, they had never seen buildings in such disrepair or people so obviously poor, and it shocked them even more than the size of the buildings they encountered at the riverside.

Jed noticed Kylla touching the Tellandor stone hanging at her chest. Whether she was doing it consciously or not, Jed thought it was a fine idea and casually slipped his hand into the deep pocket of his billowy trousers to wrap his fingers around the hilt of the ancient dagger.

"Here we are," Qa'Lea said, bringing them to a halt before a four-story building covered in thin iron balconies. "Stay close to me, and say nothing."

Both instructions seemed sensible to Jed. He had no desire to find himself more than a meter from Qa'Lea in this city, and from the constant hostile looks on their faces, he couldn't imagine wanting to engage any of its citizens in conversation.

Qa'Lea led them up a short flight of cracked stone steps, through a wide wooden door, and into the lobby of the hostel. A small, white-haired woman stood behind a desk near the front. Her dress, the same ubiquitous white they had seen covering every woman in the city, was nearly as wrinkled as her face. Behind the woman sat a wall of keys, each hanging on a small brass hook.

"I need to see room four-twelve," Qa'Lea said in a pleasant but firm voice.

"You have no authority here, priest," the woman snapped. "Best you be taking your young novices and moving along."

Qa'Lea smiled and leaned in closer to the old woman, lowering her voice and sharpening her tone. "I am on official business of the Sentient. You might say I am the Sentient's direct representative in this matter, and you will take me to room 412.

There will be no discussion of authority, and you will tell no one I have been here. And you will do this all politely and without a word, because otherwise I will be forced to threaten you, and if I threaten you, it will be very unpleasant for you."

The old woman stared back at Qa'Lea a moment, her eyes filled with a mixture of utter hatred and pure fear. Making a noise in the back of her throat like a small animal being strangled, the old woman spun around and grabbed a key from the wall. She clutched it tightly in her withered fist as she walked around the long counter and led the way up a wide staircase. Qa'Lea motioned the Kellishers to follow and began climbing the stairs behind the old woman. Four flights of stairs later, each covered by an increasingly dirty carpet, they stood before room 412.

"It's rented now," the old woman said, "so mind you don't take anything. I don't want no trouble from the tenants."

"Thank you," Qa'Lea said to the old woman. "You may return to your post. If I need anything else, I'll let you know."

The old woman frowned. Seeing she was outmatched, she grunted, turned on her heel, and headed back down the stairs.

"Inside, quickly," Qa'Lea said, ushering Jed, Kylla, and Fallon into the room before following them in and closing the door.

Once inside the room, Qa'Lea walked to the center and tapped an ornate symbol at the top of her staff with the palm of her right hand. The symbol glowed slightly and Qa'Lea began to swing the head of the staff around the room.

"We don't have much time," Qa'Lea whispered. "We'll be lucky if that old woman waits until she's back downstairs before she calls the Enforcers."

"But you told her not to," Jed said.

"People rarely do what I tell them to," Qa'Lea said. Jed very much doubted that. "Search the room."

"What are we looking for?" Kylla asked, looking around at the dingy little room with a grimace.

"Anything unusual," Qa'Lea said. "Something that might have been missed when the room was searched by the city Enforcers."

Jed, Kylla, and Fallon began searching the room, checking under the small nightstand and under the bed, not entirely sure what they were looking for, but hoping to find something useful.

"Wait. Here." The Kellishers turned to see Qa'Lea bending down to dig something out of a deep crack in one of the tiles of the floor. Pulling the object loose, she turned to them and held up a ring, round in the center but square on all sides.

"What is it?" Fallon asked.

"Confirmation," Qa'Lea replied. "This is the mark of the Iron Hand — an iron ring. A symbol they use to identify other members. Your brother must have struggled with his captors and the ring became lodged in a crack in that tile."

"So, how do we find Tal?" Jed asked, leaning closer to look at the ring.

"We need to find the owner of this," Qa'Lea said, gesturing with the ring before sliding it into a pocket deep within her robes. "But at the moment, we need to get away from this building before we attract more attention than we already have. We'll take the back stairs."

Leading the way, Qa'Lea opened the door and stepped into the hallway, turning away from the stairs they had come up and walking down the grimy hallway toward a battered metal door. The door squeaked loudly as Qa'Lea opened it and made nearly as much noise when she closed it behind them.

The back stairs of the hotel were even more faintly lit than the rest of the establishment. Jed tried not to notice the things moving in the shadows along the floor, things that could have been either small animals or large insects. He saw Kylla jump out of the way of one of them and Fallon nearly stumbled to leap over whatever it was that scuttled away into the shadows behind them. Something crunched beneath Jed's feet and he refused to look back to see what it had been.

By the time they reached the bottom of the stairs, Jed, Kylla, and Fallon were nearly frantic to get outside, but Qa'Lea stopped them suddenly, standing before another battered metal door, one presumably leading to the alley behind the hostel. She tilted her head a moment as though listening, but not at what lay beyond the door. "Stay close to me. Do not run. Stay calm. Defend yourselves if you must."

With no warning, the head of Qa'Lea's staff glowed bright blue, and with a powerful kick she thrust the metal door open and leapt into the alley. From behind Qa'Lea, Jed glimpsed three men, all dressed in black, one of whose head was markedly more square than the other two.

Qa'Lea's sudden, forceful exit from the hostel startled the three men. A blast of blue light from Qa'Lea's staff threw the man in the middle back against the alley wall. The square-headed man recovered first and swung a thin, black, metal baton, knocking Qa'Lea's staff from her hand. Spinning sideways, Qa'Lea thrust her leg out, kicking the square-headed man in the solar plexus and knocking him to the ground.

Continuing to spin, she caught the arm of the third man as he swung his metal baton toward her head, rotating the man's arm from his elbow, disarming and flipping him to the ground in one swift motion. Striking the man on the side of his neck with the hard edge of her hand, the man went limp. Qa'Lea turned to see the square-headed man standing, preparing to charge. Her staff too far away to reach in time, Qa'Lea planted her feet and bent her legs slightly.

Jed stepped from the hotel doorway just as the square-headed man attacked Qa'Lea, swinging the baton at her from every direction he could manage. Jed pulled the dagger from his pocket and the blade burned blue, just as Kylla stepped up behind him, the ancient stone held firmly in her hand. Their intentions were to help Qa'Lea, but she was so close to the square-headed man, dodging his swings and blocking his attacks, that they could not risk interfering.

Even as the square-headed man's attacks were repelled, Qa'Lea repeatedly landed strikes against him. He shrugged them off as though they hardly mattered. The square-headed man swung again, and this time Qa'Lea moved in an unexpected direction, toward the attack, swinging her body into his chest and grabbing his outstretched arm as she bent low and flipped him over her back.

The square-headed man had little time to recover before the golden head of Qa'Lea's staff smashed into his forehead, leaving him unconscious. Fallon stood above the square-headed man, holding Qa'Lea's staff.

"Well done," Qa'Lea said, standing and taking her staff from Fallon.

"It was all I could think of," Fallon said a bit sheepishly.

"I wish I'd thought of it," Jed said as he and Kylla joined them.

"You've saved us again, brother," Kylla said, giving Fallon a hug.

"Mind you don't touch the tip of that stun stick," Qa'Lea said, pointing to the head of the black baton lying near Jed and Kylla's feet. "If it touches you, you'll be asleep for hours and wake with a splitting headache.

"Quickly. We need to get out of here."

Qa'Lea turned and began walking down the alleyway when something caught her eye, and she stopped. Bending down next to the man she had knocked unconscious with a blow to his neck, Qa'Lea pulled a silver chain from his shirt to reveal a round iron medallion engraved with a seven-layer spiral. Tucking the chain back into the man's clothes, she stood up and walked rapidly down the alley. The Kellishers ran to follow her long strides.

"What about them?" Jed asked, looking back at the three unconscious men in the alley.

"Hopefully the city Enforcers will find them," Qa'Lea said. "The old woman at the hotel is sure to have called them. Which is why those men were using stun sticks instead of something more powerful. They didn't want to attract attention. This way." Qa'Lea cut down a side alley. "They probably have three more men out front. We don't want them following us."

"Where are we going?" Kylla asked, giving a worried glance down the alleys they passed.

"Back to the bridge," Qa'Lea said.

"Back to the *River Queen*?" Fallon asked, running to keep up and glancing back over his shoulder frequently.

"No," Qa'Lea answered. "The *River Queen* left long ago."

"I thought you said we had to find the owner of the ring," Jed said, a hint of anxiety creeping into his voice.

"That was before our good fortune of being attacked," Qa'Lea said.

"That's your idea of good fortune?" Jed asked, incredulous.

"It is," Qa'Lea said. "One of the men who attacked us was wearing an amulet of a Tellandor School."

"More Tellandor traitors don't sound like luck to me," Kylla said.

"It's lucky," Qa'Lea said, leading them out of the alley and onto a main street, "because it is an amulet of a school found only in one temple in one city in all of Wyconna. The Apaahand Tabernacle of New Alexandria."

"But how will we get there now that the *River Queen* has left?" Jed asked, still looking around as he spoke, expecting to see a square head appear at any moment.

"We will take the *Regent of the Sky*," Qa'Lea said, quickening her pace. "It should ready to depart by the time we make it back to the bridge."

CHAPTER 23
THE REGENT OF THE SKY

Excerpt from Jed's Journal:

"She reminds me of my grandfather in a way. Not that she's like a grandmother. I don't mean that. I can't imagine any grandmother like her. But she has some of the same qualities as Grampa. Or maybe he has the same qualities as her. She's much older. I can't believe she's that old. Maybe he learned to be that way from her. I wonder what I'll learn."

Excerpt from Kylla's Journal:

"I don't say this very often. In fact, I don't think I've ever said it about a woman, but I want to be like her. Not the robes and the Order and all that, but the rest of it. To know what she knows. To see what she has seen. To meet the people she must have met. Wonders stacked upon wonders and all waiting to be unwrapped like presents on my naming day."

Excerpt from Fallon's Journal:

"Finally! A teacher I can actually learn something from. It's odd, though. I'm not used to knowing less than someone, and with her I feel like I'm always skimming the barest amount of cream from a vast vat of knowledge. But what a sweet cream it is. I hope I can churn it into the butter of wisdom. Ick. That wasn't a very good metaphor at all!"

When they arrived back at the bridge, Qa'Lea still leading the way at a brisk pace, Jed witnessed a sight he was completely unprepared for. There in the sky, tethered between the support columns of what used to be the center of the bridge, floated an enormous aircraft.

"What is that?" Jed asked, pointing to the massive object hovering above them.

"That is the *Regent of the Sky*," Qa'Lea said, walking even faster.

"We're going to travel in that." Fallon said, less a question and more a statement of amazement.

"If we can get onboard before they cast off," Qa'Lea said, breaking into a slow jog.

"Brilliant," Kylla said, her eyes filled with sudden excitement. Jed knew Kylla was bursting to know how the massive craft remained floating in the air. Shaped like a giant flying wing, the aircraft stretched some three hundred meters from bow to stern and nearly four hundred meters at the widest part of the wing. The wing was not flat, but curved somewhat like an egg and over fifty meters thick in the middle.

In response to Kylla's questions, Qa'Lea explained while they ran that the thin silver and blue fabric covering the ship concealed a massive skeletal structure assembled from something called ceramic steel. The interior framework of the ship held hundreds of giant sacks of helium, a gas lighter than air. The sacks of helium allowed the airship to float.

Along the outside of the ship, giant turbines spun enormous blades. These propelled the craft. The silver fabric covering the top of the giant floating wing converted the light from the sun-tube directly into electricity to power the entire aircraft. Qa'Lea called the floating wonder a dirigible.

They ran across the bridge, the stone tiles clacking beneath their feet, drawing attention and discouraging stares from the locals. Qa'Lea ignored their looks. Shortly, Jed and the others stood at a booth near the base of one of the support columns. The booth sold tickets for both crafts of river and air. Less than a minute later, Qa'Lea guided them into a massive lift at the base of the support column. Moments later, Jed and the others exited the lift and stood on a small, railed platform tethered with thin ropes to another railed platform. This second platform hung down from the airship some twenty meters above by means of metal support beams. A crew member took their tickets and ushered them aboard the airship's platform, along with the other late arrivals. Another crew member cast off the last of the tethers.

"Last call," the first crew member said. "If you're not planning to fly, best be standing clear."

The few people gathered on the bridge platform saying goodbye to friends and relatives stepped back as the crew member pressed a large red button on a silver pedestal sprouting out of the platform floor. Silently, the platform rose upward into the belly of the airship above.

Jed leaned closer to the platform railing, looking down at the people and landscape below. He had never been afraid of heights, always willing to climb to the highest branch of any tree, but he had never imagined being this high before. He looked to Kylla and Fallon and saw a similar excitement reflected in their faces. Just as the urge to spit over the railing crept up in his mind the platform eased into the passenger bay of the airship.

The passenger bay had only seemed dark by comparison to the daylight outside. It was actually well lit, with wide viewing windows placed around the sides of the twenty-by-twenty meter room. Qa'Lea and the Kellishers followed the rest of the late passengers out through the wide doors leading into the main corridor of the airship. So enthralled were they by what appeared to their eyes that they barely noticed when the airship began to move, the gentle acceleration necessitating a slight lean in their walk along the ship's decks.

Although they were surrounded by giant balloons of helium, it was impossible to tell. The corridors and compartments of the airship were made from a thin material that seemed simultaneously too slim to support itself yet strong enough to stop a charging boar. The rooms and hallways were generously sized. There was an extra wide compartment called the Sky Plaza, with a ceiling rising nearly fifteen meters high, that was lined with shops and restaurants along both sides of what would have been a street back on the ground.

There were small churches and temples of every persuasion, and even a little park with what appeared to be real grass and trees. The ceiling of the Sky Plaza was covered in glass, revealing the light of the sky above. There were even windows in the walls between some of the shops. In the center of the small park sat a glass floor, allowing people to look down on the passing landscape below.

Their mouths agape with wonder, Qa'Lea led Jed, Kylla, and Fallon to the stateroom she had reserved for them. She felt it best if they all remained in one room for the duration of their overnight journey and had rented a large suite with two bedrooms, each with its own bath and connected by a spacious living area in the center.

"How can there be so much room in something floating through the air?" Kylla asked as she fell back into a generously cushioned couch.

"Size is not so much the problem," Qa'Lea said. "It's mass that causes issues. Everything you see is made of extremely lightweight material. That couch you are sitting on probably has less mass than you do. The only things they can't make lighter are food and water, which is why you will find that these rooms have only slow-dripping showers and not baths. A shame because I could use a good soak, myself."

Jed stifled a laugh at the idea of an old priest like Qa'Lea scrubbing in a bath. He sat down next to Kylla. "How long before we reach New Alexandria?"

"Sometime late tomorrow morning," Qa'Lea said, walking to stand near the other couch.

Fallon peeked out of the curtains through the wide viewing window at the head of the suite and looked at the ground below. "What do we do with the rest of the day?" he asked, turning back to the others.

"Practice," Qa'Lea said, proving her statement about the lightness of the furniture by pushing the other couch to the side of the room with one hand. "Our recent encounter has convinced me more than ever that the three of you must be able to defend yourselves in the event that something befalls me. It may have been reckless to allow you to come with me, but to leave you helpless to face of the enemies we are up against would be irresponsible. First, I will show you how to use Aaral to determine if someone is trying to use technology to eavesdrop on your conversations. Then, we will continue with your combat studies, and later, we will practice more meditation and refine your uses of the dagger and stone."

Qa'Lea held the gaze of each for a moment. "Stand up. Let's begin."

Jed and Kylla paused to glance briefly at each other before leaping to their feet. Not even having to ask how to be taught to fight, but being told they would learn was something almost more incredible than knowing they were on an airship filled with helium floating a thousand meters above the ground and flying swiftly toward a city they had only heard of a few days before.

Setting Aaral, the *Tannett*, to check for techne eavesdroppers turned out to be as easy as asking her to do so. Qa'Lea soon had them lined up and following her examples as she taught them the basics of the Tellandor martial arts. Qa'Lea explained the history of it as she guided them through the simple postures.

When the Servants of the *Tannettt* had first begun, nearly a thousand years before the launch of the *Celestial Pilgrim* on the Long Journey, there had been a strong stricture against priests using violence, even in self-defense. However, when the Sentient created the Tellandor Order, priests were often sent into hostile situations to help mediate disputes between different religious, ethnic, and even interspecies conflicts, and it soon became apparent that if the priests were to remain alive, they would need to know how to take care of themselves. Thus was born the Tellandor martial art known as Kendha, a simple but efficient set of physical tactics, postures, and moves that could be learned by anyone and applied with great success. It did not include the use of weapons, but it did focus a great deal on how to relieve an opponent of their weapon.

Jed, Kylla, and Fallon each practiced as best they could the moves and actions Qa'Lea explained to them. First there was the stance — a loose but balanced way of standing with knees bent, legs angled slightly to the side, but with the upper body facing forward, tilted from the waist to create a forward momentum. Then there was "clearing the space," which was like blocking an opponent's attack without aiming specifically at the incoming arm or leg.

Then there were the strikes, punches, kicks, evasive movements, grappling of joints like wrists and elbows, and finally throws. There was barely time for them to fully grasp the essence of each separate skill, much less master them, but Qa'Lea wanted to make sure they had as many combative tools as possible at their disposals in the event they might need them.

After several hours of practice, Qa'Lea went to a box on the wall with a small vis-sheet and ordered a large lunch. While they waited for the lunch to arrive, Qa'Lea led the Kellishers in a guided meditation. She began with the meditative practice they were most familiar with, watching their breathing. Then she modified it slightly.

"Imagine you are breathing in a brilliant white light that flows down through the crowns of your heads and into your hearts, cleansing and purifying your minds and bodies."

Jed followed Qa'Lea's instructions, feeling calmness wash over him.

"Now, imagine any anxiety or negative thoughts as a dark blue smoke, and breathe it out."

After ten minutes of trying to remain aware of their breathing and still their minds of any other thoughts, Qa'Lea continued.

"Imagine someone you have great love for."

Jed imagined his grandfather.

"Now imagine this person fading away, but the feeling of love remaining."

Jed held this feeling of love for a few silent minutes before Qa'Lea spoke again.

"The people you envisioned are not the source of that love, because you now hold that feeling without envisioning the people. Therefore, that feeling of love comes from within you, and can therefore be applied to anyone."

Jed contemplated this notion and realized it was true.

"This will be more difficult, but imagine now the square-headed man in black while holding that feeling of love."

Jed's face tensed as he wrestled with the new meditation. Struggle as hard as he might, he couldn't associate the feeling of love with someone who elicited such fear and anger. He began to suspect Qa'Lea was joking with them. Jed knew loving one's enemy was an ancient teaching in many faiths, but surely she couldn't be serious about loving this particular enemy. Opening his eyes a bit, he saw

Kylla's face wrinkled in consternation while Fallon's face remained calm, although his lips had lost the slight smile that usually accompanied the meditation sessions.

A knock at the door brought all of their eyes fully open at once.

"Lunch," Qa'Lea said, reassuring them with a smile. Shortly they were all seated on the couches, the small tables pulled up to hold their sandwiches and something the Kellishers had never tried before, but which they found quite delicious — sliced potatoes deep fried in oil and covered in salt.

"These are great," Jed said, holding up a slice of deep fried potato.

"Try this," Qa'Lea said, dipping a potato slice into a small dish with a thick, tomato based liquid. "So, how did your meditations go?" she asked as she popped the potato wedge into her mouth.

"Fine, until you brought up the man from the train," Jed said around a mouth of potato. Qa'Lea gave him a raised eyebrow, reminding him of his manners.

"And what happened when you thought of him?" Qa'Lea asked.

"I got angry," Jed said, waiting to speak until he had swallowed his food. "All I could think about was hitting him the way you were just teaching us."

"Me too," Kylla said with a frown. "It makes me angry just thinking about him now."

"And you, Fallon?" Qa'Lea asked, looking at the young boy.

"I was angry for a moment," Fallon said, a thoughtful look in his eyes. "Then I realized you were right. The feeling of love wasn't coming from the *people* we care about. It was coming from our minds, and that meant the feeling of anger wasn't coming from the man who attacked you, but was also coming from my mind. So, it was hard, but after a bit, I could make my mind feel love when I was thinking about him."

"Well done," Qa'Lea said. "It usually takes a novice weeks to be able to hold a mind of love when thinking of an enemy."

"But what's the point of learning to love your enemies when they're out to get you?" Jed asked, abstaining from biting into his sandwich until he had finished speaking.

"Because," Qa'Lea said, setting down a glass of raspberry flavored beverage that came with the meal, "if you do not learn to love your enemies and have compassion for them while you are learning how to defeat them, you will be guided by anger when you confront them. And if you are guided by anger, you will surely do something you will regret. The power to defeat your enemies must be balanced by the power to love them. Otherwise, you will bring unwanted harm to them, and to yourselves."

"How can you have compassion for people who are wicked?" Kylla asked, scowling as she bit into her sandwich.

"Simple," Qa'Lea replied. "By recognizing that the reason they are wicked is because they are misguided. As Fallon explained, anger and hatred are just as much states of mind we can control as minds of love and compassion. The wicked, as you call them, like our friend in black, have never realized this. Their minds are filled with hatred and anger and they have no notion that they can change their ways of being. By recognizing it is the state of mind that is wicked and not the person, you can cultivate compassion for them."

"What good does that do when someone is trying to club you in the head?" Jed asked, taking a swig of his fruity drink.

"A great deal of good," Qa'Lea said. "I'm not suggesting that simply because you have compassion for someone you let them abuse you. That would be idiot compassion. The most compassionate thing you can do for someone is show them the error in clinging to a mind of anger.

"However, in defending yourselves, you always want to maintain a mind of compassion and love so your actions do not become indistinguishable from those of your opponent. To that end, your actions should always be aimed at restraining your opponent, or, if necessary, rendering them unconscious. Your aim should not be to cause real physical harm and your intent should never be to end your opponent's life."

"What if you have no choice?" Kylla asked. "What if it's a choice between your life and theirs?"

"Or their life and someone else's?" Jed added.

"Such choices are very rare," Qa'Lea responded. "They can only be made in the moment, by the person in question. But I will tell you this — that choice will only ever be the right one if it is guided by the wisdom of compassion."

"And might that wisdom lead you to your own death?" Fallon asked, folding his napkin on his lap.

"It might," Qa'Lea said, looking across the table at Fallon. "But that, too, is a rare choice."

"And how do we do this?" Jed asked. "How do we learn to fight with compassion?"

"Not easily," Qa'Lea said. "You must learn to rely upon mindfulness and equanimity, the sixth principle, to sustain a mind of love and compassion. As I said, all seven of The Principles are connected. But mostly, practice. Which is what we shall do until dinner."

After cleaning up the remnants of lunch, the rest of the afternoon was spent learning more about using the ancient Tellandor artifacts. Each Kellisher focused on a single artifact, Qa'Lea moving from one to the other, giving tips in using each. They wanted to trade off, each learning how to use them all, but Qa'Lea insisted they had a rudimentary knowledge of all three artifacts, and time did not allow for all of them to gain an in-depth knowledge of all three.

The Tellandor artifacts were far more subtle and complex than Jed had assumed. For instance, he discovered the glowing blue blade of the dagger could be made harmless to the touch, and the blue light could extend into a leash of sorts that could be used to hold someone.

Kylla learned the stone could make one's own body hover above the ground and, with a little bit of practice, move through the air. Qa'Lea also began to teach Kylla how to use the stone to heal minor wounds, which involved great concentration, and placement of the stone on the affected part of the body.

For his part, Fallon realized Aaral, the sentient *Tannett*, could accomplish a wide number of tasks, such as pinpointing its position to within centimeters anywhere in the whole of the

Celestial Pilgrim, or acting as a means of communication between another sentient *Tannett*, such as Jaan'Ka, Qa'Lea's sentient tome.

The hours passed quickly, and soon the tube-light beyond the viewing window of the airship suite began to fade. Calling a halt to their studies, Qa'Lea led them to the window so they could look down on the darkening landscape below.

Even in the dimming light, the inner curve of the great starship was still visible, the walls of its tube-like shape rising up far in the distance. The fact that they were traveling toward the bow was apparent from the curving vista before them moving laterally past the window. Jed, Kylla, and Fallon stood silent at the sight, watching the lights of the houses and towns below wink into existence.

"You may not believe this," Qa'Lea said, "but the great curve of the inner hull of Wyconna is actually the reverse of what you would see in an airship if you were on a real planet. There, the horizon curves down and out of sight rather than upward."

"You're right," Jed said, struggling to envision what Qa'Lea described. "I can't believe it."

"I'll draw you a picture over dinner," Qa'Lea said. "Clean up. We'll go down to the Sky Plaza and have a real meal."

By the time they made it down from their suite to the window-filled restaurant in the Sky Plaza three decks below, they forgot about how the curvature of horizons on planets compared to starships. The conversation centered entirely upon more important matters.

"How does that necklace help us find Tal?" Jed said, dragging his eyes away from the windows that surrounded their secluded table on the far side of the restaurant and trying to focus on his plate of long noodles covered in a meaty tomato sauce. It was made with far more garlic than he was used to, but it tasted delicious.

"As I said," Qa'Lea began to explain, "the amulet is worn by a very particular order of the Tellandor priesthood and is only found in the Tabernacle of the Sun, a temple in the city New Alexandria."

"So you think a Tellandor priest turned traitor and is holding Tal in this Tabernacle?" Kylla asked, her concern for Tal obviously winning the fight with her hunger. Her plate was nearly untouched.

"It is worse than that, I fear," Qa'Lea said. "I suspect the entire Tabernacle has turned to the Iron Hand."

"Then how will we rescue Tal?" Jed asked, putting his fork down a little too forcefully.

"First, we will need to find the Tabernacle," Qa'Lea said, dabbing at her lips with a napkin.

"But you said it's in New Alexandria," Kylla said.

"Yes," Qa'Lea said. "But that does not mean I know where it is."

"We could use Aaral," Fallon offered, taking the last bite of his meal. "The *Tannett* should know."

"I'm afraid not," Qa'Lea said. "You see, the Tabernacle of the Sun is hidden. Its location is known only to those of the Apaahand School."

"Hidden," Jed repeated. "Why?"

"Because it is in New Alexandria," Qa'Lea said. "New Alexandria was founded at the launch of the ship to be an example of how faith and science could exist peacefully together. The founders insisted the city council be led equally by representatives from each major faith, as well as by scientists from each major branch of knowledge. This arrangement worked well for a while, but when the Great Upheaval began, the rift between science and religion was used by a few power hungry people to create divisiveness among the passengers of Wyconna. New Alexandria became the epicenter of violence. It was at this time that the Sentient established the Tellandor Order, sending priests throughout the ship to act as mediators in the conflicts.

"This was when the Tabernacle of the Sun was founded. Originally, it was a moving temple, more a caravan that went from city to city trying to help citizens find a workable local peace. But the Tabernacle was converted into a formal, permanent temple in New Alexandria a few years later. Unfortunately, over the next hundred years, the situation in New Alexandria grew worse, and eventually all open religious worship was banned by the city council, which had come to be dominated entirely by a clique of scientists who, unlike their ancestors, felt that true science must be atheistic.

"It was shortly thereafter that the Tabernacle of the Sun moved to a hidden location within the city. The Apaahand School remained in hiding, watching over the city and trying to bring about positive results for the citizens, but never openly revealing itself. The high council of New Alexandria made a mistake, though. Following the *Tannett* does not require a faith in the Divine, only a faith in the ability of human beings to transform their lives, to become more fully human. There is nothing in the *Tannett* that denies science or reason. Everyone can benefit from practices such as universal love and compassion. Regardless, New Alexandria, not surprisingly, has become a hotbed of recruitment for the Iron Hand."

"So how do we find the temple if it's been hidden and only the priests of the Apaahand School know where it is?" Jed asked, anxiety filling his voice.

"By following the riddles," Qa'Lea said. "Only the priests of the Apaahand School know where the temple is hidden, but there are a series of riddles and clues that will lead any Tellandor priest to its location. I have never been there myself, but the first clue is known by all Tellandor priests. By following three riddles one can find the temple, and then by solving three more, one can gain entrance to the temple."

"What is the first riddle?" Fallon asked a little too loudly. The challenge of the situation clearly appealed to him.

Qa'Lea looked at each Kellish child in turn as she recited:
"The seeker seeks
What all faiths follow.
The heart of each
Is the heart of all."

"A religious riddle," Jed said, trying to puzzle out a meaning from the words.

"All of the riddles are religious," Qa'Lea said. "To help deter anyone in New Alexandria from finding the temple. Each riddle leads to a location in the city where the next riddle can be found. But you need to know the starting point."

"So where do they start?" Kylla asked, leaning forward with such intensity that her hair nearly fell onto her plate.

"I'm not sure," Qa'Lea said. "As I said, I have never been to the Tabernacle of the Sun, but I have been to New Alexandria several times, and I know someone there, someone we can trust, who might be able to tell us where to start.

"Finish your meals. Dessert will follow shortly and then we will all need to get a good night's rest. Tomorrow will be a long day."

She turned to Jed and caught his eye. "At the end of it, Fate willing, you will see your brother."

Qa'Lea slid the last forkful of her noodles into her mouth and motioned the waiter to bring dessert. As it arrived several minutes later, a confection of cheese and sugar called a cake, but swirled with berries and looking more like a strangely thick pie, Qa'Lea's words still reverberated through Jed's mind.

Tomorrow, he would see his brother. Looking to Kylla and Fallon, he could see by their faces the words had meant just as much to them.

CHAPTER 24
THE TOWER OF
KNOWLEDGE

"Nanotechnology is the manipulation of matter on the nano-scale, the molecular and atomic scale. A nanometer is one billionth of a meter. First suggested by physicist Richard Feynman in 1959 CE, nanotechnology is the building of machines on the molecular level from individual atoms. This construction is accomplished by nanobots, small robotic machines, themselves constructed on the nano-scale. A self-replicating nanobot is the size of a large molecule and is not only able to assemble more versions of itself, but given the proper instructions, can assemble nearly anything, atom by atom, molecule by molecule, from the bottom up.

"Many of the structures of Wyconna were created using this technology. Other portions of the starship, such as the hull, were created using matter-energy conversion technology known as Flowing or Flowtech. The hull was created by first converting the mass of a lifeless solid planet into elemental energy and then back into matter in the refined form of a nearly indestructible material called weel, *which was then fashioned into the shape of the ship's hull. Flowing technology was first developed by the Androcen species and was used to create large interstellar craft. It was also used for the propulsion of such craft, prior to the discovery of Sentient-guided warp-jump travel."*

From *The Encyclopedia Wyconnica, 112th Edition*

The next morning, after a breakfast of raspberry pancakes and scrambled eggs delivered to their stateroom while they were still blinking sleep from their eyes, Jed, Kylla, and Fallon stood next to Qa'Lea on the glass observation deck at the forwardmost point of the airship. Looking down through the glass windows, Jed watched as the landscape below changed from lush forests to wide fields of grain, to houses and streets, and finally to the city of New Alexandria.

The city was well planned and its streets flowed in straight lines outward from an exceptionally tall building in the center. Seeing it from so far above, the city looked like a giant wheel, the massive structure in the middle like a central axle and the eight main streets joined at regular intervals by straight cross-streets, creating the effect of a repeating octagon. It was soon clear from the bearing of the *Regent of the Sky* they were headed directly for the singularly soaring edifice in the center of the city.

"That is the Tower of Knowledge," Qa'Lea explained, pointing to the massive building that had captured Jed's attention. "It is a library, but as it is also the tallest building in the city, it doubles as an airship landing platform."

There were a few other passengers spread around the observation deck, and Qa'Lea lowered her voice for what she said next. "I have told you a little about New Alexandria, and by and large it is much safer than a place like the Twin Cities, but it has its own features that pose a danger to us. Because the culture here so embraces technology, almost the entire city is under some sort of surveillance at nearly all times.

"There are devices so small you would never see them planted all over the city, some smaller than a grain of sand. They can see, and in some cases, hear you. These devices feed their information back to a central computer, a lesser sort of sentient, that monitors all of the images for irregularities. I assume the Iron Hand has access to this central data bank."

"Then how can we go anywhere?" Jed asked.

"While you were still sleeping this morning, I took the liberty of making certain adjustments to Aaral so she will be able to cloak you from the surveillance devices. In essence, it will intercept the signals from the surveillance devices back to the central computer and it will simply paint you out of the picture the devices see. It will work for most of the surveillance apparatuses in the city, but some may be too primitive to be affected. For that reason, stay away from small animals, birds, and even insects that seem to follow you."

"You mean to say they have techne insects in this city?" Kylla asked, her face showing both fascination and disgust at the idea. Jed looked toward her briefly. For all her courage in other things, Kylla had never been particularly fond of insects.

"Exactly," Qa'Lea said. "We should go. The ship will be docking shortly and we have much to do."

Qa'Lea led the way through the ship, arriving at the passenger platform just as the *Regent of the Sky* docked with the upper level of the Tower of Knowledge. Moments later, the bay doors opened and a covered walkway descended from the passenger compartment to the greeting deck of the Tower.

Qa'Lea led them down the walkway to a long bank of lifts. Crowding in with other disembarking passengers, they were soon on the main floor of the building. They walked past a large crystal sphere in the center of the great domed lobby and stepped out through two massive glass doors onto a wide plaza surrounding the Tower.

The Grand Plaza was a wide, octagonal space with flat, paved areas alternating between plantings of small trees and flowers. At the head of each of the eight sides of the plaza a street headed straight out into the city like the spoke of a wheel. Where the streets met the plaza, there stood eight, ten-meter-tall stone statues, seven of a man and one of a woman.

Choosing one of the streets flowing out from the plaza seemingly at random, Qa'Lea walked quickly, a chilly morning breeze fluttering the fabric of her robes. Walking beside her, Jed, Kylla, and Fallon took turns holding each other's knapsacks as they struggled into their new jackets. Jed noticed a name on a plaque beneath one of the statues they passed that said, 'Sir Isaac Newton.' Qa'Lea explained that each of the statues represented a famous scientist from the Origin World.

The streets of New Alexandria were a striking contrast to the towns and cities they had seen so far on their journey. The buildings were all nearly identical, varying little in shape, size or color, and apparently constructed from the same flat, gray material that looked far too flimsy to support the weight of the structures.

The buildings all had wide windows displaying the purpose of the rooms within. This section of the city was lined exclusively with eating establishments. Additionally, large swaths of vis-sheet covered many of the structures, displaying advertisements. These seemed to be designed to convince people to purchase different types of products, from food to clothes to techne gadgets Jed could only guess the purpose of.

As Qa'Lea briefly explained, the entire city was highly regimented in the placement of buildings. Shops were all in one section, housing in another, manufacturing somewhere else, and schools or research facilities in yet another. In addition, the city was as clean as it was regimented. The streets showed little sign of use. This, Qa'Lea explained, was because all traffic other than by foot was conducted below the street level by automated cars on tracks called transit sleds.

Above ground, only people used the wide streets, which explained the absence of sidewalks. When people needed to get from one part of the city to another, they took the subterranean transit sleds.

By the time the Kellishers had finally arranged their jackets, Qa'Lea stopped short in front of a café with a wide stone patio full of black iron tables and matching chairs. Speaking briefly to a waiter, Qa'Lea led them to a table at the edge of the patio near the street.

Waiting until their server had walked beyond earshot, Jed turned to Qa'Lea. "We've already had breakfast. When do we start finding Tal?"

"Soon," Qa'Lea said. "First I need to make contact with my friend so we can figure out where the initial riddle begins. Unfortunately, where I am going in the city I cannot possibly bring the three of you without attracting far more attention than would be healthy for us right now. The Iron Hand is looking for us. Thanks to our efforts to hide from their techne eavesdropping methods, they may not suspect we are here in New Alexandria. However, there are still many places where human eyes are just as effective a means of spying."

"You're going to leave us here?" Fallons asked, worry ringing clearly in his voice.

"Just for a short time," Qa'Lea said. "I should be back in an hour or less. While I'm gone, you can order some warm muffins and tea. I've never met children who couldn't manage to eat a second breakfast when it was offered."

"But what if you know who shows up?" Kylla asked, instinctively looking around the plaza.

"I doubt that," Qa'Lea said, smiling reassuringly. "Regardless, they won't try anything here in public. There are too many people and too much surveillance. While New Alexandria may be a stronghold for the Iron Hand, they by no means enjoy the support of the Enforcers or the City Council. If something does happen, use Aaral to contact me."

"Eat well. I'll be back soon." Qa'Lea stood and walked out of the restaurant, heading down the street, turning a corner, and vanishing from sight.

Jed stared after her for a moment, but his thoughts were interrupted by the arrival of the waiter. Following Qa'Lea's advice, they ordered an assortment of chocolate and fruit-filled pastries with cups of hot tea. As the waiter walked away, Jed noticed the small leather bag of currency still sitting on the table and grabbed it, stuffing it into the deep pockets of his pants.

"I still don't understand why they would kidnap Tal," Kylla said, looking over to see the waiter returning with a tray of delicacies.

Jed waited to reply until the waiter had placed the tray down and walked away. "I think Qa'Lea is right. His journal talks about seeing someone murdered. I think they took him to keep him quiet, and now they are planning on using him for something."

"What could they use him for?" Fallon asked, not entirely certain he wanted to know.

"Qa'Lea said the Iron Hand is trying to incite violence throughout the ship." Jed took a bite of a chocolate filled pastry. "Maybe they plan to use him to blow up a building or kill someone."

"Tal would never do something like that," Kylla said, her voice defensive on Tal's behalf.

"Not normally," Jed said, taking a sip of tea. "You've seen what sort of technology people use outside the valley. Is it so hard to imagine a technology that could control people's actions?"

"You think they might do something to control his mind?" Fallon asked, his face twisting in disgust.

"He isn't much use to them otherwise," Jed said, suddenly finding his appetite for pastries lacking.

"I don't understand why he went to the Twin Cities in the first place," Kylla said, not-so-subtly fishing for answers to questions that had apparently been on her mind for the last two days.

"I'm not sure," Jed said. "Qa'Lea may be right about him following a girl, but in the journal he only mentions her once. He says he met some girl named Mirra and that she had great things to say about Onnimas. Then the next entry has him on a train to the Twin Cities."

"It was probably a trap," Kylla said, tossing down the pastry she hadn't yet taken a bite of.

"But how could it be a trap when seeing the murder was a complete accident?" Jed asked.

"I don't know," Kylla snapped. "I just don't trust that girl. Who would lead a boy to those Cities unless they were up to no good? Men are so gullible."

"Tal is not gullible," Jed said.

"Tal is a very trusting person," Fallon said. "You remember how he agreed to help Lawfer Hannis build a fence after Lawfer tried to steal his bow?"

Jed considered that incident for a moment and then agreed. His brother *was* altogether too trusting. It came, Jed suspected, from having such an entirely good nature. Tal was constitutionally unsuited to imagine the worst of other people since he rarely encountered the worst in himself.

"Whatever the reason," Jed said, "he's in this city now. And as soon as Qa'Lea gets back, we're going to find him."

"She's already back," Fallon said, nodding in the direction of the street behind Jed.

Jed turned to see Qa'Lea walking hurriedly toward them. She stepped up to the edge of the patio, leaned over the thin chain fence separating the restaurant from the street and spoke in a low voice.

"Don't say anything," Qa'Lea whispered. "Don't ask any questions. Just leave the table and follow me."

"What's wrong?" Jed asked, ignoring Qa'Lea's instructions.

"I said no questions," Qa'Lea answered. "Something has gone wrong. We need to leave this place immediately."

"Isn't there time for one word?" Fallon asked, looking worriedly at Kylla, whose eyes were fixed on Qa'Lea.

"No," Qa'Lea said. "We must go now." Reaching out, she made to grab Jed's arm, but he moved to the side, sliding his chair back and standing up as he grabbed his cup of steaming tea and threw it in Qa'Lea's face. She dropped her staff and cursed as she raised her hands to her eyes.

"Run!" Kylla shouted, snatching her knapsack and grabbing her brother, hauling him along behind her as she jumped the low chain fence. She pulled Fallon over the fence, his knapsack in hand. Jed was right behind them, his hand pulling the dagger out of his knapsack as he leapt the fence, leaving Qa'Lea, or something that looked a great deal like her, bent over, clutching at her face.

"Hurry! This way!" Jed yelled as he dodged down a side street, glancing back to see two men dressed in black, one with a cube-like head, running up to the fake Qa'Lea.

"She must have been captured!" Fallon panted between breaths as he struggled to keep up.

"What was that thing?" Kylla said. "It looked just like her." She had the ancient Tellandor stone clasped firmly in her hand.

Jed cut down another side street and looked back, not yet seeing anyone behind them. "I don't know, but it wasn't her. She would never have given us a safe-word and then not use it. It must be technology of some sort. Maybe they made someone look like her, or maybe it's a machine that can change shape."

"We'll have to find Tal ourselves now," Kylla said.

"We'll have to find Qa'Lea, too," Fallon added. "We can't just let the Iron Hand have her."

Jed turned another corner and stopped to catch his breath. Kylla and Fallon came to a halt beside him. "You're both right," Jed said. "If the Iron Hand is holding Tal in this Tabernacle of the Sun, that's also the most likely place for them to hold Qa'Lea. First chance we get we'll use Aaral to send a message to the Sentient, and then we'll start looking for the temple." Jed chanced a peek around the corner they had come from. "All clear."

"Maybe the Sentient can help us," Fallon said as he looked around Jed's shoulder.

"No one can help you," a voice from above said.

Jed just had time to look upward as the false Qa'Lea, the square-headed man in black, and another ebony-clad assailant leapt from the rooftop two stories above them. All three landed easily on their feet, their bodies clearly enhanced to enable them to fall such distances without injury.

Jed and Kylla barely hesitated before holding out their ancient Tellandor artifacts. A blaze of blue light flashed out from the dagger in Jed's hand and struck the square-headed man full on the chest. Even as the blue light reached the man, a glow of green light surrounded him, deflecting the blue energy of the dagger away, charring a nearby wall.

"Not this time," the square-headed man snarled in a low voice.

Jed was stunned, and the fake Qa'Lea used that opportunity to swing her staff at his hand, knocking the dagger from his grasp. As the fake Qa'Lea lunged to grab Jed, Kylla squinted her eyes in concentration, and suddenly the fake Qa'Lea bounced away from an invisible wall that appeared between her and the three Kellishers.

Jed quickly reached down to pick up the blade, but it was clear the only escape from the small side street was blocked. The fake Qa'Lea picked herself up from the ground as the two men in black stepped closer, each holding a stun stick in outstretched hands.

"Come with us and you will not be harmed," the fake Qa'Lea said.

"Give us my brother and Qa'Lea," Jed said, glaring at the imposter.

"If you do not come with us," the square-headed man growled, "they will both die."

"We're not going anywhere with you," Kylla said, slowly trying to edge down the side street to the main avenue, Jed and Fallon at her side.

"They're shielded, Lakk," the fake Qa'Lea said, turning to the square-headed man. "And the Enforcers will be here soon."

"I'll deal with the Enforcers," Lakk said.

"Like last time," the fake Qa'Lea said. "I'll handle it." She turned to face the three Kellishers and raised the staff, aiming the ornate head directly at Kylla's outstretched hand. "This is far more powerful than those old toys."

"No!" Lakk yelled. "You don't know…" He was silenced by an explosion of blue light erupting from the head of Qa'Lea's staff. The blue light did not strike Kylla, Jed, or Fallon but instead flowed backward, engulfing the fake Qa'Lea and throwing her across the street where she struck the wall with a deep thud and fell, unmoving, to the ground.

The shockwave shattered the windows of buildings along the street, throwing Lakk and his companion to the ground. Jed watched as the fake Qa'Lea slowly began to change shape, her face becoming gray and indistinct until she looked like a waxy imitation of a human being.

Turning to Kylla, Jed said, "Kendha."

Kylla nodded and dropped her arm, releasing her concentration and the shield that had protected them.

Lakk was just struggling to his feet when Jed kicked him in the face, swinging his dagger out like a true knife and cutting the hand Lakk held the stun stick with.

The other man was quicker to recover, but Kylla planted her foot firmly in his solar plexus, and the man doubled over, groaning, while Fallon swung his leg up and into the man's nose.

Lakk reached out and grabbed Jed's arm, but Jed was ready and pulled the man's thumb back, firmly grasping his open hand and twisting it against the normal rotation of his wrist. Lakk groaned as he was flipped backward against his will, his head striking the pavement. Lakk raised his head almost as soon as it touched the ground, but Jed's foot was there to meet Lakk's temple, and this time when Lakk's head bounced against the pavement, his body slumped with the distinctive signs of unconsciousness.

Jed turned just in time to see Kylla strike the other man in black with his own stun stick. The man convulsed briefly and then slumped to the street. Jed ran up to Kylla and Fallon, careful to avoid getting near the fallen fake Qa'Lea.

"Hurry, we have to get out of here," he said. "You heard them. Enforcers will be here soon."

"We should take Qa'Lea's staff," Fallon said, starting toward it. Jed grabbed Fallon's arm to stop him.

"You saw what it did to them," Jed said. "Who knows what would happen if we touched it?"

"We don't have to use it," Fallon said. "Qa'Lea will need it when we find her."

"She can find it later," Kylla said, dragging Fallon down the street. "Besides, we stand out enough in this city already. If we go running around with the staff of a Tellandor priest, someone will notice us for sure."

"But won't the Enforcers already be after us?" Fallon asked, running hard to keep up with Jed and Kylla as they emerged onto a street filled with citizens going about their normal business.

"Maybe not," Jed answered, slowing to a fast walk so as not to draw attention. "Qa'Lea said she had set Aaral to fool the city's surveillance systems, so maybe all they will see is Lakk and the fake Qa'Lea."

"At least we know his name now," Kylla said.

"That one's name," Jed said. "There may be others that look just like him."

"I'll give them numbers," Kylla quipped as they turned another corner, rushing past late morning pedestrians.

"Right now we need to figure out that first riddle and find the Temple," Jed said, lowering his voice so people walking past wouldn't hear.

"How do we do that?" Kylla asked, glancing back to see if they were being followed.

"Think I know where to start," Fallon said, waiting a moment before stepping in front of the other two to take the lead. Fallon led them back to the Grand Plaza at the heart of the city.

CHAPTER 25
PATH OF RIDDLES

Christianity

"Christianity is founded upon the teachings of Jesus of Nazareth (4 BCE– 29 CE), a Jewish rabbi who offered a new interpretation of ancient Hebrew teachings. He is often referred to as Jesus Christ, Christ being the English translation of the Greek word Christós, *which, in turn, is the Greek translation of the Hebrew moshiach, or "anointed one." Christians believe Jesus was the Messiah predicted by the Hebrew Bible, that he was crucified to redeem the sins of all humanity, that he arose from the dead two days later, and that he will return to usher in the Kingdom of God."*

From *The Kellish Book of All Faiths*

Islam

"Islam, which means 'submission' in Arabic, is a monotheistic religion that evolved from the teachings of Judaism and Christianity. Islam was founded by the prophet Muhammad (570 – 632 CE). The word Muslim means "One who surrenders to God." The central teaching of Islam is that there is no God but God (Allah), that God created the universe, and that Muhammad is his final prophet. Allah, the Arabic name for God, is the same god worshipped by Jews as Yahweh (YHWH), and Christians as Jehovah."

From *The Kellish Book of All Faiths*

(More information about Christianity and Islam can be found in the *Brief Summaries of the Nine Major Human Faiths* at the back of this book.)

Jed, Kylla, and Fallon sat on a bench at the aft end of the Grand Plaza in silence. The enormity of their predicament had finally set in as the adrenaline of their escape wore off. Alone in a strange and potentially hostile part of the ship with no allies and little resources beyond the ancient Tellandor artifacts and their own wits, the three young Kellishers somehow needed to find the secret temple taken over by the mutinous Iron Hand, free Tal and Qa'Lea, and escape without being caught.

Jed sighed loudly. "At least we're not trapped under a giant door in the dark."

Kylla gave Jed the merest sliver of a grin as she turned to Fallon. "What's your plan to save us this time, little brother?"

"I don't really have a plan," Fallon said, wiping what might have been dust from his eyes.

"Just a hunch. The riddle said:

The seeker seeks
What all faiths follow.
The heart of each
Is the heart of all.

"I figured since the city is so geometric in the way it's laid out, we should go to the heart of it, to the center of the city, which is the Plaza and the Tower of Knowledge. But now that we're here, I'm not sure where to begin." Fallon stifled a sigh, his lip quivering with the effort.

"I think you may be on to something," Jed said, raising his head to look around the plaza. "All religions follow what?"

"I don't know," Kylla said, thinking through the riddle again. "Faith, maybe. Or God."

"But they don't all have faith in the same thing *or* follow the same God," Jed said.

"But they do all follow knowledge," Fallon said, perking up as he considered the thought. "They all seek knowledge of the Divine or knowledge of the self, but they all seek knowledge."

"And the heart of the Grand Plaza is the Tower of Knowledge," Jed said. "Maybe the next riddle is in the middle of the Tower. That would be the true heart of the plaza."

"There was that giant glass globe in the middle of the lobby when we were walking out," Kylla remembered aloud. "Maybe that's what we are looking for."

"Let's go," Jed said, standing up, ready to dispel his fears with immediate action.

"Maybe we should find out more about it," Fallon said.

"How?" Kylla asked. "We don't know anyone here to ask."

"We can ask Aaral," Fallon said.

"Of course," Kylla said, smacking her forehead. The notion of a book that could talk was so strange they often forgot about it completely. Fallon dug the ancient *Tannett* out of his knapsack and opened it on his lap, closing his eyes slightly in concentration.

"Hello, Fallon," the voice of Aaral said.

Jed and Kylla looked around to see if anyone was close enough to overhear their conversation with the book. Fortunately, no one was.

"We need to know about the Tower of Knowledge," Fallon said.

"First we need to send a message to the Sentient," Jed interrupted.

"Right," Fallon agreed, visibly embarrassed he had forgotten.

"What message would that be?" Aaral asked.

"Qa'Lea has been kidnapped," Kylla said, leaning closer to the ancient *Tannett*.

"I will advise the Sentient immediately," Aaral said, concern tinting her voice. "I cannot locate Jann'Ka or Qa'Lea. The Iron Hand must be shielding the signal from the tracking device on Qa'Lea and within Jann'Ka."

"But the Sentient will send help," Jed said, not sure if it was a question.

"I'm sure the Sentient will do everything in its power to find Qa'Lea," Aaral said. "And it will do everything in its power to protect the three of you."

"We're going to find Tal," Jed said, his hands unconsciously balling into fists.

"And Qa'Lea," Kylla added, her own hands gripping the hem of her jacket.

"That is not the wisest course of action," Aaral said, the tone of her voice clearly disapproving.

"We have to," Jed said. "There's no one else. Now that they have Qa'Lea, they must know the Sentient is aware that The Iron Hand has taken over the Tabernacle of the Sun. They'll be sure to move both Qa'Lea and Tal soon. We have to find them before it's too late."

There was a pause of silence, in which it seemed to Jed that Aaral was considering his statement. Thinking about it. *Could machines think like humans?* Jed wondered. *Could* she *think like humans?* He always thought of the sentient mind of the techne *Tannett* as female because of the womanly voice. He had little time to ponder the question because Aaral spoke again, her voice filled with resolve.

"It will not be the first time I have helped someone follow a less-than-wise path," Aaral said. Jed only had a moment to realize Aaral was talking about the ancient Tellandor priest Apa'Tu Kana-Shaan before Fallon interrupted.

"What can you tell us about the Tower of Knowledge?" Fallon said. "We think it's the key to solving the first riddle that leads to the Tabernacle of the Sun."

"The Tower of Knowledge," Aaral began, "is situated in the exact middle of the Grand Plaza in the center of the city of New Alexandria. It was constructed when the city was first built in the year 42 AL. Although it is used for the docking of airships on occasion, its primary purpose is as a library. The library contains every known scientific, historical, and philosophical work from all of human history and from the majority of the known Galaxy as well.

"Although all its volumes are stored holographically for consideration of space, it is also the largest repository of physical books in the whole of the *Celestial Pilgrim*. While the majority of the tower is off-limits to all but dedicated scientists and historians, the main lobby is open to the public and is a frequent highlight for the few tourists New Alexandria sees.

"In the center of the lobby is a special monument called the *Sphere of Destiny*. The name refers to the belief that all sentient life, especially human, will one day know all there is to know about the universe. The monument is capable of projecting within its glass sphere any location in the known universe that the person using it requests. The Tower first became a center of controversy during the Kadmus Affair in 195 AL when..."

"That's all we need," Jed said, cutting Aaral off.

"Are you certain?" Aaral asked. "I have access to nearly four million words about the Tower of Knowledge. I've only just given you the briefest of introductions."

"Any more and we might not know what to do with it," Jed said.

"No one ever wants all the details," Aaral said, sounding almost dejected for a sentient device.

"It was very helpful," Fallon said in a consoling tone.

"I'm sure we'll need to know more things only you can tell us," Kylla added.

"Yes," Jed said, "We'll have all sorts of questions for you today, I'll wager."

"I am at your service," Aaral said.

Fallon closed the book in his hands. "The lobby?"

"Right," Jed said, nearly bursting into a run as he stood up and faced the main doors of the Tower.

They did not run, of course, as that would attract too much attention, and attention was exactly what they did not want. They slid past citizens and walked through the massive glass doors of the entrance. There were few people in the lobby, and none near the *Sphere of Destiny* in the center. All appeared to be citizens, discerned from the tourists by the simple color overalls they wore. Most were loose fitting and in one of the eight primary colors of the spectrum of light.

Moving slowly and trying to notice everyone around them while attracting no notice to themselves, the three walked to where a slender plinth emerged from the floor in front of the giant glass sphere. Although the monument looked cloudy and filled with colored water from a distance, up close it was clear that a three-dimensional image of the universe was projected within the spherical glass. Billions and billions of galaxies crowded together.

"It's beautiful," Kylla said. "It reminds me of lying on my back and looking up at the stars near the hollock tree back home."

"It's so big," Jed said. "I never imagined it could be so large."

"I read in Aaral's pages a few days ago that our galaxy, the Milky Way, has over two hundred billon stars," Kylla said. "And there are more than a hundred-fifty billion galaxies."

"Wow," Jed said. "A hundred and fifty billion galaxies. That makes my brain hurt."

Fallon stepped up to the thin column rising from the floor and leaned close to an indented section covered in mesh that had the words, "*Tell me what you want to see,*" inscribed above it.

"Show me the Milky Way galaxy," Fallon said.

Suddenly the image before them shifted, one of the billions of galaxies growing larger and larger until it filled the sphere. A written label floated near the image reading '*Milky Way Galaxy.*'

"Show me the Origin World," Jed said, leaning in beside Fallon.

The scene within the sphere shifted again, seeming to dive into the galaxy of stars and come to center on one along a spiral arm of the galaxy. Moving closer and closer to the star, planets appeared, first one labeled '*Neptune,*' followed by a similar sized planet called '*Uranus.*' Then came a giant gaseous planet with rings around its orbit called '*Saturn*' and another massive gas planet with fewer rings called '*Jupiter.*' Then followed a reddish planet, called '*Mars,*' and then the motion of the image stopped and rested on a medium-sized planet of mostly blue water, with continents of brown and green that the floating label named '*Earth.*'

Beyond it could be seen two more planets, a cloud-filled one called '*Venus,*' and another, a small reddish dot called '*Mercury,*' which was the closest planet to the star labeled '*Sol.*'

The three Kellishers stared breathlessly at the image of Earth.

"That's where we all began," Jed said, awe in his voice.

"It's funny," Kylla said, her eyes watery. "I feel like I miss it, and I've never seen it before."

"It pulls at your heart," Fallon said, taking his sister's hand.

"Show me where we are now," Kylla told the sphere, rubbing her eyes.

The image of the sphere changed, the planet Earth receding into the distance, followed swiftly by the star labeled 'Sol' and its solar system of planets. Then the galaxy of the Milky Way receded until another galaxy came into view, one marked '*Andromeda.*' There, almost the entire distance between Andromeda and the Milky Way, floated a small dot of light labeled '*Celestial Pilgrim.*'

"We're a long way from home," Jed said. They were silent for a moment, taking in just how small and insignificant their starship was against the vast backdrop of the universe. It always seemed so enormous, this artificial world they inhabited, but it was infinitesimally small compared to a galaxy of stars, much less the whole of the cosmos.

"Show us God," Fallon said, leaning forward. The image in the sphere churned and suddenly there were words floating before the original image of the universe: "*Location impossible to verify existence for.*"

"What did you expect in this city?" Kylla asked, looking over at her brother.

"It was worth a try," Fallon said, a sheepish grin on his face.

"Show us the heart of all," Jed said, speaking to the monument. The image in the sphere suddenly went black and was replaced by a string of words. Panicked that the words might be seen by passersby, Jed stepped to the side and immediately the image in the sphere returned to that of the universe.

Stepping back to join Fallon and Kylla, the words hovering in a black background returned. Apparently only the questioner could see the result of that particular request. Quickly, Jed read the words and tried to memorize them.

"Four yokes pull the plow,
One furrow always wider.
Four good seeds meet the sun,
Eight trees bearing fruits eternal."

"Show me the center of the universe," Kylla said as a citizen began to walk around the monument. The image quickly shifted to the original of the universe with new words floating in the middle reading, "*The universe has no center.*"

"How can it have no center?" Jed asked as the citizen, a tall man in blue overalls, stepped up beside them.

"Because every part of the universe is constantly expanding away from every other part," the citizen said. "I see you are enjoying our *Sphere of Destiny.*"

"Yes, very much," Jed said, stepping between Kylla and Fallon. He had hoped to avoid interacting with the citizens of this city as much as possible, but if they were going to, it was best that Jed did the talking. Kylla and Fallon could be fine liars when pressed, but fabrication came as naturally to Jed as running to Kylla and memorization to Fallon. "It's a lovely city, too. We're here visiting from Concordia with our aunt. She's a writer. She's writing a history of the ship, so she came to use the library."

"I see," the citizen said with a smile. "And so she's left you all on your own for the day?"

"No," Jed said with a smile to match the man's. "We're supposed to be sitting at a café across the plaza waiting for her, but we got bored and decided to take a look around. We should actually be getting back. If she comes through the lobby and finds us, we'll be eating cold liver for dinner for a week."

"You aunt sounds very strict," the man said, his eyes widening slightly.

"Oh, she is," Kylla said, chiming in.

"You won't tell on us, will you?" Jed asked, a pleading look on his face.

"Oh, I wouldn't think of it," the man said. "Besides, you're perfectly safe here in New Alexandria. It's probably the safest city in all of Wyconna. There are surveillance monitors everywhere. You couldn't get into trouble if you wanted."

"Oh, we would never want to get into trouble," Fallon said innocently.

"I'm sure you wouldn't," the man said as he walked them to the door. "I'm Garrick, the Tower Custodian. If you need anything while you're here in our little city of light, you let me know. I can point you in the direction of all of the interesting things in New Alexandria."

"Thank you very much," Jed said with a wave as he stepped out onto the plaza. "We'll stop back if we get bored again." Jed glanced over his shoulder as they walked away, seeing Garrick turn and go back into the Tower.

"You don't think he suspected anything, do you?" Kylla asked, looking over her shoulder as well.

"With my brilliant acting, how could he?" Jed said, grinning lightly.

"You do have a talent." Kylla smiled back.

"But the talent important right now is remembering things," Jed said, turning to Fallon. "You can recite the riddle, right, Fallon?"

"Of course," Fallon said, excitement tinting his voice.

"Good," Jed said. "We need to find someplace where we won't be seen. That man might not be with the Iron Hand, but everyone else we meet could be. And I think I know what the first part of the riddle means."

In the starboard corner of the Grand Plaza, they found the perfect place to hide. A small group of wide trees hid them from view of anyone on the plaza, while a row of manicured bushes a meter tall hid them from anyone on the street. Sitting with their backs against the largest of the trees, they went over the riddle line by line.

"A yoke is what you use to draw a plow with an ox or a horse," Jed said. "But I've read in the *Tannett* that it is also related to the word yoga, as in the four Yogas of Hinduism. Because you yoke the ox to the plow, and with spiritual practice you yoke mind, body, and spirit together."

"Qa'Lea said the riddles were all about religions," Kylla said. "So it only makes sense this riddle has clues from Hinduism."

"And Buddhism," Fallon said. "I think the 'four good seeds' are the Four Nobel Truths of Buddhism."

"Which would make sense," Jed said, "If the 'eight trees bearing fruits eternal' refers to the Eight Fold Path."

"But what is the 'one furrow always wider'?" Kylla said, resting her chin on her fist to concentrate.

"Maybe it's one of the four yogas," Fallon said.

"What are the four yogas?" Kylla asked.

"Well," Fallon said, obviously thinking back to his late night reading of the *Tannett* and their weekly classes in the House of Light in their home town. "The four yogas are four paths or ways of achieving liberation, or what the Hindus call Moksha, which is similar to what the Buddhists call Enlightenment. The first yoga is Karma yoga, which is the yoga of action and service to others. Finding liberation in helping others. And the second yoga is Bhakti yoga, or the yoga of love, where you cultivate a love for all beings, and especially a love for God."

"The third is Janna yoga," Jed said, remembering his own time spent in weekly classes with Pastor Vannesh. "It's the path of knowledge, particularly self-knowledge."

"And the fourth is Raja yoga," Fallon finished. "Which is sometimes called the Royal path because its meditative practices lead to realizations about the ultimate nature of reality."

"There's something about eight there as well," Jed said, trying to remember.

"Yes," Fallon said. "Raja yoga is sometimes called Ashtanga yoga, and Ashtanga means eight limbs and refers to the eight limbs, or practices, of Raja yoga."

"So the riddle is talking about a single path with eight limbs like in Hinduism," Kylla thought aloud.

"There are eight paths in Buddhism as well," Fallon said.

"But what's the connection?" Kylla asked.

"In Buddhism, the Four Noble Truths are first, that suffering exists for all beings," Jed said, happy to know the answer before Fallon. "The second is the cause of suffering is desirous attachment, or clinging to external things in the hopes they will bring happiness. Then the third is that we can end our suffering by dissolving our desirous attachment and, instead, cultivate inner peace rather than outward craving. And the final Noble Truth is the Eight Fold Path, the eight practices that lead to ending suffering."

"So which one of you showoffs wants to explain the eightfold path?" Kylla said in a sarcastic tone.

"It's not our fault you're only ever interested in science," Jed said with a grin.

"Humph," Kylla said in reply.

"So the eightfold path," Fallon began, ignoring Jed and Kylla's rivalrous exchange, "is right view, right resolve, right speech, right conduct, right livelihood, right effort, right mindfulness, and right concentration."

"Hmmm," Jed mumbled. "I don't see how that helps us. We need to know where to go next."

"Maybe the path we need to follow is the same in Hinduism and Buddhism," Fallon said. "Maybe that's what it means."

"But we need a real path to follow," Kylla said. "Something that will lead to another location in the city. To the next riddle."

"Maybe it's one of the streets," Jed said, sitting up a little straighter. "There are eight streets leading out of the city center. Eight streets, eight limbs, and an eightfold path. It makes sense."

"That does make sense," Kylla said, excitement in her voice. "But how do we know which street?"

"All of the streets have statues," Jed said. "I saw an inscription at the base of at least one of them. Maybe something about the statues, who it is, or the inscription, will tell us which street to choose."

"That's a great idea," Kylla said. "But how do we check them out? We can't go running around the plaza looking at statues without attracting attention from somebody eventually."

"Aaral," Fallon said, digging the leather-bound techne volume out of his knapsack. Concentrating briefly as he opened the cover, he said to the book, "Aaral, what can you tell us about the statues in the Grand Plaza of New Alexandria?"

"Probably more than you will ever want to know," Aaral said, its pages displaying an image of the Grand Plaza from above.

"Just stick to the basics," Jed said, leaning over to better see the pages of the *Tannett*.

"Yes," Kylla added, bending over as well. "Just tell us about the statues at the head of each main street."

"Originally," Aaral began, "there were sixteen statues in the Grand Plaza, each of the current eight statues of great scientific figures from human history accompanied by eight statues of great religious figures. The statues were all created by the same artist, Jaccapo Ferretti, and they were intended to symbolize the harmonious balance of religion and science that the city strove for at the time. However, when the city banned religion in 477 AL, the religious statues were destroyed, leaving only the eight scientific heroes you see today. Starting in the sternmost corner and going clockwise around the plaza, the statues are the Greek philosopher and taxonomist, Aristotle, 384 BCE to 322 BCE; the next..."

"What about the inscriptions?" Jed asked. "What does the inscription on the statue say?"

"You said to be brief," Aaral replied. "I was going to skip over that. However, the inscription for Aristotle says, 'All men by nature desire knowledge.'"

"Mother always says that all father really wants is a second helping," Kylla said, a smirk on her lips.

"The next statue," Aaral continued, "is of Rene Descartes, the French scientist and philosopher, 1596 to 1650 CE. His inscription reads: 'Dubito ergo cogito; cogito ergo sum,' which is ancient Latin for, 'I doubt, therefore I think; I think therefore I am.'"

"Again, not helpful," Jed said.

"The third statue is of Albert Einstein, 1870 to 1955 CE, a German-American physicist who formulated the theory of relativity, which explains how space and time are really two aspects of a single thing. His inscription reads, 'All religions, arts and sciences are branches of the same tree.'"

"That sounds out of place," Fallon said, a hint of hope in his voice.

"It could just be left over from the time when the religious statues stood next to it," Jed said, not wanting to get too excited.

"The fourth statue," Aaral said, "Is of Nicolas Copernicus, 1473 to 1543 CE, a Polish astronomer who first confirmed the heliocentric theory that the planets revolve around the sun. His inscription reads,

'To know that we know what we know, and to know that we do not know what we do not know, that is true knowledge.'

"Fifth around the Plaza is the statue of Galileo Galilei, 1564 to 1642 CE, the Italian scientist who was imprisoned by the Roman Catholic Church of the time for the heresy of believing the Earth rotated around the sun. The Church was under the impression the planet Earth was the center of the known universe."

"Were they ever wrong," Kylla said, her eyes rolling.

Aaral continued, "His inscription reads, 'In questions of science, the authority of a thousand is not worth the humble reasoning of a single individual.'

"Next comes Isaac Newton, 1642 to 1727 CE. An English scientist, he was the first to deduce the mathematical laws for gravity and motion. In addition, he invented the first refracting telescope and created the branch of mathematics known as calculus, although another scientist, Gottfried Leibniz, is also credited with creating calculus independently at about the same time. Newton's inscription reads, 'I do not know what I may appear to the world; but to myself I seem to have been only like a boy playing on the seashore, and diverting myself in now and then finding a smoother pebble or a prettier shell than ordinary, whilst the great ocean of truth lay all undiscovered before me.'"

"That doesn't sound very promising," Jed said, impatient for the next inscription.

"The following statue," Aaral said, "is of Sir Francis Bacon, 1561 to 1626 CE. An English philosopher and scientist credited with creating much of what was to become the framework for the scientific method. His inscription reads, 'A little philosophy inclineth man's mind to atheism, but depth in philosophy bringeth men's minds about to religion.'"

"That sounds like it might be what we're looking for," Fallon said.

"Maybe," Jed said. "We still have two more. What's next, Aaral?"

"The seventh statute is of Charles Darwin," Aaral continued. "Another Englishman, he lived from 1809 to 1882

CE and developed the concept of natural selection, which indicates that change over time, through mutation, or evolution as it became known, explained the diversity of all life on the planet Earth. His inscription reads, 'Ignorance more frequently begets confidence than does knowledge: it is those who know little, and not those who know much, who so positively assert that this or that problem will never be solved by science.'

"The final statue is of the Polish born French chemist, Marie Curie, 1876 to 1934 CE."

"Why is there only one woman?" Kylla interrupted, clearly indignant at the unfairness of the exclusion.

"Because the scientists for the statues were all chosen from the early part of Earth's history," Aaral explained. "And much like women were oppressed and excluded by men from art, literature, politics, and philosophy, they were also excluded from science. It was only with the beginning of the twentieth century when women began to find social, political, and economic equality with men and were able to pursue interests in such fields as science. Of course, it wasn't until the end of the twenty-first century that such rights were obtained by all women of the planet Earth."

"That's still not a good excuse," Kylla said, a deep furrow in her brow.

Jed knew one of the things Kylla hated most about Kellish society was being treated differently because she was a girl, and she loathed the idea of becoming like her mother or her aunts, relegated to domestic affairs while the men were allowed to farm and build and generally have more fun, or so it seemed to her.

"What did Marie Curie do?" Jed said, hoping whatever it had been would impress Kylla enough to lighten her suddenly darker mood.

"She discovered the element radium, and much of the early knowledge of radioactivity, which is the atomic decay of certain elements, for which she received the Nobel Prize, the highest scientific prize at the time. Her inscription reads, 'You cannot hope to build a better world without improving the individuals. To that end each of us must work for his own improvement, and at the same time share a general responsibility for all humanity, our particular duty being to aid those to whom we think we can be most useful.'"

"Well, at least she has a good inscription," Kylla said, leaning closer to see an image of the statue on Aaral's pages.

"But which inscription will lead us to the next riddle?" Jed said, trying to remember them all.

"Maybe it will help if we know where the streets go," Fallon suggested.

"That's a great idea, little brother," Kylla said. "Can you show us a map of the city, Aaral?" The image on the open page of the *Tannett* changed to display a map of the city, the Grand Plaza in the center with eight main thoroughfares radiating out in straight lines. All streets seemed to run away from the Grand Plaza in a continuous line. Except one. That street ended in a park. "What's there?" Kylla said, her finger touching the page.

"That is *Pilgrim's Park*," Aaral said. "It is famous throughout the ship for being the resting place of the Launch Tree."

"What's the Launch Tree?" Jed asked.

"The Launch Tree was planted when the *Celestial Pilgrim* officially began its journey," Aaral said.

"*Eight trees bearing fruits eternal*," Fallon quoted from the second riddle.

"Are there eight Launch Trees?" Kylla asked, her breath quickening.

"No," Aaral said. The Kellishers sighed aloud.

"But the Launch Tree is surrounded by eight trees."

"That has to be it!" Jed said. "Which statue is at the head of the street that leads to the park?"

"That street, Ganfallow Avenue, is headed by the statue of Albert Einstein," Aaral replied.

Jed and Kylla turned to Fallon, knowing he would remember the inscription as quickly as they could ask for it from Aaral. "*All religions, arts and sciences are branches of the same tree*," Fallon quoted, smiling. "That's got to be it."

"Now, how do we get there without being noticed?" Jed asked aloud, peeking around the tree they sat against and looking out across the Grand Plaza toward the statue and street that would lead them one step closer to rescuing Tal and Qa'Lea.

"I believe I may be of some assistance with that," Aaral said, drawing Jed's attention back to the ancient *Tannett*.

CHAPTER 26
THE LAUNCH TREE

"If a man will begin with certainties, he shall end in doubts; but if he will be content to begin with doubts he shall end in certainties. "
Sir Francis Bacon (1561-1626)

"What is commonly called the scientific method is a series of procedures for investigating and gaining knowledge about the observable universe in an empirical and provable manner. The scientific method, as commonly practiced, has seven stages. First, one defines the question or phenomenon to be examined. Second, the researcher gathers information about the phenomena. Next, the researcher develops a hypothesis to explain the phenomenon. Fourth, the researcher creates and performs an experiment to test the hypothesis and collect data regarding the results. In the fifth stage, the researcher analyzes the data. In the sixth stage, the researcher interprets the data to determine if the hypothesis has been proven, or whether a new hypothesis and experiment are necessary. Finally, the researcher communicates the results of the experiment and the data from it with other researchers so they can attempt to duplicate the results, either continuing to prove the hypothesis, revising it, or disproving it. A hypothesis that has been proven repeatedly by the scientific method is often called a Theory. Theories that have been proven over extended periods of time are sometimes referred to as Laws."
The *Wyconna Book of Science for Students*, New Alexandria Publications, 12th edition.

With Aaral's help, they were able to navigate their way through the city to the Pilgrim's Park, using mostly side streets and alleyways. It took a great deal longer to reach their destination than simply walking down the wide avenue would have, but by the time they arrived at the center of the park they were reasonably certain no agent of the Iron Hand had identified them.

The park was well-groomed, a pleasing mixture of wide lawns, dense stands of trees, and long patches of multihued flowers. In the center of the park sat a large hill, at the top of which stood the Launch Tree, a massive redwood with a trunk nearly five meters wide and climbing over a hundred meters into the air. It was surrounded by eight smaller trees, each of a different variety. Across the hill-filled park, on the other side of a small wooded valley, lay a large and well-groomed cemetery. A few people walked through the park or sat on benches of wood and stone, but fortunately, none were wandering near the Launch Tree.

As Jed, Kylla, and Fallon walked along the stone path leading up the hill, they looked closely at their surroundings for any hint of the next clue, and marveled at the height of the Launch Tree. Once at the crest of the hill and within the ring of eight trees, the stone path broke into a circle surrounding the Launch Tree. Walking slowly around the circular stone path, the three tried to keep their eyes simultaneously on the trees, stones, grass, and sky all at once.

"This has to be the place," Jed said, coming to a stop after the first circumnavigation of the Launch Tree and leaning backward to stare at its upper branches.

"Maybe it's something on the tree itself," Kylla said, squinting at the massive tree. "In the bark maybe."

"The riddle talks about the fruit of the tree, though," Jed said, rubbing his neck as he thought about it.

"We'd never be able to reach the fruit of this tree, even if it had any," Kylla said, looking up to the lowest branches of the Launch Tree some ten meters above their heads. "I could try using the stone, but I don't know if I could get up that high."

"There's fruit on that tree," Fallon said, pointing to a tree opposite from where they had ascended the hill. "In fact, it's the only one that does have fruit on it."

Jed and Kylla followed Fallon's outstretched arm and saw what appeared to be a simple apple tree. Jed stepped off the stone path and crossed directly through the grass to the tree. "Maybe the next clue is Biblical."

"The Tree of Knowledge," Fallon agreed.

"The tree of what?" Kylla said.

"In the Bible, in the book of Genesis, the Jewish story of creation, Yahweh makes the first man and woman, Adam and Eve, and tells them they can eat anything they want except from the Tree of Knowledge and the Tree of Life."

"I remember," Kylla said. "A snake tempts Eve and she and Adam eat the fruit from the Tree of Knowledge and God expels them from the Garden of Eden."

"Right," Jed said. "And usually the fruit of knowledge is depicted as an apple."

"So you think we need to eat one of the apples?" Kylla asked, looking up at a large red fruit dangling from a branch.

"As long as there're no snakes involved," Fallon said, checking the grass around his feet. "I hate snakes."

"You first," Jed said, gesturing to the apple hanging in front of Kylla.

"Very funny," Kylla said, snatching the apple from the branch and throwing it at Jed. Jed grinned as he caught the apple, pausing only a moment before taking a large, crunchy bite. He chewed the apple loudly, taking another bite, juice running down his chin.

"Nothing," Jed said after his fifth bite. "But it tastes good. Here, have one." Pulling two apples from a nearby branch, he tossed one each to Kylla and Fallon.

"The riddle has to be in the apples," Fallon said. "I'm sure of it."

"Well, there's nothing in these apples but seeds," Jed said, taking the last bite and looking down at the seeds in the apple core. Holding them up close to his face, he squinted at them. "If there's a message in these, I don't know how we'll ever read it."

"Maybe it's not in the seeds," Kylla said, taking a bite of her apple.

"The skin!" Jed and Fallon said simultaneously, turning to each other.

Jed quickly pulled a pocketknife from the deep recesses of his pants. His first instinct had been to reach for the ancient dagger, but it occurred to him that one probably shouldn't use a sacred blade nearly two thousand years old for cutting apples. His pocketknife had been given to him by his father, and to him from his father, for several generations. While it was old, it snapped open easily and its blade still kept a fine edge.

Jed reached up and snagged another apple from the branches above. He slowly began to peel the skin from the fruit, cutting in a deliberate circle all the way around the apple. Jed soon held a dangling spiral of apple skin. Setting the skin down on the stone of the path, he carefully used the blunt edge of the knife blade to scrape the remaining pulp away until there was only the thin red membrane that once encased the apple.

"Does it have something on it?" Fallon said, uncharacteristically bursting with impatience.

"I can't tell," Jed said, holding the apple skin up to the light.

"It does," Kylla said, leaning over Jed's shoulder. With the tube-light behind it, patches of darkened texture could be seen in the cellulous matter of the skin. Patches that resolved themselves into words when looked at with the proper perspective.

"Read it out loud," Fallon said, joining Kylla to lean over Jed's shoulder as he knelt on the stone walkway.

Jed cleared his throat of an errant piece of apple and read aloud:

"Three names name what cannot be named,
Two stones of ten roll away with the one,
Revealing the sun for all to see,
While five columns support the sky,
Sheltering all beneath and beyond,
The line twixt day and night."

"What could it mean?" Fallon said, standing up to think.

"How did it get there?" Jed asked, reading the riddle from the apple skin again.

"The Tellandor priests must have altered the tree somehow to grow with that message in the skin," Kylla said, thinking it through. "Few people would be likely to eat an apple from this tree, and it would be almost impossible for anyone to notice the markings on the skin since you can only see them from the inside with light behind it. A perfect place to hide a riddle."

"Let's just hope the next clue isn't hidden this well," Jed said, starting to eat the skin. Kylla gave him an odd look. "No evidence if the Iron Hand finds where we've been. Besides, Fallon has it memorized, I'm sure."

"I think it's talking about God," Fallon said, turning as his name was spoken. "About the three names of God in Judaism, Christianity, and Islam."

"'Three names name what cannot be named,'" Jed recited with excitement. "Yahweh, Jehovah, and Allah are all names for the same unnamable God. So maybe we're looking for the same thing."

"We're looking for God?" Kylla asked, a confused look crossing her face.

"No," Fallon corrected. "We're looking for something with no name."

"What about the rest of the riddle?" Jed said. "The two stones of ten. If this is a Jewish or Christian riddle, that might refer to the two stone tablets Moses brought down out of mount Sinai with the ten commandments carved into them. What are the ten commandments, Fallon?" Jed knew it was easier to ask Fallon than try and remember them himself.

"Not to worship any other god," Fallon began, "to create no image of the divine to worship, not to take God's name in vain, to remember the Sabbath, to honor your father and mother, not to kill, not to steal, not to commit adultery, not to lie about others, and not to desire another belongings."

"I don't see how that helps us," Kylla said, staring up at the apple tree.

"Maybe all the lines together mean something," Jed said. "If the Ten Commandments were the two stones of ten, then the one that rolled away might be the stone found rolled away from Christ's tomb by his disciples."

"Which would mean what?" Kylla asked.

"I'm not sure," Jed said. "The central teaching of Christianity is that Jesus of Nazareth was killed, God sacrificing his only son so all sins of humanity would be forgiven."

"The next line is definitely Muslim," Fallon said. "'While five columns support the sky' has to refer to the five pillars of Islam."

"This I remember," Kylla said with an obvious hint of satisfaction of recalling at least some of her lessons from the House of Light. "The first is that there is no God but God and Muhammad is his prophet. Second is to pray five times a day facing Mecca, the holy city of Islam. The third is paying alms, or donating to the poor, while the fourth is the practice of fasting throughout the day during the holy month of Ramadan. And the fifth is to make a pilgrimage at least once during your life to Mecca."

"Nice job, sis," Fallon said with a smile.

"Not so easy to accomplish the fifth pillar these days," Jed said, frowning. "'Sheltering all beneath and beyond the line twixt day and night,'" he recited. "How does that connect with the other lines?"

"The line 'twixt night and day' could be twilight," Kylla said. "Or maybe a sunset. They have those on real planets. The planet rotates and the star it orbits appears to set beyond the horizon."

"We don't have a horizon," Jed said. "How could twilight be what we're looking for?"

"Maybe not literal twilight," Kylla said. "The twilight between night and day might mean the time between life and death."

"'Sheltering all beneath and beyond,'" Jed quoted, "might mean all beneath the ground and beyond the grave. So then what are we looking for?"

"I don't know." Kylla frowned. "We seem just as far from finding the next clue as when we started."

"But the next clue has to be a place," Jed said, looking out over the park, trying to clear his head.

"I still think it's something without a name," Fallon insisted.

"Maybe you're right," Jed said, his voice raising an octave against his will. "Look there." Jed pointed beyond the boarder of the park to a field of stones.

"A cemetery," Kylla said.

"And I'll bet we're looking for a grave with no name," Fallon said, bouncing on his toes.

"But how do we find the right grave?" Kylla asked. "The tube-light will start to fade any minute. We don't want to spend all night running through a cemetery."

"It wouldn't be the first time," Jed said, turning his head back and forth between the Launch Tree and the cemetery and then looking up in the sky in frustration. "Wait," he said, stepping to the side and turning around to face the cemetery again. A wide grin split his face as he turned to Kylla and Fallon. "The line 'twixt day and night.' The sun-tube."

"What?" Fallon said.

"Oh," Kylla said, turning around to the Launch Tree and back to the cemetery.

"What?" repeated Fallon, a look of clear discomfort on his face at not getting the meaning of the riddle.

"The Launch Tree and the apple tree are on the same line as the sun-tube," Jed said. "Which might just be coincidence, except if you follow that line straight out to the cemetery, it ends at the large crypt out there."

"The one that looks to have a roof supported by five pillars," Kylla added.

"And surrounded by ten grave stones in two clear rows," Fallon finished, seeing exactly the spot in question.

"I wish we could tell if it has no name without walking all the way there," Jed said.

"We can," Fallon informed him and began to dig Aaral, the sentient *Tannett* out of his knapsack once again. Concentrating briefly as he opened the cover, he said to the book, "Aaral, can you show us the front of that crypt over there?" Fallon held the book in the direction of the tomb across the park.

"I have no maps or images of that part of the cemetery of New Alexandria in my records," Aaral said. "However, I do have imaging abilities. I can show you what it looks like closer up." The open pages of the book suddenly filled with an image of the crypt from what seemed to be a few meters away. No burial name or inscription marked the smooth, stone door.

"I knew it was a place with no name," Fallon said with satisfaction.

"We should eat something quickly so we can get there before nightfall," Kylla said, grabbing another apple from the branch above her head.

"Let's eat while we walk," Jed said, impatience causing his stomach to tighten. "Every step brings us closer to Tal, and I mean to find him before morning."

"And Qa'Lea," Fallon added, taking an apple from Kylla.

"And Qa'Lea," Jed said with seriousness as he caught an apple from Kylla and began to walk toward the cemetery.

They stayed sheltered behind the trees, avoiding the open spaces of the park, as they made their way to the cemetery in the rapidly dimming tube-light. They walked briskly but did not run, knowing that too much movement might draw attention.

As Jed parted the low hanging branches of a tree, leaves brushing his face, he suddenly noticed something was different. It took him a moment to figure out what it was — silence. Just moments ago the woods they were sneaking through had been alive with the normal sounds of small animals and insects, and now there was only the rustling of the leaves in the breeze. Then he felt that familiar tingling on the back of his neck that always told him when someone was watching him. He quickened his pace as he glanced behind them, the ancient dagger sliding effortlessly into his hand.

"What is it?" Kylla asked, seeing the dagger and the look on Jed's face.

"Something's following us," he said.

"Who?" Fallon asked, looking around through the trees.

"Not who," Jed said, sniffing the air. "What."

"Gore-hounds," Kylla said, slipping the ancient stone on the necklace from around her head and grasping it in her hand, wrapping the leather thong around her wrist.

"I think so," Jed replied.

"No. Gore-hounds!" Kylla nearly yelled. "I saw something blue behind those rocks," she continued as she broke into a run.

Jed and Fallon wasted no time in joining Kylla sprinting the final hundred meters through the woods to the cemetery. Jed didn't look back for fear of tripping and falling, but he was sure there were gore-hounds behind them. He could hear large things crashing through the trees, snarling in deep guttural voices and making the ground shake as they drew closer and closer.

Once through the cemetery gates, they ran straight for the crypt. Dodging between headstones and mausoleums, Jed could hear the sounds of large, padded feet smashing into the ground and thick claws scraping against gravestones. As they reached the crypt, Jed turned and focused his mind on the dagger. The blade glowed a bright blue as it extended to the length of a short sword. Kylla and Fallon turned as well, Kylla holding out the ancient stone necklace.

Even though it was already dusk, they could see two gore-hounds bounding through the cemetery at them, blue eyes glowing in the dim light. Moving faster than Jed thought possible, the gore-hounds leapt at the Kellishers, mouths open, throats roaring, saliva flying, only to find themselves bouncing back through the air, their attack deflected by the invisible shield of the stone in Kylla's hand.

"Thanks, Ky," Jed whispered, out of breath, as he watched the gore-hounds scramble to their feet and slowly approach the three Kellishers again.

"Anytime," Kylla panted. "I love gore-hounds."

"We have to get into the temple," Fallon said, turning to examine the front of the crypt, searching for the next clue.

Up close, the crypt looked like an ancient Greek tomb with the oddity of having five stone columns supporting the weight of its triangular slate roof. Jed and Kylla glanced over their shoulders as Fallon examined the door to the crypt. Constructed of some copperlike metal with a rusted, blue-green patina, the door faintly reflected the light of the glowing dagger blade. There was no handle, but there were fourteen metal disks embedded horizontally in the door, each with numbers etched into them. The disks, Fallon found as he touched one, moved freely, spinning to reveal numbers from zero to nine. Above the disks, printed in a script too small for them to have seen through Aaral's magnified image from across the park, was a simple poem.

forever
follow
the way
the way beyond
always present and always silent
the ways number many but are always one

"It's a combination code of some kind," Fallon said, touching the first disk to the left and spinning it slightly. "We have to enter the right numbers before the door will open."

"But what does the riddle mean?" Jed asked, looking back at the gore-hounds, now approaching slowly from opposite sides.

"It mentions 'the way' several times," Fallon said, glancing anxiously at the blue eyes in the darkness. "So maybe it has to do with Taoism. There's a famous Taoist saying from the Tao De Ching that says, 'The Way that can be known is not The Way.'"

"Part of the teaching of Taoism is finding harmony and balance between opposites," Jed said, thinking back to his lessons while trying to keep an eye on the two gore-hounds. "The balance between male and female, between dark and light, between hard and soft, between action and inaction." He noticed the unpleasant balance between the gore-hounds on either side of him and licked his lips nervously.

"The yin-yang symbol," Kylla said, sneaking a look at the riddle on the door. "The black and white drops curling into each other with a circle of black in the white drop and a circle of white in the black drop."

"Right," Jed said, "But what does any of it have to do with the riddle and the lock?"

"Is there some sacred number in Taoism?" Fallon wondered aloud.

"Not one that would be as long as thirteen digits," Jed said, holding the dagger out at the gore-hound nearest him. He could smell it now, its foul breath drifting to him on the breeze.

"What if this isn't a religious riddle?" Kylla said, looking quickly between the door and the gore-hound closest to her. If they didn't solve this riddle quickly, they would soon find out if a gore-hound's teeth were as sharp as they looked.

"What do you mean?" Jed asked, backing closer to the door.

"We know the Iron Hand has taken over this school of the Tellandor priesthood, and the whole of the hidden temple," Kylla said. "So what if they changed the riddles? This riddle seems to unlock that door, and the door leads somewhere. It isn't like the other riddles. It probably won't lead us out of the cemetery, but beneath it."

"And maybe the Iron Hand changed the remaining riddles leading into the temple," Jed finished for her.

"Which means this riddle might have nothing to do with Taoism," Fallon added, switching his gaze between the door and the approaching gore-hounds.

"Maybe it did originally," Kylla said. "Or maybe the Iron Hand changed it to mislead anyone who made it this far."

"So," Jed said, "if the riddle were made by the Iron Hand, it would have to do with science and technology, right?"

"Maybe," Kylla answered, turning to look at the riddle again.

"What would 'the way' have to do with science?" Fallon asked, swallowing deeply as the nearest gore-hound licked its chops and growled.

"Maybe it's a particular branch of science," Jed offered, edging slowly closer to the door. "Like physics or chemistry or biology."

Kylla suddenly laughed aloud. She turned back to Jed and Fallon, a smile on her face. "Math!"

Jed looked at Kylla's grinning face, saw the excited gleam in her eyes, and sighed. "You know I hate math."

And then he yelled as he saw the gore-hound behind her leaping through the air. Without thinking, he raised the dagger over Kylla's shoulder even as she screamed and thrust her arm out past his head. The darkness erupted in a blast of blue light from the dagger, sending the airborne gore-hound tumbling and crashing into an elaborate statue of a woman in long robes above a grave. Fearing what he would find, Jed spun around to see the other gore-hound suspended in midair, held like a toy, as Kylla glared at it.

"Bad dog," Kylla said as she squinted her eyes in concentration, and the gore-hound suddenly flew backward twenty meters and struck a tree.

"Good work, Ky," Jed said.

"Good work, yourself," she said as she turned and handed the ancient stone to Fallon.

"Why give it to me?" Fallon asked.

"Because," Kylla said, turning to face the door of the crypt, "Jed can't use both of them at once and as he said, he won't be much help with this riddle."

"I was plenty of help with the other riddles," Jed said defensively as he eyed the recovering gore-hounds.

"Which is why it's my turn," Kylla said, staring at the numbers.

"What do you mean by math?" Fallon asked, looking up at the numbers again, attempting to glimpse what his sister had apparently seen.

"Math," Kylla repeated. "The one discipline that all other scientific disciplines rely upon."

"Okay," Jed said, stepping closer to Kylla as he tried to keep an eye on both gore-hounds at once. "I can see how math might be involved since we obviously need to find a combination of numbers, but how does that help us to find the right code?"

"The code is in the poem," Kylla said, clearly enjoying the need to explain the solution to Jed.

"Oh, I see," Fallon said with a grin. "How simple." Which was exactly what Jed was hoping Fallon wouldn't say. If there was one thing Jed hated even more than the threat of being torn apart by gore-hounds, it was being the only one who didn't understand something.

"How can we decipher a code in a poem that long?" Jed asked, hazarding another glance at the riddle again in an attempt to figure it out before the gore-hounds launched another attack, or worse yet to Jed, before suffering the indignity of Kylla's explanations.

"The code isn't in the words," Kylla said. "It's in the number of words. One in the first line, one in the second, two in the third, three in the fourth, five in the fifth, and eight in the sixth."

"Ah," Jed said, finally seeing it. "One and one makes two, one and two makes three, two and three makes five, three and five makes eight. It is easy."

The gore-hounds were closer now, moving slowly but steadily toward the three Kellishers. Fallon held out the ancient necklace, clasping it in both hands.

"It's called a Fibonacci sequence," Kylla said in an anxious voice as she began to enter the numbers by spinning the metal discs to the correct position. "It was discovered by Leonardo Fibonacci, an Italian mathematician back on the Origin World. Apparently it shows up in all kinds of places, especially in nature. I read about it in a restricted book I snuck out of the town library. The final sequence for the door is one, one, two, three, five, eight, thirteen, twenty-one, thirty-four, and fifty-five."

"That's fascinating, but I don't think the gore-hounds care," Jed said, watching as the two beasts pushed up against the invisible shield, digging their claws into the ground, muscles bulging as they slowly edged closer and closer to the Kellishers.

"They're pushing it back," Fallon said, as his feet slid toward the crypt. Jed's arms shook as he held out the dagger and let the blade burn a brilliant azure. He worried that if Fallon's grip on the shield faltered, the blade might only stop one of the creatures, leaving the other free to rip human flesh from bone.

"Almost got it," Kylla said, her hands trembling with tension as she spun the last metal dial.

As Kylla rotated the dial into place, there was a sudden hiss of air and the massive metal door lurched inward, pulled straight back by some unseen force. The darkness within the crypt would have seemed frightening were it not for the beasts growling at them from the blackness of the cemetery.

Jed grabbed Fallon by the shoulder and pushed him into the crypt as Kylla dashed through the door. As they moved, the gore-hounds leapt and Jed jumped backward, holding the dagger with both hands, a wall of flaming blue light erupting in the doorway as Kylla grabbed his arm and pulled him inside. Tripping as he stumbled backward, Jed fell to the ground, the light of the dagger winking out.

As soon as they crossed the threshold of the door, it quickly began to close behind them. They could see the blue eyes of the gore-hounds leaping at the entrance. The sound of their massive bodies striking the copper door reverberated in the small, dark chamber. Gloom engulfed the interior of crypt as the massive copper door slid fully into position. In the darkness, the sound of the tumblers on the lock spinning back to zero could be heard along with the claws of the gore-hounds scraping against the stone of the crypt wall, the beasts relentlessly seeking some entrance to their prey.

"I don't like this," Kylla said, the sound of claustrophobic panic rising in her voice. She reached out and grasped her brother's hand.

"It's okay," Jed said as a dim blue light began to fill the room. Jed held the ancient dagger before him like a lantern in his right hand, the low level of energy from the blade casting enough light to see several meters in front of them. Inside the crypt, there was nothing but a spiral stone staircase descending into the pitch black shadows beneath the floor.

"Why is it always a spiral staircase going down into darkness?" Jed asked rhetorically. "Why not something straight and well lit?"

"Because then we wouldn't be scared, silly," Kylla said, noticeably trying to calm her voice.

"How far down does it go?" Fallon asked, looking down the curve of the stairs.

"Only one way to find out," Jed said, placing a hand on Kylla's shoulder. "Want to go first?"

"I found the way in," Kylla said with a swallow. "I think someone else should go first."

"I'll go," Fallon said and started to step forward. Jed put his arm out to stop him.

"Not yet," Jed said. "Get Aaral out. If the whole city has some kind of techne surveillance, then surely the Iron Hand has some way of watching the entrance to their hidden temple."

Fallon pulled the techne *Tannett* from his knapsack. Jed took it from his hands and closed his eyes to concentrate while opening the front cover. "Aaral, can you hide us from surveillance devices of the Iron Hand as well as the city?"

"I can try," Aaral said. "As long as the Iron Hand is using more advanced technology I should be able to cloak you from their imaging, in most circumstances. However, if they are relying on older technology that has a direct, hard-wired feed from a camera to the central computer rather the than more typical nanotechnology methods, I won't be able to do anything about it."

"Just do what you can," Jed said, trying to remember what a camera was and wondering what nanotechnology might be. Closing the *Tannett*, he handed the volume to Fallon and stepped toward the spiral staircase. Kylla and Fallon hesitated for only the briefest of moments before following him.

Kylla and Fallon each placed a hand on Jed's back, as much for balance as for reassurance. The stairs went down only twenty meters or so.

They ended in a large, circular room some fifteen meters in diameter with seven corridors leading out of it. Jed, Kylla, and Fallon slowly looked around, staying close to the light of the dagger and examining the room for any clues to the next riddle. A series of letters was carved in stone above the entrance to each corridor — H, HE, NE, AR, KR, XE, and RN.

"Another code?" Jed wondered aloud as he held the dagger higher to read each set of letters.

"But where's the riddle?" Kylla asked, scanning the wall between the corridors for any sign of writing.

"Here," Fallon said, pointing to the floor beneath the final step of the staircase. "We walked right over it." Jed and Kylla gathered close to read the single sentence carved into the floor of the room.

"*Follow not the noble path.*"

"That doesn't make any sense," Kylla said, frowning.

"It does if you're the Iron Hand," Jed said, turning around to look at the corridors.

"But what does it mean?" Fallon asked. "How does that have anything to do with the letters above the corridors?"

"Maybe one of the paths, one of the corridors, is noble," Kylla suggested.

"Or maybe all but one are noble," Jed countered.

"What are the letters?" Fallon said. "They aren't Roman numerals."

"No," Kylla said, squinting her eyes to see them in the dim light of the dagger. "They're elements."

"Elements?" Jed asked.

"The abbreviations of elements on the periodic table," Kylla said.

"Another book stolen from the library?" Jed said with a teasing but admiring tone.

"Now you'll be glad all I read about is science," Kylla said with a grin.

"'H' is hydrogen, isn't it." Fallon said as more of a statement than a question.

"Yes," Kylla said, looking again at the letters above the other corridors. "He is helium, and Ne is neon, and Ar is argon. I think Kr is krypton and Xe might be Xenon. I don't remember the last one. Maybe Radon for Rn."

"Those are all gases, aren't they?" Jed said, trying to add to the progress of deciphering the riddle with his limited knowledge of science.

"They are," Kylla said. "So maybe we follow H for hydrogen, which would make sense, as it's the first element on the periodic table."

"Or maybe that is there to trick us," Fallon said. "Maybe hydrogen is supposed to be noble because it's the most common element in the universe and we're supposed to follow one of the other corridors."

"No," Kylla said a little more firmly. "Jed's right."

"Of course I am." Jed said with surprise. "About what?"

"They are all gases," Kylla said. "And except for one, they're all noble gases. If a gas is noble, it doesn't react. Hydrogen is the only one that isn't a noble, or inert, gas. Hydrogen will react with other elements. That's the corridor we take."

Kylla, excited by solving the riddle, started down the corridor without hesitation. She only stopped when she realized Jed and the light from the dagger weren't following her.

"What are you waiting for?"

"Nothing," Jed said, surprised Kylla's fear of small spaces could be overcome by a few moments of intellectual curiosity. Placing an arm around Fallon, he stepped quickly to catch up with Kylla. Together, the three of them walked cautiously down the corridor, the light of the dagger soon illuminating yet another circular room.

Five meters in diameter, the chamber contained only the door they had entered through. The walls of the room were smooth stone and revealed no evidence of writing.

In the center of the room sat a wide circular dais standing a little over a meter tall with a single, round, green glass crystal the size of a fist embedded on a flat, altar-like surface. To the right side of the crystal rested a vertical row of eight metal dials, much like the numbers on the door they had passed through up at the crypt. Each dial could be spun and had words written around its circumference, with a blank space between them. Jed reached out a hand to spin the dial at the top of the row. It had only two words written on it: *Eukarya* and *Bacteria*. The second dial had four words on it: *Animalia, Plantae, Fungi, and Monera*.

"They seem to be classifications from biology," Jed said, spinning the other dials slowly, tripping over the words as he tried to pronounce them.

"Maybe we need to classify something to solve this riddle," Kylla said.

"What riddle?" Jed asked. "There's nothing written anywhere."

"Maybe it isn't something written," Fallon said, reaching out a hand and placing his palm on the green crystal of the dais. Suddenly, an image in brilliant, three-dimensional color flickered into being several centimeters above the surface of the dais. The fifteen-centimeter image of a human being standing naked suddenly shifted to the image of a fly, then a pea, then a fruit fly, then a mass of tubular-shaped objects that seemed to have a cellular structure. Then the image of the human man appeared and the series started to flash through again from beginning to end.

"We classify one of these," Fallon said, yanking his hand back just as the human appeared again. The image of the human remained hovering above the dais.

"What happens if we get it wrong?" Kylla wondered aloud.

"The roof probably falls in," Jed said, looking up to the ceiling to check for cracks and finding none.

"Each dial has a blank space," Fallon noted. "So as long as we don't turn the last one until we're sure, we should be fine."

"As long as we get each level right," Jed said with a sigh. "The only thing I hate worse than math is biology."

"Well," Kylla said, leaning closer to the dials, "the first one is definitely 'Eurkarva' because it certainly isn't 'Bacteria.'"

"And the second is probably Animalia," Jed said, bending close with the dagger to provide more light.

Jed spun the third dial and they read them silently together: "Arthopoda, Chordata, Magnoliophyta, Basidiomycota, Eubacteria."

"Arthopods are insects," Fallon said. "And Eubacteria is bacteria."

"I think it's chordate," Kylla said. "If I remember right, it means having a hollow nerve cord. That only fits humans from the images we saw."

Kylla spun the dial into place and then turned the next dial to show 'Insecta, Mammalia, Magnoliosida, Homobasidiomycetae, Proteobacteria.'

"Mammalia, for mammals, right?" Jed asked.

"Yes," Kylla said. The next dial read: 'Diptera, Enterobacetriales, Fabales, Agaricales, Primates.'

"Primates," Fallon said, excitement in his voice. "Like monkeys and apes."

"Right," Kylla agreed, turning the dial. The words on the sixth dial read: 'Fabaceae, Hominidae, Enterobacteriaceae, Amanitaceae, Drosophilidae.'

"Just three more," Jed said, tensing his grip on the dagger.

"I think it's Hominidea," Kylla said, sounding less certain than she had before. "It means being bipedal and having big brains. I think."

"It used to," Fallon said, almost shyly. "I read the same book when you were asleep. But Hominidea, or Hominid, still refers to humans and apes."

"Glad to see I'm not the only one whose books you read when they weren't looking," Jed said, smiling at Fallon before looking back to Kylla. "Just two more."

Kylla spun the next-to-last dial to reveal the words: 'Amanita, Pisum, Drosophila, Homo, Escherichia.'

"That's easy," she said.

"Homo as in hominid," Jed finished.

"Exactly," Kylla said, already beginning to turn the last dial.

"It also means 'man' in Latin, an important ancient language of the Origin World," Fallon said almost absentmindedly.

"How could you possibly know that?" Jed asked, momentarily forgetting all about the riddle as he stared at Fallon.

"I read a lot of people's books while they aren't looking," Fallon said. "And I've been reading the *Tannett* as much as I can. Oh. I should have thought of that."

"The last one is easy," Kylla said, looking at the words on the dial and reading: 'D. melanogaster, P. sativum, H. sapiens, E.coli, A. muscaria.' "It must be H. sapiens." She spun the final dial into place and a low rumble reverberated throughout the room.

"Are you sure that was right?" Jed said, looking around nervously. "Maybe we should have chosen the bacteria to classify since all the names seem to have some form of the word bacteria in them."

"They're right. I'm sure of it," Kylla said as the rumbling grew louder.

"We should have just asked Aaral," Fallon said. "I don't know why I didn't think of it."

"Look!" Jed said, pointing toward the door with the light of the dagger. A wall of stone slowly covered the door. They ran, but it was too late. The stone blocked the doorway.

"I don't know what was wrong!" Kylla said, angrily slamming her hand against the rock now covering the doorway. "Ouch," she said and looked at the wall again. "It's still moving."

"What?" Jed asked, holding the light from the dagger closer.

"The room is turning," Kylla said.

"The doorway must be spinning to another corridor," Jed said in a near-whisper.

"That's the last of the riddles," Fallon added.

"Unless the Iron Hand has added more," Jed said.

"We'll find out soon enough," Kylla said, pointing to the doorway where the first crack of a new corridor was coming into view as the room continued to rotate.

Light from the corridor filled the chamber. They watched breathlessly as the turning of the room finally stopped. They looked down a long, metal hallway. Thin strips of glowing white material lined the ceiling as the corridor stretched out before them. The end of the passageway was lost in a haze of bright light obscuring its end point. Jed walked tentatively into the corridor, Kylla and Fallon slowly stepping behind him.

"I wonder what's at the end of it," Kylla said.

"Tal and Qa'Lea," Jed said, letting the glow of the dagger fade, but keeping it firmly in the grasp of his right hand. He walked down the brightly lit hallway toward the ancient Tabernacle of the Sun — toward Tal and Qa'Lea and the Iron Hand.

CHAPTER 27
THE TABERNACLE
OF THE SUN

Iron hand: noun

"Rigorous or despotic control."
The New Wyconna Dictionary, 97th Edition

"For too long, the reasonless masses have held the destiny of our species captive in an iron hand of ignorance. This steel grip can only be broken by another iron hand. The Iron Hand of Reason must be closed to forever crush the rule of the superstitious. We must replace faith with logic, belief with knowledge, and religion with science."

Excerpt from the *Iron Manifesto*, the founding document of the Iron Hand, recovered from a memory scan of the captured and convicted mutineer Ballus Hadrote, 1987 AL (5298 CE)

Jed, Kylla, and Fallon walked along the metal corridor toward the source of the brilliant light at the end. They kept a steady pace, walking briskly, but not too fast, unsure of what might happen with every step closer to the light. Soon, light began to fill the corridor, and what lay beyond the opening before them became clear. Jed could see what looked like balconies and walls of glass. Before long, they reached the end of the corridor, and Jed stared through wide stone arches at a cavernous chamber beyond.

The end of the tunnel had no door and Jed, Kylla, and Fallon crouched down as they crept closer to the entrance. The temple Jed beheld was not at all what he expected and unlike any temple he had ever heard about.

The Tabernacle of the Sun was constructed in a large, underground chamber, circular in shape, with seven levels of stone balconies reaching from the courtyard in the center upward. Each balcony was wider than the one below it, making the temple seem like a massive bowl, carved out of the hull of the ship. The backsides of the balconies were lined with doors, each apparently leading to some room or hallway within the temple itself. Above the shaft of temple balconies hung a massive dome glowing with light, much like the sun-tube of the ship above ground.

Jed peeked out of the corridor to make sure they weren't seen, then snuck out to the edge of the solid metal railing at the rim of the balcony. The corridor exited onto the third of the seven levels. Looking around, Jed could see that, although his position was exposed to the balconies above, no one was standing or walking on them. It took him a moment to realize that for a Tellandor temple, it was oddly sterile. In certain spots large statues, probably of a religious nature, had been violently removed. The new occupants of the temple had stripped it of all religious symbols and relics.

Jed motioned to Kylla and Fallon, who silently joined him. Sliding his head above the railing, he got a better look at the courtyard below and had to slap a hand over his mouth to stifle a gasp.

The bottom two balconies of the temple were filled with men and women in long white robes, all staring intently at the people entering the courtyard below them.

A dark-suited Lakk thrust Qa'Lea into the courtyard. Although her hands were bound behind her back, she held her head high. Lakk shoved her to the center of the courtyard where an old stone altar sat. Behind him stood another henchman in black, holding Qa'Lea's staff and her *Tannett*.

A flurry of whispers erupted throughout the crowd of white-cloaked men and women. Jed was not sure what they were, but he was certain they were not priests. No Tellandor priest, regardless of School, had ever worn robes of white. Most likely, they were all agents of the Iron Hand.

"They have Qa'Lea," Jed whispered to Kylla and Fallon. Exchanging glances of surprise, they each shot their heads over the railing for a quick look. Jed pulled them back down almost as soon as they were up. "We might be seen."

"There," Kylla said, pointing along the curve of the balcony they were on to a pedestal of stone that must have once held a religious statue of great size. Silently, they crept along the floor of the balcony, careful not to let their heads pop above the railing, until they reached the stone pedestal. The top of the pedestal was smooth, as though the statue had been cut away with some incredibly sharp blade. Its girth and height created a perfect shadowed vantage point. As they stood up into the shadow of the pedestal, hidden from the view of those below, the crowd beneath them suddenly fell silent.

Jed had only moments to realize the crowd had quieted because a man walked into the center of the courtyard, heading straight for Qa'Lea and Lakk. Tall and thin with long, jet-black hair and a round face, the man stepped calmly toward Qa'Lea. He also wore a white robe, although his was adorned with a metal belt that made it seem both functional and slightly uncomfortable. The man stopped in front of Qa'Lea and gazed at her for a moment. No emotion registered on the man's face, at least not from where Jed could see. Then the man turned away from Qa'Lea and addressed the audience above.

"It is good to see the faithful so well in attendance." The man laughed in a deep booming voice which rose up easily through the balconies, aided, no doubt, by the natural acoustics of the space. "I am honored today to present to you one of the enemy's chief counsels — a woman you all know by reputation, if not by name. Fortune has given us Shann'Ka Qa'Lea, the Sentient's right hand, if it were to have a hand. Her presence here, in submission to us, is a sign of our progress. This is a sign I wanted all of you to witness so you might not only quell any doubts of your own, but so you can return to your flocks and spread the word among all the faithful. You will reassure them not only is all going well, but things are going better than expected."

"You will never succeed, Drakkor," Qa'Lea said, her voice carrying as easily up through the balconies as that of her captor.

Drakkor turned slowly away from the crowd to face Qa'Lea, his eyes filled with dark fury. "I hate being interrupted. Especially by savages."

"Only savages resort to violence to press their demands," Qa'Lea countered, the glare of her eyes every bit a match for Drakkor's.

"Only savages believe in that which science has disproved," Drakkor said, a murmur of assent rising among the crowd above.

"Science cannot answer all questions," Qa'Lea replied.

"This is not a debate, old woman," Drakkor said with a smile. "Your opinion is not required."

"The Sentient knows all about the Iron Hand," Qa'Lea said.

"The Sentient knows far less than it suspects," Drakkor replied. "And what it does know is irrelevant, as it can prove nothing. Without proof, it can take no action. Which is why the Sentient and the First Generation Crew will soon be as forgotten as the primitive beliefs that once dominated this hall."

"You have defiled this temple with your presence," Qa'Lea said.

"This temple was in near ruins when we found it," Drakkor said. "There were only a handful of primitives to maintain it. Without the followers of the Iron Hand, it would have been forgotten."

"Your false priests make a mockery of what this hall was built to express," Qa'Lea said with clear disgust.

"We have held this hall for nearly two decades," Drakkor said. "And when the Iron Hand has taken the ship it will be remembered as a bastion of light in a time of darkness. It will become a center of a new class of priests devoted not to superstition, but to science."

"Abandoning your faith in the Divine for atheism," QaLea said, "doesn't mean you must abandon your humanity."

"One cannot be truly human," Drakkor said, "until one transcends human frailties like emotion and superstition for logic and empirical knowledge. These twin guides will lead us to a greater human condition. One where we are free to be what we choose to be rather than what random chance has made us."

"You realize, of course," Qa'Lea said with a hint of sadness, "that you are really quite insane."

Drakkor's hand flew out and slapped Qa'Lea across the face. The surprised gasp of the crowd masked the similar but louder noises made by the Kellishers hidden in the shadows above. Drakkor composed himself, forcing the rage reddening his face to subside.

"While I would love to execute you under my own authority, which I assure you is nearly absolute, the Iron Council has other uses for a favored pet of the current Sentient. Take her to the holding cells."

Lakk shoved Qa'Lea roughly toward one of the several doorways exiting from the courtyard as Drakkor turned to the crowd above. "Our time is at hand," he said, his voice filled with passion. "We have been denied our proper place for too long. For ages, the influence of the primitives has held sway. Knowledge will be returned to its rightful place at the head of society and superstition will finally be banished forever. Now that our long journey nears its end, it is more important than ever that we of the Iron Hand control the destiny of the ship. When we take control of the ship, we will take control of our destiny. Return to your places in Wyconna and spread the word. A New Age of Reason is about to begin!"

Drakkor bellowed his last words and the crowd exploded in response, people applauding, shouting agreement, and raising their fists. Drakkor bowed slightly to the crowd and then walked out of the courtyard. It was only a few moments before the crowd began to disperse, exiting through the main doors at the four points on each balcony.

Within a few minutes the balconies of the temple were empty, and Jed turned to Kylla and Fallon. "We have to follow them and see where they took Qa'Lea." The three ran toward a set of stairs leading down to the next level of balconies.

"There must be another way into this place," Kylla said as they sprinted. "How else could all those people get here?"

"How could it be this big?" Fallon asked, stretching his legs to keep up. "How thick is the hull of the ship and how thin is it beneath that courtyard?"

Running down the nearest flight of stairs, Jed said, "I think it's under the Launch Tree. The Launch Tree was on a big hill and I think the corridor from the cemetery leads back here, under the Tree. So the hull doesn't have to be that thick."

"What do we do if someone sees us?" Kylla asked, pulling the leather lanyard from her neck and clutching the ancient stone in her hand.

"I don't know," Jed said, adjusting his grip on the ancient dagger as they raced down the last set of stairs. They dashed across the courtyard toward the door where they had seen Lakk take Qa'Lea.

Suddenly, a heavyset man in a white robe stood in the doorway facing them.

"What the…" the man said in surprise.

Jed skidded to a stop, looking up into the man's jowly face. The man opened his mouth to shout but suddenly flew backward through the air, striking a wall and falling in an unconscious heap to the floor. Jed turned to see Kylla standing beside him with her arm outstretched, the Tellandor stone clutched in her hand, her face a mixture of fear and surprise.

"You're getting pretty good with that thing," Jed said, stepping into the room beyond the courtyard.

"I was just going to push him out of the way," Kylla said, following Jed. "I guess I used more energy than I planned."

"What do we do with him?" Fallon asked as he closed the door to the courtyard behind them.

"Harrish Gatter," Jed said, referring to a classmate from home who had run afoul of them once by stealing a loaf of raisin bread and getting Jed blamed for it.

Jed reached in his knapsack and pulled out a length of twine he quickly cut with the dagger. Tossing the dagger to Kylla, he began tying the man's hands and feet while she used the blade to cut a strip of cloth from the man's robes and stuffed it in his mouth. The room had only one other door, but it did contain several large cabinets. Fallon opened one of these and began shifting stacks of papers and small metal boxes. It took all three of them to roll the rotund form of the unconscious man across the room and shove him into the cabinet.

"That'll have to do," Jed said, leaning with all his might against the cabinet door to force it shut. Kylla and Fallon opened the inner door to the hallway beyond as Jed joined them and pulled the door closed. The hallway was well lit and had several other corridors intersecting with it. Doors lined the corridors, each looking the same as the next.

"Oh no," Jed said, desperation in his eyes as he looked down the corridor, crisscrossed with more corridors. "How will we ever find them?"

"We can't check every room," Kylla said, her voice reflecting the desperation of Jed's face. "We don't have time. Someone will find us."

"Maybe Aaral can help," Fallon said, pulling the ancient *Tannett* from his knapsack. Hardly pausing to concentrate his mind, he opened the cover of the book and addressed it. "Aaral. Can you show us the insides of the rooms behind these doors the way you could show the crypt from a distance?"

"No," Aaral said. "I cannot see through walls."

"We have to check them all," Jed said with determination.

"However," Aaral continued, "by viewing the infrared spectrum I can show the heat signature within each room, and you will be able to see if there are people in them."

"Can we tell what the people look like?" Kylla asked.

"No," Aaral answered. "But you would be able to see size and shape, and I should be able to discern between male and female. I assume we are looking for Qa'Lea and Jed's brother."

"Yes," Jed said, looking at the first door hopefully.

"Then point me in the direction of the door and we shall see what we can find," Aaral said. Fallon held the ancient *Tannett* up to the first door in the hallway and an image appeared on the pages of the open book. The image was in dark blues and greens.

"The room is empty," Aaral said. "Humans and other beings giving off heat will appear in shades of red and orange."

"Right," Fallon said and moved to the next door. Jed and Kylla took up positions on either side of Fallon, one looking down the hallway and the other looking backward, waiting for the arrival of anyone in a white robe or a black suit.

The next room proved to be empty as well. And the next, and the next, and the next. They moved along the hallway, room by room, as fast as they could. A door to one of the rooms began to open, and they slipped around a nearby corner into a side corridor as a woman in a white robe stepped out. Clinging to the wall and grasping the ancient artifacts in their hands, they watched as the woman walked away without noticing them. Waiting until she was out of sight, they hurriedly resumed their search.

The next corridor proved little better. The first room was clearly occupied, but the size of the human being within, appearing as a giant red shape outlined in orange and yellow, was clearly too large to be Tal. Quietly they slipped past the door and moved to the next one across the hall.

They went on like this for thirty tension-filled minutes, checking rooms with Aaral, ducking into side corridors when people in white robes appeared, and breathlessly hoping each new room would reveal some reddish-orange shape who might be Tal. Finally, at the last room in the fifth hallway, they saw a shape projected on Aaral's pages that gave them hope.

"It's certainly a male," Aaral said, "although it is difficult to judge the age of the individual as he is lying down on what may be a bed or cot. He may be sleeping."

Jed tried the handle of the door. "Locked."

"What do we do?" Kylla said, looking back down the hallway.

Jed shrugged and knocked quietly on the door. The image of the person on the pages of the *Tannett* moved. Jed knocked quietly again, and the reddish-orange image of the person sat up. Jed knocked a third time and watched as the colorful image walked to the door.

"Tal?" Jed whispered.

The image of the person behind the door momentarily jumped back and the then lurched forward.

"Jed! Is that you?"

CHAPTER 28
RELATIVE RESCUE

"Do the duty which lies nearest to you, the second duty will then become clearer."
Thomas Carlyle (1795 – 1881 CE)

"Honor is the reward of virtue."
Marcus Tullius Cicero (106 – 43 BCE)

"Man's enemies are not demons, but human beings like himself."
Lao Tzu (6th Century BCE)

"Science tells me how the universe is and why it is this way, but not how I should live in it, or why I should live that way. But I'm thankful for science all the same."
Shann'Ka Linneay Gal Sallon of the Paris School,
Tellandor Order

Tears welled up in Jed's eyes at the sound of his brother's voice. He turned to see equally teary faces of Kylla and Fallon.

"What are you doing here, Jed?!" Tal whispered from behind the door.

"We're here to rescue you," Jed said, trying to sound as matter-of-fact as possible.

"We?" Tal asked from behind the door. "Who's with you?"

"Me, Tal," Kylla said, leaning in close to the door. "And my brother, Fallon."

"You fools, you shouldn't be here, it's too dangerous," Tal said, sounding angry and relieved at the same time.

"Stand back," Jed said, ignoring his brother as he always had when Tal wasn't making sense. "I'm going to open the door."

"How?" Tal said. "The door senses something about the person's hand and only opens for the people guarding me."

"Just stand back," Jed said, holding the dagger up as it began to glow a deep cobalt blue. Jed plunged the tip of the dagger into the metal door a few centimeters above the point where the handle connected with the wall. Kylla and Fallon glanced back down the opposite ends of the hallway as Jed focused the whole of his mind upon the blade.

Slowly, he pulled the blade through the metal of the door, cutting a half-moon-shaped hole around the handle. The metal of the door offered little resistance to the glowing blade, and it felt to Jed much like cutting through a thick loaf of his mother's bread. As Jed removed the blade from the door, the bluish glow faded away. Tentatively, he touched the door, finding it was not even warm. He pushed it inward.

His brother Tal stood before Jed in the center of a small, dark room, staring with utter disbelief. Jed rushed to his brother and embraced him. Tal was taller than Jed remembered, having gained a few inches in the year he had been gone, but he still had the same rugged good looks, dark wavy hair, boyish smile, and innocent eyes.

"It's good to see you, brother," Jed said, wiping tears from his cheeks. Kylla was next to embrace Tal, almost knocking him and Jed over with the force of her enthusiasm.

"I'm so glad we found you," Kylla said, placing her hand on Tal's face.

"I'm glad as well," Fallon said, looking up at Tal.

"How did you find me?" Tal asked, rubbing his watery eyes. Lowering his hands from his face, he ruffled Fallon's hair affectionately. Tal was the only person besides Kylla who Fallon ever allowed to mess with his hair that way, and he beamed widely at the familiar gesture.

"It's a long story," Jed said,

"What is that blade?" Tal asked, looking at the ancient dagger.

"We don't have time to explain it all right now," Jed said. "A Tellandor priest helped us find you. We followed your journal and she helped us track you down."

"She's being held here as well," Fallon added.

"We have to find her," Kylla said. "The leader of the Iron Hand is planning on taking her away in a few hours."

"You know about the Iron Hand?" Tal said with surprise.

"We know everything," Jed said.

"They were going to make me do something horrible," Tal said, his face darkening at some memory. "They did things. They have this…machine, or something. It's alive almost, and it can get inside your mind…and afterward, you don't feel like yourself anymore."

"You're safe now," Jed said, seeing the fear building on Tal's face. He held his brother's arm reassuringly.

"We have to get out of here," Tal said, his voice lowering in seriousness.

"Someone's coming," Fallon whispered and quickly pushed the door closed. Jed, Tal, and Kylla slowly crept to the door and leaned in to listen to the voices in the hallway.

"I thought he was taking her in the morning," the first voice said.

"Plans change," the second voice said. "The shuttle in the service corridor showed up earlier than expected. If it stays here too long it might be noticed." Jed recognized that voice. Lakk.

"What about the boy?" asked the first voice.

"He stays until the programming is finished," Lakk said.

They heard a door opening down the hallway. Jed used the tip of the dagger to pry the door back open, swinging it just a crack, backward into the room, so he could see down the hall. Two men turned from the corridor down another hallway.

"They must be holding her in the next corridor over," Jed said. "They're taking her now."

"How many guards were there?" Kylla asked.

"Lakk and one other," Jed said, opening the door a little more and peeking out.

"If there's only two we can take them," Kylla said, her eyes blazing with confidence.

"We have to get closer," Jed said.

Leaning back, Jed saw the men step to the far end of the corridor, guiding Qa'Lea before them, hands bound behind her back and a blindfold wrapped around her eyes.

Jed saw another man trailing behind Qa'Lea and her captors. This man, who had not spoken, carried Qa'Lea's staff and *Tannett* in his arms. The men guided Qa'Lea around a corner, back toward the main courtyard of the temple. Jed gently opened the door and stepped into the hallway, gesturing for the others to follow. Silently, they trailed the men and Qa'Lea through the corridors, staying as close as they dared and moving as quietly as possible.

"If we can get Qa'Lea free in the courtyard," Jed whispered, "we might be able to use the corridor back to the cemetery to escape."

"What if there are people in the courtyard?" Kylla asked. "Maybe we should try to take them now. I might be able to use the stone at this distance."

"We have to be sure," Jed said, pausing at a turn. "If they see us coming, we'll lose the advantage."

"What stone?" Tal asked.

"Later," Jed said. "As soon as they go through the door to that small room before the courtyard, run." Turning the next corner, Jed watched as Lakk and the two men herded Qa'Lea through the door to the room where the unconscious man was hidden in the cabinet.

"Now," Jed said, as the door closed behind the men and Qa'Lea.

They rushed down the corridor as fast as they could, Tal easily taking the lead and opening the door of the small chamber for the others to run through.

They raced across the small storeroom, barely giving a glance to the cabinet where they had hidden the man in white. Jed threw open the door to the courtyard, the ancient dagger glowing brilliant azure in his right hand.

Lakk and the men with Qa'Lea were already on the far side of the courtyard. Lakk turned just in time to be hit in the chest by a blast of blue light from the dagger in Jed's hand, while the man holding Qa'Lea tumbled backward after an invisible blow from the stone Kylla held in the fist of her outstretched right arm.

The third man, still behind the others and only halfway across the courtyard, turned and swung Qa'Lea's heavy staff — only to be met with Tal's powerful and well-placed knuckles to the face. The man fell back and Tal snatched the staff from his hands. The man struggled up but was hit in the head by Fallon, swinging his fist like a cudgel.

Fallon quickly snatched Qa'Lea's *Tannett* from the man's hand and stood up as a loud voice boomed through the open space of the courtyard and echoed off the walls and balconies above.

"So these are the Kellish children who have been you giving such trouble, Lakk."

Skidding to a stop, Jed and the others turned to see Drakkor standing directly behind them, aiming a dark black rod at them. It was noticeably thicker than the stun sticks they had seen before.

"It seems they have bested you again, Lakk." As Drakkor spoke, minions of the Iron Hand, some in white robes, and some in black like Lakk, stepped from the doors around the courtyard. Each held a black rod in his or her hand.

"Leave the children alone," Qa'Lea said from the far side of the courtyard, still bound and blindfolded, but looking directly at Drakkor. Lakk and the other man in black stood to their feet and grabbed Qa'Lea by the arms.

"Had they stayed in their primitive little village, they would be safe," Drakkor said. "Now, they are in my way."

Drakkor raised the black rod and a beam of reddish-white light burst forth, flashing toward Jed and the others. Jed flinched, but the beam of energy did not strike them, sliding away from them as though repelled by some invisible sphere.

Jed saw Kylla gripping the ancient stone in both hands and staring at Drakkor. "Interesting," Drakkor said, lowering the black rod as the beam of light ceased. "I didn't realize they were training priests so young these days. Drop the shield, girl, and you will not be harmed. Defy me, and I will turn every shock rod in this room against you."

"Can you make a hole in the top of the shield?" Jed said quietly to Kylla.

"Maybe," Kylla said. "If they aren't attacking."

"Do it now," Jed said.

"I'm waiting for an answer," Drakkor growled.

"Leave them be," Qa'Lea shouted from the other side of the courtyard.

"Here's your answer," Jed said, raising the dagger above his head with both hands. The blade blazed as a bolt of brilliant blue-white energy shot upward and stuck the light-dome seven stories above their heads. Instantly the light-dome exploded in a massive fireball of blue and red light, immense sheets of glass falling to the floor in a shower of sparks. The people below, Drakkor included, ran for cover as the central hall of the temple plunged into darkness, giant glass shards falling everywhere. A huge knife of glass shattered on the shield of energy Kylla still projected around them. Jed flinched as he watched by the light of the dagger.

A figure in white rushed past them, and Jed turned in time to see Drakkor running for the same door Lakk pushed Qa'lea though. She struggled against them, but four other men grabbed her arms and shoved her into the corridor beyond. The other white clad minions of the Iron Hand raced through the door as well.

"How did you do that?" Tal said, staring at both Jed and Kylla with amazement.

"We'll explain later," Kylla said with a reluctant grin as she lowered the stone. She obviously enjoyed impressing Tal, but clearly didn't appreciate the circumstances of it.

"Quick," Jed said, running toward the corridor Drakkor and Qa'Lea had disappeared down. The corridor, unlike the temple hall, was still well-lit, and Jed could just see Qa'Lea being shoved through a doorway twenty meters ahead. Lakk stood in the doorway and smiled as he closed the large metal door, the thud of a massive deadbolt sliding into place, audible even over their footsteps.

"I've seen doors like that here," Tal said as they ran. "They're thick as my arm. We'll never open it if it's locked."

"We don't have to open it," Jed said, not pausing to slow down as he raised the dagger in front of him in both hands. "Hit it as hard as you can, Ky."

"Say when," Kylla said, excitement raising her voice a near yell as she clasped the stone in her right hand.

"Now!" Jed shouted as column of blue-white light exploded from the dagger and struck the hinges of the metal door. An unseen force slammed into the massive door, blasting it off its hinges and hurling it into the chamber beyond like a giant metal leaf caught in a windstorm of extraordinary power. The light of the dagger faded as they rushed through the doorway and were immediately struck by beams of red-white energy from twenty assorted shock-rods. Skidding to a stop, Kylla held the stone in both hands and slammed her eyes closed in concentration. Jed and Tal bounced back toward her, repelled by the inner edge of the invisible shield Kylla projected around them.

Jed looked at Kylla and then around the chamber. They stood on a wide platform at the end of a large service corridor stretching as far as the eye could see. Massive pipes and conduits lined the corridor flanking a small set of tracks down the center.

At the edge of the platform sat a boxlike vehicle similar in shape to the train cars they had seen days ago. Drakkor stood beside the open door of the service sled. Ten meters away, Lakk and four henchmen struggled to push Qa'Lea inside. For some reason, they could not seem to move her from the spot where she stood.

"I can't hold this for long," Kylla said, panic ringing in her voice as sweat began to bead on her brow. The invisible shield around them grew smaller, slowly forced inward by the red-white beams of energy from the shock-rods of the white-robed agents of the Iron Hand assembled between them and the service car. Around them, the air seemed to glow with reddish brilliance as though they were being encased in fire.

"I'll help you," Fallon said, reaching up to clasp Kylla's hands in his own as he closed his eyes in concentration. The sphere of energy ceased shrinking, but did not recover in size.

"If we can get behind that column, I can strike back at them," Jed said, pointing to a support column a short distance down the platform.

"I can't walk," Kylla panted. "I can't move or…"

"Just keep doing what you're doing," Tal said, picking up Kylla in his arms. Seeing what his brother had done, Jed turned and picked up Fallon. Kylla and Fallon's hands still clasped around the ancient stone, Jed and Tal carried them across the platform toward the support column. They could hear Drakkor yelling from the service car.

"What are you doing, you fools?" Drakkor screamed.

"We can't move her," Lakk yelled back.

"Then knock her unconscious." Drakkor fumed.

"The power-rod will kill her and I don't have a stun stick," Lakk said with frustration. There were now seven men trying to push Qa'Lea toward the open door of the service car, but her feet seemed to be welded to the floor of the platform.

"Then use your hands," Drakkor shouted. Lakk turned to do as instructed only to find himself struck in the face by Qa'Lea's forehead as she thrust her upper body toward him.

Lakk fell backward and Qa'Lea turned, shoving the man on her right side with her shoulder. The man fell back nearly three meters. The other men struggled with Qa'Lea, her blindfold coming off. Her eyes finally free, she looked across the room to see Jed and the others taking safety behind the support column.

"No!" she shouted at Jed, catching his eye and looking behind him.

The support column briefly shielded them from the attack of the power-rods of the Iron Hand agents and Jed glanced behind himself. He swallowed hard at what he saw. A meter-wide white pipe ran behind them emblazoned at regular intervals with the words, "DANGER: PRIMARY ENERGY CONDUIT." As Jed turned back, he saw the energy blasts from the power-rods still aimed at them, deflecting away from the shield Kylla and Fallon continued to maintain and striking the power conduit.

"Everybody down!" Jed shouted as he guided Tal, still holding Kylla, to the ground. As their knees touched the floor of the platform, the entire chamber suddenly exploded with searing white light gushing from the energy conduit and engulfing most of the agents of the Iron Hand.

The energy from the conduit, like a molten form of liquid light, rolled across the platform, enveloping everything in its path. A moment later, the metal of the conduit slowly began to seal itself up, like living tissue repairing a wound. Within seconds, the energy of the conduit was once again safely contained.

Jed looked up with surprise to see he and his friends were still alive. The shield from the ancient stone had protected them from the blast. Turning, Jed saw the blast from the pipe had knocked the men struggling with Qa'Lea across the platform, some of them falling into the channel housing the tracks.

Qa'Lea herself remained on her feet, a look of relief on her face as she saw Jed and the others had survived the blast.

"You are still coming with me," Drakkor said, stepping from the train car, a power rod in his hand. "Alive or otherwise."

"No, I am not," Qa'Lea said calmly as she turned to face Drakkor. She stared at the power-rod in Drakkor's hand as he aimed it at her. The power-rod flew from Drakkor's grip and skittered across the room.

"How could you do that?" Drakkor shouted, his voice quivering in rage and surprise.

"By believing in things you say don't exist," Qa'Lea said, staring intently but peacefully into Drakkor's eyes.

Kylla released the shield around them and Jed ran to Qa'Lea, the others following close behind. Racing toward Drakkor, Jed saw all of the followers of the Iron Hand were either unconscious or badly wounded, many probably dead from the energy blast of the ruptured conduit. Drakkor looked around as well, and then, smiling, stepped backward onto the service sled, the door of the vehicle closing in front of him.

The car swiftly accelerated down the tracks as Jed and the others reached Qa'Lea. Jed tried cut at her bonds with the ancient blade, but she shrugged him off.

"Forget about me," Qa'Lea said. "You must stop him."

"Right," Jed said, running to the edge of the tracks and seeing the service car rapidly gaining speed. Holding the ancient dagger in both hands, Jed thrust it out toward the service car, the familiar blue-white glow engulfing the blade. Down the tracks, Jed could see Drakkor opening a small emergency door at the rear of the speeding service car.

"Hurry," Qa'Lea said from behind him.

Jed focused on the blade and looked down the tracks at Drakkor in the open doorway of the service car. He knew he could create a blast with the blade strong enough to stop the car by destroying it, but at this range he would have little control over where the energy from the blade struck. With Drakkor standing at the rear of the car, there was no way to stop the service shuttle without killing him. The service car would be out of range in seconds. He had to make the choice, the right choice, before it was too late. Kill the man who had kidnapped his brother and who would wreak unknown havoc if left free, or let Drakkor escape.

Jed sighed.

And lowered the dagger.

Qa'Lea and the others stepped up behind him.

"I'm sorry," Jed said.

"You had him," Tal said, shaking with anger.

"I couldn't stop him without killing him," Jed said, unable to meet his brother's eyes. The others were silent for a moment.

"You made the right choice," Qa'Lea said. Jed cut through the bonds wrapped around Qa'Lea's hands with the dagger, the wire-like ropes offering little resistance to the blade as it glowed pale blue.

Tal put a hand on Jed shoulder and looked in his eyes. "You did make the right choice, little brother."

An explosion rumbled down the tracks from the direction the service car had gone, a ball of flame visible several hundred meters away.

"Drakkor has sealed off the service tunnel," Jed said, staring down the tracks in shock.

"The way back to the temple is blocked as well," Qa'lea said, looking back the opposite direction. Jed saw the energy blast from the ruptured conduit had totally destroyed the entrance to the temple.

"We're trapped," Kylla said, her voice filled with frustration.

Glancing around, Jed saw some of the followers of the Iron Hand beginning to regain consciousness. He watched as the square-headed Lakk lift himself up on one arm and rubbed his forehead.

"Not yet," Qa'Lea said, turning to Tal. "You must be Jed's brother. Introductions will have to wait. Right now, I need my staff." Surprised to discover he was still holding the staff, Tal handed it to Qa'Lea without a word. "Follow me," Qa'Lea said, jumping into the track pit and running in the direction of the explosion.

Blinking at each other in momentary bewilderment, Jed and the others hesitated only a second before leaping down and following Qa'Lea.

CHAPTER 29
DAYRISE REUNION

"The beginnings and endings of all human undertakings are untidy."
John Galsworthy (1867 – 1933 CE)

"There is no end to the adventures we can have if only we seek them with our eyes open."
Jawaharlal Nehru (1889 – 1964 CE)

"What we call the beginning is often the end. And to make an end is to make a beginning. The end is where we start from."
T.S. Eliot (1888 – 1965 CE)

"Where are we going?" Jed asked, looking back to see Lakk and several of the followers of the Iron Hand standing in the center of the tracks, seemingly unsure whether to follow.

"Back to the surface of the world," Qa'Lea said as she ran. "This service corridor runs parallel with a communications corridor. There are junctions every two kilometers where they are joined by a door. Once through the door, we can follow the communications corridor until we reach a service lift."

"What about the Iron Hand behind us?" Fallon asked, glancing back.

"With Drakkor gone, they don't have nearly the same incentive to face us as before," Qa'Lea said with certainty. "They'll stay back."

They continued running down the train tracks, trying to keep their footing in the dim glow provided by service lights mounted in the corridor ceiling. Jed saw Kylla running stride for stride with Tal and smiled. A moment later, Qa'Lea stopped short.

"What is it?" Jed asked.

"The door," Qa'Lea said, pointing to a melted mass of metal in the corridor wall. It looked nothing like a door. The blast from Drakkor's explosive had fused it to the wall. Qa'Lea looked down the tracks to where the ceiling of the corridor had collapsed some twenty meters ahead. "Our exits have been closed."

"I can cut through it," Jed said, raising the ancient dagger in his hand, the blade already beginning to burn bluish-white.

"It's too thick for you alone," Qa'Lea said, placing her hand on Jed's arm. "It would be too thick even for me."

"We can do it together," Fallon said, stepping forward and placing a hand on the dagger.

"Yes," Qa'Lea said, a whisper of pride in her voice. "The four of us together. Tal, hold my staff, please." Tal accepted the staff from Qa'Lea and watched in fascination as she and Kylla both added hands to those of Jed and Fallon already holding the dagger.

"Let your minds float free and mix like water mixing with water," Qa'Lea said. "Then focus on Jed and the blade. Jed will guide the flow."

Feeling the others' hands upon his, and something flowing into his mind, calming him, Jed touched the blade to the edge of what had been the metal door and focused.

The glow of the blade blinded Jed and forced him to squint as he guided the dagger around the edge where he thought the door had once been. After several minutes of intense work, he finally brought the blade back to the point where he had started. Releasing his concentration, Jed felt suddenly exhausted. He had never used the blade to create that much power, and even with the help of Qa'Lea, Kylla, and Fallon, he could tell how much it had drained him. Drained all of them. Fatigued, he stepped aside and Qa'Lea turned to Tal.

"My staff," Qa'Lea said, with outstretched hand. Tal placed the staff in Qa'Lea's hand and watched with surprise as she turned to the outline of the door and touched it with the headpiece of the staff. A flash of blue light surged from the golden sphere of the staff and struck the warped metal door, thrusting it back into the corridor beyond with a squeal of grinding metal. Qa'Lea lowered the staff and leaned on it, clearly weary from the exertion of cutting through the door.

Jed looked through the newly cut doorway and was amazed to find it was nearly a meter thick. The ancient dagger was even more powerful than he had suspected.

"Quickly," Qa'Lea said, stepping through the doorway into the corridor beyond.

Only two meters wide, this second, much smaller corridor was filled with hundreds of small, clear, light-filled pipes, several of which had been severed when Jed cut through the doorway. As soon as the others were all through, Qa'Lea stepped to the far side of the metal plug and again used her staff, this time to push it back into the opening they had just come through. The metal mass slid across the floor with a loud screech and then suddenly came to a halt half a meter from the wall. An arm, clad in black, slipped into the gap, followed quickly by the blocky and smoke-smeared face of Lakk.

Qa'Lea squinted as she redoubled her efforts to push the door and Jed swiftly lifted the dagger as Lakk looked at Qa'Lea and spoke, his voice raspy but urgent.

"Theodicy."

Qa'Lea blinked and lowered her staff, reaching out to place a hand on Jed's arm and push the outstretched dagger away.

"He's a friend," Qa'Lea said, stepping closer to Lakk. The space between the plug that had been a door and the wall was too thin for Lakk to squeeze his wide shoulders through and he stepped back a bit. He visibly relaxed as Qa'Lea approached him.

"He's no friend," Tal said, stepping forward to attack Lakk. "If you only knew what he did to me."

"Not me," Lakk said.

"Not him," Qa'Lea said, placing her hand on Tal's chest to stop him. "One just like him."

"Copies," Jed said.

"Clones," Kylla said.

"A spy," Fallon said.

"Exactly," Qa'Lea said. "I knew we had someone inside, but I didn't suspect it was one of your kind," she said to Lakk, or the clone that looked just like him.

"I'm Rakk," the man said. "There are eight of us, all working in different places. Three, including myself, were here."

"What do you want?" Qa'Lea asked.

"I had to look like I was trying to follow you," Rakk said. "The others, particularly my brothers, would become suspicious." Rakk said the word 'brothers' with a dripping sarcasm. "I had arranged to go with you, so I could protect you. They're planning something. Something in Helios. I don't know what. They were going to use the boy."

"I'm not a boy," Tall said, still bristling with anger.

"I thought I should warn you," Rakk said.

"Thank you," Qa'Lea replied. "We should go now. We can't be seen together."

"Yes," Rakk said. "You'll need to make your escape convincing."

"Certainly," Qa'Lea said. "Sorry." Qa'Lea swiftly raised her staff and a blast of red light struck Rakk in the chest, sending him flying into the transit corridor. Qa'Lea again aimed her staff at the melted door. With a wail of metal against metal, the door slid back into the hole in the wall.

"That will hold for now." Qa'Lea strode down the corridor. The others followed silently. They walked for what must have been several kilometers before anyone spoke.

"So he was a spy," Jed said.

"The Sentient has eyes and ears everywhere," Qa'Lea replied.

"But was he the one who tried to capture us?" Kylla asked, frowning.

"It's difficult to tell," Qa'Lea said. "Even a spy would follow orders to capture you so as not to reveal his true nature."

"I don't care what or who he is," Tal said. "If I see a face like that again, I'm going to punch it."

Jed blinked and looked at his brother. Violence was not just frowned upon, but renounced in Kellish society and, until just a few minutes ago, he had never seen Tal take a violent action or even think of threatening someone. Jed began to realize just how much Tal's experience had changed his brother.

"Considering there are seven more just like him who aren't friends of the Sentient," Qa'Lea said, giving Tal a curious look, "that might be a good idea."

"We saw someone who looked just like you back at that café," Fallon said.

"Yes," Qa'Lea said, her voice soft. "I apologize. I never should have left you alone. This was all my fault."

"It turned out okay," Jed said, smiling.

"What was that thing?" Kylla asked, looking up at Qa'Lea.

"A doppelganger," Qa'Lea replied, her mouth twisting in distaste. "A creature genetically modified from a human embryo and then further augmented with techne to be able to mimic the appearance of nearly anyone, able to change size and shape and even sex."

"Who is Drakkor?" Tal asked, a hard glint in his eye as he mentioned the name of his captor.

"He is one of the leading figures among the Third Generation Crew," Qa'Lea said. "He has been advocating greater political power for the Third and Fourth Generation Crews for over two hundred years."

"Is he the leader of the Iron Hand?" Jed asked.

"Yes," Qa'Lea said. "The Sentient has always suspected Drakkor to be the guiding force behind the Iron Hand, but could never prove it. There is also some sort of central council I was unaware of that must be comprised of similarly-minded people in powerful positions throughout the ship. Most likely they have a representative from each of the twelve species aboard the *Celestial Pilgrim*."

"What will happen to the Iron Hand?" Jed asked.

"Thanks to the four of you, we will finally have proof of the Iron Hand's existence and the plan for mutiny," Qa'Lea said with a thin smile. "The Sentient will have noticed these explosions and will be sending the ship's Enforcers and repair crews. They may have arrived at the service corridor already.

"The supporters of the Iron Hand will be trapped and interrogated. A full investigation will follow. Although I imagine at least one of the captives will manage to escape. The High Council of the *Celestial Pilgrim* and the First Generation Crew will finally be made aware of the danger we all face.

"Here we are."

They stepped into a circular room within the corridor. To one side of the room sat a slender metal door. Qa'Lea waved her hand over a glass disc beside the door and it immediately slid open to reveal a smaller chamber beyond. Stepping inside, she gestured for the Kellishers to follow. Once within, she placed her hand on another glass disc and the door to the small room slid closed with the slight *whoosh*.

"Service lift," Qa'lea said by way of explanation.

Jed immediately sensed the upward motion of the room. The movement stopped and the door slid open again. They stepped into a cave of dark black and roughly hewn rock with a low ceiling. Looking around in surprise, the Kellishers followed Qa'Lea through the cave toward a bright light around the curve of the walls. Moments later they walked out of the cave and stood on a hill two kilometers outside the city of New Alexandria.

The tube-light of a new morning brighten the sky, the lights from the city slowly winking out as daylight grew more intense. Jed took a deep breath of cool morning air and smiled.

"What happens now?" he asked.

"We have to warn Helios," Tal said firmly. "They had this machine, this living machine, and they were using it to twist my mind so I would do it. They were going to make me do it."

"Do what?" Jed said with concern.

"Destroy Helios!" Tal nearly yelled. "They were going to make me carry it."

"Carry what?" Qa'Lea asked, frowning with concern.

"I don't know," Tal said. "All I know is it would kill every living person in Helios. And I was supposed to be the one to do it." Tears were in his eyes.

"It's okay now, Tal," Kylla said, placing her hand on Tal's shoulder in comfort. "The Sentient can stop them."

"Yes, it can," Qa'Lea said, smiling reassuringly at Tal and the others. "Thanks to you all. I'll alert the Sentient about the plan to attack Helios. And then I will see you home."

"Home?" Jed said, a pleading tone in his voice. He wasn't sure how he felt about their adventures coming to an end. Part of him yearned to return to his parents and the comforts of the farm and the valley, but another part pulsed with a desire to help the Sentient defeat the Iron Hand.

"Yes," Qa'Lea said, smiling at Jed in a way implying she knew his inner contemplations. "You have done quite enough to save the ship and your part in this adventure is over."

"But we could help save Helios," Jed said, not sure how they might do that, but certain it was true.

"Yes," Kylla said, her voice firm and strong. "We could help find Drakkor."

"And continue our training," Fallon said, stepping up between Jed and Kylla as they faced Qa'Lea.

"I'm sure you could," Qa'Lea said, grinning openly at the thought. "But your parents are worried about you and they will want you home with them, not out risking your lives."

"All I want is to go home," Tal said, his voice weary as he looked out at the vista of morning light dawning across the valley and the ship.

"I have requested a transport craft from the Sentient," Qa'Lea said, glancing briefly at the sky. Jed had no idea when Qa'Lea had managed to contact the Sentient, but knew enough not to doubt her. "You will all be home shortly."

"Thank you," Tal said, visibly relieved by Qa'Lea's words.

"Here is our ride," Qa'Lea said, gesturing up and drawing everyone's attention to the sleek, needlelike aircraft of silver floating down gently from the sky above them. Jed heard Kylla gasp with excitement beside him. The aircraft ceased its descent and silently hovered a meter above the ground as a hatch opened and a small set of stairs unfolded to the grass.

Qa'Lea led them across the hundred meters of rock and hillside weeds to the aircraft and ushered them inside. Jed barely had time to admire the plush black fabric seats and the wide, square windows before the door to the hatch slid shut and the aircraft rose swiftly and soundlessly into the air. The only sensation of movement was the feeling of being pressed back into his chair. Jed stared out the window as the ground rapidly receded below them. He could see the top of the Launch Tree and behind it, the Tower of Knowledge and the city of New Alexandria dwindling into the distance. Then they passed through a cloud bank and he lost sight of it.

"Wow," Kylla said, voicing Jed's own assessment as she stared fixedly out the window at the valley below, seeming smaller every second.

Jed noticed Tal wasn't looking out the window, instead staring down at his own hands. Jed wondered about all the things that had happened to his brother and how they might have changed him. Was he contemplating what might have happened if Jed and the others hadn't arrived to save him? Was he thinking of the Iron Hand's machine and the attempt to make him destroy Helios? Or was he thinking of something else?

"What happened to Mirra?"

Tal snapped his head up and stared at Jed in dazed curiosity. Kylla's neck did not swivel so swiftly, but she did turn her attention from the window toward Tal.

"You mentioned her in your journal," Jed said. "Is she okay? Did the Iron Hand kidnap her as well?"

"Mirra," Tal grunted with barely contained disgust. "I thought she liked me, but all she really wanted was someone to pay for her ticket home. To see her boyfriend. One more lesson I learned on Landdesh."

"I'm sorry it didn't work out," Kylla said. Tal seemed oblivious, but Jed noted the wide smile slowly spreading across Kylla's face as she looked back out the window.

The remainder of the flight home barely lasted twenty minutes. Jed could hardly fathom how fast they must be traveling. Qa'Lea instructed the automated craft to land in a field between Jed and Tal's parents' farm and the home of Kylla and Fallon's parents. Strictly speaking, bringing technology like the aircraft into the Notesch Valley was forbidden. However, Qa'Lea assured them their parents would not mind.

Indeed, Jed's parents hardly seemed to notice the slender chrome craft hovering above their wheat field as they ran through the waving grain to embrace their children. Kylla and Fallon's parents, working in their garden like all good Kellishers at midday, arrived moments later, sweeping the children into their arms.

"Thank you, thank you, thank you," Jed's mother said to Qa'Lea between sobs as she embraced her two sons.

"The thanks are owed to Jed and Kylla and Fallon," Qa'Lea said, gesturing to the three young Kellishers.

"They saved me," Tal said, smiling and holding his parents tight.

"They rescued me as well," Qa'Lea said.

"What?" Jed father exclaimed, wiping tears from his eyes.

"Doesn't surprise me in the least," Jed's grandfather said as he walked through the waist-high wheat and clasped first Jed, and then Tal in an embrace.

"We're sorry we ran off," Fallon said to his mother and father.

"Sorry we ran off without permission," Kylla said, making it clear she wasn't at all sorry for their adventures.

"I'm sure you thought you were doing the right thing," Kylla's mother said.

"But you must never do such a right thing again," her father said, blinking as he tried to makes sense of his own words.

"I promise we won't run off to save Tal if he promises not to get into trouble again," Jed said, as usual, leaving room for contingencies.

"I won't be going anywhere more dangerous than the swimming hole for a long, long time," Tal said, affectionately tossing his arm around Jed's shoulder.

"Apologies are all very well and good," Jed's mother said, "but don't think for a moment that just because you saved your brother and brought him home means you won't be making restitution for leaving us worried sick about you for days and days and days."

"There will be time enough for punishments after the celebrations," Jed's father said.

"Can there be pie with the celebrations?" Jed asked, realizing how much he had missed his mother's baking.

"I'm sure I can manage a pie or two to celebrate my sons being alive," his mother said with a laugh. "There may even be pie for the punishments."

"Will you stay with us and celebrate their return, Shann'Ka?" Jed's grandfather asked, absentmindedly sticking a thin stalk of wheat in his mouth.

"I'm afraid I cannot," Qa'Lea said, her eyes a mixture of delight and sadness. "Jed and the others have uncovered a dangerous plot that threatens the Sentient, the people of Wyconna and the whole of the ship. Unfortunately, I must begin helping the Sentient deal with this threat immediately."

"Can we make you a breakfast for your journey?" Jed's mother said before blushing as she realized the ridiculousness of offering a woman who could command a floating airship a basket of bread and cheese.

"No, thank you," Qa'Lea said with a smile. "I must go."

"But you will come back?" Jed said as he abandoned decorum and rushed to throw his arms around Qa'Lea.

"Yes, you must come back," Kylla said as she and Fallon joined Jed in embracing Qa'Lea.

"Yes, we have to continue our training," Fallon said.

"Training?" Fallon's father asked, staring at his son.

"It's a long story," Qa'Lea said. "I'm sure they will enjoy telling it to you. But whatever you do, you must promise me you will let them keep the artifacts."

"What artifacts?" Jed mother asked, giving Jed a concerned stare that he was all too familiar with.

"The ones they used to save me," Tal said, grinning at his brother.

"I'm sure Jed will explain everything we need to know," his grandfather said.

"All you need to know is that these three are special," Qa'Lea said, gently pushing Jed and Kylla and Fallon in the direction of their parents. "I will return when I can, and as often as I can. They must be prepared and you must prepare yourselves. One day they will each leave the valley on Landdesh, and Wyconna may never be the same."

Qa'Lea laughed at her own words and made her final farewells. She walked back to where the aircraft floated, glistening in the sun, fields of wheat reflected along its silvery surface. Jed watched as Qa'Lea climbed into the aircraft and turned to wave. He and the others waved back. The hatch sealed up as Qa'Lea lowered her arm and the aircraft rose quietly and quickly into the air.

Jed watched with the others in silence as the fleet silver craft receded into the distance, over the tops of the Pinak Mountains and out of the Notesch Valley, carrying Qa'Lea back to Wyconna proper and out of their lives.

His heart ached with the pain of missing the old Tellandor priest, even though she had only just left. *But she wouldn't be out of their lives forever,* Jed thought defiantly to himself as he wiped a tear from his eye. She said she would return, and he was certain she would continue to help them train with the ancient Tellandor artifacts.

Jed walked over to stand between Kylla and Fallon, placing his arms around their shoulders as the three of them continued to stare past the mountain tops, where Qa'Lea's aircraft had disappeared from view. Jed knew Kylla and Fallon were thinking the same thoughts as he.

"Drakkor and the Iron Hand won't be easy to defeat," Kylla said, her voice too low for their parents to overhear.

"I think one day, she and the Sentient will need our help again," Fallon said, his face serious, but calm at the implications of his words.

"And when that day comes," Jed said, a smile breaking out across his face, "we'll be ready for it."

And who knows, Jed thought, grinning even wider, *maybe that day will come soon.*

BRIEF SUMMARIES OF THE NINE MAJOR HUMAN FAITHS

From *The Kellish Book of All Faiths*

(Note: All locations refer to the human Origin World. All dates are in Origin World nomenclature prior to The Great Journey.)

Buddhism

Born a prince, Siddhartha Gautama, (490– 410 BCE) of the Shakya clan in India, became the founder of Buddhism. Buddha means "One who is Awake," and enlightenment, the goal of Buddhist practice, is considered to be awakening to the Ultimate Nature of Reality.

Buddha's core teaching was the Four Noble Truths.

The first noble truth is that the nature of human existence is suffering — being denied that which we desire, being forced to experience that which we dislike, as well as aging, sickness, and death.

The second noble truth is that the cause of suffering is desirous attachment, or grasping at external objects, people, and phenomena as sources of happiness.

The Third Noble truth is that the way to end suffering is to extinguish desirous attachment, seeking instead to find inner peace by calming and pacifying the mind.

Lastly, the Fourth Noble truth is the Eight Fold Path, or the eight practices that will lead to liberation, or enlightenment. These are: 1) Right View, or correct understanding of the four Noble Truths and the true nature of reality; 2) Right Resolve, or the intention to practice the *Dharma*, or Buddhist teachings; 3) Right Speech, or wholesome truthful speech; 4) Right Action, or avoiding harming others; 5) Right Livelihood, or making no income from harmful actions; 6) Right Effort, or applying oneself wholeheartedly to the Path; 7) Right Mindfulness; striving to attain an ever-present awareness of all phenomena; and 8) Right Concentration, the single-pointed concentration necessary to attain enlightenment.

Buddhists do not believe in a creator god, or soul, containing memories and personality, but they do believe in reincarnation with the *very subtle mind*, passing from one life to the next based upon the *karma*, created by the actions of the person. The cycle of rebirth is called *samsara*. *Nirvana* is the escape from *samsara* and the goal of Buddhism.

Christianity

Christianity is founded upon the teachings of Jesus of Nazareth (4 BCE– 29 CE), a Jewish rabbi who offered a new interpretation of ancient Hebrew teachings. He is often referred to as Jesus Christ, Christ being the English translation of the Greek word Christós, which in turn is the Greek translation of the Hebrew *moshiach,* or "annointed one."

Christians believe that Jesus was the Messiah predicted by the Hebrew Bible, that he was crucified to redeem the sins of all humanity, that he arose from the dead two days later, and that he will return to usher in the Kingdom of God.

The Christian bible is divided into two halves, the first being the Hebrew Bible (*The Tanakh*), and the second being composed of letters and four narratives of the life and teachings of Jesus (*The new Testament*).

Christianity is monotheistic, as is the Jewish faith it evolved from, although later teachings by the apostle Paul put forth the idea of the trinity, or a single being existing in three separate persons of God, Jesus Christ, and the Holy Spirit.

The belief in an afterlife of reward in heaven for those who take Christ as their savior and an eternal punishment in hell for the wicked is one of the central beliefs of Christianity.

Different Christian sects flourished throughout the three centuries following the death of Jesus. In 325 CE, the Roman

Emperor Constantine, a convert to Christianity, called the first Council of Nicaea to unify Christianity. In 1054 CE, the Church split between the eastern Orthodox and western Roman Catholic churches. Further divisions and sects arose throughout the centuries, giving Christianity a wide range of theological and philosophical schools of thought and forms of worship.

Confucianism

Confucianism is often considered an ethical philosophy for living rather than a religion. Ostensibly founded in China by K'ung Fu Tzu (551– 479 BCE), usually pronounced Confucius, Confucianism focuses on personal conduct and social governance rather than the worship of any particular god or gods. The examination of individual and collective life led Confucius to several core teachings. The ethical teachings are as follows: Li: rules for ritual and etiquette; Hsiao: love between family members; Yi: righteousness; Xin: honesty and trustworthiness; Jen: benevolence towards others; and Chung: Fealty to the government.

Confucius's *Great Learning* was a series of steps to attain harmony within a person, between people, and within a state. These steps are: Investigation of phenomena, Learning, Sincerity, Rectitude of purpose, Self-development, Family-discipline, Local self-government, and Universal self-government.

Confucius also held that Society was comprised of five prime relationships: husband and wife; parent and child; the elder and the younger; Ruler and subject, and between friend and friend.

Confucian beliefs are collected in a series of texts called the *Analects*.

Hinduism

Hinduism is the oldest of the human religions still in practice, originating in the Indus Valley (in what became Pakistan) from 2500 BCE to 1500 BCE.

Hinduism has many deities, but all are considered a manifestation of the single Absolute or Ultimate Reality known as Brahman. Popular deities that are worshipped are Brahma, the creative force of the cosmos, Vishnu, the preserving force of the cosmos, Shiva, the destructive or transformative force of the cosmos, and Shakti, the divine mother.

Hindus believe in reincarnation, the rebirth of the soul, or *Atman*. All actions, or *karma*, reflect upon the *Atman*, and will lead to either positive or negative rebirths.

The central teaching of Hinduism is that through *dharma*, or right conduct, human beings can purify their negative *karma* and attain union with Brahman, the Ultimate Reality, thus escaping cyclical rebirth, or *samsara*. This union with Brahman, the Ultimate Reality, is known as *moksha*.

There are four paths, or yogas, by which one may attain *moksha*, each suited to a different temperament. The first is *Karma yoga*, which is a practice of finding liberation in action, or service to others. The second is *Bhakti yoga*, the yoga of love, where one cultivates love for God and others. The third is *Janna yoga*, or the path of knowledge to union with God. The fourth is *Raja yoga*, also known as the royal path, focusing on meditative practices that lead to *moksha*.

The central Hindu Texts are the four Vedas, *The Baghavad Gita*, and the *Upanishads*.

Islam

Islam, which means 'submission' in Arabic, is a monotheistic religion that evolved from the teachings of Judaism and Christianity. Islam was founded by the prophet Muhammad (570– 632 CE). The word Muslim means "One who surrenders to God."

The central teaching of Islam is that there is no God but God (Allah), that God created the universe, and that Muhammad is his final prophet. Allah, the Arabic name for God, is the same God worshipped by Jews as Yahweh (YHWH) and Christians as Jehovah. Abraham, of Judaism, and Jesus, of Christianity, are considered as earlier prophets whose teachings are superseded by the revelations of the prophet Muhammad.

Muhammad's teachings are recorded in the Koran (sometimes spelled Qur'an), the central and most holy text of Islam. Muslims believe that the Koran is the word of God and should read in its original Arabic. Many Muslims learn to recite the entire text by heart as an act of devotion and a practice of submission to the word of Allah.

The cornerstone teachings of Islam are called the five pillars. These are: *Shahadah*, The belief that there is no God but God and that Muhammad is his prophet; *Salat*, To pray five times each day facing the holy city of Mecca (in Saudi Arabia); *Zakat*, Almsgiving, or making charitable contributions to the poor; *Sawm*, Fasting between dawn and sunset during the holy month of Ramadan; and *Hajj*, The commitment to make a pilgrimage to the holy city of Mecca at least once in a person's lifetime.

Jainism

Founded by Nataputta Mahavira (599– 527 BCE), also called Jina, or "Spiritual Conqueror," Jainism is believed to have originated with twenty-three previous spiritual teachers, or "Tirthankaras." Mahavira is considered the twenty-fourth Tirthankara.

Jainism teaches a path toward spiritual awakening based on renunciation of not only violence, but of materialism, and worldly affairs as well. Jains do not believe in a creator god and instead focus their practices on self-transformation rather than exterior worship.

A fundamental doctrine of Jainism is that of two eternal categories known as jiva, or living matter (the enjoyer), and ajiva, or inanimate matter (the enjoyed). Contact between jiva and ajiva results in suffering.

Jains believe that all human actions cause karma, which binds the soul to an endless cycle of reincarnation and suffering. The path to becoming free from the effects of negative karma is through ascetic practice, particularly *ahimsa*, or the practice of causing no harm to any living creature. Liberation from suffering and the cycle of rebirth is called *Moksha*.

Judaism

Judaism is the second oldest religion still practiced, founded by the prophet Abraham circa 1800 BCE. Judaism was the first monotheistic religion, believing in a single God, responsible for creating and maintaining the whole universe. Often translated from the original Hebrew as Yahweh (YHWH), the name of God is never spoken aloud in Judaism.

The Jewish faith is guided by 613 mitzvot, or commandments, governing every aspect of Jewish life from worship and diet to justice and personal conduct. These 613 mitzvot are summarized by the Ten Sayings (often translated as 'ten commandments') brought down out of Mount Siani by the Prophet Moses on two stone tablets. These are: To worship no other god but God, to create no image of God, to never use God's name in vain, to remember the Sabbath, to honor one's father and mother, not to commit murder, not to steal, to never commit adultery, to never bear false witness, and not to covet your neighbor's possessions.

A central belief of Judaism is the coming of the *moshiach* or 'annointed one' who will be sent by God to end all evil and usher in a new world.

While Judaism does not strictly believe in an afterlife, it does posit the resurrection of the righteous upon the arrival of the *moshiach*.

Judaism has been highly influential upon Christianity and Islam, both religions finding much of their origins in Jewish history, belief, and philosophy.

Sikhism

Influenced by the *Bhakti yoga* of Hinduism and the Muslim sect of Sufism, Sikhism was founded by Guru Nanak (1469 – 1539 CE), the first of Sikhism's ten Gurus, in the Punjab region of northwest India. The word 'Sikh' comes from the Sanskrit word for 'disciple' and Sikhs are considered disciples of the gurus, who are held to be mediators of divine grace.

Sikhs believe that the cycle of *karmic* rebirth can be transcended through spiritual union with God. This spiritual union is to be accomplished through the meditative repetition of the divine name of God, given several names by the Sikhs; Sat (truth), Sat Guru (true Guru), Akal Purakh (timeless being), Kartar (creator), and Wahi-Guru ("praise to the Guru").

Sikhs also emphasize charitable works, acts of service, and avoidance of the five ills: Kam (lust), Krodh (anger), Lobh (greed), Moh (worldly attachment) and Ahankar (pride). Sikhism rejects such religious rituals as fasting, vegetarianism, pilgrimages, idol worship, or superstitious acts.

Sikhism is a very community oriented religion with a strong tradition of householder, rather than monastic, worship.

Taoism

As much a philosophical way of life as a mystical religion, Taoism (sometimes spelled Daoism) is concerned with bringing human life into harmony with the natural cosmic principle of all existence. The word Tao usually translates as 'Path' or 'Way,' and refers to the Ultimate Reality and the act of bringing human action in alignment with it.

Although commonly thought to be founded by Lao-tzu, (sometimes translated as Lao-Zi), in the 3rd century BCE, most historians doubt that any such person existed. Lao-Tzu is said to have written down the essence of Taoism in the collection of sayings and poems called the *Tao De Ching*, commonly translated as "The Way and its Power."

The 'Way' of Taoism is accomplished through contemplation, meditation, and following a practice of *wuwei*, or the process of seeking harmony through non-action, and abiding with the ebb and flow of the Tao, or Way.

ABOUT THE AUTHOR

After a childhood spent whizzing through the galaxy in super sleek starships and defeating treacherously evil monsters in long forgotten kingdoms, G.L. Breedon grew up to write science fiction and fantasy novels. He lives with his wife in Brooklyn, NY.

He is also the author of:
The Wizard of Time (Book 1)
The Sword of Unmaking (The Wizard of Time – Book 2)
The Edge of Eternity (The Wizard of Time – Book 3)
The Dark Shadow of Spring (The Young Sorcerers Guild – Book 1)
Summer's Cauldron (The Young Sorcerer's Guild – Book 2)
The Dragon Star Saga (Books 1-4)

For more information or to sign up for G.L. Breedon's mailing list, please visit:
Kosmosaicbooks.com

Word of mouth and recommendations are essential in helping an author's work find new readers. If you enjoyed **The Celestial Blade**, please consider writing a review at Amazon US or Amazon UK. Even a few words would be helpful.

www.ingramcontent.com/pod-product-compliance
Lightning Source LLC
Chambersburg PA
CBHW062116170626
46813CB00002B/468